For My Sins

Alex Nye

For My Sins
Alex Nye
© Alex Nye 2017

Cover illustration: Graeme Clarke
Published by:

Fledgling Press Ltd,
39 Argyle Crescent,
Edinburgh,
EH15 2QE

www.fledglingpress.co.uk

ISBN 9781905916788
Printed and bound by:
Bell & Bain Ltd, Glasgow

For Martha and Micah,
With much love

"Royal brother, having by God's will, for my sins I think, thrown myself into the power of the Queen my cousin, at whose hands I have suffered much for almost twenty years, I have finally been condemned to death by her and her Estates...

Today, after dining I was advised of my sentence: I am to be executed like a common criminal at eight in the morning... The Catholic faith and the assertion of my God-given right to the English throne are the two issues on which I am condemned..."

From the last letter of Mary Queen of Scots,
Fotheringhay Castle,
8 February 1587

Fotheringhay Castle
September 1586
Fragments and Memories

*T*he Crown of Scotland was placed upon my brow when I was six days old. It bit into my baby flesh like a crown of thorns. No other crown in Europe is as thorny as that of Scotland.

I have seen men murder, scheme, even forfeit their lives for the sake of a crown, but only I know that it is nothing in the end but a heavy circlet of precious metal marking the forehead with a raw and bloody scar.

From the barred windows of this fortress where my dear sister and cousin Elizabeth so kindly allows me to remain as her 'guest', I can see the dreary countryside of England stretching away, endlessly flat, dull and grey. I am a captive here, with nothing but a dark past of memories to keep me company. As a royal sovereign I am provided with little luxuries, gifts to relieve the monotony – boxes of sweetmeats, lengths of Holland material to make clothes with, soap, Spanish silk. Only yesterday I received a small blue box of taffeta full of 'poudre de santeur'. Such a kind thought. But the one gift which I constantly crave is never ~~*forthcoming. I am provided with satin clothes, perukes of*~~ *false hair, gold and silver thread for my embroidery, but as I ply my needle through the stiff linen it is my freedom I dream of – my freedom and my return to absolute sovereignty.*

The facts are these.

I was born with the burden of sovereignty thrust upon me – and I will die the same. As I languish in this lonely cell, quietly stitching my tapestries, I am haunted by the ghosts of my past. They visit me here while the rain beats a painful tattoo against the bars at my window. Shadows and firelight surround me; hangings and draperies soften and obscure the turret walls, small compensations to calm an unquiet soul. I have had twenty long years in which to reflect on the way Destiny has treated me. Jane Kennedy, my faithful servant, has urged me to write my memories down, commit them to paper.

"Tell the truth, at last," she says.

The truth?

I think of Pilate's question: "What is Truth?"

John Knox thinks he knows the answer – but I do not believe he does.

I am not alone in my captivity. As well as my faithful servants, Elizabeth Curle and Jane Kennedy, there are others here: shadows, phantoms, fragments of memory. No one else sees them. Only I...

Some are less welcome than others. They parade before me, whether I will them to or not.

I have no control over their exits and entrances. It is as if I occupy an empty stage, and I wait for them to appear from the wings.

Here they come now, a motley crowd. They appear before me with all their vices and idiosyncrasies. My half-brother, Moray; Maitland; Morton; Lindsay; John Knox; Rizzio; Father Mamaret. And Darnley, of course. Quite a cast of characters.

They are my guests, and I am their reluctant hostess.

They stand before me, icy-clear at times, their clothes glimmering with bright colours and jewels, rings on their fingers, eyes direct into mine, lips parted. They fill the darkened chamber with their ghostly clamour. Still voicing their many grievances, still filled with pride, they boast chains of office, fur and gowns, costumes of state. Even now they still crave what they cannot have. They are greedy for power. Ambition marks the destiny of each and every one of them – especially the pious and sanctimonious Knox. He was not immune to the same mortal cravings as the rest of them. Never was there a more judgemental or hypocritical man – other than Paulet, my present gaoler.

A single candle burns low at my side. Jane lit the fire some hours ago. There have been many times when they have denied me even that small request – to have a fire in my room.

Paulet is the worst. A bitter Puritan, he guards me with the ferocity of a wolf. He is like a reincarnation of Knox himself – angry, vicious, keen to judge. He has been my gaoler now for several months. When I am forced to move to a different castle, Paulet moves with me now. They know I hate him. And he hates me. He is not happy about any of the gifts I receive from my cousin Elizabeth, and he threatens to remove them.

Let him try...

I have seen better castles than this. I am kept in a small turret chamber. A narrow aperture in the wall allows me to glimpse the damp fields. They are flattened by mist and rain. I think of other windows onto other worlds: leafy glens in Scotland, or high fortresses with a view of the mountains. Then I stop thinking...because the regrets tumble in and that way madness lies.

Elizabeth and Jane have been allowed to remain with me and they are a great comfort to me. Geddon, my Skye terrier, sits close to my skirts, sheltering. I feel his warmth close by.

I am still allowed my chaplain, De Preau, for the time being, although Paulet has threatened to deny him access. Sir James Melville, my secretary, visits me often as does my physician, Burgoing. Didier, my porter, came with us to this desolate god-forsaken fenland, but he seems nervous and afraid. A sombre mood infects us all.

As my needle flies in and out, my eye is drawn to a parchment letter lying on the table beside me.

Jane gives me a warning glance.

She shakes her head slowly from side to side. "It is not wise, Madam."

Her voice is quiet, barely above a whisper.

"What is not?" I say, catching at the parchment.

She offers no reply.

"I know not what you speak of."

I pick up the letter and slide it quickly between the pages of my breviary, out of sight.

She says nothing, but a knowing look passes between us.

My stitches may be quiet and the room I live in may be wrapped in silence, but a tumult exists inside my head.

Voices clamour. Memories taunt me. Injustices still burn where I cannot put them to rest.

Over the years I have learned the art of patience – or the semblance of patience. I have learned to sit and wait.

As a nightly silence falls upon the many gloomy corridors of this castle, I quietly lay aside my embroidery silks. Jane has left me in peace. The servants are all abed, where I should be. The fire is dying down in the hearth. By its feeble light I slip out the letter from between the pages of my prayer book and read the French script with a curl of delight on my lips.

This is all I have left.

For a long time I still waited for the ring of horse's hooves clattering on the cobbles below, a speedy rescue of some kind. They would not leave me to languish here alone, I thought.

It is many years now since I stopped waiting for Bothwell. I realised my error quickly enough. He tried to exonerate my name in the immediate aftermath of our disaster, writing to the King of Denmark from Dragsholm Castle where they kept him: for ours was a very public scandal that lapped around the shores of Europe. The gossip winged its way across borders, as the rumour-mongers spread their poison far and wide. He wrote the truth.

But it was too late by then. The damage was already done.

His is the only ghost who refuses to haunt me here. How I wish sometimes to hear his tread on the stair. Wherever his spirit roams, it is not to my dank castle chamber that he flits.

Perhaps I never owned his soul at all.

I never speak of him to my servants here.

A secret code enters my French correspondence, slipped

between the lines and the hastily expressed sentiments.

Jane warns me against it.

"They will set a trap for you, Madam."

"I know you worry for me, Jane, but there are many people out there – Catholics – who would be willing to further our cause."

The shadows flutter with unknown presences.

"Walsingham will be watching," she whispers.

"Walsingham," I hiss, "is always watching. He has nothing better to do."

"There are rumours that he has double-agents working for him, people who will ensnare you."

I think of Charles Paget. Then there is Thomas Morgan, my chief cipher clerk, who deals with all of my French correspondence. I have heard the whispers, the rumours, that he is a friend of Francis Walsingham, that they grew up together. I know of Walsingham's plots, his underhand scheming, but this time I am sure.

"I have Anthony Babington on my side."

"He is just a young man. They will entrap him and execute him."

I shudder.

"My Guise uncles are still fighting my cause. I have proof of it."

I touch the parchment at my side.

Letters have reached me from France. They appear to be full of polite platitudes, urbane details enquiring after my health, discussing my predicament, offering sympathy in a distant, formal tone. But underneath the polite French is another message – the language of conspiracy.

These letters reliably inform me that the French will be on my side in the event of a Catholic uprising against the Protestants.

But Jane's expression fills me with doubt.

"We live in dangerous times, Madam," she murmurs.

I am a pawn in the power struggle between Catholics and Protestants. Yet I have a cause of my own.

Is it wrong to hope?

Perhaps my servant Jane is right.

I feel the net tightening around me.

Night after night, I am entertained by the ghosts of my past.

When John Knox appears before me, clamouring for attention, I laugh in his face and share with him the secret of my plotting. It drives him insane.

Sometimes I think my loyal servants, Jane and Elizabeth, fear for my sanity – so I have stopped telling them about these nightly visitations. I wait until everyone else is asleep before I dare to look into the shadows and see my ghostly companions come.

I must be patient. There are still people out there willing to help me. I am not forgotten. I will always be a thorn in Elizabeth's side. She may wish me gone, but she hesitates to rid herself of a sister Queen. We female monarchs must stand together, shoulder to shoulder, facing down the great army of hypocrites. However, Jane oft reminds me that she may not want to put my head on the block, but others will execute her will for her.

Can I out-fox my enemies one last time?

In my younger years, I had many adventures escaping from the snares they laid for me. It began in my infancy, right from the days when my mother kept whisking me out of the reach of the greedy King Henry – Elizabeth's father. He wanted

me for a bride for his son. But Edward did not last long, weakling that he was, and he was replaced by his Catholic sister Mary. When she died there were many who believed I was next in line to the English throne. After all, Henry had no right to put aside his lawful wife, Catherine of Aragon, in order to marry his mistress, Ann Boleyn. There were many who considered Elizabeth to be illegitimate, and therefore not entitled to be his heir – and many still do. Henry's oldest sister, Margaret, was my grandmother. She was sent up to Scotland to marry James IV. According to the laws of inheritance therefore, she was next in line to the throne and so were her offspring, but King Henry was a law unto himself and decided to rule her out of the line of succession for reasons best known to himself. Nevertheless, the fact remains that my own grandmother should have been next in line to the throne of England, and there are those who have not forgotten this.

As a result my early years were marked by anxiety and the fear of being kidnapped by King Henry. Strange to think that he was actually my own great uncle – I saw him only as some distant monster who wanted to destroy my childhood idyll. He loomed large on my horizon for many years, a terrifying ogre.

My mother, Marie of Guise, was having none of it.

I often think of the high turrets and lofty castle walls of Stirling, how they enfolded me like an encircling womb. My mother kept me there until I was five years of age, fearing for my life. My earliest memories are of those darkened corridors, frightened faces looming up at me out of the darkness, lit by flame, as they hustled me away into secret places.

I can remember the Great Hall, the vast fireplaces, the courtyard, the Chapel, and my mother's anxious, saddened face.

It must have been so hard for her. She wanted to keep me close, but she feared to lose me. In the end she had to think of my safety.

Then one evening the guards came to say that they had spotted movement on the horizon. Stirling Castle commands a panoramic view in all directions. A garrison of English soldiers were rumoured to be heading our way.

My mother wrapped me in a cloak, and a small party of us hurried down a flagged corridor away from the main entrance. We fled from a postern gate at the rear of the castle grounds, a secret tunnel leading below the crags. Horses were waiting for us and we galloped through the night. I remember the speed and the tension, the dark air whipping the cloak from my face, someone's arms encircling me tight.

It was a strange sensation. A mixture of fear and delight. Exhilaration at the movement of the horse beneath me, the wind in my hair, and yet apprehension.

We transferred to a small boat and I was rowed across to a tiny tree-covered island. By daylight Inchmahone Priory was revealed to me in all its glory. We sheltered there for a few weeks, days spent exploring the little island, nights of torchlight and tension. But it could not last. The threat of danger appeared to increase. My mother could not hope to keep me safe on a tiny island forever, so we left this little sanctuary and rode out towards the coast again.

I did not want that journey ever to end.

Because the end of it meant this: a tearful farewell from my mother.

She put me on a boat bound for France, the only place where she knew I would be safe. She entrusted me to the care of her French relatives. Little did she know…

I saw my mother only once more after that – when she came to stay with us in France for a year. Much later, she tried to attend my wedding in Notre Dame, but the Protestant nobles were stirring up trouble and rebellion and it was too dangerous for her to leave. She suffered much in trying to keep my kingdom free for me. But I have never forgotten the efforts she made, or the tearful sorrow with which she bade me farewell. I had to be torn, crying, from her arms.

Versailles
1551

The sea was rough, I remember that, and we were thrown about on the deck of the ship like skittles. I did not mind. I had already been drowned by my mother's tears when we parted, but I felt certain that I would see her again. I did not think our parting would be forever. Maybe she knew differently.

A lot of the passengers were sick from the roughness of the journey, but I was too young to suffer much. I watched the rise and fall of the waves with fascination. I had never been on the sea before and it was a new experience, an exciting one despite the ever-present threat of shipwreck or an attack by English ships. We rode a crest then plummeted down as if we were diving to the bottom of the ocean, ploughing our way to the depths. At times there was a wall of water in front of my face which I could have punctured with a fingertip, had I reached out. But the storms held no terrors for me. I had little knowledge of how easily ships could be tossed asunder in seas like this.

By the time the shoreline of France came into view we were all eager to reach land. My mother had taken great delight in talking to me about her own country, its people and customs and the world she had left behind, so I was excited to see what I would make of it.

That was before I met Catherine de Medici, my future mother-in-law.

The grand Parisian palaces, sculpted from blocks of white tufa, were very different to Scotland's dark castles. The weather was warmer, no need for roaring fires in every room. There were huge mirrors on the walls, long shining corridors instead of tunnelling passages lit by flaming torches.

Catherine de Medici greeted me with these words.

"Ah, the little half-caste!"

Did she mean me? I glanced over my shoulder, but there was no one else to whom she could be referring.

I did not know what she meant.

Her black Italian eyes narrowed with envy and spite, a look that would become familiar to me over the years as her dislike of me grew.

"How delightful!" she said silkily, bidding me step forward.

I shyly subjected myself to her inspection.

She was the King's wife. I was to become part of their household; the House of Valois. I would eat with the royal children, share their nursery, their schoolroom, their routines and rituals, and whatever else came my way. King Henri insisted that I be treated like one of his own. I do not think this arrangement pleased his wife.

The Medici woman studied me as if I was an insect – one to be feared. Her own children were special to her, of course, and she was not overly keen on having to take me under her wing.

I was treated as a novelty at first, and I took pleasure in that initially. I missed my mother, but in time I began to adjust and adopt the foreign ways of France. Scotland gradually – over the years – became a distant memory, vague and dreamy, obscured by mist and cloud. Bright vignettes would break through from time to time, fragments of memory, but like all children I learned to adapt. My future father-in-law, Henri, insisted that I speak French instead of my native Scots. But I clung quite tenaciously to my Scottish identity. I was not to be as easily biddable as they imagined. My mother had taught me the importance of maintaining always my dual nationality, and my birth-right to the Scottish throne.

"Oh, show us how you dress in Scotland again?" I was surrounded by a semi-circle of well-fed, shining-faced siblings in the royal nursery.

"And speak Scots for us again. It sounds so funny!" they laughed.

The Medici woman broke their ranks. "Don't mock Marie, my dears. It does not become you. Although the foreign tongue does sound unusually guttural, does it not?"

I eyed her suspiciously. She held an air of dark menace for me, even as I adjusted and fitted into the royal nursery and its way of life. I was never quite sure of her affection, even when she pretended to like me.

When they teased me like this not all of the royal children joined in. Little Francois held back. He was pale and thin. He was never one to taunt me. I liked him for his kindness.

"Did your father speak with a rough tongue?" they asked me.

"I don't know. I can't remember him."

"Did he tear meat from the bone with his bare hands?"

"Scotland is a rugged barbarous hill country. I heard the Cardinal of Lorraine say so."

I stared at them. A memory flew into my head – of wind and speed and movement, of a heathery terrain flashing beneath the hooves of a galloping horse, the splashing of mud and water at a lochside, the powerful breath of the animal conveying us. It ended quickly. I looked up. The memories would become more muddled over the years, harder to disentangle reality from fantasy.

Francois's pale face regarded me.

"She does not wish to speak of it," he said gently, with a surprising authority. The others turned to him. The spell was broken, the semi-circle of sibling relatives drifted away to seek other amusement.

Although I sometimes revelled in the novelty lifestyle, the comforts and the luxuries which had been unknown in Scotland, I was under no illusions. Part of me was always aware how spoiled and indulged were the children of the House of Valois. They were pandered and fussed over like a menagerie of tame birds. There was a hothouse atmosphere about the French court, an air of unreality. It did not always compare favourably with my native Scotland.

It has been said that I loved France and wept to leave it.

But no one knows how much I missed my mother, and how in doing so I came to love my native Scotland. During these years of captivity in England, is it France I dream of?

By the time I celebrated my ninth birthday at the French court I had grown used to the fact that the only communication I had with my mother was by letter. Letters flew back and forth across the ocean that separated us. She advised me, cajoled me, kept me informed of proceedings in Scotland, told me to seek counsel from my Guise uncles. She said that I would prosper and benefit from the education they could give me. I shudder to think of those words now, how misguided her prophecy, how forlorn her hope. My poor mother had entrusted me to her relatives because she had no choice. She thought – by doing this – she would rescue me from a worse fate.

Meanwhile, the Medici woman made it clear where *her* real loyalties lay. She cosseted and cherished her own children, tolerated and criticised me. Whatever King Henri's wishes, she made it obvious I was there on sufferance.

On my birthday I received the present of a small pony and was filled with delight. These tokens were making up for the absence of my mother, it is true, and at first I looked forward to the party that King Henri insisted they should throw for me.

A maid stood behind me and threaded tiny, opaque seed pearls into my hair. I stood admiring the jewel-like glimmer, turning my head this way and that to catch the light. Suddenly another face loomed behind me in the mirror. I jumped. Her dark witch-like eyes held mine.

"If you look in the mirror too often, God will wither that pretty face of yours, my dear. Remember, *'Sin is a beast lurking at the gate.'*"

Then she flashed a malicious smile and was gone.

No one witnessed this little exchange or noticed the way my face fell. I did not enjoy the party after receiving this sharp rebuke and little Francois wondered why I was so subdued. He did not know that his own mother was the cause of my gloom.

Later, as we skidded across the parquet floor playing musical chairs, I saw the Italian witch appear in a doorway. I withdrew from the game and stood half-concealed behind a pillar, pretending I did not feel well.

It was in subtle ways like this that the Medici woman made her presence felt in my life and increased my unease. I was happier in the company of Diane de Poitiers, mistress to the King, which of course did not please my future mother-in-law. I had made friends with her enemy – accidentally. I simply accepted whatever kindnesses were offered to me.

My mother's own family, the Guises, were a powerful clan at the French court, and she had entrusted me to their care and protection. There was my grandmother Antoinette and then there were my uncles, but one uncle figured larger than all the rest. The Cardinal of Lorraine fixed on me from an early age, although his influence was double-edged, poisonous. When my mother wrote to me asking questions about my education in the business of statesmanship, she could never guess at the secrets I might be forced to keep. And when I wrote to her in reply I remained mute on the subject. I did not lie, but I distorted the truth, withheld information. For how could I do otherwise? And who would have believed me?

The Cardinal loomed large in my universe.

He frightened me with his lecherous looks and his camphorous breath. He wore huge capes, and when I was a child I thought he had black velvet wings and flew at night above the spires and pinnacles of Joinville.

In Paris we used to attend Mass every morning – Francois and I. After this we were allowed breakfast, but I ate sparingly because I was dreading what was to follow. I had to go to my uncle's study for lessons. He was a ruthlessly ambitious man; he steeled me against the possibility of treachery and deceit.

"You are the jewel of our family," he told me. "We invest our greatest hopes in you. Watch. Be on your guard. That is the secret of success."

Rise high and I shall rise high with you. A leech sucking my blood.

The purpose of these private sessions was to instruct me in the art of politics. He took upon himself the responsibility of my education, but I was miserable all day until I had left that darkened chamber. The smell of camphor took hours to fade away.

When my mother was at last able to travel to France to visit me, I was ecstatic. We were very close, despite our years of enforced separation. She spent a full six months at the French court, but only days before she was due to depart for Scotland again, learned of a conspiracy to poison me. Terrified, she and my Guise relatives ensured that the perpetrators were executed, but she decided to prolong her stay and refused to leave my side. She remained with me for another six months after that. I was too young to fully understand the implications of this incident, though my mother hinted darkly that there was more to a plot like this than the immediate perpetrators' involvement. In other words, who else had been behind this dreadful scheme?

I watched my mother's eyes swivel towards Catherine de Medici. It was said she resented the influence my Guise relatives had at the court. I thought of my uncle's words during our lessons.

"Watch. Be on your guard."

I was a precious commodity in his eyes, his passport to future power and success.

My mother – wisely or unwisely – left me in his care

again, as she finally boarded a boat for Scotland. Trouble was brewing in our faraway kingdom, and she could not delay her return any longer.

She bid me a tearful farewell, but her brave smile hid her dark concern and fears for me. I do not often try to recall the moment of our parting. I prefer to let it rest in peace. Her face was strained and pale, concealing the pain she no doubt felt. She returned to Scotland to manage the warring factions of the lords in my absence. She had a mammoth task ahead of her, which she stuck at for another nine years or so. She kept my throne safe for me. It was an act of love, sacrifice and devotion – I know this now.

I never saw her again.

My memory of my mother has never faded – she has remained a strong, absent presence in my life, if there is such a thing. Her bright, courageous spirit and the example she set me were always with me. And I knew one thing for certain. Had I remained at her side throughout my childhood she would have equipped me for ruling a kingdom like Scotland much better than my French Guise uncles ever could.

She underestimated her own talents and strength.

She should have kept me by her side – in Scotland – where I still belong. But I do not resent her decision, or berate her for it. She did what she had to do as a mother, and I appreciate her sacrifice. The bond I had with her is the strongest I have ever known.

Paris
April 1558

As I prepared to marry Francois, heir to the French throne, my mother became Regent of Scotland and ruled in my absence, struggling to keep the kingdom in relative peace. The Protestant nobles of the Reformed Kirk now had a stranglehold, and once John Knox returned to his native land he increased the pressures against my mother. He was determined that Scotland should become a Protestant country, by violence and any other means. He encouraged the people to tear down statues, destroy monasteries and abbeys.

Meanwhile, nuptial preparations were underway for my marriage to the Dauphin – which had been agreed upon when I first set sail for France at five years of age. My mother was unable to attend the wedding in Notre Dame. Knox was stirring up more trouble, and it would have been unsafe for her to leave Scotland at that time.

I wrote to her often, describing every miniscule detail of the event. I thought it marked a new beginning for me, a dazzling future as Queen of France.

I wore a grey, velvet train borne by thirty pages, and my jewels flashed in the sunlight as I moved slowly towards a canopy of blue Cyprus silk, spangled with golden fleur-de-lis. Musicians clad in red and yellow satin poured their music into the air. Before me I could see the great twin towers of Notre Dame rising up darkly into the sky.

They cast a long shadow.

This was what my uncle had dreamed of. I was to become the Dauphiness, married to the heir to the French throne, one of the most powerful kingdoms in Europe.

I had been reared for this.

I was sixteen years of age. I glanced at Francois at my side. He was younger than me. I would look after him, protect him. Together, side by side, we would succeed in living up to what was expected of us.

The memory of our short time together is strange to recall. We were playmates together in the nursery; he was like a brother to me. We slept side by side like children in the giant bed, but our marriage was never consummated. It did not occur to either one of us to break the spell of the childish bond between us, and in truth I do not think we really knew how. All we knew was that we had loved each other as children and so could love each other now.

When King Henri was killed in a jousting accident a year later, the court went into mourning. Catherine de Medici grieved. Overnight Francois had become King of France. And I was his Queen.

I was barely seventeen when they crowned me in Rheims.

My uncle's eyes were gleaming, fixed, glutted with greed as he watched those gems sparkle on my brow. I was caught in his web, netted.

His assumption was that he would be able to control me – it is a common assumption made by men – so he was rather surprised when I stood up to him. When I began to resist his efforts to 'educate' me and sought to make my own decisions independently, he was greatly displeased. I don't think he ever forgave me.

He tried to subdue me, made excuses to arrange meetings in private, but as the Queen of France I refused to attend.

I began to loathe him, his touch, the great black cape waiting to enfold me in its musty embrace, the smells, the odours of defilement.

Francois and I tried to support each other in our difficult new role but it was an irksome task.

For there was yet another who sought to control us.

Catherine de Medici.

Versailles
December 1560

This was a year of profound and bitter loss for me. News of my mother's death in Scotland arrived ten days after she had passed. Instead of the usual correspondence from her there was a letter from the ambassador, telling of her passing.

Soon after this, Francois, who had often been unwell when we were children, contracted an ear infection which turned into an abscess on the brain. I watched him struggle for his life on the huge bed, a marmoreal slab bearing his slender frame, but it was my mother I was thinking of.

I waited with him in the closeness and cloying misery of the sick-room for death to come. He died one morning at dawn, after a long night of watching, and when I woke I saw his mother grieving over his lifeless body.

I knelt at the bedside and wept.

The Medici woman looked at me strangely.

"Enough time for tears, Marie. You have packing to do."

I looked up at her, aghast.

"There are jewels to be replaced in their coffers."

Still I did not understand her.

"You are no longer Queen of France, my dear. I fear it was a very short reign for you, after all."

I was shocked at her words and the sentiment behind them. I stared at her, waiting for some kind of confirmation that I had misheard or misread her intention. But none came.

This was a woman who knew – even in the depths of her grief – what she wanted. She had been content to sit and wait, and her waiting was not in vain.

Catherine de Medici, the new Regent, ruled.

She had other children to console her and assuage her grief. My mother had only me. And she had lost me to this life of pettiness in the French court.

Paris
July 1561

A period of mourning followed in which I avoided my Guise uncles and was acutely aware of their disappointment in me. I had been their brightest hope, borne the burden of their ambition, but it was not to be.

I sat in lonely silence in my darkened rooms, considering my future. I was entitled to a queen dowager's pension but would be expected to lead a quiet life in the shadows, on the fringes, while the Medici woman ruled.

I was not yet ready for a quiet life.

I thought of my mother, her intelligent rearing of me and all that she had done to make Scotland secure. I missed her deeply. While I grew up in the pleasure-loving Renaissance court of France, a part of me had been left behind with my mother across the ocean, where she struggled to govern Scotland for me in my absence. Now that she was gone, there was a vacuum.

There was an empty throne waiting for me, and a country in need of governance. I was beginning to understand that destiny was pulling me away from the home where I had lived for the last twelve years, and taking me back to my beginnings.

I would go where Fate directed me.

As if to confirm this belief my half-brother, Lord James Stuart, stepped into the breach. He arrived from Scotland, bringing the tang of sea-mists with him and the ring of his Scottish dialect.

I was still in deep mourning at the time and ordered my attendants to bring in some light. Candles were lit and the dark room began to flicker and glow. Umber shadows retreated into the corners as my brother stood in the doorway, tall and fair in the manner of our Scottish ancestry. He hesitated, then gave a courteous bow of the head.

"Lord James," I cried. "I am so pleased to see you."

"The pleasure is all mine."

Once the awkward pleasantries were over he told me the reason for his visit.

"I have a specific purpose in coming here."

"I did not doubt it."

"Have you considered your future here in France?" he asked bluntly.

"I have," I replied. "And it is bleak."

"I have come to urge you to return to Scotland. It is unwise to leave the throne empty for much longer. There is a power vacuum, which is never advisable in a country like ours, filled with hot-headed nobles as it is. Factions may develop."

When I think of his words now, an ironic smile plays on my lips.

He offered me the possibility of escape, back to my former home and away from my uncle, the Cardinal.

I had not yet learned that we cannot always run from our memories.

"Well," I admitted, "you are not the first to ask me to return."

"No?"

A few weeks earlier the Catholics had urged me to return to the north of Scotland in a military capacity, and help them to overthrow the Protestants. They had assured me that Catholic nobles in the north-east would support me with their troops.

"You refused?" Lord James asked.

"Of course. It is not my desire to bring discord."

He looked surprised. But there was something else in his eyes, admiration. Respect.

I was impressed by my half-brother back then; I trusted him. I liked his single-mindedness, his determination. I quickly grew fond of him.

Did he see me as just another pawn in the game of power and diplomacy? I was ready to trust him and turn to him as a key adviser.

Hindsight is a wonderful thing.

Lord James was a strict Protestant and a clever statesman.

"Are you surprised that I am not prepared to throw in my lot with the Catholics?" I asked him, point-blank.

He hesitated before answering. "A little. But I am very glad to hear it from your own lips, Mary. I confess that I was not sure how easy it would be to reach an agreement. It is true that Scotland is insecure without a monarch," he went on. "Indeed, the Scottish people have almost forgotten they have a queen."

I stared at him, and blinked my eyes once or twice.

Careful, I thought.

"They must have awfully short memories."

"An absent queen is not a real queen in their eyes."

"Then we must remedy that fact," I snapped back, quick as a flash.

"It has been twelve long years since you set foot on Scottish soil, Mary. In addition to this fact, they see you as an absent *French* queen..."

I was taken aback.

"Lord James," I said calmly, "I am a Scotswoman born and bred, and my mother – God rest her soul – never allowed me to forget that. The people of Scotland will be waiting to receive me. Besides, I am no longer a French queen – as you can see," I reminded him bitterly, indicating my black gown.

"With respect, you were but lately."

"Oh, I am well aware of my position. I am still a Queen Dowager of France, but I was crowned Queen of Scotland at six days old. In all that time my mother kept the throne secure for me, battling against all the troubles that the lords brought her with their endless rebellion and factionalism. It is perhaps worth reminding you, brother, that I am as Scottish as yourself. I am one of those who can claim a dual nationality as part of my good fortune. It is rather limiting to belong to one country alone, don't you find?"

He smiled thinly, then lifted his long white fingers to his lips, prayer-fashion.

"It's all a question of priorities and perspectives."

"Is it?"

"It is."

"And they are?"

"Well, and I speak on behalf of my fellow countrymen, of course, we would need to know your intentions. You have spoken of a policy of religious toleration, but what does that in fact mean? How could we trust that you would continue to respect our Protestant Kirk in the future?"

I looked him squarely in the face. "You have my word upon it. The word of a monarch ought to be sacrosanct."

Again, I had the impression he was a little nonplussed. He had hoped to find in me a biddable half-sister he could manipulate, but I was proving to be more fiery and single-minded than he had bargained for.

"What I am proposing Mary is this. I do not know how easy you would find it – as a Catholic, I mean – to rule a Protestant country."

"Oh, I would find it perfectly well," I assured him.

"It might be expedient for you to consider a change of religion."

"You mean Scotland change?"

"I mean you to change, Mary."

I knew of course that this was what he meant.

"Lord James, I am a very tolerant and broad-minded woman, as you have rightly pointed out. But I change my religion for no one. If I come to Scotland, I come as a Catholic queen."

"Then perhaps it may not be possible…"

"Possible? You speak strangely seditious words, my brother. Treasonable, in fact."

"That was not my intention."

"Religion is not a matter of expediency, Lord James. It is a matter of faith."

He persisted with his point, notwithstanding. He was a very determined man. "As a Catholic queen you may feel tempted to introduce Popish ways and laws into the land – perhaps not at first, but after a period of time. We want no change of that sort in Scotland. The people would brook no interference with their Kirk. They would rebel. You must understand that Scotland has only just lifted the yoke of Catholicism."

I regarded him coolly and lifted a hand to stop him. "You have my word that I will recognize the Reformed Church, but I expect to be able to attend Catholic services on my return. I shall respect your Kirk, but in return I must be free to worship as I please."

He held my gaze for a long moment. "Excellent. But let us not argue about religion."

"No, let us not."

He smiled grimly. "We have so much else to discuss."

"Do I have your word, then, that I will be able to practise as a Catholic?"

"In private...yes, you do indeed. I shall make it my business to ensure that you be allowed to worship in freedom. I shall keep my side of the bargain...for as long as you can keep yours," he muttered.

I did not like the sound of those final words, but I let it pass.

I decided that my actions would have to speak louder than my words.

Scotland
August 1561

Waves smacked against the creaking bows of the ship. It was a journey in reverse – reminding me of my absent mother. A mist came down and wrapped itself around the rigging and masts. A bell clanked eerily, indicating the approach of a port. It sounded oddly funereal, melancholic.

I peered through the fog, trying to make out the coastline. My half-brother, watching me, cleared his throat.

"We get these sea-mists from time to time."

He appeared to be apologizing, but I assured him there was no need. I did not hold him responsible for the climate of his native country, or the behaviour of the elements.

"I remember the mist," I said.

"Do you?" he sounded surprised. "You were so young when you left...I thought perhaps you remembered very little."

"I remember," I said.

But I chose not to share with him exactly what it was I remembered, whether those memories were good or bad. In truth, they were tinged by sadness. I remembered principally hiding from an unseen, amorphous enemy which lurked always beyond my ken; being borne in haste away from castles in the dead of night, just as dawn was lightening the edges of the sky. I remembered flaring torches, the hush of muted voices, whispers of urgency from the adults hovering just above my head. And I remembered my mother's face, tear-stained but brave, smiling with courage, promising me we would see each other again soon. And I had believed the adventure was only just beginning, that all would end well. I looked at her sorrowing countenance, and then turned in the hull of the boat to face the direction of my future with the heartlessness of the very young. That's what I could remember.

None of this I shared with Lord James.

The port of Leith came into view, appearing gradually through the haar like a haunting apparition. I gazed in fascination.

"My goodness, how quaint!" one of my French servants said.

"I didn't expect…"

"It's a sea-mist, is all."

"*Well…*"

Everyone seemed at a loss for words, but I secretly smiled to myself.

"Where is everyone?" I heard another say as we disembarked.

"What do you mean?"

"Well – where are all the people?"

"Yes, where all the crowds to greet Her Majesty?" Lord James was demanding of one of his party.

A few boatmen and fishwives were standing on the quay, staring at the spectacle before them, their eyes wide as saucers as if they could not quite believe what they were seeing.

"My sister came here expecting at least a welcome of some kind."

"We couldn't rustle up any of the crowds, I'm afraid. It's the weather."

"Damn it, aren't they used to the accursed weather by now?"

"Well, no one knew what to expect."

"What can you mean, man? I sent word we were arriving. Surely they knew to expect the return of Her Majesty."

"It's not quite as simple as that."

I gazed about me, the grey cobbles greasy with fog, the heaped barrels and coils of sticky rope on the quay, the downright poverty of Leith in comparison with the Paris streets I had come from. Gulls wheeled and gave out a desolate ghostly cry in the silence.

"Transport?" I heard my brother say, in a weary tone of disbelief. "What! You don't expect Her Majesty to walk into Edinburgh, I take it?"

"It's all we've got I'm afraid."

I was quite sure I heard my half-brother mutter under his breath "Someone will pay for this."

Then I heard a familiar sound – hooves clopping slowly, heavily on the damp cobbles. A tired-looking horse hung its head in front of me; I laughed.

Heads swivelled around and they turned to stare at me.

"She's laughing," a voice murmured in the mist, as if they considered me to be either mad or about to launch into an attack of French proportions on their lack of deference.

What they failed to see was that I was amused and charmed.

There was no lavish pomp and ceremony, no fanfare, no pageantry, no Guise uncles to chastise and control me.

I was my own mistress.

I could see clearly through the mist, and I could see my way to the future.

So it was a humble return to the kingdom of my birth, on the back of a tired-looking nag. I stroked its neck and spoke to it encouragingly as it bore me over the rough cobbles.

We made a steady, slow progress into Edinburgh. I was five years of age when I left these shores and I was not entirely unfamiliar with the sights. My memories were blurred. I did not, for instance, remember the tall grey tenements, crowded with people, the outside stair-heads where the odd square of laundry fluttered – in the vain hope that it would dry in this mist. Nor did I remember the closes and wynds that divided the tall buildings, winding out of sight. It was daylight, summer time in late August and yet the town was painted with darkness and shadows.

It was certainly different from what I had known in France. It was bleaker, colder, and there looked to be more poverty. We children of the royal nursery were cosseted from all of that. The House of Valois liked to rear its children in a soft fantasy land, far from the ravages of reality. I see that now.

In Scotland, a ruler is more closely acquainted with the ordinary lives of the people, aware of their sympathies and loyalties. The Scottish spirit is hard to subdue and I had no intention of subduing it. I wanted to rule with compassion, which has always been my way. I never wanted to repeat the tyranny I had seen under Catherine de Medici.

Edinburgh appeared much quieter than Paris. The streets here were muddied where they were not cobbled, and the people looked poor, but ruddy of complexion, used to the cold winds and the sea-mists.

At the top of the hill we turned left, away from the city boundaries. A rough mountain known as Arthur's Seat reared up through the mist, its black crags darkening against the sky. In its shadow lay Holyrood Palace, smaller than I remembered.

Rows of windows regarded me blankly.

The sun came out for a moment, and the shapes of clouds moved in the thick distorted windowpanes. We clopped into the courtyard, and my half-brother began sending out orders while I gazed all about me.

I dismounted and stood in the courtyard while the horses were led away.

Lord James glanced at me and there was a look of vague unease and disquiet in his eyes.

"It will all seem very different from what you are used to, Mary," he said gently.

I met his gaze. "Yes, that is true. But it is not as unfamiliar to me as you might imagine."

In truth, memories I did not know I possessed rose to the surface of my mind. I did not share them with anyone. I simply observed all around me with growing interest.

"The palace will have been made comfortable for your arrival," he added.

Then he made a deft but brief movement of obeisance as he showed the way to the entrance of the Palace.

The gesture touched me.

We entered the great echoing hall – less of a palace, more a castle, with its rough walls and dark turrets.

There was a commotion, footsteps resounding down

corridors as my half-brother took command of the details of my welcome. I had switched to speaking in my native Scots, but my French servants who had accompanied me were of course not able to oblige.

The air was chill inside the palace, and when one of my ladies made a move to take my cloak, I stopped her.

"There are no fires lit," I observed, looking about me.

Lord James caught my eye. "It is August."

"But it is freezing," I murmured.

My half-brother turned and shouted an order along the corridor.

"Get the fires lit, can't you? It's too cold for Her Majesty."

There was a flurry of movement, and then I was escorted up the main staircase and shown to my private apartments, a vast bedchamber with table, chairs and sturdy four-poster.

One or two servants set about creating a blaze in the fireplace. The panelled walls were bare, but the furniture was good solid oak. I had brought tapestries with me to hang on the walls.

"What's this?" I said, noticing a doorway in the corner. I stepped through it into a tiny turret chamber, the windows of which overlooked Arthur's Seat. There was a table in the centre and tapestries already covered the walls.

In the winter months, I was told, I would benefit from retreating into this turret room for warmth. With a fire roaring in its hearth, I could imagine it would be warmer than my larger audience chambers.

"You will be tired after your long journey, Ma'am," one of my French servants said.

I agreed that I was.

It was a journey across time. I had travelled backwards into my own past. When I stood on the rocky shore of the Forth twelve years ago, bidding farewell to my mother,

France had been my future. Now everything was in reverse order.

But I had escaped Catherine de Medici, and I had escaped my Guise uncles. This was the alternative left to me, and I was determined to rise to the challenge.

Holyrood Palace
August 1561

It was early evening, and I lay down to sleep, exhausted. What did my future hold? Anxiety knotted in my stomach, and sorrow, for what I had left behind in France. I would need to adapt to Scotland. Its people were a mystery to me still. In France I had been paraded as a little Scottish maiden, a figure of curiosity, a novelty. But here I could not boast that claim. I could already see that those Scots I had come across since we landed at Leith regarded me as a foreigner. I would need to remedy this and prove a point.

It was still light outside when I heard a strange dirge drifting up to my windows. I recognized that sound – the wail of the bagpipes. Usually an instrument which moves me profoundly, it can resonate through my bones when I hear its lament. But this was not the case that night.

I rose from my bed. In the courtyard beneath were gathered a group of people, mainly men, singing along to the dirge.

Others had joined me and peered down. Lord James had appeared at my shoulder and gave a sigh. "You see, they are welcoming you, Mary."

One of my French servants began to laugh.

"What is it they are singing?"

Lord James coughed. "It is a psalm, Madam."

"A psalm?"

"That's right, Your Majesty."

He nodded.

"And why cannot they sing something a little more… appropriate?" I trailed off, not knowing how to finish my sentence politely.

Lord James met my eye, and I was certain I saw a twinkle of mirth there. "They are only allowed to sing hymns or psalms. Profane music has been forbidden."

"Forbidden?" I stared at him. "By whom?"

He coughed again. "John Knox."

"John Knox?"

I had heard that man's name mentioned before.

"That's right, Ma'am."

My half-brother paused for a moment.

I stared down at the drab crowd gathered in the courtyard below. "And do they take all their orders from John Knox?"

"Well, it appears so." He corrected himself slightly. "They listen to their Calvinist ministers at any rate."

I gazed down. White faces were turned up to me in the gloaming twilight below, and they sang on, trying to sound as cheerful as they could under the circumstances.

"But it's ridiculous. They sound awful."

Lord James shrugged.

I said nothing, but I was interested to meet this man who regarded his influence as superior to his appointed sovereign.

When they had done, I opened the casement window and one of their number shouted up to me.

"Welcome home, Your Majesty."

"Thank you," I replied.

There were a few cheers and hats thrown in the air.

The next morning, I remarked on the incident to my brother. "I couldn't help noticing that their numbers were a little thin on the ground, considering their sovereign has returned to take up her duties as Queen."

"Knox has a powerful sway over the people. What you must understand, Mary, is that in their eyes you are French, and you are a Catholic."

"Not just in their eyes, brother," I corrected him. "That is exactly what I am. Half-French, the other half being Scottish."

He laughed and added, "Perhaps they are uneasy with that."

"But there are Catholics here in Scotland too, Lord James. Not just Protestants."

He shot me a quick resentful glance. "Remember our bargain, my sister."

I hesitated. "Oh, I remember. But do you remember yours?"

A note of acerbity had entered our dialogue which reminded me of the dangers which might lie ahead.

Holyrood Chapel
August 1561

I was wrapped in shadow and there were cold, stone flags beneath my feet. I could smell the solid oak, the dust on the air. I had chosen to come to the chapel at Holyrood in order to immerse myself in solitude. In my rooms my ladies and servants always accompanied me, but I craved a moment alone.

It was late evening. I lit a candle in the darkness, and its light rippled against grey stone walls. The glassy eyes of Our Lady looked down upon me, trying hard to be real.

Idolatry, John Knox would have called it, but the statues remained untouched. His sabotage could not reach here. I could smell the oil paint on the paintings, a heady intoxicating aroma which never seems to fade with age and always fills me with inspiration and wonder.

Knox does not like the presence of art in any religious building.

For myself, I think art celebrates life and God and everything that is beautiful in the world.

I knew that beneath these flags were the vaults containing the bones of my ancestors. It was a sobering thought. The remains of my own father and grandfather lay here – men I had never met. I wondered for a moment what advice they would give me.

But it was my mother, Marie of Guise, I missed most of all. She had proven herself to be a strong ruler. How would I be able to emulate her example?

A footstep on the flags behind me made me turn and I saw Father Mamaret, my French confessor.

"Forgive me, I have no wish to disturb you, Ma'am," he said.

I shook my head and greeted him.

"I hope you realise how indebted I am to you, Father, for agreeing to leave France with me?"

"Nonsense. It is my duty to serve you, Ma'am. I could do no less."

"I would have been quite alone without you."

"Not alone, Mary, surely?"

It was with a vague sense of unease that I noted his slightly patronizing tone. I chose, however, to ignore it.

"Who else would serve me so well?"

He took a deep breath. "There are plenty of Catholics in Scotland who would be as ready to serve Your Majesty."

"I do not think my brother would agree with you there."

He gave me a long steady look. "On the contrary. I think he *would* agree. That is what he is so afraid of. The heretics have the upper hand for the time being, but Scotland was a Catholic country until recently. Your brother knows this."

I glanced over my shoulder nervously.

But Father Mameret went on. "They are content to listen to John Knox and his kind for the moment, but it will not last."

I smiled, and thought of the promise I had made to my brother back in France – that I would allow Scotland to continue in its Protestant beliefs. His words came back at me now "...*for as long as you can keep your side of the bargain.*" My half-brother, Lord James, had not believed that I would remain true to my word.

"I made a promise to the people of my country, Father."

"Of course," he muttered.

"I will do everything in my power to honour that promise."

Father Mamaret watched me patiently. "You always were wise for your years, Marie."

"I hope so."

"But you have had much to contend with."

"I consider myself to be very fortunate," I replied.

"Yes..." he murmured reflectively then broke off as if there was more that he could say.

On my first Sunday in Holyrood, Father Mamaret prepared the Chapel Royal at my request. Word had got out that I would be celebrating Mass in the evening. It was no secret. Lord James had assured me that I would be free to worship.

So when the fight broke out in the courtyard, I was appalled.

My almoner was crossing the courtyard when the candles were snatched from his arms, and he was beaten about the head.

I confronted my half-brother with the news.

"This is outrageous," I declared. "You promised me. What about your side of the bargain, brother?"

He looked surprised by my fiery outburst, of which he had seen no sign before – but I was more than a match for him.

"It was an oversight," he told me. "It will not happen again."

"Oversight?" I cried, my voice echoing along the corridors of Holyrood. Several pale faces turned in our direction, observing the outburst from afar with growing consternation.

"When I came here to take up my duties as Queen I did not expect to find my servants beaten about the head by criminals when trying to carry out my orders!"

"They have not taken kindly to hearing that you are to celebrate Mass this evening, Mary."

"You promised!" I roared. "Do you expect me to honour my side of the bargain when you cannot honour yours? This is rebellion, brother. In another country it would look like treason – and I would be required to deal with it accordingly."

He met my gaze, but said nothing. He was beginning to understand who he was dealing with.

Later, when it was suggested that I should consider cancelling the Mass in view of the disturbance, I refused. We assembled in the Chapel Royal at eight o' clock sharp, although my brother warned me that a riot had broken out in the streets of Edinburgh.

"And who organized this little rabble, James?"

He paused before answering. "I assured Your Majesty that you could worship in peace, and I will see to it that you may."

As Father Mamaret's Latin chanting filled the dark air of the chapel, it did not succeed in drowning out the noise beyond. We heard shouts and cries, mostly incoherent, but occasionally calling for the blood of the Papist priest.

Father Mamaret's hands shook as he lifted the sacrament, and I glared straight ahead, refusing to acknowledge the disturbance in any way.

It was at this point that a loud hammering began on the doors of the chapel.

As the host was elevated an undignified scuffle broke

out and I turned in my pew to witness Lord James forcibly ejecting two old men and slamming the door shut in their faces. He stood firmly in the doorway, legs apart, arms folded.

Afterwards, as I left the chapel, Lord James caught my eye. "You see I am doing my best to observe my side of the bargain, Mary?"

I hesitated. "A little less noise next time perhaps?"

His stern face broke into an involuntary smile for a moment, like sunshine appearing from behind clouds.

Although I spoke with humour, I was alarmed at what I had witnessed. And I did not then – nor do I now – believe that it was representative of what the whole of Scotland wanted. Knox might have arranged his little rabble of protest, but there were plenty of others, Catholics and Protestants alike, who would rather not adopt his narrow-minded methods. I had only to win them round.

St. Giles' High Kirk
August 1561

John Knox, when I met him, seemed impervious to charm. I established this quickly; he was distressingly open in his hostility and rebellion.

After all, this was the man who was engaged in writing a pamphlet called *THE FIRST BLAST OF THE TRUMPET AGAINST THE MONSTROUS REGIMENT OF WOMEN.*

My sister-queen, Elizabeth, fared little better in this treatise of his – he hated us all equally, forbore to condone the idea of any woman in power, and he especially hated myself. At least Elizabeth was not a Catholic, and at least she was not half-French.

The cobbles were slick and wet beneath the hooves of the horses as we rode up the Canongate towards St. Giles' High Kirk. Crowds gathered to watch us passing. There was some laughter from the servants behind me and we rode on, smiling at those I saw along the way. This was my attempt to make peace.

Knox's rabble had not approved of my celebrating Mass in private, in my own chapel, but I would attend his service. At the same time, I could allow myself the opportunity to watch him and judge what kind of man I was dealing with.

The shadowy interior was filled with people, and there was a buzz in the air. Heads turned at our arrival. There were even one or two dogs gathered there, next to their owners, milling about in the dense fug. I could feel the curiosity of those around me, eager to observe their new Queen for the first time. I rose to their inspection, nodding and smiling as I took my place at the front, along with my ladies-in-waiting and companions.

Then I looked up.

A dark oak pulpit loomed over us all and I felt his eyes upon me before I saw them. I returned his stare. It was one of blank disapproval and he had no intention of keeping this private. Tact, diplomacy, any attempt at conciliation were completely beyond him. I saw that at a glance.

His sermon began with a tirade of abuse against what he saw as the 'Popish' religion. His eyes were fixed on me, and there could be no mistaking the target of his wrath. I was appalled. My cheeks burned, while the congregation about me fidgeted in their seats in discomfort and boredom. His powerful invective sliced the air and went on and on interminably. Someone behind me coughed, and there were embarrassed glances in my direction.

This was something my mother's anxious letters had not prepared me for, despite her best attempts.

What kind of man was this, I wondered, studying his great flowing beard, his voluminous garments, his heavy brow as he harangued the people from his giant pulpit? His dark-blue eyes were beetling and angry.

What motivated him? Was it all down to piety, truly? *He*

certainly believed so. I had heard he was married to a woman with grown-up daughters. His step-daughter Margaret was particularly close to him. Not so '*monstrous*' after all, then? Or was it only the women who had authority over him that made him chafe?

Once his tirade of a sermon was over, I breathed a sigh of relief – as did everyone else. We were free at last to file back out into the sunshine. But first the crowds.

They parted to let me through, but I saw eyes staring, wonderingly, some in awe, a few with naked curiosity.

"Make way," my half-brother James ordered – always in front of me in those days, to pave the way. "Make way for the Queen."

I struggled through into the daylight.

Then we rode back down to Holyrood.

"A fiery sermon, was it not?" Lord James said.

"I didn't much care for it."

"I did warn you," my brother said.

I took my brother by surprise then. "I want to see him. In private."

"Who?" Lord James asked.

"Don't be facetious, James. You know who I mean."

There was a meaningful silence.

"I request that a meeting should be arranged with that man in my audience chamber, here at Holyrood."

"For what purpose?" my brother asked in a low voice.

"To give him the opportunity to explain his actions. We shall see what manner of man he really is."

John Knox responded to my invitation immediately, but only in order that he could make his opinions clearer than ever.

He strode into Holyrood Palace with an air of defiant self-importance.

I glimpsed his arrival from an upstairs window of my private apartments and prepared myself for the interview.

What manner of man is this? I wondered.

I was to have my answer soon enough.

Knox was difficult, stubborn, but ultimately disappointed by life. He craved martyrdom, I know this much. He would have loved for the Catholic Church to make a martyr of him. Instead he died peacefully in his bed of old age, waited on hand and foot by his 'daughters'.

He distrusted life and pleasure and art, and he distrusted himself – his own weakness.

"Master Knox," I said, when we met. "I had occasion to listen to your sermon last Sunday."

Knox raised his chin an inch or two. "Aye. What of it?"

I blinked once, astounded by his abrasive tongue and rude manner. This was not a gentleman.

"I have to confess I was surprised at its content."

Knox glared at me.

"It appeared to me that you were inciting my people to rebellion."

He stuck his bottom lip out so that it protruded from the mass of his grey flowing beard, which fell like a great waterfall over his chest. He appeared to be reflecting on how to answer.

I spoke for him. "Tell me, Master Knox, why do you incite my people to revolt against their royal sovereign?"

He stared at me, and after a short pause finally spoke. "Because I am no' so sure you hev a right to call yourself that…Ma'am."

I gaped at him, astonished by his complete and utter audacity.

"The statement you have just uttered is a treasonable offence. Would you care to explain yourself further?"

"I do not believe that any woman has a right to rule this kingdom – least of all a Papist French woman. It is an unnatural state of affairs for a country like Scotland. Ye were no' bred to rule this country. Neither was your mother afore ye…My people…"

I stopped him there. "Excuse me? *Your* people?" I said. "I had no idea when I arrived here that Scotland already had a ruling monarch."

His brow furrowed. "'Tis not a treasonable statement to declare that my people owe their allegiance to the true Kirk, first and foremost."

"I have absolutely no wish to interfere with the worshipping habits of my people, Master Knox. They may worship *when* they want, *where* they want, *how* they want. I believe in tolerance."

There was a short silence, while we eyed each other.

"That is perhaps an idea you are not overly familiar with, from what I have observed of you. But what I do object to is that you should incite my people to rebellion. It is not in their best interests, and neither is it in yours."

He remained silent.

"I hear you are writing a book, Master Knox."

"That is right."

"Could you tell me a little about it? Its title, for example?"

Of course, I already knew the title, but wanted to hear it from his own lips.

He cleared his throat momentously.

"It is called *THE FIRST BLAST OF THE TRUMPET AGAINST THE MONSTROUS REGIMENT OF WOMEN.*"

"How extraordinary. And how beguiling."

There was a suppressed titter from others present in the room. I caught my half-brother smiling to himself.

"Why do you regard us as monstrous, Master Knox? I am at a loss to understand."

"I have nothing against you personally," he began, shifting heavily on his widespread feet. "It is not intended to be a personal attack in any way. I'm merely voicing my opinion – and the view of many others present in Scotland today – that it is a weaker kingdom if we let women govern. It is not natural for women to rule. Being the weaker and fairer sex they know not the political ways, and have a leaning towards ungovernable, unreasonable...hysteria."

"Hysteria?"

He nodded grimly.

"That is very interesting. When I lived in France, Master Knox, I was forced to witness the torture and execution of many men and women who happened to be of a different religion to the one espoused by the ruling House of Valois – of which I was a part. It was decreed that – being a Catholic – I would approve of this violence."

I paused for a moment.

"I did not. I still frown upon such methods of controlling people, as I do not believe that cruelty is what God wants. If you bothered to examine the pages of the Good Book you are gripping so tightly in your fist, Master Knox, you might see that it tends to recommend kindness and compassion."

I could see he was angry. His dark eyes were beetling with barely suppressed rage. He wanted to roar at me, but contained himself.

"Forgive me, Ma'am, but I do not require to be lectured on the contents of the Scriptures. I am familiar with its contents, chapter and verse, after years of studying it in Geneva. The fact remains that women do not make adequate rulers. The Bible testifies to it, and so do I."

There was a splutter from someone behind me, who then struggled to conceal their mirth. I stared at him, this new adversary of mine who had spent years tormenting my mother, Marie of Guise, and now seemed set to torment me.

"You and I will never agree over religion. I am not for burning men, Master Knox, but be warned. There are many rulers who would have you hung, drawn and quartered for what you have just said to me. If you incite rebellion in my kingdom again, I may be forced to reconsider my views on religious tolerance."

I realised I might have gone too far. There was a ripple of unease from the corner of the room where I knew my half-brother stood.

Knox glanced towards Lord James and it seemed there was a glimmer of communication between them from which I was excluded.

Then it slipped out, words he might easily have regretted speaking. "You'll no' scare me. Your mother didn't freeght me, and she was more brawn than yerself."

I stared at him, aghast. I should have struck him down then, while the iron was hot. I should have sworn to demolish his purpose before he could undermine me further. But I was mindful of the promise I had made to my brother.

I bid John Knox a good afternoon and demanded that he be escorted from my presence.

The palace rang with gossip afterwards. I could hear them discussing it in subdued voices, wondering how I would react.

After our meeting that day I sat down on a low stool before

the fireplace, where I wept tears of frustration.

"Calm yourself, Mary," Mary Livingstone comforted me, a hand on my shoulder. "You must be strong."

"How can I appear strong when I have an adversary like that ranting against me from the pulpit every week? How did my mother bear it?"

"She struggled, and she rose to the challenge – as will you."

I looked up.

It was James Hepburn speaking.

"I had not known you were there, Bothwell," I said.

He came forward into the light. "You will succeed, Ma'am."

The atmosphere was tense suddenly.

"My mother wrote of you often," I said.

"Did she?"

"She told me how loyal you were."

He said nothing.

"A ruler needs to find out early who are her enemies – but also her friends."

Mary Livingstone watched this little exchange with a wry look on her face which I could not quite fathom.

I went to bed that night trying to suppress the vision of John Knox's face before me, his flowing beard, his angry eyes, as his mouth worked on and on in a torrent of terrible invective and abuse.

Edinburgh
February 1563

During my first year in Scotland I transformed the
Palace of Holyrood, making it resplendent with
furnishings brought from France. I covered the walls
with rich gold tapestries; I filled the dull, forbidding rooms
my father had built with oaken and marble tables, furnishings
of velvet and damask, brocade sofas and porcelain, cabinets
and silver lamps, gorgeously canopied beds.

I lived mostly in the north-west tower. I imported my
own library from France, glad these precious volumes had
survived the journey across the high seas – texts in French,
Latin, Greek, Italian, Spanish, and of course my native
Scots. I was fortunate in receiving an education which most
young women are denied.

My brother frowned at these attempts to soften my
surroundings. *He* declared it an extravagance.

I reminded him that no money had been parted with.
The coffers of the Exchequer remained untouched.
I had simply brought from France what was already mine,
and made good use of the items. I could not see that this

should be a problem for my brother, but he used it as an excuse to complain of my lavish excess.

I was often absent from Edinburgh during these years, continually on the move, my brother by my side, as we sought to put down rebellion. I rose to the challenge, thinking often of my secret heroine, Joan of Arc, who had been inspired to lead her people into battle.

There is one incident, a fragment of memory from this time, which burns clear after all these years. We spent a memorable few nights at Cumbernauld Castle and one night the roof of the main hall caved in. It collapsed unexpectedly while we were dining. My brother was quite put out, but even more so when he observed my response to the incident, for I did tuck my skirts into my breeches and set about helping the servants to clear the hall of debris. We were hard at the task all day, and when night fell, I slept with them on the floor of the chamber as there was nowhere else to rest. The servants were full of gratitude, and did tell me how great was my kindness, but what I recall most about the incident is that it made me long for an ordinary status such as theirs, for it was a comfort to join in with them and be on good terms with those who work hard. There was great warmth and comfort in sharing their company that night, and I have longed ever since for such conviviality.

During my absence from Edinburgh, Knox, of course, continued to preach against me in the pulpits, ranting about idolatry and implying that a French Jezebel could not be trusted to rule. His screams echoed above the rooftops and tenements of the city in a silent frenzy which – thankfully – only met my ears in muted whispers and rumours.

"Did you know…?"

"Have you heard…?"

"What was it this time?" I asked.

"The man is a fool," Bothwell said. "Ignore him."

"But I thought you were a Protestant, Bothwell?" I chided him.

"So I am, Your Majesty – but that does not mean I have to agree with everything Knox says."

Meanwhile relations with my brother became gradually strained over time. At first we presented a united front, but if I happened to disagree with him, he objected.

"Why can you not accept that I know what is best for this country? I could have been…"

He stopped.

We both knew what he could have been. My brother was born out of wedlock, illegitimate, therefore ruled out completely from the succession.

"I like not the direction of your thoughts, Lord James," I told him.

This exchange introduced a tension into our relationship.

There came a time when I began to doubt the loyalty of my own brother.

I did not know who to believe.

I still do not know who to believe.

Fotheringhay Castle
September 1586

My lady-in-waiting, Jane, has just entered the room. She stands, folding clothes and placing them by the fire to warm.

The past tires me.

She glances down at my writing book.

"I am confessing here, Jane," I tell her, patting the thick leather binding. "I have taken your advice."

Jane smiles. "It is between yourself and God, Madam. No one else. But it will be a comfort to you."

"I will entrust this book to you for safekeeping when the time comes, Jane. When I am gone, you can be the guardian of this volume. And you can decide what will happen to it."

Jane Kennedy's eyes brim with tears and she looks sad. "No, Madam. You will not die soon. We have many years together yet – all of us."

"And are you content to remain trapped alongside me between these dank castle walls?"

"I am content enough to serve you, Madam."

"You are very kind, Jane. And loyal."

"I am not the only one," she replies.

Perhaps she is right and Mary Queen of Scots has not been forgotten. There are many beyond these walls who would risk their lives to further our cause, to see me released and returned to Scotland. I used to believe that my son waited for me there, and that he would demand my release so that we could endeavour to rule jointly. But, sadly, that is not the case. He broke my heart. He thought only of himself and did nothing to secure my release.

That is another bitter pill I have had to swallow during these terrible years of captivity.

"It is sometimes a little hard to believe that anyone cares," *I offer in a tired voice.*

"You will see, Madam. But we must tread carefully."

She pauses and adds carefully, "Forgive me, Ma'am, but I do not always believe that the letters you receive from France are genuine. I think you must be wary."

"I trust Babington."

"So do I, Madam. But what if he too has been tricked?"

I shake my head. "All will be well," *I tell her.* "You will see."

Jane looks worried as she watches me put aside the writing book and pick up my tapestry.

"But how do you know your replies have not been intercepted, Your Majesty?"

I give her a long level look.

"I do not know. But I trust to God."

Jane does not look convinced by this.

She continues to fold clothes and pours a few more coals

onto the fire. It knocks apart the little pyre we have built, and the burnt-out pieces crumble into ash before it revives again.

I am ringed around by Walsingham's threats and his spies. Sometimes I find myself even doubting Jane. How easy would it be for Walsingham to turn my closest friends and servants against me with the threat of torture? Who would not consent to turn double-agent when threatened with the rack, the boot and the screw?

"These are evil times we live in, Jane."

She stops what she is doing at the fire, and her back is rigid.

"Indeed, Your Majesty."

"I am very grateful to you, Jane. I hope you know that. I would be lost without you."

She makes a hasty motion, thrusting the poker back into its cradle. "Don't be silly, Ma'am. We are all your friends here – Elizabeth, Didier and I. And don't forget little Geddon," she laughs. Then adds on a more serious note "We will never desert you, Ma'am."

A piece of kindling cracks in the hearth, like a pistol-shot in the darkness.

Sparks fly.

As I watch the flames lick the coals I think of how many perish in this fashion. Catholics are being burned throughout the land – at Queen Elizabeth's orders, just as in Mary Tudor's day. Knox hated Catholic monarchs because of what happened to his friends, but the Protestants are no better in their methods.

Walsingham is cunning and sly. Will he find me out?

I pick up my embroidery silks and stab my bright tapestry

with the needle. *My life is a web on which sorrow and pain stitches itself.*

It is incomplete. I study the picture with a wry smile on my lips. I have stitched a cat with evil, gleaming yellow eyes; there is a mouse between its paws. Elizabeth is the cat and I am her victim, being teased and toyed with. Every tapestry of mine is a narrative alive with symbolism.

The stitches are miniscule and delicate. Although my eyesight has suffered over the years and my shoulders have become rounded, no one doubts the skill with which I execute these tapestries. It is sometimes said that the pen is mightier than the sword, but there is also power in my needle.

I watch the thread grow taut as I weave my anxiety and sorrow into the tapestries I create, in and out, in and out.

In the corner of my chamber there is a spider's web, stretched tight across the cornice. For weeks now I have studied the intricate weave of that web, like Robert the Bruce in his cave. It has pockets and cradles, strung like a hammock from several hooks. It is a work of art, the architecture of the spider. I heard it once said that spider's web is stronger than silk. It bends, but it does not break. I imagine winding a whole sticky spool of the stuff to use in my embroidery.

How strong would it be then? How inviolate?

Crookston Castle and Stirling Castle
February 1565

It was the year of the Big Freeze. The lochs froze like plates of glass. Trees became statuesque forests of spindly white with winds whistling through them. The cold was interminable and ruthless. Coal fires were lit throughout Holyrood and they greedily swallowed up our supplies of fuel. No matter how much wood was chopped or how much coal was heaped in the scuttles, the fireplaces devoured it.

I wore voluminous cloaks of velvet and damask, lined with soft white sable fur to keep out the chill. Despite the freezing conditions I continued to take delight in getting to know Scotland. The royal court was constantly on the move, riding across country to stay in the various residences and castles dotted about my kingdom.

The more I was seen in evidence by my people, the more I could count on their support. I visited both Protestant and Catholic lords alike, keeping the nobility on side no matter what their religious leanings during this turbulent time. We all heard stories of what was taking place in England, terrible atrocities.

There had been continuing negotiations about whom I should marry. I was surrounded by male advisers who brought pressure to bear – all insisted I should marry well to provide an heir for the throne.

I think now of my wily sister, Elizabeth – how she submitted to the negotiations, hummed and hawed, kept suitors dangling, and then somehow never finally agreed to marry anyone. She remained the Virgin Queen, married to her country. Do I now wish I had done the same, avoided marriage altogether?

A life without love?

Without pain?

Without disappointment?

That winter Darnley rode over the border into our territory. Elizabeth sent him, I believe.

I was invited by his father, Lord Lennox to visit them at Crookston Castle.

No mention was made of Darnley at first, but I could not avoid noticing him. He struck me as a fine-looking young man. I was twenty-four years of age. Darnley was nineteen: tall, lean and lusty-looking. He gave the impression of being well-educated, refined, and made a welcome change from the gruff Scottish lords I was surrounded by. He played the lute and the virginals, he could sing and dance and play cards. He was amusing – I could tell that at a glance. My eye was caught, but not my heart.

As I left Crookston Castle with my entourage, I thought about how my advisers did urge me constantly to find a husband.

It was not long before our paths crossed again.

We were at Stirling Castle. The Great Hall was filled with guests. All four fireplaces were blazing and the long trestle tables were laden with food. Music was playing; the sound of the lute and the virginals hung in the high wooden rafters above. There was snow outside. Through the small diamond panes, I could see a white sugary coating over the mountains. Flaring torches lit the cobbles and the air in the courtyards outside was bitter – but inside here we were warm as toast while darkness fell.

Lennox had made sure that I encountered his son at Crookston Castle. He then drove home the advantage, I believe, by insisting that Darnley follow me to Stirling and make himself amenable. I saw him now among the guests, without his father this time, but attended by a couple of valets.

Bothwell was there too, watching, as was my half-brother, Moray.

When Darnley approached and led me onto the dance floor, I was happy to oblige. I love to dance and when I was young I could have danced without stopping, until dawn rolled in over the mountains.

He was an excellent dancer, a skill which was not lost on me. He wore sky-blue satin, a shining cloak that swished with his swift movements, and a high collar which showed off his good looks to perfection. The slashed velvet of his doublet and hose revealed the faintest of blue silks beneath.

I could feel eyes upon me as we danced. Lord Lennox would have been delighted had he been there; Bothwell and Moray were less so.

After several hours there was a lull in the dancing and I took a break, cheeks still aflame and eyes wide. Darnley acquired a lute from one of the musicians and began to pluck its strings – with the same delicacy of skill with which he could dance. I watched him, entranced. I will admit he had succeeded in holding my attention.

He played a quiet melody, softly singing a few notes in a low voice which sounded surprisingly intimate despite the crowded hall. The entire court was watching us, while pretending not to, of course, but it was obvious that all present would be keen to know where my interests lay.

I was not completely won over at this point. My heart was still my own.

There was a moment, as he sang, when he lifted his eyes and looked straight into mine. I was the first to look away.

Bothwell and Moray exchanged knowing glances with each other.

The next day Moray came to visit me in my private apartments. Most of the guests were still present, and Stirling Castle rang to the sound of blacksmiths and ostlers, horses being led across the courtyards. The Great Hall was being swept, the debris from the night before cleared by scores of servants. The kitchens were always busy with activity, kitchen boys and porters, steaming, simmering, chopping, plucking, kneading and baking. The smells wafted across the courtyard and found their way into my rooms.

"Did you enjoy the festivities yesterday, my brother?" I asked him cheerfully.

"I did, Ma'am."

He regarded me coolly, and I think I almost knew what was coming next.

"You appeared to be enjoying yourself too, Mary. Are you aware that Lord Lennox's son is a Catholic?"

I shrugged. "It has been mentioned to me."

He frowned and chewed his lip for a while.

When I said nothing he launched into his main point.

"You know, Mary, I have stood by you all these years, supported you…but I am afraid I cannot answer for your safety if you should decide to marry a Catholic."

"Marriage? Who said anything about marrying him? You are a little quick off the mark, brother."

He gave me a long piercing look and pursed his lips. The silence between us spoke volumes.

Of course, once he had planted the idea in my head it began to take seed, festering away like a little wound.

Perhaps I would never have considered Darnley as a serious contender if my half-brother Moray had not laboured the point. If he had kept his thoughts to himself I might have allowed Darnley to pass on by after a little frivolous flirtation.

After all, there was something a little light and insubstantial about him, something I could not quite put my finger on. It was as if he lacked substance.

I stood at my window watching the snow fall.

"It never snows in France," I observed later that afternoon.

Lady Jean Stewart, my half-sister, glanced at me.

"Never, Ma'am?"

"Not like this, no. I believe this is the worst winter since I arrived."

Flakes began to swirl and eddy from a low-scudding sky.

"The guests are staying overnight again. The weather does not promise to be lifting."

I loved Stirling Castle.

I could see the shrubbery partitioned into beautiful

terraces below, though bleak and austere. We were so high, the land falling away, a panorama of mountains marching across the skyline. Deer and elk could be glimpsed in the plains far below, and up here the wind was cutting. It blew through the narrow, stone passageways and wound its way into the courtyards.

The fires were built up as darkness descended, the raised baskets in the hearth piled high with black coal.

Lord Lennox would have been delighted. Another evening of music and dance during which Lord Darnley could display himself to his best advantage.

"Lady Jean," I asked, turning back to the room where a fire burnt in the grate. "What do you think of Lord Lennox's son?"

"What do I think of him, Ma'am?" she asked.

"Yes – as a person."

"Well, as a person he is… very charming, I suppose. He can sing and he can dance and he can be… entertaining…"

"And?"

"And what, Ma'am?"

"Well, is there anything else you can say to recommend him?"

Lady Jean looked distinctly awkward.

"Recommend him for what, Ma'am?"

I laughed.

"The lords have been urging me to find a husband, Lady Jean. And so I must oblige, but it is difficult to be certain about one's options."

"He is a Catholic, Ma'am."

"So my brother was telling me. I am a Catholic also."

There was a small silence. When Lady Jean did not reply I grew bold, and went on.

"He has other factors to recommend him."

"Such as?"

"He has a very strong claim to the English throne."

"Ah!"

"He has Tudor *and* Stuart blood running in his veins. His grandmother was sister to King Henry, Elizabeth's father. That makes him – technically – Elizabeth's heir."

Lady Jean was sitting on a low stool by the fire, sewing. She looked up as I said this.

"Why do you seek my opinion? It sounds as if you have already made your decision."

"Anyway, none of it is of any consequence at all," I added lightly. "I have no intention of marrying the man – despite my brother's fears."

Lady Jean stabbed a needle through her tapestry and winced. "Ouch!"

She sucked at her pale finger where a drop of red blood had appeared.

There was another banquet that night. Platters of food appeared from the kitchens, borne on servants' shoulders. It takes an army of staff to keep the castle equipped and functioning. As the snow fell on the cobbles, the candles and fires continued to burn and Lord Darnley made himself ever more amenable.

In a lull between courses I glanced at him across the crowded Hall. We were a merry party, food and drink being consumed, firelight and candlelight flickering against the high stone walls. I thought back to my days with Francois back in Versailles, that early marriage bed where neither of us had known what it was to love. We played at being grown-ups but at no point had passion or romantic love ever entered into the way we saw each other.

Now I began to wonder if life could be different, if there was an experience I was yet missing.

I had been struggling to rule Scotland on my own now for nigh on five years. I had put down rebellion, mustered support, made my presence felt among the people, tried valiantly to steer an even path between the Catholics and Protestants while throughout Europe a Reformation raged. As I watched Darnley dance, and play the lute, and speak to me with such wit and charm, I began to believe that he could stand by my side and help me in this herculean task of mine. I convinced myself that he would be worthy. And all the while my brother Moray watched, as did Bothwell, and they knew what they knew.

Within a few weeks I made my intention to marry Darnley known.

Moray was furious.

He refused to speak to me for days on end, and when this had no effect and it became clear that I intended to marry Darnley anyway, he took off. Made himself scarce.

This was the beginning of our rift.

Fotheringhay Castle
September 1586

I sit in silence, surrounded by the absolute darkness of my chamber, listening to the walls creak, the mice in the wainscoting. Time passes slowly – or not at all.

Memories are all I have left.

It is with a shock that I realise I am not alone.

A figure is standing in the corner, his back to me. He was not there a few moments ago.

Fear creeps down my spine in ice-cold trickles beneath my heavy garments, my kirtle and silk petticoat, my gown and cloak.

The figure does not move or speak. I cannot make out his features. He is a black silhouette, merging with the shadows.

There is something oddly familiar about his outline.

He begins to turn his head very slowly, and terror grips my soul.

I wait, my needle poised in mid-air.

I do not want to cast my eyes on it; I do not want to look.

It is my half-brother, Moray.

His ghost cuts a sad and sorry figure.

"Are you real?" I whisper, but he does not reply.

I attempt to ignore him, but the figure moves closer.

"What do you want?"

I try to remain calm, steel myself against these visions. Why must I be tormented by my memories? What is it they seek?

I pick up my needle again and begin to sew, as a form of distraction. The action soothes me, settles my nerves.

He moves closer, puts his head on one side and stares at me accusingly.

"You were such a brilliant politician, brother, but it did you no good in the end."

To my surprise, his ghost speaks.

"Your son remains grateful to me to this day," it replies.

"My son is a fool. He was your puppet. I know about puppets and masters."

"Do you?"

"You paid a heavy price for becoming Regent over my son. No one lasts long in the Scottish court these days – so I hear."

For they killed my half-brother in the end, stabbed him in the back, while another villain – Morton – took the role of Regent over my son.

The door to my chamber opens suddenly, letting in a band of yellow light from the corridor outside and a candle borne aloft.

"Madam," Jane whispers, reappearing on the threshold. "You were talking to yourself. Be easy in your mind now."

When I glance back over my shoulder I realise that the room is empty.

"Did you see anyone just now, Jane?"

She shakes her head.

"No one passed you in the corridor?"

"Of course not. How could they?"

Holyrood Palace
June 1565

It was a wet June. The endless rain provoked boredom. Perhaps that is why I agreed to Darnley's plan.

It was ten o' clock at night when I stood in the darkness of my room, straightening my doublet and hose. I had changed into a suit of Darnley's, velvet doublet, silk hose and leather jerkin, and wore a large cap on top of my head, with my auburn hair tucked neatly away out of sight.

We looked like brothers standing there beside each other and Darnley erupted into laughter.

"Shush!" I warned him. "You'll wake everyone."

He stifled another outburst, and then grabbed me by the wrist. "Come on," he said.

"But you don't know the way," I reminded him.

I pushed in front of him and led the way down a back staircase, out into the Edinburgh night.

"Are you sure about this, Mary?" he asked me.

"Of course I am sure. It will be an adventure."

It was dusk outside and a pale yellow moon hung low in the sky, in readiness for nightfall.

"What if someone recognizes me?" I asked nervously.

"It will be dark soon and no one would guess." He looked me up and down. "You look like a man."

"Thank you."

"A long, lean lad of healthy build," he corrected himself.

As we walked side by side toward the postern, I felt an incredible sense of freedom. I could go anywhere, do anything, be anyone I liked. Disguise is a powerful thing.

As we strolled together past Kirk o' Field, I glanced at the silent square of houses, desolate and grim in the fading light, and a shiver ran down my spine.

We neared the city wall, and passed through the gate without any difficulty. Then we headed through the Cowgate and up towards the closes and vennels of the High Street.

"Come, Mary, I will show you some of my old haunts."

"But you have been in Edinburgh but a few short months," I remarked.

"I waste no time in making myself familiar with the locals. You will see, people know me."

"If they know you then they'll recognize me as well."

"People only see what they want to see. You'd be surprised how remarkably blind people can be."

These words would come back to me later, when I would find myself leading Darnley to the houses in Kirk o' Field for a very different purpose other than a night of revelry.

The dusk had grown thicker by this time and torches flamed on the walls of the narrow closes, flickering against the stone walls. The cobbles were slick with rain and mud, but I didn't care. I was beginning to feel a delicious sense of excitement.

A knot of people stood blocking our way along the passage.

Darnley pushed through them.

I hesitated, unsure.

"Ah, Darnley," someone cried, "good to see you this evening."

Then there was a short silence, followed by, "Who's yer young friend, then?"

"My cousin," Darnley replied without batting an eyelid. No one would be any the wiser.

"Your cousin now, is it?" I felt invisible eyes looking me up and down, assessing.

"Well, ye mind how ye go, Darnley, my boy. Don't be getting into any fights this night."

I frowned and glanced at Darnley, who avoided my gaze.

"Do you usually get into fights?" I asked him when we had passed through the crowd.

He changed the subject, stopping in front of a rough-looking tavern with mermaids painted on its sign.

"I'm not really sure about this, Darnley." I hesitated, but he propelled me forward with a hand gently placed in the small of my back.

"Come on, Mary. Let's take risks. Dare to be different."

The fumes of alcohol and body sweat inside were overwhelming. I watched Darnley down his first jug of ale. He placed a frothing pewter jug before me on the gin-soaked table – the wood was sticky with spilled drink. I must have looked unsure, because he winked encouragingly and whispered in my ear, "Remember Mary – the most fun you will ever have in your life. No protocol here."

I lifted the jug and sipped gingerly. It washed to the back

of my throat. I spent the next while pretending to drink the rest, but leaving the liquid largely untouched.

A 'friend' of Darnley's joined us at the table, which alarmed me at first. He and Darnley seemed to speak in a secret code, as if they were sharing a private joke from several nights ago.

"Ye no' gambling tonight, man?"

"Maybe not tonight," Darnley replied, glancing at me.

His companion was introduced as Scythe "on account of the fact my nose looks like one," accompanied by raucous laughter.

I was aware of this stranger watching me, as I fastidiously sipped at my drink.

"You're no' drinking, man'?" he said then and clapped a heavy hand on my shoulder.

I spluttered into my foaming jug and glanced at Darnley.

"My cousin is not used to being out this late. He's young yet. It's his first time," Darnley said, trying unsuccessfully to steer the conversation away from me.

"Well, ye've brought him to the right place then, if it's a woman yer after," and he gave me a sly wink.

There was mockery in his look as he leant closer to Darnley and whispered loudly in front of me, "Not much of a lad, is he? More a lassie by the looks on him. Maybe it's not the lassies he'll be after, eh, Darnley? Eh?" He snorted and chortled with pleasure at his own ribald joke.

Glad of the shadows, I glanced at Darnley uneasily, trying to communicate a silent request for help.

That was when the women arrived, dressed in foul-smelling rags with ribbons and frills to soften the impact. Their faces were heavily rouged, like masks. They sent a shudder down my spine. I felt heart-sorry for them. When Darnley shot a look in my direction he realised he had gone too far.

He stood up swiftly, took my elbow and led me away, back out into the fumes and mud of the passageway.

"Mind how ye go, Darnley, man!" shouted Scythe after him, but Darnley took no notice.

Once we were outside, under the swinging inn sign, he looked at me in the flickering torchlight.

I glanced at the sign. "So that's what the mermaids indicate is it? I should have known."

"Everyone knows. 'Tis only a bit of fun, Mary."

"Is that what those women call it?"

"Perhaps I have gone too far," Darnley murmured. "I see that now."

"Is that the kind of place you often frequent?"

"Of course not."

"That man seemed to know you very well."

Darnley shrugged. "Come, Mary," he urged, trying to make up to me, "this was supposed to be a night of adventure. Let's go somewhere else."

As we wove our way through the night-time vennels I began to smirk to myself.

Darnley glanced sideways at me. "What is it?" he asked.

"That man – Scythe or whatever he's called. He doesn't know it, but he just slapped his sovereign on the back and told her to drink up. What would he think if he knew?"

Darnley laughed.

It was a novel experience, to be loose in the city. The disguise seemed to work. No one appeared to recognise me, because no one would expect the Queen to dress as a man and wander the streets of her capital at night, accompanied only by her lover, without a train of ladies-in-waiting and men-at-arms acting as bodyguards. It alarmed me how well-known Darnley appeared to be in a city he had only arrived in three months ago. He had lost no time at all in making himself familiar with the night-time crowds. They all knew him for a rogue and a party-man in the most unlikely of places – drinking dens and taverns where you'd not expect to find a member of the nobility.

"I'm a man of the people, Mary," he told me, smiling. "If you marry me, you'll have a popular ruler at your side."

I felt uneasy at his words. A warning ripple troubled my mind, but I was too busy enjoying the novelty of his company to take proper heed. I persuaded myself that it would be good to wed a man with such a strong sense of adventure and mischief, one who knew how to talk to ordinary folk and who was glad to escape the confines of Palace life. The thought gave me a thrill of excitement. This was a man worth being married to, not to mention his claim to the English throne, which could only strengthen my own claim.

I silenced any misgivings about what I had seen and heard that night – hints that his behaviour could perhaps deteriorate to levels I might not want to see, or know about.

We were outside the city walls now, in open fields.

Kirk o' Field loomed on our right again. Its gable ends looked desolate under a pale yellow moon and one or two of the houses looked abandoned and half-derelict. Fenced-off fields stretched away behind them.

I stood and stared at it in the stark shadows.

Darnley threw an arm around my shoulder.

"Come on, Mary," he sang, pulling me after him.

It should have been Darnley who stood there shuddering with a sixth sense. Neither of us yet knew that this would be the scene of his murder – and a plot against him which would have earth-shattering consequences.

We laughed together as we crept back through the city postern in the early hours. The guard on duty was asleep – for which I was grateful.

The Palace was dark and silent when we returned. No one had noticed our absence. None of my servants or ladies-in-waiting knew. I had asked them not to disturb me, claiming that I needed an unbroken night of sleep and would appreciate the solitude.

As we re-entered the Palace with such ease, through a back stairway, it did not occur to me to question the security of the Palace guards. If we could so easily slip unseen into Holyrood in the early hours, how easy would it be for an enemy to do so, one with a murderous intent?

There is a back staircase connecting the apartments at ground level with my own private apartments above. It gives egress into the tiny turret chamber just off my larger bed-chamber.

This was how we made our way back into my rooms without being seen. The unmade bed with the pillows stuffed under the quilts was just as I had left it. Darnley held me in his arms, laughing.

I felt giddy with the audacity and daring of it. This was the sort of freedom I had always craved. Oh, to be a man for a day. What woman would not crave that?

Fotheringhay Castle
October 1586

Knox has appeared in my cell. I have no choice but to entertain these ghostly guests of mine. They emerge from the shadows as they please. I have no control over these nightly visitations.

The old man watches me scratch my signature at the bottom of a letter with a flourish. I leave the parchment to dry while he observes me narrowly, his great grey beard frothing over his chest, his shoulders square and his broad feet splayed apart.

A man of judgement and ire.

"Ye are here fer yer sins, Mary, may God have mercy on your soul."

I glare at him.

"What sins would those be, Master Knox?"

I must lower my voice lest Jane should hear me.

He doesn't answer – because only I can answer that.

"Ye murdered yer own husband."

"What proof do you have of that?"

"There's evidence aplenty," he retorts.

"You are a fool. There was never any proof."

"Aye, that's what you think. Ye should be ashamed o' yerself," he roars.

His roar echoes and resonates in an empty room. There is no one else here.

I do not regret those nights I spent with Darnley, creeping into the city, wrapped in male disguise.

It is easy to be a man in this world. Men walk freely, live freely, think freely. They do not take kindly to being ruled by...what was it Knox called us?...the Monstrous Regiment of Women?

Life is hard for women, unless you can out-fox the men who stand guard around you.

I think now of the painted women in the tavern with the mermaids on its sign. From the lowest of us to the most high-born, we suffer the consequences of being female.

I think of Anthony Babington out there, desperately striving to secure my release, and I shiver with excitement and hope.

Dare I believe?

In the dim light of the candle, moonlight lancing through the casement windows, I murmur a quick prayer. The beads of my rosary click together with a comforting sound and my fingers explore their smooth roundness. Those beads are worn down with my hopes and fears, my constant pleading with God.

One day He will hear me and respond. Not the god of John Knox who is all fire and brimstone, but the God of love and peace.

He will hear me now.

Holyrood Palace
July 1565

Preparations for our wedding began. The Palace was oddly quiet without my half-brother about and I missed his constant presence, although I never voiced this out loud.

I had other friends, however. Lord Robert Stewart, my half-brother, and my half-sister Jean. There was Rizzio, my Italian-born musician, and there were men who stood by me and continued to counsel me – Maitland of Lethington, for one.

I always liked Maitland; he was a man of good sense and calm reason. He did not hold with extremism and radical thought, but usually erred on the side of tolerance. For that, I liked him.

"There are rumours that Moray has been seen in England," Maitland told me now.

"Why?"

"He has taken the idea of your marrying a Catholic very hard, Ma'am. He is seeking Elizabeth's favours."

"In what form?"

"Men, maybe? Arms? Support?"

I was furious.

"How dare he raise an army against his own people, his own sovereign and sister?" I cried.

Maitland said nothing.

The plans for our wedding continued and I silenced any misgivings with frenzied activity.

Life was never peaceful; there was ever a storm brewing somewhere in those turbulent years, just out of sight but never out of mind.

The date of our wedding drew near. What I had seen and heard during our nights of freedom in the city should have rung an alarm bell for me. What exactly might my future husband be capable of? But I chose not to heed the warnings. I was too far gone and set upon my purpose.

"Ma'am?" Mary Beaton woke me with a shake of the shoulder. It was dawn, first light.

The tip of Arthur's Seat caught the gold rays of the sun.

No fire in the fireplace.

Twenty-ninth of July.

I began to dress quickly to keep the chill from my body. They helped me into a voluminous gown of unrelieved black which I wore over my silk petticoats and kirtle. It was my choice. Its layers covered me like the plumage of a bird of ill omen. I rustled as I walked along the long dim corridors. Windows flashed past to my right, giving views onto Arthur's Seat and the great relentless sky of Scotland awakening under a grim new dawn.

My ladies and courtiers fell into place behind me and once we were set, we processed in state to the Chapel Royal.

It was six o'clock in the morning and my ladies-in-waiting looked tired and pale in the feeble early light.

Darnley was waiting for me there and my heart took a lurch at the sight of him. He turned at the altar and watched me process down the aisle towards him.

Father Mamaret wed us according to the rites of the Catholic Church – which I knew some of the lords may not approve of – but I had insisted it should be done this way.

"I am not a Calvinist and nor can I make myself one to please one or two of my lords. I promised my brother I would respect this country's religion and I have done so. I was also promised that in return I could worship freely. I will therefore be married in the Chapel Royal according to the rites of the Catholic Church."

No one had dared to dispute this. My brother had vanished. No one else sought to contradict me once I had made my plan known.

The chapel was wrapped in early morning gloom. Candlelight rippled against the stone of the walls and the wood of the pews, and unbroken statues stood in their niches, watching us in silence. The Reformers had not destroyed them yet.

I stood beside Darnley and took my vows, dressed in mourning.

This is the last time I will wear widow's black, I told myself. *Once this day is over, I will be a bride once more and will wear what I please.*

The vows were over fairly swiftly, after which Darnley turned to me and, with a quick peck on the cheek, murmured "There. I shall see you later, my love."

I stared at him.

"But…where are you going?"

"To our bedchamber. It is early yet, is it not?"

I glanced at the altar where Father Mamaret was poised, looking painfully awkward. The guests tried to avoid my eye, aware of my humiliation, Maitland and Bothwell among them.

"We haven't heard Mass yet," I reminded him.

"You stay, of course," Darnley said politely, as if he was giving me permission. "I shall be waiting for you." He had an air about him that was both insensitive and blind.

I turned back to face the altar and listened to the rest of the Mass alone. I was conscious of a veil of loneliness falling down upon my shoulders at that moment, swamping me from head to toe. Perhaps I have never yet shrugged off that mantel.

I was listening to the service on my own, newly-married – the loneliness of my situation was not lost on me. The rap of Darnley's heels against stone faded off into the distance, disturbing any sense of peace I sought from the service.

I watched Father Mamaret elevate the host, lost in my own stunned silence and disbelief. I tried desperately hard to conceal my thoughts and feelings from the others in attendance.

Afterwards I caught Bothwell's eye. There seemed to be a sympathetic gleam there. "Darnley was never a very devout Catholic, Ma'am," he offered as we turned to leave the chapel.

"So I gather," I replied.

I thought for the first time of my absent brother. *Was Moray right? Had he only been trying to warn me of what he already knew?*

Too late now to wonder! I walked back to my bedchamber where I found Darnley waiting for me.

He surprised me by being an attentive and gentle lover and it was he who removed every last layer of my widow's clothing – which my ladies-in-waiting had fastened that morning.

I had worn black since Francois' death.

"You are no longer a French widow, Mary," Darnley whispered. "You are a Scottish bride. *My* Scottish bride."

The disillusionment and disappointment of the ceremony faded in favour of these more pleasant exchanges. In the privacy of our bedchamber we were united as any young couple must be, and I allowed this to dictate what I felt about Darnley over the next few months.

I had nothing to resent yet. Almost nothing.

Fotheringhay Castle
October 1586

The fire has burnt low and I am alone again, except for my faithful Geddon who hides beneath my skirts.

Jane Kennedy and Elizabeth Curle have both retired to their own rooms, and Didier too.

I light a candle from the fireplace and set it on my escritoire. Then I open my psalter, flick through its pages and carefully remove a letter I received from France a few days ago. Thomas Morgan, my cipher clerk, helped to decipher the hidden message encoded here. According to this letter, there are those in France who would seek to remove Elizabeth and rescue me from her clutches.

Freedom is what I dream of.

The word breathes fire through my soul.

I have hesitated to write a reply before now. Jane is forever warning me of the perils of engaging in this kind of communication. She does not trust Morgan.

I gather together my writing utensils then smooth out a

fresh sheet of parchment. I dip my quill in the ink, lower it and watch the violet-blue squiggles begin to bloom. I love the sound it makes, a pure clean scratching.

Sometimes I scribe poetry, songs of love and longing, of sorrow and regret. But tonight I write a letter instead – in French to my brother-in-law, the King of France, and to my Guise relatives. Our secret code weaves its way in and out of the sentences as deftly as my needle flies through linen.

All that can be heard in the silence is the faint scratching of my quill against parchment.

Outside an owl hoots, and I lift my head. There are bars at the window behind the casement of glass – rumours of my skill at escaping in the past have forced Lord Burleigh to take extra measures. A silver patina of moonlight finds its way into my chamber.

I ignore the owl and resume writing.

I continue for some minutes, head bent over my desk, before I realise that I am being watched. Glancing up quickly I see a long thin shape out of the corner of my eye.

I freeze.

Darnley is standing behind me, his vague outline shimmering in the moonlight.

I gasp.

He fixes me with a long stare. Our eye contact seems to last for minutes before he slowly raises a finger to his lips. He doesn't speak but the silent gesture indicates a whispered intimacy.

I glance down at my letter, briefly, and when I look up again he is no longer there. Geddon has run out from beneath my skirts and is barking furiously at the spot where he stood.

It is not the first time Darnley has visited me and doubtless it will not be the last.

The ink has dried. I fold it neatly, drop a blob of melted wax on the fold and seal it with my ring. A secret message curls inside that missive. Not even Walsingham will find it, even if he should break open the seal.

I will hand it to Morgan when he comes in the morning.

Holyrood Palace
September 1565

And so we began our married life.

In the early days we were distracted by the need to deal with my brother who was stirring up trouble and rebelling against my decision to marry.

I took to the field, with my new husband beside me. Wearing a pistol and armour I rode across my kingdom seeking my brother out. He had a small rabble of men to support him and I chased them across the lowlands and over the border again, where he could turn to Elizabeth for as much support as he liked.

Those days of riding in the field, with my new husband at my side, were a welcome distraction and brought us closer together. We were united in our purpose. At night we made love, in whichever of the castles we found ourselves in, and by day we rode to arms.

However, on our return to Edinburgh, I noticed the cracks begin to show. My new husband seemed restless, increasingly demanding. When we signed official documents he made sure his signature was larger and bolder than my own. He wanted the privilege to be able to call himself King in his own right, and was angry at my reluctance to grant him his wish.

A new coin emerged from the royal mint – in honour of our marriage – but I sent it back with the instruction that they were to withdraw it immediately from circulation. They had had the audacity to show his name in the ascendancy, as if he was the ruling monarch and I merely his consort or paramour.

When Darnley got to hear about it, he grew angry. I was still of a mind at the time to try and appease him with gifts, so I bought my new husband a bed. It was magnificent, hung with violet-brown velvet, cloth of gold and silver, encrusted with elaborate monograms and flowers, sewn with delicate gold and silver thread. It was draped with curtains of damask, adorned with plump pillows of white satin, and covered with a blue taffeta quilt stitched with crimson, as well as layers of linen sheets imported from Holland. I supervised its installation myself while Darnley was away on a hunting trip. It was to be a surprise for him on his return. I smoothed the sheets and admired the finished work. It was a fortress of a bed – a bed to build dreams upon.

His own private apartments were directly beneath my own and a secret staircase connected us. The doorway was obscured by a hanging tapestry in the small turret chamber just off my bedchamber. Not many people knew of its existence.

Now I waited anxiously for his return. I had been feeling unwell of late. I rested on the new bed in Darnley's room, away from prying eyes. It was more elaborate and luxurious than anything I had in my own bedchamber and I hoped he would receive it as a token of my love for him.

Darnley was late in returning and I fell asleep where I was, exhausted by the bouts of sickness I'd suffered. I suspected I might be pregnant.

I woke with a start when the door banged open. Darnley crossed the room in the dark.

"Is there no light, dammit?" he mumbled. His voice seemed slurred with drink and an ominous smell followed him into the room.

I roused myself and tried to light a candle while Darnley stumbled into the bed. One of the curtains became entangled in his legs and there was a ripping sound. He cursed loudly, and struggled with the bedding.

"What the...?" He hadn't expected to find me, or the new bed, in his chamber.

"You here, Mary? Cannot resist my charms, eh?"

I backed away from him and succeeded in lighting the candle. Light flickered and bounced around the room.

He looked surprised at the sight of the bed.

"I fell asleep here," I said. "I have been feeling unwell."

"Ahhh..." he grinned "and you've been waiting for my return!" He leant in close, but I reacted instinctively and pushed him away.

His brow darkened, and there was a glint in his eye I did not like.

"That's no way to receive your husband is it, Mary? Am I not good enough for you, perhaps?"

"Don't be silly, Darnley. You smell of the taverns."

"Since when has it been a crime for a husband...a *king*, in fact, to visit his old friends?"

I rose from the bed where he lay sprawled against the plump soft furnishings and pillows. Disappointment flooded me.

"I bought you this as a gift." I added, "It was to be a surprise."

He gazed about him drunkenly. "Surprise!" he echoed in a high weak voice.

"I'll go now, Darnley, and receive you in the morning."

"Don't go," he mumbled. "Come, Mary, you and I can have a little fun."

"When you're sober, perhaps," I replied, and opened the door to our secret staircase which led up to my own apartments.

I wasn't sure if he would even remember the incident in the morning.

I watched my own slippered feet as I climbed the dark stone staircase, struggling against the great weariness I felt. I had taken the candle with me, leaving Darnley in darkness. I did not trust him with a candle in that room.

I lay down in my own bedchamber and placed my hands across my stomach. I could sense the new life stirring there and my heart gave a flutter of fear.

What have I done? I thought now, watching the darkness deepen around me. It was hours before I slept that night.

As Darnley and I grew more remote with one another there was one in my inner circle who filled the gap, as it were. Davie Rizzio had started his life as a courtier, sleeping on an oak chest in the corridors of the Palace, and making himself useful where he could. As the weeks went by, his ready charm and wit made him indispensable in our company, and it was a short step from there to becoming a constant presence in my inner circle.

Rizzio was fun, mischievous, warm and witty. He made me laugh, and I turned to him for advice and reassurance. I was not attracted to him, and there was nothing physical between us. If truth be told, I do not think it was women he was particularly interested in.

Darnley himself seemed drawn to Rizzio, and at one stage

they appeared to be firm friends. They would walk along the corridor with an arm thrown across each other's shoulder. Their friendship flowered to such an extent that I even found myself standing outside of it, wondering at their closeness. Then suddenly their bonhomie evaporated, as quickly as it had begun. Where once they had sought each other out and laughed and even shared a bed at times, when the Palace was particularly crowded, suddenly they were icy with one another, cold, as if their purpose had been served.

Darnley began to be jealous of Rizzio's time spent with me.

I wondered at that. Was he jealous of me, or jealous of his new friend Rizzio?

Perhaps he felt I had come between them.

I have had plenty of time in which to dwell on these niceties of behaviour.

When I broke the news of my pregnancy to Darnley in front of our friends, he seemed sullen and guarded. Mary Livingstone and Mary Beaton were there, Lady Jean Stewart and Lord Robert and Rizzio, of course.

There was an awkward silence after I spoke.

"Well done, Ma'am!" Rizzio cried, and clapped his hands together.

There were cries of delight from the others in the room, but Darnley was noticeably silent.

"Darnley?" I murmured quietly. Still, there was no response. "I thought you would be pleased."

He spun round then and shot me a quick glance. "I am, Mary. I am!" Then he strode out of the room and left us alone.

I looked at my friends for advice.

None dared give any.

No one would meet my eye except Rizzio who shrugged and said comically, "Men!"

This caused a ripple of laughter which lightened the mood somewhat, and relieved the awkward tension.

It was not something I forgot, however, and the incident troubled me. Dark storm clouds began to gather on my horizon.

Fotheringhay Castle
October 1586

"Did they now, Mary?"

I jump in alarm.

He is here again – in the darkness of my lonely cell.

His ghost often slips in without warning, suave in sea-blue satin to match his eyes.

Angel-face.

He looks not a day older than when I first met him. A white ruff frames his pale countenance.

He leans in close and points at the parchment on my writing desk.

"What are these?" he asks.

"Letters," I reply.

"Still plotting are we, Mary?"

"Why couldn't you have been happy with what we had, Darnley? You always wanted more."

"More than you could give?"

"More than anyone could give."

He leans forward and kisses me gently on the forehead. I can almost feel the feather-light touch of his lips. But when I reach out my hand there is no one there.

Am I dreaming?

Am I mad?

Am I hallucinating through lack of sleep?

I pick up my needle and thread, and begin to sew.

Edinburgh
November 1565

D arnley's nights apart from me became more frequent, despite the secret staircase and the elaborate new bed, and my heart turned slowly to stone.

Often he was drunk and I could imagine how he spent his evenings. What had seemed daring and risky during those early days – when I accompanied him into the darkened closes of Edinburgh – now seemed sordid and fraught with danger. I thought of his friend, Scythe, and the other men and women who had already seemed to know my husband so well, greeting him like an old friend; and I thought of the tavern with the mermaid sign, and the painted women in their rags. I was not so naïve as to believe he was faithful to me. I wept in my bed at night for what I thought I had lost.

However, it was not only the women I had reason to be jealous of. Darnley was often described as 'lady-faced' in my hearing and I once overheard some of my courtiers calling him Angelica – behind his back. I did not fully comprehend what they meant at the time. But now I know. Now I begin to understand.

Although I tried to hide my disappointment, my friends were not blind.

And then there were the nights when he seemed repentant. He would come to me and apologize, promise to change.

I had grown used to his absence and was therefore surprised when he appeared suddenly in my bedchamber one night, swaying in the shadows.

I had not heard him approach.

"Mary, may I come in?" he spoke from beyond the sweeping bed-curtains that partially obscured my view.

Surprised by his courteous tone I murmured, "Of course," and held the bed covers open for him.

He climbed in beside me and we held each other for a moment. Neither of us spoke, and in the stillness I listened to the sound of his heartbeat, his breath in my ear. The warmth of physical contact soothed away my fears. It seemed as if our grievances even now could be put aside, daring me to believe in his regret, but then he broke the silence.

"Why are you so cold with me nowadays, Mary?"

My heart sank like a stone.

"I am not cold, Darnley."

"You have a heart of stone."

"I don't mean to be cold, but you make it difficult for me. If only you behaved normally..." I said.

"How do you know what is normal for me?"

His words made my blood run cold.

"I don't," I replied.

He had moved away from me now.

"You pay more attention to Rizzio nowadays, than you do to me."

"Davie?" I said. "You cannot be jealous of him, surely? He is my friend. Yours too."

"I've noticed! And so has everyone else."

"What do you mean?"

He shrugged. "Rumours grow. Even Knox gets to hear of them."

"And you would know about that, of course," I said icily.

I had heard that Darnley had begun attending some of Knox's Protestant services in the High Kirk. Did he take delight in listening to the sermons against me?

"You're becoming quite the Protestant, I hear!"

"I like to keep an open mind," Darnley said. "I never said I was a devout Catholic. It was you who made that assumption. There are a lot of powerful men in this country who are Protestant."

"So you sit on the fence?"

"It pays to appease both sides. That's always been your own policy, Mary, has it not?"

I said nothing.

"Why have you come here? Only to reproach me?"

"I was trying to make peace."

"And so you accuse me of…of what? I don't even know what it is you are accusing me of."

"Rizzio," Darnley snarled. "He spends too much time in your presence."

"He is in my service. I pay him to be my secretary and if he keeps us entertained at the same time, and makes our evenings more pleasing with his music, then what is wrong with that?"

"Knox has a great deal to say about what is wrong with that."

I turned away from him, exasperated.

"Why do you have to be like this?"

"It is you who drive me to it," he said and rose from the bed.

Blame and reproach came easily to his lips.

"Why must you always spoil what we have?" I asked him.

He stood on the far side of the room now, glowering at me.

"If anything ever happened to you Mary – God forbid – there are many in this country who would be happy to see me crowned in your place. You know that, don't you?"

"And that's why you married me, is it?"

There was a long guilty silence.

"You may think you are powerful, Mary, but I don't depend on you for my title. I have royal blood on both sides of my family – Tudor and Stuart."

"You've never borne the responsibilities of kingship," I murmured. "You know nothing of what it means to be a king."

"I have a right to rule Scotland on my own terms," he said, shocking me into momentary silence. "Either by your side – or not."

"You would have no right if I hadn't given you that right, fool that I was."

Only moments before, we had held each other in a tender embrace of forgiveness. Now we were sworn enemies again.

"And now you tell me you are with child," he added slowly, nonchalantly. "The question is…can I be certain it is mine?"

I fell silent as the implications of what he was saying sank in. A wave of comprehension and fear flooded me in an instant. So this was why he resented our unborn child? This quivering life inside my womb, as yet unseen, would become my heir. Next in line to the Scottish throne – before Darnley.

My hand moved instinctively to the flat of my stomach in a protective gesture.

He watched me and turned away.

Horror filled my soul from top to bottom.

Where was the dashing young man in sky-blue satin who had led me onto the dance floor in February? What had happened to him? Had he ever existed, or was he a mirage?

The following night Darnley was contrite, but I hadn't forgotten our earlier quarrel. His mood was enigmatic, mysterious, as if he was on the verge of some strange new confession.

He kissed me gently on the forehead.

"Mary," he whispered. "Is it possible that you can ever forgive me?"

"That would depend on what you've done," I said carefully.

I was wary of him now and felt inclined to handle him as one might a dangerous animal, appeasing him while waiting nervously for the next attack.

He shook his head. "It's not what I've done. It's what I am about to do."

"You're drunk," I told him.

"Oh no, I'm stone-cold sober."

Inspired by greed, what atrocity would he commit against me? How far would he go?

Alarmed by his behaviour, I confided in my friends. All of them sought to reassure me.

"Darnley is all bluster," Lethington told me. "He won't do anything that would risk his own position. You have nothing to fear – but fear itself."

So fear ate away at my peace of mind.

Edinburgh
March 1566

David Rizzio played the lute and the lyre like a dream. He was Italian-born and had first entered my circle as a court musician, but within a short space of time he was promoted to being one of my secretaries. As the years passed he became more and more indispensable to me. He spoke fluent French and dealt with all my French correspondence, and also entertained us in the evenings when the long winter nights closed in. He was small, mischievous of temperament, with a slight hunchback which increased with age. He loved me, and I loved him, but not in any romantic sense.

The long echoing corridors of Holyrood Palace grew darker and colder as the winter progressed. One of my only comforts was to huddle in the small turret chamber off my main bedchamber of an evening, and play cards or listen to music with those who were closest to me. Darnley was sometimes included, often not. He chose to spend his nights elsewhere.

The Scottish winters were harsh and it was a struggle to keep the rooms warm, even with the fireplaces roaring.

As I grew larger with child, Holyrood was where I spent most of my time. It lay outside the boundary of the city wall and I thought nothing of this. The whispers of conspiracy did not reach me.

I knew there were those who resented what they called the 'foreigners' in my midst. They did not like French or Italians being amongst my number, and they did not like Catholics either. Knox's Calvinist grip on the country was strong. I had promised never to impose Catholicism on Scotland and I had observed that promise, even if the Pope and my relatives abroad should urge it. Religion is a matter between an individual and God, and I still see no reason for it to be otherwise.

As I sit here in semi-darkness and listen to the wind howling outside, it recreates in my mind another memorable night. It was March and the wind battered against the walls of my turret chamber, making us glad of the warm hearth.

We were clustered together in the room I favoured – a handful of us – with a peat fire blazing in the hearth. There was a large green baize table in the centre, and my half-brother Lord Robert Stewart was dealing out a deck of cards.

The howl of the wind made us glance at one another uneasily and I turned to Rizzio.

"Play the lyre for us, Davie. It will cheer us."

He smiled and, lifting the instrument into his lap, began to pluck the strings. I listened to the pure sound filling the air, competing with the roar of the elements outside. It tinged my thoughts with melancholy and I smiled at my guests to reassure them.

Again we heard the wind sigh and moan above the turrets.

The walls were lined with rich tapestries for warmth, and

it felt safe and pleasant to be here with my friends. There was my half-sister, Lady Jean, the Countess of Argyll, my half-brother Lord Robert Stewart, Mary Livingstone, Mary Seton, and of course, Rizzio. There was a world out there that I was afraid of, but inside, for a few hours, we formed a tight circle of intimacy that no one could break.

So I was surprised when I saw the tapestry move aside and Darnley appear from the secret doorway to our staircase which connected his private rooms to my own.

"Darnley?" I said. "I didn't expect you to be home tonight. Come and join us." I made room for him at the table. He sat down with his arm around my shoulder and I smiled at him, warmed by the unexpected gesture of affection. Ah, I was so quick to forgive in those early days.

"Mary, you are winning again?" he asked me.

"Of course," but he seemed a little tense, so I squeezed his hand and laid his fingers to rest gently on the small mound of my belly where our unborn child grew. He gave me a quick guilty look which I was unable to read. A puzzled frown lit my brow.

"Why so tense, Darnley?" I whispered.

"I'm not tense," he replied.

The others were busy playing cards, and the exquisite sound of Rizzio's playing drowned out our low voices and kept our exchange private.

Darnley had to lean close to hear me – so close – and he must have felt the brush of my lips against his earlobe. Time seemed to slow down and I stared for the longest moment into the elaborate seashell whorl of his ear. This was the moment – the precious moment – before our world exploded apart. I remember it well.

I can see myself glancing up as the tapestry was moved aside for a second time, and another figure emerged.

Lord Ruthven, dressed in black armour, with a face as pale as death. His ghostly countenance alone was enough to shock us – he had not been well for months, and he still bore the marks of the illness that had ravaged him. I heard Lady Jean draw in a gasp and Rizzio stopped playing.

We all looked at the intruder. His fist moved menacingly towards the hilt of his sword.

Time stood still and our future hung in the balance.

No one spoke.

It was clear that Lord Ruthven had not used my private staircase for a courtesy visit, but had some other, more nefarious, purpose in mind.

"What is it you require of us, Lord Ruthven?" I asked, finding my tongue at last, and deciding to assert my own authority.

He avoided my eye, but looked instead in Rizzio's direction. Poor Rizzio had grown pale.

"Our business is not with you, Ma'am. It is with Davie."

There were more gasps from around the room.

"Would it please Your Majesty to allow Davie to accompany us?"

"Why?"

"We wish to escort him outside," Ruthven answered blackly.

I knew instinctively that Rizzio should remain with us in this room; I would protect him with every last ounce of my dignity.

"No, we prefer Davie to stay among us for now. There is no need for him to leave."

"I think there is every reason," Lord Ruthven growled.

I glared at him.

"He has already been in your private chamber far too long."

There was an uneasy silence; I wished suddenly that my half-brother Moray was not so far away in England but had stayed by my side in Edinburgh, that we had not quarrelled. I missed his support now.

"He has done nothing wrong."

"I beg to differ."

"What offence has he committed?" I said, standing up now and shielding Rizzio with my own body.

"Great offence! An offence deserving death!" Ruthven roared.

At this Rizzio trembled, and I suffered a terrible dawning of revelation. Of course, I knew it.

I spun round and confronted my husband.

"What do you know of this?" I cried. How else could Ruthven have gained access to our private staircase, except through Darnley?

My husband shot me a look of triumph mixed with shame. He had succeeded in having his revenge for whatever I was supposed to have done, or not done.

I heard the thunder of heavy footsteps cascading up the stone staircase, accompanied by the clash of steel weapons. Suddenly the room was filled with dangerous men, armed to the teeth, and my poor friend Rizzio was vulnerable to attack. His precious lyre lay discarded and broken on the stone flags. I struggled against Darnley's embrace and cried, "If he has done anything wrong, then put him to a court of law – not this!"

But no one listened.

Rizzio was still behind me, and I had presumed no one would dare strike him if I stood in his defence. But I was wrong.

The first blow was struck over my shoulder by George Douglas, narrowly missing myself. Drops of Rizzio's blood spattered my gown. Darnley held me back and then – amidst all the confusion and noise there was a moment of terrible clarity – I saw someone produce a pistol that was pointed and jabbed at my stomach where our unborn child lay. I held Darnley's eye, and again time seemed to slow down, holding us in that moment forever, while the world around us exploded in chaos.

"Dare you?" I snarled, looking him in the eye. "Dare you?" The rage I felt then was so loud it drowned out the horror of the fighting around me and the howling of the March winds outside.

The room was now filled with men, armed and bearing daggers. In the confusion the table was overturned, but Lady Jean had the foresight to grab one of the candlesticks before it crashed to the floor and plunged us all in darkness.

Rizzio was screaming and had been dragged along the floor away from me, while men struck blows at him with their daggers, stabbing with such force that the life was beaten out of my poor friend. I can hear those terrible punching blows even now.

They dragged him out of my turret chamber, across the floor of my bedchamber where his body left tracks of blood, and out into the main hall beyond. They then thrust him from a high window and his corpse lay mangled and bloodied on the cobbles below.

As his screams died away I stood helpless, Lady Jean and Lord Robert both shocked into silence at my side. Darnley still held me back.

"Traitors!" I sobbed.

Then I turned to my husband.

"You will pay for this."

In spite of his bravado, he appeared alarmed by what he had done.

I picked up Rizzio's lyre from the floor.

"He was my friend. He had done nothing wrong," I said.

I turned on Darnley once more.

"You will live to regret this day. I promise you that."

Darnley had released his hold on me now and looked uneasy. As I held my arms across my rounded stomach, shielding it from his touch, I saw what I fancied were the first flickerings of remorse in his eyes.

Throughout the rest of the palace I could hear the pounding of heavy footsteps running up and down the corridors, and men shouting.

The danger to my life – and that of my child – was not yet over.

After some moments I went with my half-brother and sister to the door of my room, but we found our way barred by George Douglas, standing four-square at the entrance. He was armed.

"I demand to leave this room," I ordered, looking him in the eye.

George Douglas met my gaze with a look of such deep disrespect that it sent a cold wave of fear through me.

"I cannot allow that," he said, without addressing me with my proper title.

"I demand that you address me by my proper title," and when he still refused to budge, I made a move to lift his dagger aside, but he responded by pointing it directly at me.

"What? Am I a prisoner now?"

"Leave this room and I shall cut you to pieces," he snarled.

I paled in shock. The point of his dagger was still smeared with my own dear Rizzio's blood.

At that moment I heard a commotion of voices in the courtyard below my windows. I ran across the room and would have leaned out, but my assailants would not allow it.

The whole area below was filled with the flickering of lighted torches and I heard the Provost of Edinburgh shouting up at the Palace, demanding to see the Queen.

"They fear you have taken me hostage," I cried. "They have sounded the tocsin."

George Douglas and his nameless minions slammed the shutters closed.

"This is treason."

"We act in the name of Protestants everywhere, and of Knox's Kirk."

"And you think they listen to you?" I cried, indicating the window from where the townspeople were gathered below to check on the safety of their queen.

"You are nothing but an upstart, Douglas. A rebel and a traitor. And one day you will die a traitor's death for what you have done this day," I spoke in a low hate-filled voice.

"Calm yourself, Mary," I heard Lady Jean whisper. "Think of the child."

I turned then, and became aware that Darnley was no longer in the room with me. He had slipped away unnoticed, coward that he was.

Lady Jean and Lord Robert were then ordered to leave, and I was to spend the rest of the night alone in my bedchamber – a prisoner – guarded by dangerous armed men, Douglas cut-throats mostly.

I paced my room all night – a prisoner in my own Palace – and as I watched the grey beginnings of a new dawn filter into the room across the blood-streaked boards, I felt Darnley's child stir inside me. A tiny curled-up bud of being, quivering uncertainly. I laid a hand across my belly and gave myself up to my fears. It would be a child born not of love, but hate. This is what I feared.

Holyrood
March 1566

"You have a visitor," a voice said.

I turned my head and looked back at the doorway in surprise.

"My brother!" I rushed towards him then stopped. We regarded each other in silence.

"I thought you were in England?" I asked, perplexed.

"I was," Moray replied. "But I came back."

I looked at him shrewdly. It must have taken him more than a week to ride from London. What had brought him back here so suddenly, at this particular hour, when I had need of him most?

Coincidence?

I had banished him from my land, and yet here he was again. He must have heard of my incarceration in the Palace. Instantly I suspected him of having foreknowledge of the plot to kill Rizzio, but I was not about to let him know that.

"What drew you back so soon?" I asked.

"I was already on the road. And when I arrived back in Edinburgh, I heard that Holyrood was in turmoil."

I kept control of my temper.

"Turmoil? Conspiracy, you mean."

"I am sorry for you, my sister."

I glanced up at him. He appeared to be sincere for a moment. Could I trust that sentiment?

"Thank you, but I need a little more than your pity, Lord James. Perhaps..." I considered my words carefully for a moment. "I am ready to concede that perhaps you were right about Darnley, after all."

He watched me in silence.

"When I chose him for a husband, I had no idea he would betray me."

"He is a jealous fool, but it has been to the advantage of others to make him jealous. He is their play-thing, their tool. They have used him – he is simply too foolish to realise that yet."

My blood froze.

"And you?" I asked. "Are you among their vile ranks too?"

"I am here to help you, Mary."

I observed him narrowly.

"It's outrageous the way you have been treated. I would never have allowed them to incarcerate you like this. If I had been here at the time, Morton and Ruthven would not have dared..."

I smiled. "I need your help, brother."

I pride myself on being a woman of resourcefulness. There have been many times when I have found myself a prisoner and yet managed by stealth, duplicity and sheer force of will to effect an escape. If only I could be so inventive now.

After Moray left, I remained alone in my bedchamber,

waiting. It wasn't long before I received a visit from Darnley. I had urged my brother to contrive an excuse to be alone with my husband and speak with him urgently; I was confident that this *tete-a-tete* would have the desired effect.

Darnley was afraid of Ruthven, Morton, Lindsay and Douglas – the very men who had encouraged him to turn traitor against me. They had used his jealousy of Rizzio and his insecurity about being named King. Now he was more afraid of them than he was of me.

"I am sorry, Mary," he begged. "I have made a grave error."

"You come to me now?" I wept. "After what you have done?"

"I did not think it would end in this way, with you being treated so brutally…"

"Our child could have died."

He sat on the edge of the bed and refused to look at me.

"Is that what you wanted?" I cried.

When he didn't answer at first I added quietly, "But of course it is. You wanted our child dead, because the poor unborn mite will obstruct the way for you. You are driven, Darnley, driven by your own ambition – and if either myself or our child stand in your way…" The truth dawned on me with a sickening lurch of emotion. Any child of ours would be first in line if anything happened to me. "Isn't that right, Darnley?"

"I made a consummate error and I regret it."

"Yes, you have erred. You chose to throw in your lot with evil men. And to trust them instead of your wife, the queen."

He glanced over his shoulder towards the wooden panels of the closed door, beyond which we could hear guards marching in the corridor outside. He was afraid. Those same men who had told him to overthrow his wife and queen could now just as easily turn traitor against him. He was pale with nerves and fear.

I wiped away the tears that sprang from my eyes. *Enough tears*, a voice inside my head said clearly. *I must think on revenge.*

"You should have trusted me," I murmured, mellowing slightly, swallowing back my rage. I spoke my next words smoothly and sweetly. "You should trust me now, and maybe together we can escape, and turn the tide of events in our favour."

He stared at me. "What are you proposing?"

"Poor Darnley," I whispered, "you never loved me."

"If I had never loved you, I'd have no need to feel jealous of our poor friend Rizzio."

I flinched at the mention of that name. Then I studied my husband calmly. Let him believe that it was love motivating him, if that's what he wanted. But I would never trust Darnley again. I would play him like a fish in order to secure my own release. A fat carp hooked on the end of my line, to be landed and gutted.

"Mary, I know there is nothing I can do or say to make you believe me."

I withdrew my hand from his grasp and he gave me a look then that I could almost believe.

"I will forgive you, Darnley," I said carefully. "But I will never forget. If you promise that you are willing to change, then there is a way out of this."

He lifted his head hopefully.

"I need your help, Darnley."

His eyes gleamed.

"Of course. I'll do anything," he said excitedly. "We'll stand together again."

The sight of his enthusiasm repulsed me somewhat, but

I hid it well. If I was to escape this den of lions that paced the corridors of my Palace, I needed Darnley's help and assistance. I could not do it alone.

I sat down at my desk and wrote a letter to the two individuals I knew I could rely upon.

"What is it? What ails the queen?"

It was midnight and my wails were filling the empty rooms of the Palace, echoing to the rafters. George Douglas stood in the shadows looking pale and perplexed as others gathered in the doorway behind him.

I emitted a deep groan from the depths of my being and clutched my belly.

"I need a nurse," I spoke breathlessly.

"She needs a nurse," Darnley echoed.

"Fetch the midwife."

"No!" I cried. "Fetch Lady Huntly. She will deliver me."

Footsteps pounded away.

Darnley mopped my sweating brow while the others looked on.

"Give her privacy," he demanded, and slammed the door shut in their faces.

Lady Huntly was sent for and eventually arrived amid much bustle and confusion.

"How is she?" she asked. The door was opened and a funnel of candlelight fell forward into the room. She was led into our midst and immediately began issuing orders.

"Stand back, man," she murmured, forcibly pushing Darnley aside. "This is woman's work."

Darnley backed away while Lady Huntly knelt beside the great bed where I lay marooned and clutching my abdomen in pain.

The door closed on our little tableau.

Once we were alone I opened my eyes wide and sat up straight. Lady Huntly observed us both with a wry look on her face, then nodded wisely.

I took out the letter with haste, slipped it into her hand and whispered, "Please, pass this to your son. And to Lord Bothwell."

She smiled and hid it in the folds of her clothing.

"Not even a Douglas would dare to look here," she said, patting her chest.

"Come along now, Your Majesty," she urged. "Keep up the performance or they'll think our business here is done. And we cannot have that." She spoke with positive glee, as if she was rather rising to the occasion and enjoying the drama of it all.

While that good lady and Darnley watched, I broke out in cries again, and I must admit that I indulged in the performance. I could see that Lady Huntly did too; Darnley was too distracted by his own terror to notice or appreciate much. He kept glancing nervously towards the door, as though afraid one of them might enter at any moment and beat him.

We waited a while, and once my mock groans of pain had subsided, she made a hasty exit, with my letter secreted away. We watched her leave nervously.

I heard raised voices in the corridor outside, then Lady Huntly's voice rose clear and confident above the clamour.

"Her Majesty is calm for now, but you have risked her life and that of the child. She needs absolute quiet."

Another voice spoke then I heard her add, "I am warning you, if you attempt to harass her again, that child will not survive, and the consequences will be grave for all."

I listened to this exchange, and then heard her footsteps

fade. She was taking with her my secret missive, with its instructions to meet me the following night beneath the shadow of the churchyard wall.

I was left in peace, as Lady Huntly had instructed, despite the fact that George Douglas and Ruthven were itching to make their presence felt. Darnley left as well, to avoid rousing any suspicions. Part of me still suffered a twinge of suspicion and unease at letting him go; I wondered how far I could trust him. Had I really won him over? If he was a turncoat once, then he could be so again.

While they assumed I was taking my rest, I dressed myself in a riding cloak and lay beneath the covers of my bed, waiting for darkness to fall.

At half past eleven I rose and entered the small turret chamber off my main bedroom. One of the heavy tapestries moved and Darnley appeared. We regarded one another in silence. This was the same aperture through which Ruthven had appeared... The memory still echoed in the recesses of my mind, but I had no time to pay it heed in the urgency of the moment. All my thoughts and energies were focused on the task in hand. Everything else faded into obscurity for now, to be mulled over and dwelt upon later when I had the leisure.

Together we crept down the narrow stone staircase to his apartments, using the same route that Ruthven and my enemies had taken.

"We are fortunate. There are no guards set below," Darnley informed me.

I was relieved to hear this. His private chambers beneath, were empty. My enemies had relaxed their guard. Stealthily, we cracked open the door and emerged into the darkness of the passage beyond. The wall sconces were not lit.

"What if they hear us?" Darnley whispered.

"Then we must be very quiet."

I could tell that he was frightened. If those ruthless men discovered him helping me to escape, his life would be forfeit. His terror grew with each step we took as he began to realise the implications of helping me to flit the cage.

We felt our way cautiously, fearing that someone would hear us or grow suspicious, but the downstairs corridors were empty. They had not thought to set a sentry here, and fearing that a miscarriage was due, had relaxed their guard somewhat after my performance earlier. Such womanly matters tend to make men distant and afraid. They trusted to the fact that I would be too ill to escape.

"Come," I whispered to Darnley. "I know the way through to the servants' quarters, and from there, down into the cellars beneath."

Darnley was nervous, starting at every sound. We made our way in the dark, without the aid of torches. We did not want to alert anyone to our presence.

Down in the cellar I found the entrance to a dark tunnel leading beneath the vaults of the abbey and from there into the churchyard beyond, where I hoped my rescuers would be waiting with horses.

We groped our way forward, assaulted by the charnel-house smells of the burial vault. Dank stone and centuries' old trapped air assaulted my nostrils. Darnley gagged and held a cloth to his mouth. I steeled myself and lit a torch. Light flared out in the shadows, picking out the detritus of bones and old graves lying around.

"This is where my own ancestors are buried," I told Darnley.

I had no wish to join them just yet.

We stumbled on, surrounded by the final resting-place of

my grandparents and great grandparents. I tried not to think about my poor mother. The air became cold and clammy, and wet stone shone before my eyes. When I missed my footing in the dark, Darnley automatically gripped hold of me to save me falling. The sudden intimacy struck a spark, moved me almost, but I knew better than to trust it. It was the final flowering of our love for one another, before it died for good.

I was surprised to feel him throw an arm around me as he led me protectively past stone coffins and tombs, surrounded by the smell of decay. Then we moved into single file, the better to negotiate the tunnel. I looked at his dark, cloaked shoulders just ahead of me. This was Darnley – my husband – and he had betrayed me in the worst possible way. He had allowed armed men to threaten my person in my own private room and had sanctioned, approved, conspired with them in the slaughter of my own dear friend. Rizzio had kept me company these past few years, sleeping faithfully on a chest in a corridor of the Palace, never far from my side. Now he was gone forever. Worse than this, Darnley had watched as they held a pistol to my womb where our unborn child lay vulnerable and unprotected. Now he had become weak and scared, afraid of his own shadow.

I had loved him too, and the disappointment was hard to bear. I felt scooped out, excavated by loss and sorrow, but at the same time realisation dawned. I lost any final illusions I had about Darnley; I was no longer his victim, happy to wait for him to come home, to overlook his faults. Instead I was the one in control. All of this transformation took place silently as we moved in stealth and darkness beneath the Abbey. The immense building bore down on us. I could feel its weight and its history – and I began to reflect that all of this was what Knox and his Protestant supporters sought to tear down and dismantle, stone by stone, removing statues from niches, leaving altars bare and stripped of their adornments.

How can you dismantle so much history?

How can you wish to destroy beauty and art? Knox takes a hammer to the past and wants to smash it to bits. He wants to rewrite the history books, declare himself the King and Master, masquerading under the banner of religion. He is radical, extreme, ready to operate through terror and judgement.

Knox and Darnley: they are two of the troubled souls who haunt me here in damp, dismal Fotheringhay. Whatever it was they wanted of life, they are not at rest. They have not found peace. This much I know…

But it was another who waited for me on the far side of the churchyard wall, under the shadow of the overhanging trees.

As we emerged from the subterranean depths of the burial vaults into the moonlight, I heard the jangling of a harness. The silhouette of a man on horseback rose above the wall.

"Quick," Darnley urged me, dragging me after him where I was stepping carefully for fear of stumbling. He was full of cowardice and desperation. He did not want the conspirators to find him in the act of escaping – and what is more – helping me to escape.

Our cloaks brushed against the damp grass and I could see clouds of mist escaping from the horses' nostrils, rising like steam against the brightness of the moon.

"A full moon is not what we wanted," a familiar voice said.

Darnley recognized the voice too and hesitated a moment.

"That ruffian Bothwell is here?" he asked.

"That ruffian, as you call him, saved my mother's life on many an occasion. He was loyal and steadfast."

I spoke with not a little trace of reproach and bitterness, which I am sure was not lost on my young husband.

"Make haste, Your Majesty," came the familiar voice again from the darkness. "There is no time to lose."

We mounted the horses that were waiting for us, endeavouring to silence the jangle of harness and bit. Then we moved with stealth through the trees on the edges of the churchyard, bending low to avoid creating a silhouette, hugging the wall. I glanced upwards at the many windows of the Palace. Did I detect movement in those narrow panes? It was hard to tell.

Bothwell was right. What we did not need was a full moon, which was picking out our silhouettes in movement. The white orb hung low in the sky, like a lantern lighting up our figures. Thankfully, a sudden cloud crossed before it and we were doused in darkness. Breathing a sigh of relief we took advantage of the brief respite and broke cover, then headed for the boundary wall of Edinburgh. As we clattered through the cobbled streets, I glanced from left to right at the shuttered houses on either side of us. Would anyone suspect or recognize our little troop for what we were – a queen on horseback, in flight from Rizzio's killers? I pulled my cloak closer about my face.

The people of Edinburgh had shown great concern for the safety of their Queen earlier, when rumours of the incident had reached their ears. If they did suspect me of fleeing, they would not move to stop me or help the rebel lords. Those scheming conspirators – Morton, Ruthven and Douglas – were no friends of the people. They operated only in the interests of their own rise to power – like so many before and after them.

By the time the moon reappeared we had left Edinburgh far behind and were on our way to Dunbar. The clouds had saved us from detection.

We listened anxiously for the thunder of hooves behind us. How soon would my absence be discovered? I had left clothes and pillows stuffed beneath the coverlet of my bed and Lady Huntly had left instructions that I was not to be disturbed, but how long would it be before the guards grew suspicious and sought to check on me?

After an hour or two exhaustion caught up with me in my frail state; when it was clear that we were not being pursued, I pulled my mount to a halt.

"Mary," Darnley cried, "what in God's name are you doing?"

"I am unwell, Darnley," I replied. I felt my stomach heaving and, leaning forward over my horse's neck, I retched from the saddle.

"There isn't time for this," he cried, glancing over his shoulder into the distance.

"I'm sorry if my sickness inconveniences you, Darnley, but it is beyond my control."

He glared at me in frustration, urged his horse on, but when I did not follow suit he rode back again.

"You have to make haste. We are going too slowly."

"I am with child, Darnley. I cannot go any faster. If you are so concerned for your own safety then why do you not ride on ahead? I will go at my own pace. I care about the safety of this babe, even if you do not."

He glared at me once more then spurred his horse forward.

Bothwell, who had been watching this exchange, moved to ride beside me. He made no comment but I was aware of his presence. And his silence.

He kept pace with me throughout the rest of that long journey.

The moonlight was unsettling. In truth I was afraid that Rizzio's murderers would discover my empty chamber and ride out to detain me; but I spoke the truth to Darnley when I said that I could not ride any faster. I was in some discomfort and had to stop several times more on the journey, to empty the contents of my stomach, retching in an undignified manner from the saddle. Darnley rode on ahead.

Bothwell gave me a shrewd sideways glance.

"His Grace is very keen to save his own skin," he remarked.

I nodded.

"I must apologize," he murmured.

I waited a moment, wondering.

"For what?"

"It is not my place to criticize your husband."

"No, it is not," I replied quietly.

After a while he said in a soft voice, "You are sad."

I did not turn to look at him.

"Would not anyone be in my position?"

We rode in silence for some moments more before I added stiffly, "I do not understand why they murdered my friend."

He considered his words carefully before he spoke.

"In their eyes poor Davie was not aristocratic enough, and what was worse, he was a foreigner. Two black marks against him. He appeared to have Your Majesty's ear. They did not like it. Jealousy, Ma'am, plain and simple."

"And you?" I glanced at him. "Were you jealous?"

"Of what?"

"Of the influence others have over me?"

He did not answer me.

"Every courtier seeks the queen's ear. Everyone wants

to be my adviser. I am a female monarch, weak in their eyes. But who can I trust? That is the question."

There was a long silence during which I listened to the husky breath of our horses and the soft rhythmic thudding of hooves against the earth.

Eventually Bothwell spoke in a low voice that arrested my attention. "You can trust me, Ma'am."

I did not reply.

There was a moment between us, a silent dialogue of understanding.

Fotheringhay Castle
October 1586

"There was a moment between you, was there? Ahhh...how sweet..."

Angel-face is back again, watching me from the shadows.

I ignore him. Pale and whey-faced, Darnley occasionally breaks his silence to taunt me.

"Do you think the world cares about you any longer? Do you think anyone would care if they lopped your head right off your shoulders?"

I continue to sew, in silence.

I do not understand how these ghosts find me here.

When Jane or Elizabeth bustles in to attend to my needs, I breathe not a word of these encounters. I will confide in them everything else, but of the ghosts I say not one word. I fear to be thought insane, for then any last shreds of my credibility are lost.

The Duke of Norfolk lost his head for me. He wanted to marry me with the blessing of the Pope and the Catholic

Church, but Elizabeth saw fit to deal with him. Men have loved me in droves before now. Boys and old men, eager to please, to rescue a maid in distress locked in a tower, sewing for her life.

Where is my knight in shining armour?

I once thought Bothwell was that man.

Where is he now?

The truth is he is nowhere to be found. Even his damaged spirit does not visit me here.

So many of the men who played their part in my drama have met their bitter end. My half-brother Moray was murdered after a few short years acting as Regent over my son, to be replaced by Morton, who was murdered in his turn. Plots and counter-plots, betrayal, conspiracy and intrigue...

I have outlived them all.

And still my sister-queen, Elizabeth, hesitates to sign my death warrant. She will avoid it if she can.

Anthony Babington is my final hope. My last knight in shining armour.

I wait for him here, for his letters and whatever influence he can afford.

But it is Bothwell I long for still. I remember those moments we had together, those first sparks of intimacy when he rallied to my side. He was my staunch defender: quiet, steadfast, but always there in the shadows, off-stage as it were.

Why can I not persuade him to haunt me here? Why must I only have traitors for company? The grey-bearded Knox and his fanatical demons?

The shadows shift uneasily in my narrow chamber.

I turn my face away from Darnley's pale ghost. I snap the silver thread with my teeth, and feel the squeak of pain. It reminds me I am still alive.

Dunbar Castle
March 1566

The journey was a long and arduous one that night, and by the end of it my own feelings had undergone a transformation, but one which I was barely aware of.

We made slow progress and I feared at any moment to hear the distant pounding of hooves behind us. Tension and fatigue took their toll, and I felt the last of my strength ebbing away. Bothwell glanced at me with kind concern from time to time, and I noted his courtesy and warmth.

He has many critics, men who deride and reproach him for his rash actions, but I remember these small kindnesses which others were slow to offer.

We reached Dunbar by dawn. When I saw that stark black fortress rearing up on the horizon ahead of us, with the morning sun rising over the sea, my spirits lifted.

"At last," I breathed.

"We will be safe here, Your Majesty," Bothwell said.

We rode up the narrow causeway and beneath the portcullis. Far below us, the waves crashed against the black rocks and the sea stretched endlessly. I made to dismount, but Bothwell moved to assist me, followed by others I recognized in the dawn light.

I was exhausted.

"Where is Darnley?" I asked.

"He arrived before you," I was told.

"Of course," I muttered darkly.

I was led to a room made ready for me, and fell to my rest, a dark relief washing through me, tinged with sorrow. I had done it. I had out-manoeuvred my enemies, Rizzio's murderers.

I lay for many hours on my bed, falling in and out of a deep slumber, my dreams punctuated by the slough of the waves beneath. In the courtyard I heard the steady commotion of armed guards and horses mustering under my banner. In spite of the noise I slept on, and the ring of horses' hooves and steel weapons penetrated the thin veil of my dreams. It was the best sleep I was to enjoy in months. The sound of their mustering comforted me.

And beyond the sound of men at arms rushing to my defence was the persistent murmur of the waves beating a perpetual tattoo against the castle ramparts. My sleeping thoughts were awash with reminders of the ocean, as gulls and cormorants pierced the air with their cries.

When I woke the sickness had passed and I felt reassured that the child in my womb was safe. I joined the others in the main hall for a meal. From time to time I caught Bothwell's eye across the crowded chamber. Halfway through the meal I called him to my side.

"My Lord Bothwell," I began. He inclined his head politely. "You served me well yesterday."

He nodded. All his actions towards me were calm and understated.

"My mother wrote to me in France, telling me how she

could rely upon you. She mentioned your name often and urged me to remember that I could trust you. I believe she was right."

Bothwell met my gaze briefly, but said nothing.

"I wish to show you my gratitude by making you warden of this castle."

"Your Majesty is very kind."

"Kindness has nothing to do with it," I said. "Dunbar Castle is a safe fortress to retreat to. It has offered us protection and may well do so again in the future if I have need of it. To have you named as warden of this castle can only be to our advantage."

I tapped the side of my wine glass and the assembled company ceased their chattering.

A silence fell and all eyes turned to me.

"I wish to make an announcement," I declared.

The crowd hesitated.

"I wish to make our friend here – James Hepburn, the Earl of Bothwell – warden of this castle, in reward for his services."

There was a ripple of applause, glasses were raised, and the announcement passed unremarked as the murmur of conversation started up again. It was all in the ordinary way of things, but then I chanced to glance in Darnley's direction. He was standing transfixed with a strange look on his face. I could read his thoughts like a book. He was consumed with resentment that he made a poor show of concealing from me.

Fotheringhay Castle
October 1586

"Jealous of that oaf?" Darnley explodes. "That rough Border laird, strutting about the corridors like he owns the place?"

I pause, thread held taut for a moment, listening. He is here again, hovering in the passage beyond. My servants and ladies have left me in peace. I am alone. Almost...

Darnley's voice rattles on.

"He was more of a liability than I ever was, and that's saying something. Where is he now?" His sea-blue satin rustles in the shadows as if he is real.

"I don't see him here? Do you?" he adds, making as if to seek out Bothwell's ghost in the corners of the room.

I lower my tapestry onto my knee and concentrate on the delicate weave – tiny infinitesimal stitches that glitter and gleam in the dark. Silken threads, silver and gold, pick out the detail with such effortless skill. I need a steady hand for this elaborate fretwork, and a careful eye.

Darnley is right.

Bothwell's ghost has never appeared in this chamber, neither to reproach nor comfort me.

He offers nothing now.

In the corridor outside my room I hear guards marching, stamping their feet. They make so much noise they keep me awake at night. My sleep is always troubled, disturbed by visions of the past and fears of the future.

When I look up again the room is empty. Darnley has vanished. I stare at the spot where he stood. Not even a shadow or a footprint in the dust remains. My needle is still held mid-air, my careful stitching arrested.

I do not know if he is real or a figment of my imagination sent to torment me.

Perhaps I am being driven mad by lack of sleep and worry as I wait patiently for the end that never comes.

Dunbar Castle
March 1566

When I close my eyes I hear again the endless crashing of those waves against the rocks below. I imagine myself standing on that exposed parapet, as the wild winds whip my face. I can see the wide North Sea stretching toward the horizon, all the way to distant rocky islands one has never even heard of, where human beings have barely set foot. The foggy marshlands of Norfolk are tame in comparison. I long for those bracing winds, the pounding of that ocean.

It was a happy few days I spent at Dunbar Castle, despite the circumstances that had brought me there, and the terrible crime I had recently witnessed. I felt determined, sure of my own power. I look back upon those years of my youth with bittersweet nostalgia. Although in peril, I could rise to the situation with spirit.

After a hearty breakfast in the Great Hall I summoned those closest to me. "Send out messengers throughout the north of the country, warning them of what has happened to me, and requesting their help."

"And if no one responds?"

I turned to look at my husband, for it was he who had voiced this doubt.

"They will," I replied. "They must."

"Have no fear on that score," a quiet voice murmured.

I caught Bothwell's eye and smiled.

Darnley glowered and – turning on his heel – swept from the room. I watched him go with a sinking heart. I had no time for his petulance; it was exhausting trying to keep him docile, and now was not the time. Right now I needed to focus on my goal – reinstating myself at the centre of my own kingdom, back in my own Palace, with my enemies routed.

"They will not get away with this," I told Huntly and Bothwell. "I will see them to the edges of the borders… and beyond."

From my room I watched as several riders left the castle in haste, racing across the hills, spurring their mounts on until they were no more than a blur on the horizon, hooves pounding into the earth with relentless purpose. They would spread out and rally my supporters to action.

Once they had left the castle fell to quiet again and I waited tensely for news, wondering what events were taking place in Edinburgh in my absence. How had they reacted when they discovered my empty chamber, that their prisoner had flit the cage? I imagined their blind panic and disbelief, their frustration.

I was reliant now on my own people for their support. If they did not rally then I was lost.

I attempted to rest and also to appease my errant husband Darnley, to soothe his unpredictable moods. He was jittery with nerves.

He voiced his fears in my private chamber. "What will happen to me when they find out I helped you?"

"Have no fear, Darnley, you have done the right thing."

"And will you stand by me always, Mary?" he asked. "Can I trust your word on that?"

A flame of anger leapt like fire in my belly. "You have no right to ask that of me, after what you did."

"I did not think you were the sort of person to bear grudges," he whined. "I thought you were bigger in spirit than that."

I choked back my anger; I knew it would do no good. Was this husband of mine always to be a burden, a problem I needed to contain?

"Do not reproach me, husband," I said in a low voice. "I thought we were reconciled. Let us leave it at that."

"I have seen the looks you give another," he said in a quiet undertone. I glanced across at him. At last, he had voiced the unspoken thought between us. But I did not deign to reply.

"None of this would have happened," he murmured "if you had simply granted me what was rightfully mine."

"Rightfully yours?"

"I am your husband. As such, it was your duty to grant me the Crown Matrimonial, and make it absolutely clear – in front of all your courtiers – where I stood in the matter."

"Next in line to the throne of Scotland?"

"Exactly. It is, after all, only what I am due. I have an impeccable birthright. Is that not one of the reasons you married me, Mary? For my claim to the English throne?"

I gave a small dismissive shake of my head. "I married you, Henry, because I thought I loved you…"

Even he was shamed into silence for a moment. "Past tense, I see?"

"I need time, Darnley. And at this moment, I have other more pressing matters to consider."

I pushed open the heavy oak door and ran straight into Bothwell in the corridor outside. He bowed his head slightly.

I struggled to regain my composure and brushed past him.

He said not a word, but I could feel him watching me. When I glanced back over my shoulder, I could see him hesitating at the door to my chamber. When the door was flung open again and Darnley emerged, they regarded each other in silence. I was too far away to hear what was said, and besides, I did not wish to hear it.

Down below there was a rising commotion. One or two of the messengers had returned.

Rather than returning to the fray so soon, I wanted time to calm my jangled nerves, to subdue my anger with Darnley. I resented him more bitterly than I cared to admit – even to myself.

A narrow winding staircase opened up to the left of me and instead of joining the others below, I mounted the stairs. They twisted up into darkness until the last curve where light poured through from the top.

Here I emerged suddenly onto the castle ramparts. I took a dizzying step backwards and caught my breath. The view was dazzling, the ocean stretching away to one side, the land and the cliffs to the other. The wind buffeted me. Exhilaration caught me unawares.

I looked below and for the first time felt a lightening of my troubles, for there across the plain, I could make out a long line of raggedy troops making their way to Dunbar and pouring in through the portcullis.

They had come. They had answered my call for assistance.

A sense of indomitable determination lit me from within. This kingdom was mine, and no one would displace me or take it from me. I would serve my people and they knew it.

A footstep on the parapet behind me made me turn and gasp.

A familiar soft voice spoke. "Ma'am?"

"Are you checking up on me, Lord Bothwell?"

"I needed to reassure myself that you were not in any danger."

"Danger of what? Throwing myself from a great height?"

He hesitated.

"I sensed your husband was...displeased."

I sighed. "My husband is always displeased. I know what would please him, however."

Bothwell waited patiently.

"It would please him if I were to fall from this parapet and die, leaving him as sole heir, next in line to the throne. Taking our unborn child with me."

My palm drifted instinctively to the mound of my belly.

"I know what I know, Bothwell. He sees our unborn child as a threat to his position."

I stopped, wondering suddenly about the wisdom of having said so much.

I sighed heavily. "I have come to love this country, Bothwell, but find I need to watch my back at every turn."

"I will be watching it for you, Madam."

"As faithfully as you did my mother's?"

For answer he stepped towards the edge of the parapet.

"You see that, Mary?"

He pointed to the courtyard below where nameless men were mustering by the hundred. The castle rang with the noise and clamour of them.

"They are rallying to your call. They will not let their queen be usurped by anyone, least of all traitors."

His words sounded so confident; the sight of those many men filing in great columns into the stronghold below filled me with courage.

At the same time, I became suddenly aware of our

proximity, of my isolation away from the rest of my court circle, and the intimacy of our position. I stepped back uneasily and smiled at him.

"How is your wife, James?" I asked then, to change the subject.

He looked taken aback. "She is very well," he replied.

It was I who had arranged the union of James Hepburn, the Earl of Bothwell, with his young wife Lady Jean Gordon a few weeks previously. I had persuaded the icily serene Lady Jean that it was in her best interests to marry Bothwell instead of Alexander of Ogilvie to whom she had been betrothed. She had reluctantly agreed, but rumour had it that she was not in Bothwell's thrall.

I'll admit there was a stirring of excitement being near to James Hepburn at that time. I trusted him; we worked together towards one end, one goal.

At the end of ten days I marched back into Edinburgh at the head of an army, and when I neared Holyrood, the scene of Rizzio's grisly murder, my enemies were nowhere to be seen. They had fled across the border like the dogs they were, their tails between their legs.

Edinburgh welcomed me back and I was reinstated at Holyrood. The people lined the streets to cheer as we processed into our capital at the head of an assembled army, ready to begin a new chapter.

At my side were two men, the one skulking, by turns reproachful and remorseful; the other confident, sure of himself.

Darnley and Bothwell, vying for position.

And so it began…

Edinburgh
April 1566

I stood looking out of an upstairs window in the middle of the night. Arthur's Seat rose like some kind of mythical monster on the skyline. The Palace felt overshadowed by its presence – as did I.

All was unusually quiet. The rest of the court were in their beds. I glanced down at the evidence of my belly. It was growing larger, a small hump beneath my kirtle. The traitors had fled the Palace and fled Edinburgh, humiliated and defeated while I declared them outlawed. If they dared to return, their lands were immediately forfeit.

However, Knox remained in situ: the horned beast who governed Scottish minds from his monstrous black pulpit. St. Giles' Cathedral dominated the centre of Edinburgh and he flung his poison from its rafters, its great grey buttresses reaching across the city like the legs of a giant spider.

I was sorely troubled in my mind. Knox still held a powerful sway over people, or tried to. The rebellious lords were delighted to stir up civil unrest; it served their purposes. So Knox was a godsend to them.

My bedchamber at Holyrood was not a place where I felt safe anymore. The echoes and cries of that terrible night haunted my dreams. I would wake with a start, thinking I heard the steel of clashing weapons. I would relive again those terrifying moments when the first blow was struck over my shoulder, and blood spattered the tapestry. The stains remain there still. I would hold the cloth between my fingers and rub the weave. Mary Seton claimed it was my imagination, that the hangings and boards had been scrubbed clean. But I did not believe her.

The stain was in my mind now.

I felt suspicious of those around me.

I was relieved when Darnley began to make himself scarce, as his company was irksome to me.

"Keep him close," Bothwell advised me. "Keep him where you can see him."

"He is not an easy man to live with."

"If he is by your side, you know what he is about."

"I don't feel safe in the Palace. I wake at night thinking it is happening again, but this time it will be my unborn child they murder."

"Not on my watch!" Bothwell said quietly, a thunderous look in his dark eye.

It was not long before worry and anxiety made me ill.

Darnley stayed away.

"I think he even desires my death," I told Mary Seton, "for then his only barrier to my throne is removed. That is what he wants."

For days I languished, unable to sleep or eat, my mind at war with itself, until eventually I made it known that I would not remain at Holyrood for my confinement. It was too easy to storm Holyrood, as had been shown. I would retreat to Edinburgh Castle where I could await the birth of my child with peace of mind, knowing that we would be heavily guarded. No one could kidnap my child on that fortified rock.

Courtiers and servants were sent ahead to prepare the rooms for me and make the castle ready. I waited, eager to flee Holyrood and its nightmarish memories.

Edinburgh Castle
April 1566

We trooped in a long line up the cobbles of the High Street towards the gloomy Castle on its formidable black rock, where I planned to await the birth of my child. We were happy to occupy the south-eastern corner overlooking the rambling sandstone town beneath. An elaborately carved oaken cradle had already been crafted for the occasion and was set in place, with ten ells of Holland cloth draped over its crown. It was waiting for me in our chamber, along with a vast bed hung with blue velvet and taffeta. Would that soft velvet could dull my pain in child-birth, or still my fear of death!

Although it was spring, the winds howled across the castle ramparts and whipped up the sombre waters of the Firth into white-tipped crests. The sky was blackened by storm clouds. It was a bitter wind that blew.

I was glad to hasten inside to my apartments in the south-eastern tower where a fire was roaring in the hearth.

On arrival I sat down to pen a note to Darnley to inform him of my move to the Castle and to let him know that I had been ill and wished now to see him. The messenger was sent on his way and I then prepared to settle in. I was turning my back on the world for now. I was in retreat, but the world could still come to me. Lady Huntly soothed my fears and assured me that I had no cause for anxiety; all would be well.

"My son and Lord Bothwell have the castle heavily guarded, so there is no fear on that score."

I smiled.

"If only their protection could extend as far as saving me from the dangers of child-birth."

Her face softened and she patted my hand.

"We women know how to outwit death in the birthing chamber. We have the best midwives to hand. Have no fear, Mary."

She spoke my name with such warmth and affection it soothed me, and I felt for a moment the loss of my mother, Marie of Guise. Her spirit was ever near me. I had grown used to her absence in childhood, so it was a small feat now to imagine that she was with me still. I felt comforted and tried to push all thoughts of death aside.

After several days I asked Lord Seaton, "Was my note to Lord Darnley delivered?"

"It was certainly received, Ma'am."

"And yet he does not appear?"

My comment was met with silence.

The bitter winds continued to blow, but I did not set foot on the castle ramparts. I remained cloistered within, surrounded by my women, awaiting the first pang.

One dismal afternoon, as hail smattered the window-panes like bullets, I began to make my will. I ordered them to bring my coffers and opened each one to inspect the jewels within.

This was a little of what I would leave behind.

Was I nothing more than a heap of cold gems? Well yes,

in truth, this is often what royalty amounts to. They clamour
for my blood and my crown, but in the end my spirit will
ever escape them; that part of me they will never have, nor
tie me down.

I took out my jewels, ran their cold, cut gems over my
hands and itemized each one, entering them in my clear
flowing hand on a fresh piece of parchment. This was my
inventory; my will. I took a sort of morbid pleasure in the
task.

With diligent care I listed my cross of gold set with
diamonds and rubies, my Scottish pearls, the rings and
necklaces of enamel and turquoise and cornelian, the red
rubies I wore against crimson velvet, and my great black
Spanish pearls, strung together like a rope of ripe olives.
Each cameo and fibula and pendant was accounted for.

I dipped my hands into their richness and let their gold
chains run through my fingers like silk. The irony is that
those costly stones are now scattered to the four corners of
the earth. Most were taken from me by rebels and distributed
where they pleased, to my enemies. Catherine de Medici is
now in possession of my black pearls, I believe, a gift from
her son Francois that she ever did covet. Now they lie against
her wrinkled throat, tarnished by her sweat. My written word
as queen has been disregarded

I derived some comfort in the calming scratch of the quill
against the parchment as I wrote out my inventory. Such
work has always quieted my soul. I scribe poetry and songs
that speak from the heart, and I stitch my stories into a clear
bright tapestry of words. All of this makes sense to me. They
are my only remaining pleasures as my hours grow darker
and shorter.

The weeks continued in this fashion and still no word came from Darnley. I feared what he might be plotting. Bothwell and Huntly promised to send out men to keep an eye on him and my brother Moray did too – although how far I could trust his word was beyond me.

I waited.

And then, in the middle of the night it started. Nothing but a twinge or two at first, with gaps in between, growing steadily sharper. If this is the worst of it, I thought, then I can bear this.

My midwives were there by my side and this time Lady Huntly's services were required for the real thing, not a performed charade.

The chamber was lit with flickering candles and firelight, and I bore the first pains with dignity. My ladies comforted me with words of encouragement and I gave myself up to their know-how and experience, trusting completely in their skill.

As the pains worsened my mind flew out of my body in a panic. What had begun as minor twinges now intensified to a ripple of sheer pain until at last it was coming in waves that bore me away on their backs, one after the other. Voices broke through the wall of pain and I detected a note of alarm and hysteria in them.

"Make her lie flat on her back. It is not dignified for a queen to do otherwise."

"No! Believe me, I have seen this done in the country and it is best for all concerned!"

Strong arms manoeuvred me into a crouch upon my bedcovers, as my body urged me into a crawl, as if I could crawl away from the pain itself.

"But she cannot birth like a common animal in the field. She is a queen, not a peasant."

"Queen or no, this is the way she and the child will survive." A younger midwife had taken over; one I did not know. She seemed no more than a child herself. "I have seen my mother do it this way, when she did birth my brothers and sisters."

As the older midwives protested Lady Huntly stepped forward and bid them be quiet.

"Do as the child commands," Lady Huntly ordered.

The women exchanged looks and I was encouraged to heave onto all fours where I crouched like a pig in the fields, my posterior upended to the world, and in that way, gravity did the work for me.

After sixteen hours of intense labour – during which I truly thought I might die, and came as close to it as I have ever been – a last immense wave of pain tore me in two, and my body was split like a melon. I felt carved open, halved where I lay in the sweat and blood of my own toil. Nothing dignified about that, nothing that velvet and taffeta could alleviate. The child flopped from my womb, still attached by a tangled red cord.

One of the midwives lifted him up and showed him to me.

"It is a boy," she told me proudly, evidently delighted.

The young midwife who had saved me earlier now whipped the child from us and slapped it hard upon its bare little rump. Immediately the tiny mite sparked into life and began to cry in rage, its limbs taut and trembling.

I watched in astonishment, as if all of these strange proceedings were happening to someone else. He looked small and strong, wiry and frantic, dangling there. He looked exactly like his father …

I opened my arms and they laid him there, then I gazed down at him while the world withdrew into the distance. As voices and instructions clamoured around me, I heard nothing. My soiled bed was an island on which my son and I drifted, gazing at each other with familiarity.

"So, here you are my little man," I murmured. "It is you!"

He gazed back at me.

"It is I!" he seemed to say.

The moment lasted and stretched while the din of the birthing-chamber went on apace.

The apothecary attended to me and care was taken to remove the sack of the placenta from inside, all of which indignities I had not quite been expecting. It felt like an assault upon my body. But afterwards, when the sheets were changed and my baby washed clean, the room returned to some kind of order and calm.

"I shall call him James," I said. "For his grandfather."

I had never met my own father. He died just six days after I was born, but his spirit had never been far from my conscience. Like my mother, he made himself felt in absence.

I held my little son in my arms and a love I had never expected to feel poured out in an instant, binding me to him forever.

It has been my sad fate ever to be parted from those I love best in this world.

Nurseries and wet-nurses would intervene at first, and then the larger arena of world politics. But for now, my little babe and I were alone in the south-eastern tower of the castle, attended by my ladies and the midwives, comforted, cossetted, wrapped in peace.

Darnley appeared that day, amid the sweat and mire of the bedchamber. I lifted little James in my arms slightly, the better to display him to his father.

I do not know what I expected, but what I did not expect was Darnley's cold reaction. It shocked me to the core. He did not lean forward to peer closer, or touch, he showed no warmth or affection for this child of his own loins, the sight of which moved him not.

"Does it not warm your heart to see him?" I asked.

His cold eyes slid towards mine.

"How do I know it's mine!"

There was an audible in-take of breath around the room. All those watching dare not utter a word, of contradiction or otherwise.

I was shocked. Darnley had spoken the unthinkable.

"And exactly whose child do you think he is?" I dared to ask.

He met my gaze, but uttered not a word. "Oh, he's your child alright, Darnley. In fact, so much so that I fear for him. I would not have him grow up to be like you."

I muttered these words quietly so that it was hard for others in the room to hear this exchange, but Darnley shot me a look of pure vitriol.

"So much for your promise of loyalty, Henry," I murmured.

He did not stay long after this.

My ladies tried to comfort me with distractions. They made me comfortable, until exhaustion claimed me at last.

While I slept the battle-wounds of birth began to heal, leaving their scars behind – the scars of experience.

I woke to the sound of gunfire and explosion. I started up from my pillows in a panic, white-faced with alarm.

"Have no fear, Madam," Lady Huntly smiled. "They are simply discharging the artillery of the castle above the town, to celebrate the birth of a son and heir."

Five hundred bonfires were lit throughout Edinburgh, and their orange flames cast a ruddy glow across the buttresses and dome of St. Giles' High Kirk, softening its bleak austerity. Scotland was glad, for it had a male heir at last, having suffered a 'monstrous regiment' of French women for the past two generations. I thought of John Knox in his lair and wondered what he would be making of it all.

Then I turned to mind my son.

I leaned over the cot, but it was empty.

My cries of alarm brought a guard rushing in.

"Where is he?" I cried. "My son!"

"Calm yourself, Your Majesty," a midwife soothed. "Do not fret so. He is with the wet-nurse at the moment. We are trying to ensure you get some rest, Ma'am."

"Bring him to me at once. I can feed him myself."

And so it went on, as they conspired to keep us forever divided, from the moment of his birth.

I wanted him by my side, but the cares of estate meant that this could not always be the case. As it began, so it would end…

Fotheringhay Castle
October 1586

My son never communicates with me in this cold friendless
place. He does not answer my letters.
*   I remember the day he entered this world.*
*   He does not.*
*   I remember how I held him close and feared for his safety*
always.
*   He does not.*
*   I still fear for him.*
*   My heart is a broken vessel. It lies on the floor in shards.*
*   When he was a child I heard that his tutors beat him*
and I could do nothing to stop it, incarcerated as I was, far
from my land. He was a lonely little boy, by all accounts,
whose father was murdered and whose mother was forced to
abdicate and leave her son to the wolves. My enemies, those
who threatened my life, raised him. My brother Moray acted
as Regent over him for a while. He was vulnerable, my little
boy; they forced him to become a King who would do as he

was told, and they reared him to think the worst of his own mother.

It is not his fault if he ended up believing their lies.

I do not blame him.

I mourn for him.

I lost my little boy many years ago, and I have been pining for him ever since.

I failed to protect him from their ravages.

While my brother Moray and the cut-throat Morton treated him cruelly, I had no way of intervening, no power to change what was happening to my son.

When Sir James Melville visited me, I demanded to know the truth.

"How do they treat him? What is he like?"

Melville was reluctant to speak at first.

"He is a very dour child. He does not smile."

"They beat him?"

"They strive to teach him the ways of kingship...but harshly. I do not rate their methods. And nor would you, my lady."

When I hid my face he added "I did not wish to speak of this, Ma'am."

"I am glad you told me the truth. I am surrounded by liars. I want no more lies. What can I do to improve his lot?"

Melville opened his hands in despair.

"Is there nothing anyone can do?"

"Ma'am, you are a captive and prisoner of Her Majesty, the Queen of England. If we raise a hand to help you in this matter, we are committing treason. What can any of us do, but hope?"

"I have no room in my heart for hope anymore," I said quietly. "It is too brim-full of sorrow."

I have had my helpers and supporters, those who have fought my cause, but none were able to rescue my son from the lions' den when he was growing up. My brother and my enemies shaped and moulded him with their cruelty, using him as a bargaining tool to power.

And now...it is too late.

It is painful for me to remember those days in the castle after he was born, how the country celebrated, and how I held him close for fear of the world coming between us. Events conspired to separate us and now I know him not.

Crookston Castle
August 1566

After our son was born, Darnley kept his distance and I did not see him for months at a time. He kept to his own affairs; I kept to mine. In many ways it was a relief to be free of his company, but the drawback was that I did not know what he was about.

I avoided Holyrood. For me the place would remain forever haunted.

Once I was fully recovered from the birth, I rode about Scotland, re-acquainting myself with my kingdom. I was in the saddle for hours at a time, my Spanish riding cloak falling in folds across the flanks of my horse, compelled to keep moving, in a vain attempt to quell my anxiety about Darnley. It was as if I was possessed by some restless demon. If my people saw me, they would be more inclined to give me their loyalty in times of trouble. And times of trouble I could certainly see ahead.

Bothwell rode with me, offering the support of his retinue – fierce fighting Borderers.

We were at supper one night in Crookston Castle, not far from the Clyde, when my secretary, Maitland, took me aside.

"Madam, there are those of us who are beginning to grow anxious at the amount of influence my Lord Bothwell appears to have over Your Majesty. Do you think it wise to create such unease?"

The banqueting hall was small and secluded, and our host was not present, having gone out to request the servants bring in more firewood. Firelight flickered against the stone walls. Two candles sat at the long table, casting their shadows across our faces.

"Maitland, do I really need to answer that?"

He cleared his throat.

"I am merely giving voice to the concerns I have overheard."

My gaze lingered on the narrow window where I could see the moon – a cold coin in the night sky.

He leant forward to pour himself more wine.

"I myself do not hold with these rumours, but they grow apace."

There was a lengthy pause; a log cracked noisily in the fireplace.

"There are some who say that Bothwell wants to be King."

I looked at him.

"I cannot help what people say!"

"Even so, you can avoid encouraging it."

I stood up in frustration.

"Am I to be forever surrounded by petty jealousies and rivalries?"

Maitland flinched suddenly on hearing a noise in the passage beyond. The doorway was in darkness. We could not see who stood there.

"Come!" Maitland called, waiting for a servant or our

host to reappear. But the shadows remained still. No one moved.

"And if Bothwell does not support me with his army, who then do you propose will?"

"You have many faithful followers, Madam. You are surrounded by love and loyalty."

I gave him a wry look. "So much so they thought to threaten me in my own Palace!"

At this point my gaze returned to the doorway where I sensed rather than saw a presence in the shadows. Who was it, lurking there? To this day, I do not know. We heard a step on the flags.

"Come forward, I say," Maitland barked and rose from the table to cross the room.

Firelight streaked his boots, and the shadows rippled closer.

I watched as he pulled the curtain aside that obscured the door. He turned back to me, disappointed.

"Ghosts!" he said.

I nodded and turned back to the table.

"Are there ghosts at Crookston Castle?"

"We should ask our host that question," Maitland said.

"Where is Bothwell?" he asked now.

"I do not know his every movement. But I believe he is out with his men, seeing to the horses."

Maitland took his seat again at table.

"Have you thought any more about the little Prince's baptism, Your Majesty?"

"I have indeed, Maitland. It will be a lavish affair. I intend to impress upon the foreign heads of state throughout Europe what a noble kingdom is ours. They shall soon learn what Scotland is capable of."

"Quite so. Then you shall have need to make financial arrangements soon."

I nodded. "I will be staying at the Exchequer House on my return to Edinburgh, in order to do just that. My lord Bothwell will help me in this."

There was an awkward silence.

"Bothwell?"

"That is right. He will assist us. And you too, Maitland, of course."

"And you will stay at the Exchequer House?"

I strove to hide my impatience.

"I do not wish to stay at Holyrood, if that is what you are implying, and it means I am on hand to work as hard as need be to see the job done."

Maitland did not comment, but I could feel his disapproval. I chose to ignore it. At this point our host returned with a servant.

"Ah, more firewood," I smiled.

By the time Bothwell joined us, all talk of the Exchequer House had ended and we spoke merely polite pleasantries, while Maitland quietly fumed.

Exchequer House
Edinburgh
September 1566

Night had fallen when I arrived in Edinburgh. The
streets were deserted, the people disappearing into
the darkness of their houses and tenements.

I went to Holyrood first, spent one night there, and rode
up the High Street early the next morning, through the
Netherbow Gate, to begin work at the Exchequer. Holyrood
lies outside the city walls; it is low-lying and damp. I ne'er
did like its prospect, overshadowed as it was by Arthur's
Seat, and I was glad to escape into the town.

At the Exchequer House I met up with Bothwell and
Maitland to begin work on the financial arrangements for the
baptism of my son, Prince James. I wanted the celebration
to be a sumptuous affair. There would be invitations to all
the crowned heads of Europe, whether they came or not. I
wanted to prove to my contemporaries that Scotland was not
to be dismissed lightly, that it was a kingdom to be reckoned
with, a state player on the stage of world politics. It would

take about a week in all to complete my business. I was not overjoyed to be staying long in Edinburgh.

The Exchequer House itself sat opposite St. Giles' High Kirk, the seat of that most powerful and most despicable of men – Master Knox. I'd heard he was in Edinburgh too, but I had no wish to encounter him. He owned a tall house on the High Street, with several rows of windows and an outside staircase to the upper floors. He was a wealthy man for one so committed to the word of God. And a happy one too, by all accounts. He had recently re-married. Although he liked to compose long treatises against the 'monstrous regiment of women', and complain about us in the pulpit, he did not believe in depriving himself of the pleasures of the flesh.

"The vow of celibacy is a Papist construction," he roared from on high. "It has no basis in the word of the Lord as spoken in the Bible."

Did his young bride help him to do God's work, I wonder?

Did I feel his eyes upon me as I rode up the Canongate and the High Street towards the Exchequer House?

In the library of the Exchequer House we lit candles even in the daylight. The rooms were dark and as we set to work with the ledgers, I took up my sewing. T'was a habit of mine. I ever did take up my needle while my councillors and advisers did sit or pace around me, discussing matters of state importance. With my head bent to my sewing, I could listen carefully without appearing as a threat. My needlework neutralized me, as well as soothed me. My hands were never idle. It was a habit I had learned from Catherine de Medici.

"What can we afford, Maitland?" Bothwell asked.

Maitland gave him an uneasy glance and moved the books slightly away from him. "You are getting a little ahead of yourself, Lord Bothwell."

Bothwell looked stung and I stepped in smoothly.

"I appreciate the advice and support you are giving me, Lord Bothwell, and would not have it otherwise. I am reminded again of my mother's words to me." I bent my head, pulling the needle in and out, weaving a spell. "How well she could rely upon your services. *If ever I needed support, Bothwell was there* – she wrote. *If you have need of the same, my daughter, follow suit.* That was ever her advice to me, and I remember it."

Maitland was shocked into uneasy silence.

"I want this to be a lavish affair. It is our opportunity to prove to the rest of Europe what Scotland is made of."

Maitland looked sardonic.

"Scotland is made of many things, Your Highness, but what it is not made of is money."

I looked at him askance.

"The coffers are bare, Ma'am."

"Then how…?"

"We have means at our disposal. We can levy a tax."

"I have never levied a tax before now," I demurred.

"No. In which case, the merchants will be more likely to oblige. Let us calculate how much we need and then debate the figures."

I felt their eyes upon my needle as it wove its way through the linen, describing the most delicate of pearl-like stitches.

"Well, there would need to be masques and musicians, banquets and dancing for a period of days. If people have travelled across the high seas to be with us, we cannot send them home without some form of entertainment."

Bothwell smirked to himself.

"What is it, Lord Bothwell?" I asked.

"If Master Knox could see what we are about…"

"What?" Maitland snapped. Normally suave and urbane, he had become uncharacteristically irritable of late.

"Well, it is a very Catholic affair, is it not?" Bothwell went on. "Knox never did approve of the dancing. Is it not that which has caused him to spit vitriol about Your Grace from the pulpit?"

"The fact that I sing and dance and make music? That I am merry, and perhaps a little too French?"

"Knox never did like foreigners," Bothwell added.

"God forbid we should take pleasure in life…" I added. "Besides, I care not for what Knox thinks."

However, I did care. I never sought to displease anyone in my life before.

"I am not sure he would approve of masques and musicians as part of the baptismal celebrations," Bothwell went on.

"I seek not Master Knox's approval," I broke in. "Nor will I be extending an invitation to him."

"He is a man of the people, we are told. I doubt he would want a place amongst royalty."

"Nor does he merit one," I snapped. "I like not the man."

"With good reason."

"Let us attend to our business," Maitland said. "Do you have any objection, Bothwell, to our lavish preparations? Perhaps it offends your own Protestant sensibilities?"

Bothwell's brow darkened.

"Not at all. If it pleases Her Grace to impress the rest of Europe, then it pleases me. And it serves our purpose."

"Our purpose?"

There was a moment of prolonged tension that prickled the air and made me uncomfortable as Maitland eyed our man, Bothwell.

"It seems you speak a little too freely, my lord!"

Bothwell did not reply. He met Maitland's stare.

Maitland lowered his gaze first and said, "Madam, it is time to think about returning." He glanced towards the window where the afternoon was darkening.

"Actually, Maitland, I prefer to stay here rather than ride back down the Canongate. I believe it would be easier – and safer."

There was a deafening silence.

"I did make that suggestion beforehand? And I recall you liked it not then, either!"

"As you wish."

"If you have such concern for my safety, then I think it only wise we should remain here."

And so we did.

One week of rising early to work at the ledgers in the library, dining at night by candlelight opposite the very shadow of St. Giles' High Kirk with its beastly buttresses. We worked hard all day, blinded by figures. We could spin money from thin air, coinage to pay for banquets and feasts, masques and musicians. We agreed to levy a tax, and to borrow money from the merchants of Edinburgh to the tune of £12,000, and they did oblige. We promised to pay them back and they foresaw future benefits to themselves and their businesses if they did comply. The baptism would take place at Stirling Castle; with its high vantage point and its grand proportions, we could safely host a myriad of kings and their entourages here. And besides, it was the seat of my son's nursery. He was safe there, as I had been years ago, until the age of five when my mother sought to protect me from King Henry's ravages.

My French page, Bastien, was with us while we worked at the Exchequer – one of my favourites – but I took no other servants.

Eventually Maitland was called away to attend to some family business and left, promising to return in a day or two to finalize the arrangements.

"Do not be gone long, Maitland. I need you here."

Bothwell and I dined alone that night. Bastien served us cold meat and vegetables. As the moon rose high above Edinburgh, it painted the stark buttresses and tall tenements with an eerie silver glow.

As we ate I confessed to Lord Bothwell that I no longer trusted any of my own courtiers, the people I was supposed to rely on to help me govern.

"Even Maitland," I said. "Even he. They share my table, eat my food, live in every palace and castle alongside me. I pay their wages and yet I cannot trust them."

"Ma'am, they are not a very trustworthy bunch," he murmured.

"I suspect everyone of treason. Rizzio's murder, Darnley's changeable nature. There is someone else behind all of this, Bothwell. Someone very close to me, who wishes me harm."

Bothwell said nothing.

"Who can that be?"

Still, he said nothing.

"Protestants," I said. "They have an agenda of their own."

And I nodded my head towards Knox's headquarters across the way.

After a heartbeat or two Bothwell spoke quietly. "But I too am a Protestant."

"You?" I laughed. "You are no zealot, Bothwell."

"From your Catholic stance, do you not view me as a heretic?"

"I believe in tolerance. I have seen what extremism does to people."

I shuddered, remembering the Huguenots in Paris, and how my mother-in-law, Catherine de Medici, had forced us as children to watch when they were rounded up and publically slaughtered. She presented it as a spectacle for royal eyes to feast upon, to ensure the continued success of the Catholic monarchy.

"I do not believe in terror as a persuasive argument," I added thoughtfully, my eyes filled with the mist of those far-away memories.

"Anyway, I do not see that you are over-exercised much by religious concerns, Lord Bothwell."

He considered this for a moment.

"I have my own thoughts on what is right and wrong, what is expected of the Church and State."

I mulled over his words for a while and was surprised by his next remark.

"I suppose it is not wise for a woman in your position to trust anyone. It could be political suicide."

I dared to risk a glance. He had risen and stood at the window, staring out.

"Even you?"

He had his back to me now.

"Especially me."

I hid my disappointment as I bent my head to my needlework. I was aware that he might be studying my reflection in the opaque glass, where the candles made a mirror of our little tableau.

The occupation with my hands saved me from showing the anxiety I felt.

Linlithgow
November 1566

Once the baptisimal arrangements were made, we parted company and it was with relief that I quit Edinburgh. I rode back to Stirling to visit my son's nursery. He was still so small I feared he would not remember me. Had my touch, my smell, become foreign to him? Wet-nurses could not provide the love I did feel; the attachment, the bond. But the cares of government do contrive to break that bond, to snap it asunder with distance and time.

"He is safest here, Ma'am," Mary Seton assured me when I shed tears on leaving him again. "What good would it do to risk the little Prince by having him accompany you? It would be impossible."

"I know this, my friend," I murmured. "But still it hurts to leave him. It is the burden of my birth-right. Sometimes, Mary, I wish I had been born a wench in the field, an ordinary carter's daughter. Would my fate have been any happier then?"

She looked at me askance. "Aye, it would. If you had

survived, that is. Many an ordinary carter's child dies before they reach their majority."

I nodded. I loved Mary Seton for speaking always the plain truth.

At the beginning of November I found myself in Linlithgow Palace, the seat of my own birth. I stood regarding the elaborate fountain in the courtyard which my father had had constructed to welcome his French bride to Scotland. I wondered what my mother must have felt on first arriving here and encountering that gift. Marie of Guise was a good mother who loved her daughter deeply. We wrote often to one another and spent our lives in craven affection, ever full of longing for one another. That first sad parting when I was five years of age is one that haunts me forever more. We shared the same name. Marie.

When she first arrived at Linlithgow and met her future husband, James, could she have known the struggles that awaited her? Could she have known how strong and noble a figure she would cut? A woman of steel who could govern our unruly kingdom all on her own? And she spoke often of Bothwell. He had served her well, had been her friend and confidant, a loyal servant. How could others not therefore understand that I would expect the same of him?

At Linlithgow I began to feel the first vague stirrings of unease in my health. One morning I woke to a sharp pang, but chose to ignore it. I clutched my abdomen and was immediately beset by thoughts of gloom. I decided the best policy was to rise above the pain, pretend it was not there.

It was on that day that Bothwell's wife, Lady Jean Gordon, rode out to meet me from Crichton Castle where she did reside. I was surprised and not a little alarmed by the visit.

"My husband Bothwell lies ill in Hermitage Castle," she told me. "Perhaps you have heard?"

My face paled.

No, I had not. "Is it serious?"

"Well, I am not always the first to learn of these matters. There is aye a distance between James Hepburn and myself. But, aye, they say it is serious. He got involved in a skirmish with some cattle reivers and came off the worst for it. He lies abed."

"Is he in danger?"

"I know not." She watched me for some time. "You understand, I would never have married the man, if it had not been at Your Majesty's bidding?"

I met her gaze. "I only meant to reward the Earl for his services to our crown. And it seemed you both would benefit from the match."

She lowered her almond eyes.

"And do you not think that love should have entered the arrangement?"

I said nothing, for she knew as well as I that love has little to do with marriage for women of our standing.

"I would have been happier wed to Alexander of Ogilvie," she murmured.

"Oh...happiness?" I sighed. "Perhaps it is an over-used word."

"And you, Your Grace?" she enquired, her calm gaze keen and alert. "What of your happiness, Ma'am?"

"I have none," I replied "certainly while I rule Scotland, and with an errant husband by my side. At least, if he *was* by my side I could be sure of what he is about. I know not what he conspires to do next."

She studied me carefully.

"And my Lord Bothwell?"

"What of him?"

"How do you perceive him, Ma'am?" she added pointedly.

I hesitated.

"I regard him as a friend and acquaintance, a loyal servant and supporter of the crown. As did my mother afore me."

"And nothing else?"

Narrowing my eyes, I put my head on one side.

"Of what do you charge me, Lady Jean?" I was nonplussed.

"I think you grow over-fond of him. And he with you."

"Then you think wrong!"

"But I came here today to inform you that I care not. He is not mine to love, nor I, his."

I swallowed, shocked at her words.

I spoke what was on my mind.

"I have heard others say that Bothwell does love his wife very much."

"And that offends thee?"

"Of course not. It is what I had hoped when I encouraged you both to wed."

"You did not encourage me. You *gave* me to him. Like a chattel."

I hesitated, shocked at her straightforward manner of speaking. Her icy serenity hid a woman of steel.

"I am sorry that you see it in that light. That was not my intention."

"If my husband does love me, I do not return the favour. I want only my freedom. And that I cannot have. But I only came here to tell you the news."

"How sick do they say he is?" I asked her.

"I cannot say," she added.

My mind ran with possibilities of disaster. How would I fare in Scotland if Bothwell and his army were not on my side? To whom would I turn? Who possessed enough of the brawn and willpower about them that they could actively step in to defend my position and my honour?

I was terrified at the prospect of losing him – and she saw it.

She was a young woman of grace, with a smooth, fair complexion and lovely almond-shaped eyes, hazel of hue. She was sedate where I was fiery; she was elegant where I was too ready to leap into the saddle and ride; she was calm where I was spirited. I envied her and yet, I admired her. She did not lose her head to anything, even to her beloved Alexander of Ogilvie, whom she had forsaken at the urgings of court politics.

I did not wait for Lady Jean Gordon to return to her own Crichton Castle before I did leap in the saddle and – pains or no pains – hastened my way to Hermitage Castle where Bothwell lay in peril.

I rode for four hours without stopping, my retinue urging me to take my rest, but I listened not to them. I arrived before noon – the day after Lady Jean Gordon's visit – and burst into the chamber. I feared he had already passed.

"My Lord Bothwell?" I cried of his man-servant. "What of him?"

"He is…"

A forest of backs confronted me, gathered about the bed. I did not wait upon ceremony but pushed into his midst. I feared to see a corpse lying there, pale and blood-spattered, statuesque in white sheets. But his eyes were open upon the pillow. He was staring at the wall. At first I thought it to be the death-stare, but then I saw him blink. He turned his head towards me, but the first word he spoke was not my name. It was Lady Jean's.

I did not flinch, for that was as it should be. I was his queen and his sovereign. He owed me a great deal, but he owed his wife more…

"It is not she," I whispered. "It is I. Marie."

His gaze quickly focused.

"Your Grace? You ride all this way to see me?"

I stood up quickly from where I had knelt, and recovered myself.

"Of course," I said. "How else am I supposed to govern Scotland if I have not the support of my fiercest Borderer? You cannot afford to be ill, Bothwell. I have not the time for it."

"Nor the patience, I see!"

His servants watched us, and my retinue too, all eyes upon us, noting our behaviour. There was nothing untoward in the way we did relate to one another. I swear this upon my son's life and any who were there could vouchsafe this for me.

"It is not my time, Your Grace. I have no intention of quitting this world just yet. 'Tis but a scrape. No more."

"A mere scrape? I had not thought you could be laid low by such a slight injury."

His dark eyes glowed merrily in his poor face for an instant.

"Aye, Your Grace is right. I should hasten back into the saddle afore long. Your Majesty will have need of my efforts."

"Indeed I do, Bothwell."

I slipped a glove from my hand and laid it upon his chest.

"Lest you forget your duty!"

He picked it up and held it briefly.

With barely a half hour to rest ourselves and take sustenance, having assured myself that Bothwell was not, after all, at death's door, I did take my leave of him, mounting the saddle and riding another four hours across moorland and heath, to be at Jedburgh by nightfall where I had business to conduct.

Once there, I succumbed to the pains which had been troubling me earlier. The irony was, I became more ill than Bothwell, and neither he nor Darnley hastened to my side to ensure I was not dying.

The doctors were of the opinion that I had not recovered from the birth of my son. It was suggested to me that perhaps the placenta had not fully come away from the womb, and some remained, infected. Whatever it was, my apothecary and surgeon waited on me anxiously as a fever ravaged my body. I remember little of those dark days, only that I did fear the worst.

Of Darnley there were constant rumours filtering through, that he was urging the Catholics abroad – Spain no less – to send out an Armada to kidnap me, that he would conspire to murder me and rule Scotland in my stead. He continued to bargain for the Crown Matrimonial, to be named as my heir after my death, and when I refused, he skulked and brooded like a madman. He drank more heavily, kept bad company, and in truth I was relieved to be free of his presence. He disappeared often into his father's country. Lord Lennox and his wife had lands near the Clyde, and here it was that Darnley retreated, brim-full of his woes and grievances.

"It is I who should be King," he complained, and no doubt his mother agreed with him.

The Lennoxes had ruined their spoiled wee darling, and I was the unfortunate one who was forced to bear the consequences. I knew what it meant at first-hand. I had lived with it; seen it; witnessed its petty cruelties. The thought of leaving my son to his care terrified me.

Fotheringhay Castle
October 1586

The sun is up. It has risen above the castle ramparts and reaches long claws across the fields. Another day dawns with monotonous regularity.

Jane comes to help me dress.

It is bitterly cold this morning. A ground frost has made white statues of the bushes and shrubs. A world of spun sugar, glittering in the dawn.

Even the garden is a prison. I may only go thus far, heavily guarded of course. It is almost not worth my while, but Jane insists the fresh air is good for my constitution.

I dreamt about Bothwell last night, for the first time in years. I blame Darnley's ghost for that, setting off a train of memories that are best forgotten. What is done cannot be undone. And what is known cannot be unknown.

On our return, the chair is waiting for me, pulled up close to

the hearth. There was a time when they denied me fuel and I shivered, perishing. Now Jane has managed to correct that wrong and I am grateful to her.

My basket of needlework lies on the table, the threads laid out carefully in rows. A rainbow of silk.

I have been curiously absentminded this morn. I keep gazing out of the narrow window into the grey distance, where the mist curls off the edge of the world.

My embroidery lies discarded in my lap, the calico untouched.

The jangle of a harness in the courtyard below. My keen ears hear boots resounding on the bare staircase, circling higher.

"Ma'am," Jane whispers. "There is a messenger here from Her Majesty."

"What is it?"

"It is Lord Burleigh to see you."

Almost before I have had time to collect my thoughts he bursts upon us, without ceremony.

Cecil, the most efficient of her statesmen.

He is accompanied by diverse others who crowd into my chamber.

"How nice to see you, gentlemen. Please, don't trouble yourselves to take off your hats!"

Cecil clears his throat. "I have come on business of a high priority, from Her Majesty the Queen of England."

"And how is my dear sister and cousin?" I murmur.

He ignores me.

"Her Majesty has sent instructions that you are to receive no more letters."

"Letters?" I gaze at him in innocent surprise.

"Quite so! Letters. Walsingham and I are working to protect Her Majesty and feel that her person is ill-served by your continued correspondence with foreign heads of state abroad."

There is a long silence while I digest this.

"What does Elizabeth know of my correspondence? Am I to have no privacy?"

"You must become accustomed to having further restraints placed upon your freedom."

"Hah! What further restrains could they muster?"

"Despite the hospitality our sovereign has extended to you these past eighteen years, you have continued to show a blatant disregard for her position and – I might add – her safety."

"How so?"

"By encouraging others to plot on your behalf – as has been proven in the past."

"I have no control over what others conspire to achieve in my name."

He rises to his full height, his black eyes beetling, and clips his heels together before departing.

"You have been warned!" he calls. "Good day to you, Madam."

"Civil servant," I shout. "Lackey!"

Jane leans in to quiet me.

The corridors outside fall silent and soon we hear the ring of horses' hooves again, riding away.

"They push me too far."

"I have warned you before about the letters, Ma'am. Walsingham and his spies are everywhere."

"They cannot forbid me my rights as a Queen."

But I do not add what we both know. That they have, and they will.

In the old days I used to meet with dignitaries, men of rank and position, as we carved out the fortunes of my kingdom, struggling to maintain peace.

Now I wear plain black, relieved only by a ruff of white lace at my throat. There are no rings on my fingers; no coronets or ermined gowns as of yore. No crimson canopy of state. They took that away from me. No gleaming crown or sceptre.

But a true queen needs no crown, nor even crowds to cheer her. A true queen remains so even in exile. Even in prison.

Bare of ornaments, a crucifix at my breast and a beaded rosary at my waist, I nevertheless manage to look the part of a queen. I have innate royal dignity, innate sovereignty, bestowed upon me by God. And it is that which irks my sister, Elizabeth. I was born to be royal from the cradle upwards. It was a responsibility I was reared for and rose to.

Elizabeth fears her position, for she is the daughter of a king's mistress, as illegitimate as my brother, Moray. There are many who question her claim to the throne, even as she sits on it. Catholics would have her gone, and myself in her stead.

I know this.

And so does she…

Sovereignty comes naturally to me whereas Elizabeth tends to look of peasant stock, even in her finest robes and glittering gems. I do not know quite what it is about her, but no matter how high her collars, no matter how wide her gowns, her countenance is ever that of a peasant.

So, I am not allowed any letters.

So Walsingham says.

So Cecil says.

We shall see.

We have means at our disposal.

Does not the butcher deliver the meat and the brewer deliver his ale? They use caskets and barrels for this purpose, do they not?

I sit by the fire and wait for the moment of reckoning.

And this time the ghosts will leave me in peace.

Craigmillar
November 1566

I was lying ill at Craigmillar Castle when a formal meeting was called to discuss the problem of Darnley. They came to me as I languished in my illness, beyond the boundaries of the city walls. I did not wish to stay in Holyrood and Craigmillar offered us the seclusion we desired. Who could come eavesdropping to this dark castle sitting stark and quiet on its low-lying mound? Its high walls afforded us secrecy. None could see us arriving.

I was already ensconced in my own apartments upstairs, having rested here for the past week and a half with my apothecary in attendance. The fever had passed, but I was still weak.

Rain sleeted across the battlements and clattered down the great chimneys, and when that had passed, my councillors began arriving, in pairs, secretly, without attendants or men-at-arms, quietly through the countryside. No one would even know we were there.

By nightfall we were all assembled in the great banqueting hall. Craigmillar is a sombre seat, remote. Set against the backdrop of a harsh escarpment, it broods; and it did brood that night.

While the servants laid a few victuals at the long tables and lit fires in the great hearths, we waited patiently, making small talk.

We sat down to eat with the black windows set high in the walls uncovered to the night. Candlelight played fitfully across our faces and the fires did little to take the chill off the air.

There were a few of us present; most notably Maitland, Moray, Bothwell and Huntly, Argyll, Mar and Atholl.

"We are gathered here in the interests of national security!" my secretary Maitland began.

Moray held up a hand to stop Maitland, and gestured towards the fireplace where one of the servants still attended to the hearth. We waited for the servant to leave before continuing.

"This is a delicate matter to discuss, but we have to ask Your Grace, how have relations been with your husband of late?"

I prevaricated and Moray stepped in impatiently.

"Marie, we need to know. Have things improved on that front at all?"

I stared at my brother. I could feel Bothwell's eyes upon me too; I was the only woman in a room full of men.

"Is my private life with my husband really a subject for discussion?"

"Yes, I am afraid it is," Moray said, addressing me directly. "As Queen of this realm you have no private life. Your life belongs to the crown."

"I am aware of my responsibilities, Lord James. You have no need to remind me of my role."

"But perhaps Your Grace is not aware," Maitland broke

in carefully, "that while Prince Henry and yourself are unreconciled to one another, he poses an immediate and considerable risk to the security of the crown?"

"I know that there are rumours…"

"Rumours aplenty!"

"He is becoming dangerous, Ma'am. He is plotting against you."

"Where is the proof of that?" I asked.

"We have proof," Moray cut in.

"He writes to the Pope, to the King of Spain, asking for their support. Marie is not Catholic enough, they say."

"Not Catholic enough!"

"She surrounds herself with Protestants, they say…"

"I do so with good reason," I broke in. "My advisers are both Catholic and Protestant, yes."

"Mainly Protestant, Ma'am," Maitland added.

"That is because I have chosen advisers with the necessary experience and power to help me govern Scotland. It would be foolish of me to do otherwise."

"But others abroad may not regard the matter in that light, Your Grace."

"They know not Scotland," I said.

"Exactly. But Your Grace does. As did your mother before you. They know not the realities of governing this kingdom, with its divided history, its politics. But Your Grace does."

I looked towards Bothwell but he remained quiet throughout all of this.

I rose from the table and reached for my sewing which calmed me.

"Your husband sees himself as having a legitimate claim to the throne, Marie." It was my brother speaking this time.

"I know this."

"He cannot be left to his own devices any longer."

"What do you suggest?"

There was silence in the room. The walls were thick with shadow; the wind gusted in the chimney.

My needlework lay still in my lap.

"What can I do?"

Eyes were lowered, fingers drummed on lips.

"Divorce is an option."

Bothwell spoke for the first time.

"No. If Her Grace divorces him that would invalidate Prince James' claim to the throne. It would be tantamount to declaring him illegitimate," Maitland said, and I noticed him avoiding my brother's eye at this point. Moray, my bastard brother! It was a wound that festered in him – the painful fact of his own illegitimacy. But for that he could have made a first-rate King.

"What, then, is the alternative?"

"As long as Darnley remains outside Your Grace's circle, he will be dangerous."

I glanced at Maitland. "So you wish me to be reconciled to him?"

He hesitated. "Possibly…"

I thought of how Darnley had behaved of late, how he had responded to the birth of our son.

"But what can I do?" I cried. "I cannot control him any more than you can. What steps can I possibly take to be united with him, other than to give him what I have already refused? If I give him the Crown Matrimonial now–"

"That will not be necessary–"

"–how can I know that he will not continue in his villainous course afterwards?"

"Quite so, Your Majesty."

"Perhaps… there is another way."

We all stared at Maitland, eyes wide.

"There are ways and means of dealing with this sort of problem."

I was suddenly aware of how dark it had become. It was so quiet in the great banqueting hall once their voices had stilled. I could hear their breathing, sense their tension. A log cracked in the hearth and a shower of red sparks fizzed in the dark.

I lifted my needle again and began to sew.

"Darnley leads such a dangerous life-style, it is indeed a wonder he has not met with an accident before now."

I sought out Bothwell in the gloom, but he had risen and was standing in the far corner, away from the main table.

"Who knows what may happen to him in the future?" Maitland added.

And there it was. Put there on the table before us like a playing card. *The declaration. The promise. The threat.*

Whatever it was, it hung in the air between us, palpable as mist.

I felt a tightening in my chest; my breath came short.

Maitland continued smoothly while my brother Moray remained inscrutable, his eyes giving nothing away.

"I hear that the banished lords Ruthven, Morton and Lindsay have shown themselves entirely penitent for their past misdemeanours and are anxious to return to Scotland…"

"Traitors…" I murmured softly without looking up from my work. "They threatened my own life and the life of my child. What kind of insanity would it be to allow them passage back here?"

"They are anxious to prove to Her Grace their continued fealty and loyalty."

I narrowed my eyes. "How opportune! Where was their loyalty before, on that night in March? Am I to forget what happened?"

"Of course not, Marie. No one is suggesting you should forget!" I glanced at Bothwell who had spoken.

"You too?" I murmured, but so quietly I do not think the others heard the words pass my lips.

"With Lord Bothwell here to protect you, Ma'am, how could anyone possibly threaten Your Grace's life?" Maitland added in a soft voice.

I ignored his implied tone.

I sewed on in silence for a moment or two more, while my lords waited.

"You expect me to formally pardon Morton, Ruthven and Lindsay and invite them back to Scotland?"

"They may help to solve Your Majesty's problem."

"Traitors cannot help me!"

"Then who can?" my brother said, rising suddenly from the table, his fists clenched.

I lifted my eyes and watched him pace.

Maitland and Moray did put their heads together and murmur. What they said, I know not.

"Perhaps Her Grace needs more time?"

I felt suffocated suddenly. Great bat wings of shadow loomed in the far corners of the room and night seemed to creep around the edges of our circle of light, heavy with menace. I glanced upwards. The banqueting hall was too high to fill with light. Shadows leapt in the pillared minstrels' gallery above, creating stark images, unearthly shapes, horned figures of black against the yellow stone. I blinked my eyes slowly, wondering if my fever was causing me to imagine devilish shapes in the gloom. I rose, laying my embroidery aside on my chair.

"Wait," I whispered. All eyes followed my gaze as I pointed upwards.

Bothwell and Moray exchanged glances.

"There is no one there, Your Grace. There cannot be," Maitland assured me.

"I will go and see that we are not overlooked," Bothwell said, before vanishing towards the staircase. I watched him go.

When I sat down again at the head of the table the others were watching me, waiting. I felt weary all of a sudden.

I spoke clearly. "I do not want to be a party to any crime. I will not sanction it. Do you hear?"

I could feel the instant relief in the room.

"You may leave the logistics entirely up to us, Ma'am," Maitland said.

"I want no stain on my conscience, nothing that trespasses the law of God or the law of this land. You understand?"

Maitland and Moray smiled.

"Of course!"

"And it goes without saying that whatever measures you take must be done with the full backing of Parliament, of course."

"Of course! I can assure Your Grace that it is possible to deal with this little problem, quite efficiently, without any prejudice either to your reputation…or your conscience."

Maitland bowed his head slightly and it did occur to me then what a smooth and urbane operator he was, a master of manipulation. That is why, after all, I had chosen him as my chief Secretary of State, to assist me in affairs of government – because of his consummate skill in dissembling. He was a past master at it.

As I lifted my embroidery and began to sew, he added a comment which I have never forgotten and which has haunted me all these years.

"After all," he added, nodding his head in the direction of my brother – who remained inscrutable, "although Lord

Moray here is as scrupulous a Protestant as Your Grace is a Papist, I am sure that he will look through his fingers at the deed, and say nothing."

There were a few smiles of mild amusement as the tension in the room eased.

Look through his fingers?

"At what deed?" I asked.

The men stopped suddenly and looked at me.

Huntly advanced to my side and spoke quietly. "Maitland knows what he is about, Your Grace. Leave matters in other's hands."

My brother Moray rose and walked towards the window.

The November winds had begun to howl around the blackened castle walls.

"It looks as if it may snow tonight," he observed.

I watched his back.

And as I did so I had a sudden flashback – not so long ago in fact – to when he was ushered into my presence in my widow's chamber in France. How I had been so glad to see him then, as if he heralded the answer to my prayers. Now his back was turned to me and I could not fathom a single honest thought in his head.

As the others began to talk, I was quiet and thoughtful. The pains of my recent illness were still not far from my memory. And now I had other pains to exercise my mind.

Stirling Castle
December 1566

There were fragments of snow on the air as we approached Stirling Castle. Whenever I saw that stark fortress resting high on its impregnable rock, the mountains marching along the skyline behind it, my heart rose in my chest, because I knew then that I was to come face to face with my little son. We kept his nursery here as it was more secure, easier to guard.

Twenty years ago my mother Marie of Guise had thought the same, and I always associated Stirling with happy childhood memories, the precious years before my mother and I were separated.

Darnley did not ride with us. He was in Glasgow. He had formally requested to be allowed to retreat into exile in France, but my privy council and I had refused the ludicrous request. Once outside the borders of Scotland, what manner of plotting might he not be capable of? Requesting foreign arms and men to rise up against me.

Scotland froze that December. The lochs became white plates of ice, reflecting the mountains like glass. We rode under a weak winter sun, great white fields and moorland stretching either side of us. Behind us we left a trail of hoof prints, wheel-marks and churned-up ruts of greying snow.

We clattered up the steep causeway towards the fortified entrance, the wind keening across the plains, straight from the mountains. The air was bracing. To one side were the Trossachs, to the other the Grampians. I could see their snowy summits, speaking of far-off places yet to be visited.

Stirling Castle itself was ready to receive us. The horses were stabled and the outer close was full of bustle and business. Carts rolled in bearing goods and supplies. Smells of baking emanated from the kitchens and the bake house and the spice house – areas of the castle I would never visit, where men and boys roasted meat over the spit, plucked partridges and pheasants, cracked eggs, and kept the great bread ovens constantly stoked up and roaring. I loved the way that the courtyards rang with these distant sounds of activity. It made me feel warmed, as if I was at the heart of something cherished. The sights and sounds and smells were a welcome assault on my senses.

The windows of the palace that my father had built winked in the fading winter light, set in their ochre walls. He had employed carvers, painters and stonemasons to adorn this wonderful palace, to advertise it as a sparkling gem upon the brow of Scotland. It was the perfect place to baptise little Prince James, a showcase to present to our European visitors.

The walls and facades were thick with statuary: sculptures of fantastic and weird design. They leered down at us from the highest points and I remember as a child, craning my neck to see them, wondering what messages they bore for me.

We made our way up the high wooden steps to the entrance

of the Palace. Here were my private apartments, the walnut ceilings heavily carved and painted, bright colours depicting the kings and queens who had ruled Scotland before me – my ancestors and forebears. There was even a motif of my mother's family, the Guises, a bird pierced through with three arrows. Every attention to detail had been carefully overseen when my father attended to the building of this opulent jewel. I miss it so. And I can lovingly recall every feature as if I trod there only yesterday.

My worries and anxieties back then on that winter's day in 1566 seemed grave indeed, but how much graver have they become? I had no way of knowing what the future had in store for me, that I would spend much of my adult life as a prisoner, a captive queen!

I settled into my private apartments immediately. My bearers unpacked the chests and unrolled the rich red rugs and tapestries which always accompanied us, until the walls and floors were adorned with them. There was a desk before the great fire, so that I could sit with my back to the flames as I worked or signed documents, or met with my ministers to discuss matters of state – for there was always business to attend to. The painted ceiling above me was loud with symbolism and motifs, brightly picked out against the dark of the wood.

A prie-dieu sat in a corner, with a painted icon above it where I could pray. It would have Knox grinding his teeth if he could see it, but he was not invited to the festivities. He remained outside my inner circle, along with his radical minority, agitating for violent extremism. He liked to pretend that he spoke for Scotland, but the people were only grudgingly obedient to his example. In their hearts they still looked to the old ways.

But high on our rock at Stirling Castle I felt safe and far

away from John Knox and his ilk. This was not Edinburgh, where my nemesis could hold sway and dominate and march about the streets with impunity. This was my domain. Knox would have to knock many times before the great gates would open to him and no one would be listening to his sermons here.

My son would be baptised in the Chapel Royal according to the old rites of the Catholic religion and the world would be there to witness it. I would entertain them magnificently and show them how Scotland could rise to the occasion with its own traditions. There would be four days of feasting, dancing, masques and musicians, the great rooms of the castle filled with music and light. Candles and lanterns would flutter, fireplaces would roar, tapestries would gleam and glint, costumes would sparkle, platters of food would entice, and outside the wind might howl and the snow might fall, but inside all would be merriment and laughter.

From far away, people on the plains might see the windows flicker and catch the strain of a madrigal, but they would be too far away to smell the roasting of the meats. The only fowl they would smell would be those still wild on the carse, trying to avoid being hunted. The mountains and the stars would watch us from a distance.

Within an hour of arriving Moray marched into my chamber, smiling for once.

"You look well, my sister."

"I feel it, Lord James," I returned.

"Do we have word yet of whether your precious little husband will be with us?"

I eyed him sceptically. I had half a mind to question his disrespectful attitude towards Darnley.

"He is due to arrive, but I have no way of knowing if he will keep to that arrangement. You know as much as I."

"If he does not appear it puts us in a difficult position. I shall send another messenger to his father, Lennox, and insist his son attends. We shall see what good that achieves."

In fact, my errant husband arrived at Stirling the following day. I heard a commotion in the outer close and was aware of his presence before I saw him. I felt strangely nervous, uneasy in my mind. This was the first time in months that we had seen each other for any great length of time. It was painful to meet. We were a constant reminder to each other of our mutual failure and the ruin of our blighted hopes of two years before.

When he came into my presence I was shocked. He appeared a changed man. His eyes were darkly shadowed beneath, and his countenance was pale as if he was harbouring some sort of illness that had yet to come to the fore. He seemed agitated and restless.

He came into the chamber with a surly demeanour that did not bode well for our celebrations.

"I am delighted that you've come, Henry," I said quietly, trying to mean what I said.

He eyed me suspiciously.

"I do not feel particularly welcome."

"Is your room not to your liking? We have made every effort to ensure that you feel welcome..."

"You want me to speak truth?"

"Of course."

"It feels as if I have walked into the lion's den. I am surrounded by smiling enemies pretending to be my friends. I trust no one."

"You can trust me."

He laughed bitterly.

"You are the last person I should trust."

"Why would you say that…?" It came out as a whisper only. I reined in my fury and smothered it.

He went on… "I have no friends left. You have succeeded in turning everyone against me."

I felt a wave of indignation rise in my chest. "That is not true, Darnley, and you know it. If you are friendless and isolated, you have brought about that state of affairs yourself."

"You have never loved me, Mary…You have a heart of stone."

It was impossible to contain my despair and anger any longer, and I burst out at this accusation. "How can you reproach me when I have done everything in my power to resolve our differences, after all you have done?"

I realised we were no longer alone when my brother Moray appeared in the doorway behind us.

"Lord Darnley!" he inclined his head politely, but the sneer upon his face was not so easily hidden. "We are hopeful that you will govern yourself in a fitting manner at these festivities. There will be many there to observe what passes."

Darnley shot a look of resentment in my brother's direction, but said nothing. He brushed past him and disappeared into the outer chamber, no doubt intending to make his way to his own apartments.

Moray and I watched him go then exchanged glances.

"Let us hope he deports himself with dignity," my brother added. "If he does not, the whole of Europe will know."

I stood at the window of the Great Hall, staring out. Flakes of snow still fell beyond the tiny window-panes, speckling the cobbles. I rubbed the glass and gazed out at the mountains in the distance, their summits serene and snow-covered. It was not often I enjoyed a quiet moment, surrounded as I always was by the affairs and business of state.

The ceilings above me were arched like the ribs of a giant ship upturned on its belly, golden oak glowing in the light from the lanterns that flared from the wall sconces. My father's initials were carved and mounted on the wooden panels above the windows. He had left his mark on this castle. I could feel his presence. I imagined him sitting in the grand oak chair before the fireplace, slumped to one side, thoughtful, stern, taciturn, afraid of the future and what it might bring. He had had wars to fight, worries to consume him, children to rear...

What had he thought about my birth when I arrived? A female, a girl, a legitimate heir...

They have told me stories, tales, legends. Some say he was disappointed, afeart at what might happen to his kingdom after his death.

"Alas, it came wi' a lass and it will gang wi' a lass." They told me these were his dying words, as he turned to face the wall.

I turn my head and search the shadows of the Great Hall for his ghost.

Is that a figure in the far corner? Footsteps cross the flags towards me. Confusion fogs my poor brain. Is this Stirling Castle I sit in, or Fotheringhay? Am I in Scotland, or Norfolk?

"Your Highness, the men are looking to you for advice!"

A voice broke into my thoughts.

"Advice? But of course, I was just ..."

Mary Seton smiles and together we make haste back into the fray.

The rest of Stirling Castle is awhirl with activity. The kitchen fires belch out smoke, the stoves are red-hot, servants carry panniers of water up and down stairs and along corridors. Canopies have been beaten to expel the dust; wine and ale are uncorked and flow freely; bread and spiced meats scent the air; candles and lanterns are lit, fires built high with coal. It is bitter outside, and it will be a battle to keep the cold at bay.

After a day or two the guests at last begin arriving. The courtyards and hallways seethe with the hundreds of stalwarts who have braved the cold. Foreign ambassadors, heads of state, dukes and cardinals come in their scores as my guests of honour. Elizabeth's ambassador is there of course; she is to be godmother to be my little son, and although she is not present herself, Melville is here to represent her as proxy. My former brother-in-law the King of France and the Duke of Savoy are the other two named godparents. Neither of them will attend in person, but their ambassadors have been sent ahead, and can report back on the occasion and its lavish surroundings.

No expense has been spared – thanks to the coffers of the merchants of Edinburgh who helped us to raise the funds. I would pay them back in kind. The whole event has been planned with infinite care in a conscious effort to impress the rest of Europe. I will not have them thinking that Scotland is a poor kingdom; I intend to show my country off to its best advantage. Scotland may not have the fruits and sunshine and glinting white palaces of France or Spain, but Scotland has its own charm, its own traditions, its own ineradicable character.

Each of my nobles and their retinues were dressed in their own colours, chosen by me. I could hear them grumbling in the corridor as I passed with Mary Seton. Moray and Bothwell – who normally communicated little – had their heads together whilst viewing the aspect of the other in a slightly calculating fashion. Suddenly there was a burst of conspiratorial laughter between them, and Bothwell slapped my brother on the back.

I stared at them, amused. "It is not like the two of you to be so cooried in together. Tell me what amuses you so?"

"Oh, nothing, dear sister," my brother said. "Lord Bothwell here was just filling me in on one or two details."

"You like your costume?"

Moray glanced down at his suit of green velvet trimmed with red and gold.

"It's very fine, Your Highness."

"And you, Lord Bothwell. Like you your livery?" He was covered from head to toe in blue velvet, trimmed with silver and white, as were his men.

"Indeed I do, Your Highness. It is very… blue. And like as not our men will not get themselves muddled up if a brawl breaks out. They can easily distinguish the one from the other."

"I hope there won't be any brawls, Lord Bothwell. Not at this time."

"Exactly!" Moray said. "We want no disagreements. We shall have enough on our hands keeping Darnley from misbehaving without worrying about our own men breaking out in feuds."

I smiled. It was good to hear them engaging in light-hearted banter. The mood of the castle was becoming infected with good cheer. I wanted nothing to spoil the atmosphere.

Mary Seton and I retreated to my private chambers to see to the ordering of my own wardrobe. I would shed my plainer gowns. For the next few days I would glitter in cloth of gold with diamonds at my throat, or deep crimson velvet with great rubies like drops of blood on my fingers, or orange damask embroidered all over with silver filigree. And for the baptism itself – a gown of silver cloth, mounted with lace and covered in intricate embroidery, the like of which I would have gladly stitched myself, swirls, whorls and arabesques of silver, dove-grey and pure white. I would glitter like a column of ice.

So impressive... So cold to the touch... A warm heart beating beneath.

To finish, Scottish pearls were wound about my throat and threaded into the tresses of my hair. My own flowing auburn hair, pinned and coiffed to perfection.

Ah, then I had hair. Now I have none. My bald pate glistens beneath the wigs I wear, although none shall see it.

It was the morning of the baptism. The nineteenth day of December. Mary Seton and Mary Livingstone and others had finished my toilette. We had been up since before dawn, pulling back the bed drapes and the shutters onto a cold dark night. Candles were lit and my servant, Christina Hogg, attended to the fire until it roared up the wide chimney breast. I shivered next to its warmth in my gown.

"Be careful you don't melt, Your Grace," Mary Seton said.

I held the stiffly-embroidered cloth between my fingers. "This will never melt. Where is my son, Christina?"

"They will be bringing him soon, Ma'am."

"I like to have him sleep here in the chamber with me. Could we not manage to arrange this, Mary?"

"I see no reason why not…" Mary Seton replied.

"The wet-nurse, Ma'am. He has not yet been weaned."

"Then let the wet-nurse sleep here too. I miss my son so…I hope the others are readying themselves."

"Her Highness Queen Elizabeth has sent a huge silver font as a christening gift, Ma'am. The Duke of Bedford conveyed it himself, it would seem."

My women laughed at the vision of the duke struggling under its weight.

"Surely not?"

"It is a great, cumbersome object, covered with gems."

"Then our cousin has extended herself. It is not like her to be so extravagant with her purse."

"Ma'am!" Mary Seton chastised me.

Elizabeth has never been one for wasting money on fripperies. We all knew that. So I was amazed that she should have gone to all the trouble of transporting a baptismal font of solid silver for my son to be baptised in. I suppose she wanted to place herself conspicuously at the centre of the ceremony, even if only by proxy.

It was an hour or two later that Moray burst into my chamber.

"He's refusing to attend the ceremony!"

"What? Who, my lord?"

"Your husband…" Moray said, adding "Your Grace."

"How do you know?"

"He's refusing to leave his room. He is adamant that he will not be attending under any circumstances."

"Then let him sulk…"

"Your Grace, do you not see how that will appear to our

guests? It will be a clear statement to them. He is already suggesting that Prince James is not..." He hesitated for a moment, glancing awkwardly at the gathered company in my room, "...is not his son."

"Well, then who the devil does he *think* is the father?" I burst out, indignant and furious.

Moray cleared his throat, but no one said anything.

"This is ridiculous," I wept, wringing my hands until the rings bit into my fingers. "What does he expect to gain? He seeks to ruin everything."

Moray was enraged. "Your Grace, we shall pay him a visit. Together."

"I am almost more afraid of him appearing at the ceremony. What if he stands there before all the guests and denies our son? What then? He would do anything to embarrass and humiliate me!"

"Your Grace, we shall not give him that opportunity. Come!"

My brother Moray beckoned me to follow him as he strode to the King's apartments. Our feet rang out loudly along the stone passageways. Moray threw open the heavy oak door at once and marched straight into King Henry's presence.

King Henry, I am ashamed to say, was skulking in a corner near the fireplace, almost cowering, and part of me felt a painful twist of pity, despite my fury at his behaviour.

"Lord Darnley!" Moray began.

"King Henry – to you!"

"However you style yourself, Your Grace, I demand to know the meaning of your behaviour!"

Darnley interrupted him. "So, she gets her henchmen to deal with me now, does she?" He shot me a vindictive glance.

"Do you have any idea," Moray barked at him "how this will look?"

Darnley gave an innocent shrug of the shoulders. He was deliberately trying to be provocative.

Moray stepped forward. "I would advise you," he muttered, "to treat Her Highness with a little more respect, if only for your own sake!"

Darnley locked eyes with him. "I'll treat my wife as I please!"

My brother's eyes flashed and he said in a quiet, menacing tone, "Not in *my* presence you won't."

I was surprised and moved by Moray's defence of me. In spite of our differences he seemed intent on defending my honour.

"You have made a grave mistake, Darnley. If you refuse to take your place by Her Highness's side at this ceremony, then I cannot answer for your personal safety."

There was a sharp intake of breath. The air of the chamber seemed suddenly suffocating, poisonous with threat. The three of us were caught in a tableau that will never be erased from my mind.

As he spoke Moray pushed my husband back against the wall and pinioned him there, with one hand on his throat. I almost pitied Darnley in that moment.

"Is this a threat?" he whispered.

"Well done!" Moray hissed.

"I'll set my men on you," Darnley protested weakly, struggling against my brother's stranglehold. "I'll let everyone know how you've treated me. I'll tell them all – your precious foreign guests. I'll let them know what you're plotting, what you're up to. I'm not blind. I have eyes and I can see…"

"You see nothing," Moray spat.

Then Moray pulled back his arm and I heard the sound of a slap ringing on the air. He pulled at Darnley's open shirt.

"Get dressed!" he ordered.

The slap had sobered Darnley in an instant, and shocked me. A red weal had appeared across his cheek where Moray's ring had bit deep and drawn blood. He did not protest any more.

"You've signed your own death warrant," Moray muttered through his teeth. Then wiping his hand on his thigh, he withdrew from the room.

Darnley was left standing there, looking at me, his shirt disordered.

"Are you satisfied?" he said.

I winced.

His eyes looked incredibly sad and my heart failed me. The whole ghastly scene was disturbing to behold and shook me to the core.

"Do you honestly expect me to appear at your side now, Mary, as a dutiful husband?" he said, raising his hand to his jaw. "After this?"

"What do you expect of me, Darnley?" I said.

He shrugged. "Not this!"

"Nor I! You have undone us," I wept.

He looked at me as if in surprise at my display of grief. Perhaps he really did not comprehend how he had hurt and injured me.

"Rumours come to me all the time, Darnley, of how you are plotting to leave the country."

"I have asked your Privy Council if they might release me into exile! There is no secret!"

"But what then?"

"We are not happy, Marie. We have never been happy. What is the point in continuing?"

I noticed how he called me by the affectionate 'Marie'.

"*Never* happy, Darnley?"

He avoided my gaze. How could I win him over, this recalcitrant husband of mine?

"You can't just leave," I murmured "any more than I can. You are married to the queen of this country, remember?"

"Oh, yes, I remember," he said bitterly. "The problem is that other people don't."

I tried to fix his gaze, but he turned away.

"Will you come to the baptism, Henry?"

"I have another question for you – my sweet wife. Am I permitted to share your bed, eat at your table? Or is that reserved for your favourites?"

"You are objectionable, Darnley. You have made yourself utterly objectionable. You have brought this upon yourself!"

"And is that your answer?"

I did not reply.

"In that case, I cannot answer for my own behaviour."

I turned and left, not knowing what would happen next.

The rooms below were filling up with guests, their clamour drifting along the corridors and up the staircase. Diplomats from France, Savoy and Piedmont gathered in the courtyard and the Great Hall, their vast retinues clad in velvet, damask, silk and furs, rubbing shoulders with each other, completely unaware of the private drama that was being enacted above.

I arrived back in my own apartments to find a scene of agitation, people restlessly pacing and demanding to know what we were about. Maitland, Moray and Bothwell had all appeared.

"It is unthinkable."

"Something must be done."

"We will threaten him."

"I have already done so."

"Then we will cajole him. Your Grace can employ her feminine charms…"

I shook my head wearily. "I have tried, but to no avail. We shall simply leave matters as they are, and wait and see."

"Wait and see, Your Highness?"

"It is all we *can* do, Maitland. There is no other way."

I could hear their voices all around me as they paced the room. But no matter how much they protested and complained, no matter how much they panicked, I knew it was pointless. There was nothing that any of us could do. I would simply hold my head high and perform before my audience with a bright smile upon my face.

And it *would* be a performance.

I can ever act the part of a queen.

"Come," I beckoned Mary Seton and Livie to my side. "It is time, I think."

My ladies fell nervously into position behind me, my lords went before me and we processed along the stone corridors towards the Great Hall. We could hear the hum of voices long before we neared them, and while my stomach fluttered with butterflies, a surge of energy carried me through. I was to meet with the world's leaders and their representatives, and demonstrate to them that Scotland was a kingdom to be ranked among the best – whether they believed me or not.

Music drifted from the state rooms as we walked in kingly file along the corridors, the walkways, and down the spiralling staircase that led to the Great Hall itself.

The guests were gathered. A sea of faces glanced up. Hopefully, the cluster of maids-of-honour and companions around my person would distract them from the absence of my husband.

"It is not likely that they will notice, Madam," Livie whispered in my ear. "We are such a busy army."

She was right. Besides, the assumption might be that he would join us later. I hid my nerves.

A sigh of acknowledgement and a cheer swept through the crowd as we entered. I held my head high, smiled, and met their acknowledgements with a courtly greeting.

The gathered company bristled with wealth and rank; jewels and ermine, fur and silk. I had lived so long in the country, riding from castle to castle, that I was suddenly overwhelmed by the ocean of grandeur before me. It quite took me back to my days in France. In an instant I was transported to the past, but then swept back again.

The Duke of Bedford was at my elbow. "Your Majesty, the Queen of England sends her regards and her deepest sorrow that she cannot be with you on this auspicious day."

"Please convey to my dearest sister, the Queen Elizabeth, that I count myself blessed that she has sent such a worthy representative as yourself. I hope that you will enjoy our humble festivities – such as they are."

"Humble?" he glanced about him at the Great Hall decked in its finery, boughs of Christmas greenery, candles and lanterns burning, the four great fireplaces roaring. Despite the great expanse, it was filled with the scent of wood-smoke and spices. The diamond-paned windows flickered gold with reflected light.

The crowd parted as I processed into the middle of the Great Hall. I was aware of being watched, studied, scrutinized, but I know my own capacity to charm. I do not pretend; I do not dissemble. I am myself, always, in every aspect a queen, willing to die for her people. If my people are required to make sacrifice, then I will make sacrifice also. If my people are ready to fight for what they believe in, then I am ready to fight also. I never heard it said that Elizabeth rode at the head of an army, though I am willing to stand corrected if such be the case.

Polite pleasantries and platitudes were exchanged, murmurs of greeting, standard phrases of praise and obeisance. Court etiquette, they call it. And I can shine at the ritual if this is what is required. But what wins over my enemies, in all cases but one, is my sincerity, my genuine wish to connect with another human being, to please. I have known only one or two men resistant to this charm. Knox is one of them – impermeable to the last. Elizabeth's henchman, Cecil, here in England, is another.

May God rot their souls.

I am nothing if not obedient, respectful, courteous. I have always been guided by a firm belief that most people are open to reason and compassion. But I have been proven wrong before now. And I have ever been shocked at the realisation.

It is indeed hard to forgive, though forgiveness is at the heart of the Catholic religion.

I looked on the sight of my assembled guests with not a little pride. *All of these eminent figures have gathered here in the Great Hall of Stirling Castle at my request and invitation,* was the thought that ran through my mind. Glittering ecclesiastical vestments, garments of unparalleled opulence, bejewelled, mitred, encrusted with gems. It was hard to credit that all of these ambassadors and representatives of the most important heads of state throughout Europe had travelled through the cold and the snow to celebrate alongside us the baptism of our little son. It was a magnificent sight.

I could see Bothwell's figure among the guests, circulating, throwing back his head in laughter. I suppressed the uneasy thought that he seemed to be subtly proprietorial in his gestures. He seemed a little too expansive, a little too comfortable in his role as defender of my honour.

However, I was more concerned about my husband lurking upstairs, nursing his grievances.

Moray appeared at my elbow at one point and murmured "Any word of Darnley, Your Grace?"

I shook my head.

"Maybe it is for the best, after all," he added.

I was terrified that he would suddenly appear amongst us, drunk.

At four o' clock in the afternoon the guests formed two parallel rows along the corridors all the way from my son's nursery to the Chapel Royal across the courtyard. It was in part spontaneous, and in part organized with the utmost skill. Between their ranks my little prince was carried in state, borne in the arms of the Count of Brienne, his passage lit by the flickering of torches. It was a solemn procession we made, down the staircase, step by step, across the Great Hall, out through the palisaded walkway, between the hushed and waiting guests. I could hear sentimental sighs of pleasure at the sight of a mere wean, all bedecked in frothing lace, the burden of sovereignty already upon his brow.

The Chapel was sumptuously adorned, resplendent with its own finery. Silver candlesticks shone on the altar and richly embroidered vestments hung all about, flashing in the candlelight. The heavy silver font that the Duke of Bedford had borne all the way from England was centre stage, near the door of the Chapel where everyone could see it. It shone like fire.

Bothwell and Moray stood at the doorway rather than

participate in the actual ceremony. Apparently their religious persuasions would not allow them to proceed any nearer to the altar.

I knelt in view of the world; the courts of Europe ranged in rows at my back, and prayed for my son's future.

'King James', as he styles himself now, was a mere babe in arms then, a fleshy creature with bright questing eyes, still too young to listen to the rumours they would tell of his mother, or to condemn me for crimes I did not commit.

Fotheringhay Castle
October 1586

My needle flies in and out, feverishly stitching the fine lines which tell my own story.

I like to unravel the threads of my destiny, and dream of what might have been. It is a comfort, because the truth of what really happened hurts so. He has ended by believing in the lies and slanders which Moray fed him, the distortions and half-truths. After I was forced to abdicate, and as soon as I fled Scotland, casting myself upon my sister's 'mercy', they had my little son crowned and my brother Moray declared himself Regent.

It was what he always wanted. When we were friends, I believed in his friendship. When he defended my honour against Darnley that morning in Stirling Castle, I was genuinely moved. I thought we had a bond of blood that would prevail. But I was wrong. My half-brother achieved his ambition in the end. To rule as Regent – it was all he wanted, in the event that he could not be King.

"I was pragmatic, Mary."

A voice breaks the silence, and when I look up he is standing before me. White-faced, wily-eyed as ever.

"You betrayed me."

"Everyone betrayed you. There was only ever one single difference between you and I, sister, in the line of succession. Knox put it succinctly. Women cannot rule. You were female."

"And you were illegitimate!"

"Exactly so, my sister. It is with regret that we must acknowledge that fact. I never wanted to hurt you, or betray you. It was never personal. You must understand that."

I bend my head to my sewing, just as I always did when I was listening to my councillors discuss matters of state. Pierce the cloth, pull the thread through, apply the exact amount of tension, see where the stitch lies, and proceed with another. There is a reassuring rhythm to the art, the movement of lifting and pricking, pulling the bright thread through.

"I ever did love to see you sew, Mary!"

I drop my sewing in my lap for an instant and gaze at him.

"Is this affection you show, after all this time, after all these years of enmity between us?"

"I am a phantom, Mary. There is no 'us'. I cease to exist."

I lower my head again, and sew in silence.

"Yes, you cease to exist."

They betrayed you, my brother, just as they once betrayed me. You enjoyed, what? Three years of regency before they stabbed you in the back? Morton was next to take the reins of government, to inflict his odious rule upon my son.

They beat him, I know. I try not to think on it, because

there was nothing I could do from here. I heard rumours;
I wrote letters, implored, entreated. I wrote to my son to
reassure him of the great love I had for him.

I doubt those letters ever arrived.

Censored.

His mind erased of the memory of his mother, those few
short months we had together when he was a babe in arms.
Before they ruined him. Before they shaped and moulded
him into the monster they wanted him to become, hardening
him with cruelty.

But he is no monster, and never was.

He holds the memory of his mother dear, even if he is
unable to express it.

They showed me a portrait of him once. He did not look
a happy man. Why did the artist not choose to conceal that
look in his eye, and replace it with another?

They took him from me, and they beat him. They shaped
him until he was cowed beneath the weight of their greedy
ambition.

I know a little of what that feels like. My Guise uncles
slither and creep into the corners of my mind where I will
not let them loose. I command them to stay in the shadows.
Unlike Moray, Darnley and Bothwell, my Guise uncles are
not allowed to claw their way up from where I have buried
them. I plant a stone upon their graves. It holds them down.

I have other ghosts to contend with.

Ghosts never haunt the innocent. *Bess of Hardwick told*
me that once. The wretched woman who took such pleasure
in my incarceration. She revelled in humiliating me and
depriving me of the basic comforts needed in order to keep
body and soul together.

Ghosts never haunt the innocent.

Well, I have plenty of ghosts to contend with here.

Stirling Castle
December 1566

After the ceremony in the Chapel, I glanced over my shoulder at Bothwell and Moray who still hunkered in the doorway, refusing to enter a place where such 'Papist nonsense' was being conducted. I caught their eye and smiled. They clung so ardently to their bleak Scottish God. John Knox held sway, even here, far away from the shadow of St. Giles' High Kirk.

Those few days spent at Stirling Castle were among some of the best I enjoyed during my reign, despite the anxieties and fears I suffered concerning Darnley's behaviour. Were it not for my problematic husband, it could indeed have been said that I was happy. People I thought were friends and allies surrounded me. I had succeeded in uniting the Catholics and Protestants to some extent. I was in a position of strength, weakened only by the presence of Darnley and his impossible demands. But I had Moray and Bothwell and Maitland on my side, working in my favour.

So I thought...

There was a ripple of laughter and sympathy from the

For My Sins

crowd as little James was baptised. As Father Mamaret
held him over the font and poured water upon his forehead,
my little son opened his lungs and roared. The assembled
company responded with more murmurings of mirth.

"Ah, he is a lusty lad, as you say," the Count of Brienne
guffawed, trying out our native Scots.

I answered him in French.

When I neared Bothwell I took the time to pause and
murmur, "You couldn't find it in your heart to enter the
Chapel itself?"

"You have your beliefs, Your Grace, and I have mine!"

"Ah, a man of principle, I see! I suppose you would not
want to risk stepping any further…for fear of contamination."

"No offense is meant by it, Your Grace."

"And none is taken," I replied.

It was completely dark outside by the time we emptied
the Chapel and a banquet was waiting for us back in
the Great Hall. The guests thronged after us along the
palisaded walkway on the edge of the courtyard, and through
the tall double doors. Long trestle tables were redolent
with great platters bearing meat and fish, preserved fruits
and freshly baked bread. I had little appetite, my nerves
were too fraught, but I was happy to watch my guests
salivate at the sight of all these delicacies. The four huge
fireplaces had been built up again and were roaring. It was
a relief to be bathed in their golden warmth after the chill of
the Chapel and the courtyard.

I moved among my guests, smiling and sociable,
acting my part as perfectly as ever, but at the back of my
mind was the thought of Darnley.

"Your husband is not well?" a smooth urbane voice
murmured. I turned to see the Duke of Piedmont at my
elbow.

I hesitated a moment too long before replying.

"He did not attend the ceremony!"

"Yes, my husband has been suffering with an old complaint of his. He kept to his rooms upstairs. It is to be hoped he will appear shortly, perhaps during the evening celebrations."

In fact, I sincerely hoped not – but was not about to confess as much in public.

A dark shadow crossed my mind. Others had noticed his absence, after all, and now it was commented on. I looked up to see Bothwell watching me from across the far side of the Hall where he had just entered.

Once the Duke of Piedmont was out of earshot my brother Moray slid to my side.

"We have decided the best policy is to put about the rumour that Darnley is not well," he hissed. "It's partly true anyway. I'll go up and see him again in an hour or two and 'encourage' him to make an appearance."

"Is that wise? Perhaps we would do better to leave him be."

"How?"

"I fear what he might say in public."

"Have no fear of that, sister. I will be watching him. We will keep him contained."

A dark dread filled my chest, suddenly crushing my earlier optimism.

"Are you not hungry, Your Grace?" Livie beckoned me. "Come and eat!"

I went with my women to the tables where I took my place at the head of the Great Hall, centre stage as it were.

My eyes were bright.

I must dissemble. I must not let them see the dread that lived in my heart. I must hide it. It sat upon me like an evil spirit, trying to suck the life force out of me, but I would not let it. This was my moment – Scotland's moment – and I would shine. Never had Scotland seen such festivities in generations, and I was the author of it all.

"Your father would have been proud," Maitland said, leaning towards me briefly.

I glanced at him without replying, but he nodded his head the once, as if to confirm the truth of his statement.

The absent ghosts of my parents passed through the chamber unremarked, unnoticed by all but me. Where do they vanish to, I wondered? Why do they not stay to help their child?

I felt surrounded by people and yet suddenly alone. This is what it is to be a monarch. It is a burden which Darnley will never understand. I know men who have schemed all of their lives for the chance to become a sovereign Head of State, but they know nothing of the burdens and cares which accompany that role.

There are those who bleat about their right to sovereignty, but it is not merely a birth-right. It is a responsibility. And a heavy one at that.

Platters of food passed before me and I picked at what I was offered. Sweet and salty tastes assaulted my palate, but my main concern was for the comfort and pleasure of my guests.

None would leave this castle in a few days' time without the idea that they had been feasted and indulged to perfection. Despite the winds which blew, carrying the sting of the north, they would look back upon this time in Stirling Castle as a memory of rich red warmth, lit by candles and lanterns, fireplaces roaring.

There are some passages in the castle precincts where the wind cuts through and howls like a banshee, but one can turn a corner and the air is suddenly calm. I would often take a turn on the ramparts and battlements to admire that view, despite the protestations of my servants. And what I remember most is how the dark oily cobbles of the courtyards were slick with lantern-light, rippling where it fell.

And how the shadows held the ghosts of my parents, ever near.

And how the firelight lit the rooms, bathing them in honeyed warmth.

And how the painted ceilings did glow.

And the stone-carvers and masons had left a forest, a city of figurines, all fetched up and perched on the ramparts and rafters, lined up on the battlements, ogling the crowds below, characters of impish delight with their stony eyes goggling and their jaws working.

I loved it all.

It was a moment of triumph, and my father's Palace which he had had erected on the Rock (as an addition to what had been there before) was the perfect setting for it.

He had employed an army of skilled workers and craftsmen to design this Palace. My mother had told me often in her letters about the clamour and upheaval that had accompanied its rebuilding: the attention to detail, the bustle of painters, carvers and stonemasons labouring away to make this Palace a jewel in the crown of Scotland.

As far as I was concerned, they had succeeded.

And the fact that my father and forebear was responsible for all of this made it all the more precious to me.

As the banquet continued and we were served dish after dish of Scotland's finest fare, conjured up in the remote castle kitchens, I became aware of a mood, a certain atmosphere. I caught several pairs of eyes glancing curiously in my direction. Was it my imagination or were people beginning to whisper? I felt under scrutiny all of a sudden, but of the worst kind.

The guests had begun to entertain the idea that Darnley was lurking upstairs, but refusing to attend, and the rumour had spread that there was a rift between us.

As the feasting ended and the dancing began, I rose and clapped my hands to indicate a change in the proceedings. Chairs scraped back noisily against the flags, and my musicians began to pluck the strings of the lyre, threading a trickle of sound onto the night. Outside, the dark air pressed against the window-panes, speaking of an evil weather that blew from the mountains.

I would not have them speak ill of me. I would have them rejoice and be glad that they were here, enjoying the feast and the dancing, instead of out there in the darkness, waiting for the snow to fall.

And it did fall.

The wind howled that night and brought a blizzard with it. The guests turned to watch, pressing against the windows, and there were oohs and aahs, and exclamations about the likelihood of becoming trapped here, our horses and trains unable to negotiate the snowdrifts afterwards.

But that thought was for the future. For now, all that existed in time was this little bubble-world of blissful abandon. No one else existed outside of this drama. Stirling Castle was our theatre and our stage.

The villain of the piece was off-stage at present, threatening to emerge from the wings in the worst possible way, courting disaster.

As I passed between my guests I caught snatches of gossip, which were quickly silenced in my presence.

"Where is he?"

"They say he is ill with an old malady!"

"And what might that be? Jealousy?"

A courtier whose name I did not know – one of the English retinue – paled on meeting my eye. I smiled, and held my head high with studied dignity.

"You will not get the better of me," was the thought which ran uppermost in my mind.

It was at this point there was a murmur of anticipation and the crowd fell silent. I looked to where they all stared.

Darnley had appeared in the archway.

He looked up, surprised at the attention his appearance commanded.

I watched him from the other side of the Great Hall, my heart thumping in my chest loud enough to wake the dead.

The musicians, sensing the atmosphere, slowly drew to a halt and the last note faded away.

It was my brother Moray who rescued the situation, stepping forward smoothly, his hand outstretched.

"Ah, Your Highness has decided to grace us with his presence at last. We are delighted you are feeling so much better after your rest."

The guests watched.

Darnley stared at the advancing figure of his brother-in-law in the pause created by the musicians. I felt conscious of Bothwell's eyes on me too, studying what I would do next, and willing me to do the right thing.

I gathered myself and added to the greeting, unsure of how Darnley would respond.

He wavered a moment, his eyes blurred.

For a moment I fancied he was about to make some portentous announcement to the assembled company, to declare that he was leaving the castle as the child we were baptizing was not in fact his. It was, after all, what he had threatened to do. Sabotage the whole affair.

I watched and waited, anticipating disaster. It felt like the longest moment, wondering if he would destroy everything I had built with the delivery of one slanderous line.

The slander was a complete lie, of course, but I was a mere woman. Once tainted and tarred with the brush of scandal, who would not believe the lies? *Mud sticks! There is no smoke without fire!* All the old adages apply. A man like my father can sire a dozen illegitimate children if he so pleases, but let a woman once be suspected of committing adultery and the consequences are dire.

And I was no adulteress.

There was a whiff of scandal here for the guests to sniff and they were quick to join the hunt.

To my relief, however, Darnley did not make a fuss. He merely accepted my brother's greeting. I did not ask him to dance for fear that he would refuse me in front of all our guests. I instructed the musicians to resume, and they did, their music spiralling high to the rafters.

The guests began to relax again and I stood with Darnley, murmuring to him in private.

"I am glad you decided to join us, Henry."

He looked at me. "My sweet wife," he said in a low voice. There was a look in his eye that frightened me, but I did my best to smile and act the part of a loving wife.

Someone – I think it was Livie and Mary Seton between them – had commanded the guests to begin a new dance that distracted the attention from us, and for this I was grateful. As the guests formally requested the attention of potential partners and assumed positions for the courtly dance, I felt a sigh of relief.

The moment of danger had passed.

The villain of the piece had appeared on-stage, but had not yet disrupted the performance. The drama would continue.

For four days the halls and corridors of the castle reverberated to footsteps and the silver-noted playing of my musicians. Rooms that were normally quiet and bare were filled with festivity. Every wing of the castle, every remote corner and distant garret was thrown open to the celebrations. One night there were fireworks exploding above the battlements, great arcs and ribbons of light shooting up into the December sky, showering the guests with colour, the smell of cordite and gunpowder tangy on the night air, peppering the snow with black soot. I felt a rush of exhilaration on seeing the display. It was so beautiful, so enchanting. My son – for whom all of this was in honour – gazed up at the star-shaped contours in the sky and his little face creased in dismay at the bangs and explosions.

"Do not be alarmed, my little one," I smiled, leaning in close to comfort him. He still recognized me in those days.

The snow continued to fall, thick and fast, and there were genuine fears of being unable to leave the castle for days.

Maitland assured the guests that they could remain for as long as they needed if the weather did not lift.

There was some anxiety at being stranded in Scotland. The Count of Brienne, the Dukes of Savoy and Piedmont were delighted to have attended such a lavish event, but I could surmise that they did not relish the idea of a delayed departure.

Darnley remained an outsider at the castle throughout. My councillors and advisers, Maitland and Moray in particular, engineered events so that he was disregarded. We would thole him as much as we were able, but he was largely an outcast, isolated by his own behaviour. He resented it bitterly.

On Christmas Eve there was a masque. Guests appeared with black velvet masks across their eyes to perform their courtly dances.

Bothwell and Moray looked dour and muttered about self-indulgence, that the lavish affair had gone too far, but I assured them it was necessary to mark the occasion and teased them accordingly.

Then came the moment I had feared. Maitland reminded me of my promise which had been made in Craigmillar Castle back in November.

At midnight I silenced the guests with a gesture. A sea of faces turned to regard me.

"As we celebrate this most auspicious feast, I have an announcement to make. The Catholic religion has forgiveness and mercy at its heart. In light of this fact, I have considered the request of the former rebel lords – Morton, Ruthven and Lindsay – who have assured me of their loyalty to our royal person and who long to return from exile in England. I have decided to grant their request as a goodwill gesture, to formally pardon them and welcome them home to Scotland."

A deafening silence met this announcement. It was known these men were responsible for the murder of my beloved Davie Rizzio.

Maitland applauded loudly and stepped forward. "Well done, Your Highness. Such a magnanimous gesture will not go unnoticed, and marks Your Grace apart as a ruler of tolerance and virtue."

The guests began to move and talk again, but an abrupt

movement in the far corner caught my eye. Darnley had left the Great Hall. Before he went I noticed he was white-faced as a spectre.

A couple of hours later, as the guests continued to dance and music drifted along the stone passageways and staircases, I took the opportunity of a quiet moment to retreat to my own apartments. My brother Moray met me on the stair.

"Darnley has left," he informed me.

"What do you mean?"

"He fled, shortly after your announcement."

"In this weather?"

"He and his few men took horses and rode out into the night, Your Grace."

"Where is he heading?"

"Lennox country, no doubt. Have no fear, Ma'am," Moray reassured me on seeing my face. "It is not far to Glasgow. He will not perish tonight, although…" I glanced at him quickly. The lantern-light flickered fitfully over his features "…more's the pity. It would save us a most persistent problem."

There was no one else present to hear him say this. My brother Moray was nothing if not cautious. He would not be seen to admit to such a confession before witnesses. There were only he and I present, in a bend of the staircase, lanterns flickering on the walls. The walls have ears, they say. There was a small window set in the thick wall beside us, reflecting the flicker and glow of candlelight. Beyond that reflection was the bleak midwinter's night which Darnley had chosen to ride out into.

"I like not the way you talk, Moray. My husband causes me great grief and anxiety, but I would not have him perish."

Moray looked me in the eye. "Would you not, Marie?"

The note of intimacy and warmth took me off guard. I

felt the Devil's breath in my ear, an invisible sigh emanating from the dark.

"No, I would not."

I glanced back over my shoulder, but the corridor beyond our staircase was empty. A long tunnel of darkness.

Did someone walk across my grave that night?

Fotheringhay Castle
October 1586

I raise my eyes from my quiet stitching.

A shape in the corner attracts my attention. I glance up to see if Jane has noticed.

He who never visits me has appeared at last. A silent phantom.

I can't quite make out his features. Is it Bothwell?

Or is it Darnley?

I put down my sewing to stare.

He merges with the crimson drapes behind him so that it is hard to see...

The darkness hurts my eyes, the hours of stitching by candlelight have taken their toll.

He moves gradually forward by degrees.

It is Bothwell, I am sure.

But he is completely silent.

Not one single word passes his lips.

Jane shifts on her stool, and my little dog Geddon whimpers at my feet.

I drop my hand and let it rest on the flat of his head. A low growl still rumbles in his throat. I feel the vibration of it rising through his skull.

Jane looks up in surprise.

"What ails thee, little Geddon?"

She glances at the spot where Geddon and I both stare.

She sees nothing there, of course.

But she is unnerved, and asks to be excused for one moment.

Even after she has left the ghost does not speak.

We regard each other in silence.

Glasgow
January 1567

The winds stopped howling and the guests were eventually able to leave. Stirling Castle felt strangely empty afterwards. With the departure of the last guest the corridors fell silent. They no longer rang to the sound of livery and horses' hooves clattering on the cobbles. There were only our own courtiers and servants left in residence.

"Well, Your Grace," Maitland sighed. "The celebrations went better than we could have hoped."

"Apart from my husband!"

"We contained the problem, though, Your Highness," he added.

"And now the outlawed lords, Morton, Ruthven and Lindsay are on their way back to Scotland," I murmured, "even as we speak!"

Moray and Maitland coughed and avoided my eye.

"Exactly so, Your Grace!" Moray said. "It was the right action to take, under the circumstances."

"Under what circumstances?"

Moray was caught off-guard and did not answer at first.

"Your husband Darnley needs to be warned off his present behaviour, Your Highness. And this is one way of achieving that," Maitland said. "Besides, they have sworn their allegiance to you, Ma'am, and are heartily sorry for former misdemeanours."

"Misdemeanours…" I sighed. "Is that what you call them?"

I had had no choice in the matter. Like my brother Moray, I was learning to be pragmatic. Courtly intrigue is full of these volte-faces. One moment they are in favour, the next they are out; one moment they can be trusted, the next they cannot. It is the way of courtly life.

I decided to escape onto the battlements. A narrow stone tunnel led me out onto the ramparts and a blast of wind greeted me. The view below was astounding. The castle is perched so high upon its rock, higher even than Edinburgh. Its height has always thrilled me. The flat plains stretched as far as the eye could see, with the mountains rising in the distance. The cold air cut through me but I did not notice.

Something caught my eye. Far below I espied movement. A single rider making his way at great speed across the carse. I watched as he headed straight for the castle esplanade.

"What now?" I wondered.

I was to find out soon enough.

"Your Highness," Maitland burst out, when I returned to my apartments. "We have news of your husband, Darnley."

I waited.

"He lies dangerously ill in Glasgow where he has fled to his father's estate."

I recalled the black shadows I'd noticed beneath his eyes; the fevered look he did sometimes bear.

"How much truth is there in this message?"

Maitland hesitated, and shrugged. "We have only the messenger's word for it."

I read the missive they gave me.

"He wants me to go to him at once," I said. "He wants to beg my forgiveness."

"How can we trust this?" Moray said, pacing the room. "One moment he is writing to the Pope himself, threatening to leave the country, the next he suddenly requests his wife's presence at his bedside. It is madness."

"He is afraid," Maitland advised. "That is what motivates him. He is afraid of what might happen to him once the pardoned lords return. He turned double-traitor against them, remember. They will bear a grudge, and he knows this."

I felt suddenly heart-sore for my young husband; despite the pain and grief he did cause me. He was a spoiled child, ruined by his parents, and now his enemies were ranged against him. He was reaping the consequences of his actions.

"But why is he asking for Marie to go to him now?" Moray said. "He left in haste. If he had wanted her companionship so badly, he could have remained at the baptism with the rest of us instead of running away. It's a trap. It must be. His father, Lennox, will be behind it."

"There is only one thing for it," Maitland said. "Your Majesty will need to venture into Lennox country in order to bring him out. If he remains there, we cannot control his actions. We need him safely under our noses again, so that we can see exactly what he is about."

"But the risk to Her Majesty?"

I silenced them both.

"I will take that risk."

There was a long silence.

"We will give you enough men-at-arms, Your Grace, that they can defend your person if need be," Maitland conceded.

"Lennox and his men would not *dare* make a challenge," Moray said in a low voice that carried the sting of threat in it.

"I will be equal to the challenge," I said quietly. "I can manage my own husband."

Moray and Maitland exchanged looks of admiration. For all that we went through in the months after this, I saw the look and I recognized it for what it was.

"Come," I said. "I have a journey to prepare for. I will take only the men-at-arms you suggest and one woman with me."

"Who will that be, Your Grace?"

"Mary Seton," I replied.

I set out from Stirling Castle on a cold frosty morning towards the end of January. I was to visit my sick husband in Glasgow, a small area beside the Clyde which his father did reckon among his territories. He lay ill, and I was hastening to his bedside, a dutiful wife to the end, despite his treachery.

Bothwell and Moray both accompanied me as far as Callendar House, where they left me to complete the rest of the journey alone.

There was a white frost on the ground as I neared my father-in-law's estate, and it was bitterly cold. I have no fear of the cold, however, not when I am mounted on horseback. It is one of life's greatest pleasures, which I have been sadly denied in these latter years. I rode at the head, as feathers of snow gently drifted to the ground. I wrapped my fur-lined cloak closer about my shoulders for warmth, and we slowed to a walking pace as we entered Lennox country. The stillness of the surrounding countryside was unnerving suddenly. The horses of my men-at-arms were frisky with the cold, tossing their heads lightly. Were they nervous? What did they sense in the air? The whiff of conspiracy? I have always listened to the mood of any horse I ride.

It was a dangerous undertaking, to enter Lennox country; I knew this. I was at the mercy of Darnley and his father, should they decide to take action against me. If they were foolhardy enough. I trusted my own judgement.

Glasgow was a small town clustered around a dark cathedral on the banks of the Clyde, and as I entered its narrow streets I was surprised at their emptiness. Deserted. No one about.

The few houses were shuttered and silent, as if all had been forewarned of my arrival. I had already sent word that I refused to stay with my father-in-law but would lodge instead in the Archbishop's house across the way, where I felt marginally safer. I had also brought my own apothecary with me from Stirling to attend to Darnley.

On the afternoon of our arrival, as I crossed over the square to visit my husband in his father's house, I felt watched, spied upon. The quiet stone houses seemed to have eyes, which followed me as I walked, although I could not see them. Feathers of snow still drifted and spiralled on the air.

"I will go alone, Mary," I told Mary Seton.

"Marie, is that wise?"

"Have no fear, my friend," I reassured her. "I will return safely."

"We shall see how ill King Henry really is!" I added.

I was ushered into the dark rooms of his father's house, staircases lit by flickering torches in the gathering dusk. Darnley's man-servant led me up a spiralling flight, oak panels surrounding us as we crowded in.

When I saw him in his apartment I was shocked. The signs of illness I had observed when at Stirling Castle had blossomed into a greater malady that now ravaged my young husband's body. His arms had erupted into pustules and he wore a taffeta mask to hide his face, which was now scarred and pitted with pocks, many of which were open running sores. His breath was heavy and malodorous.

I sat down heavily on a high-backed chair at the foot of the bed, as far away from him as I could manage. I could not remain standing as my knees were trembling with shock, but I would fain hide the fact.

He regarded me in silence from beneath his stained mask.

"You came!" he said.

I nodded.

"Of course I came."

"I did not expect you."

"I had word my husband was dangerously ill. And here you are."

"And here I am!" he repeated.

"What is it that ails thee, Darnley? Have they been able to identify a cause?"

His eyes slid away from me and his jaw worked quietly beneath the mask. "It is an old malady."

"I have brought my own apothecary to attend to you. He will know what…"

"There was no need. I have my father's doctors at hand."

There was an awkward silence, while I smoothed my gown.

"An old malady…" I murmured, glancing across at him. "One wonders…"

"Syphilis, Marie. It doesn't take an expert to work it out. My brain is ravaged by it."

"You need proper attention, proper care," I said. "It is not too late to give you the treatment you need. Mercury baths."

Darnley was listening intently.

"We can attend to you properly in Edinburgh, if you return with me."

His eyes fixed on me. He blinked like a lizard.

"How can I trust you, Marie?"

I looked at him questioningly.

"Why did you pardon those men?" he asked.

"Because I had no choice."

"They are my sworn enemies. Do you think they will be happy to see me reinstated by your side, after I betrayed them?"

"None will harm you while you are at my side."

"How can you promise that, Marie? You have witnessed their handiwork before now."

I paled at the memory. I had thought to forgive Darnley for his part in Rizzio's murder, but the anger was still there.

"Aye, my husband, and so have you!" I spoke more sharply than I intended. "You had a hand in that work too, remember."

He was cowed slightly, for despite his petulance he could not deny it.

"It is beginning to grow dark outside," I added, and I got up to light more candles. They flickered into life, throwing into sharp relief his ravaged countenance beneath the mask.

I glanced out the window where I could see the blackish-grey gables of the Archbishop's House opposite. There were candles burning behind those upper panes too, figures passing to and fro. It made me feel less vulnerable, knowing that I had my supporters across the way should Lennox decide to take action against me. I had put myself at his mercy, sitting here in his house, largely unprotected. If Lennox wanted to make a striking blow against me now, he could. I had taken that risk.

"May I tell you something, Marie," Darnley said now. "When I sit here in the dark, I have these terrible thoughts. I am afraid of dying."

In spite of myself my heart was moved to pity.

I moved towards the head of the bed and laid a hand on his shoulder. He grasped it tightly between his fingers. We had never known such intimacy as this since before the birth of our son, and it shocked me. There was such a distance between us, such a gulf, and yet suddenly the gap was bridged – in a moment – through this confession of fear.

But it was not enough.

It was regret only. Not genuine remorse.

Fear of failure. Shame. All of those things.

"You will not die, Darnley," I reassured him. "You are too young. You are younger than myself by four years. Perhaps that was our trouble all along. You are just a boy." I glanced down at him sadly. "You will survive. This is just a temporary phase in your illness."

"We were happy once, were we not, Marie?"

I looked at him sharply.

Could I trust these words?

Why was he suddenly so soft and compliant when only days before he had been like a hornet in a nest of wasps?

"I have not been a good husband to you, Marie. I know. But things could be different."

There was something about his manner that made me suspicious. I did not entirely trust him.

"Stay with me here tonight," he urged. "Don't leave!"

I looked towards the narrow aperture, where I could just glimpse the outline of the Cathedral against the dark sky.

"Stay here? With you?"

He nodded. His eyes were feverish.

"But I cannot."

"You will be safe. No one will harm you, Marie. It is all I ask of you. To stay with me, at my pillow, while the nightmares ride my dreams."

"Madam," a voice spoke from the shadows. It was Darnley's own man-servant. "A lady has appeared below and insists on…"

At this point there was a clatter of footsteps on the wooden stairs and Mary Seton appeared in the doorway. "Your Majesty," she said breathlessly, "I came across…"

"Calm yourself, Mary," I said gently. "I have agreed to remain here tonight. With my husband."

Mary gaped at me incredulously. "I do not think that entirely wise, Madam."

"We will stay here. For tonight. Just this once. You can return for us again in the morning, Mary, and I will be here. I promise."

Mary Seton left us and Darnley lay back on his pillows, exhausted and weak. He appeared genuinely ill and I took pity on him. I knew it was a risk, but I was unafraid. Let Lennox do his worst. Let him try. It would only prove to all just what a treacherous animal he was.

And so the night passed.

There were long unbroken silences, during which I simply sat and watched the candles burn low. Darnley slept, but I did not. I drifted between sleep and wakefulness, wondering what the future had in store, how I would handle the mess and confusion that my personal affairs had become. I thought of my cousin Elizabeth, down in England, and how she had managed to avoid taking a husband so far, and I wondered how she had contrived to avoid the issue for so long. For it seemed that a husband was only ever a burden, rather than a cause for celebration. I envied her, although I had heard it said she envied me.

However, I would not have my son Prince James unmade. He was the happiest consequence of my bargain.

It was a freezing cold night and there was only a small fire in the hearth. I did not want to call any of his servants to attend to the blaze, as I felt too vulnerable still, being here alone. I would rather wait in the dark until morning. I wore a thick cloak of Florentine serge which I kept wrapped over my shoulders as I rested and I was glad of it now, gathering its folds close about me. The stubs of two candles flickered on the mantelshelf, casting monstrous shadows across the wall behind Darnley's bed.

He looked sordid and sad. The malodorous mask was stained and dirty, and did little to conceal the unsightly yellow sores. I was disgusted and appalled, yet at the same time he called forth my compassion. I had been closeted with him for so long I felt my cloak must have absorbed the taint of his breath.

It was a relief when morning came and I was still there, alive. No one had accosted me.

Daylight broke above the Cathedral and I looked out to see its dark buttresses stark against the sky. Still no one stirred in those quiet streets. I felt sure that Lennox's men were behind closed doors, armed to the teeth, watching me. Waiting for the word to strike.

After all, Darnley was my own cousin. I do not – and never have – disputed his claim to either throne. We shared a grandmother between us. But the fact of the matter was that I was the ruling sovereign and he was not. If anything happened to me, our son James would rule in my place and

Darnley would no doubt step in as his Regent. So I was fully aware what my husband stood to gain in the event of my own demise. However, I had little doubt that my loyal supporters would not tolerate a coup against me, should he be so foolhardy as to attempt it, along with his father, Lennox.

I knew where the land lay and I was prepared to take a risk to win Darnley over.

Well, it appears I succeeded. At the end of my short stay in Glasgow, I managed to leave Lennox country without a fight on my hands, and Darnley came with me, borne in a litter over the rough country tracks back to Edinburgh.

I wonder what his father had to say about that decision?

I do not know, because he did not once make an appearance in my presence.

Edinburgh
February 1567

It was a freezing cold February day. The ice had not melted from the Clyde, but moved in great ice-floes over the surface. Our horses' breaths steamed on the air and we gathered in the courtyard at dawn, outside Lennox's house where a horse-litter waited. Darnley was conveyed inside it, propped up by pillows and covered in blankets and furs. I think my companions wondered at my concern for him, the way I petted and ensured he was safely ensconced.

The road was rough, and he leaned out of the litter at one point and cried out against the men conveying him to be careful of the ruts. Their faces were stoical and I merely smiled patiently.

Of Lennox there was no sign.

We headed east towards Edinburgh. The forests and barren landscapes passed in silent monotony. The charms and spirits of this ancient land lived in the landscape. Stories were still told of ancient curses and grudges, spells of witchcraft and evil deeds. Wolves and bears still haunted some of the more desolate areas, and the further north one travelled the wilder that land became.

But we were heading east, not north, back to so-called civilization. I knew that Moray, Maitland and the others were all waiting for me, wondering what the outcome of my visit would be, and how well I had succeeded in drawing Darnley to my side again.

Did I have him in the palm of my hand? Truly?

Or was he playing his own game, one with a hidden agenda?

The frost had hardened the earth to iron and the horses' hooves smacked the ground unremittingly. Serried ridges of mud, crusted over, made the tracks almost impassable, but we made our way across the icy inhospitable tracts of land.

A messenger caught up with us to deliver the news that Craigmillar Castle was being made ready for Darnley's arrival.

As we saw the angular rooftops of Edinburgh coming into view in the distance, with the castle louring ominously on its rock and Arthur's Seat skulking further down, Darnley suddenly ordered the litter to be stopped. It was lowered onto the tracks and I turned in the saddle to see what the commotion was about.

His head appeared between the canopy curtains and he shouted for me to attend, waving an arm towards me.

"What is it, Darnley?"

"They said I am to go to Craigmillar?"

"That's right…"

He shook his head furiously. "On no account will I be taken there."

"But it's the best place for you, Darnley. We can treat you properly there, with mercury baths…"

He met my gaze. "It lies far outside the city limits, Marie."

"And?"

"And…I would be vulnerable to attack from traitors."

"There are no traitors wishing you ill, Darnley," I said patiently.

"If I cannot stay in Holyrood with you, then I will stay in St. Mary's-in-the-Field instead. I will take a house there."

I stared at him, defeated. "But we have not made the place ready."

"Then make it so," he snapped.

I sighed and turned my horse around, then informed our men of the change of plan.

"My husband does not wish to stay in Craigmillar," I instructed them, "so we will repair to Kirk o' Field instead."

Glances were exchanged and there was some murmuring among their ranks, but we continued our journey with this new destination in mind. I was weary and had ceased to care what happened to any of us by now. I merely wanted my rest. I had been advised to bring Darnley out from his father's protection in Glasgow, back here to Edinburgh where we could keep an eye on him. My duty was done.

I sent word to Maitland, keeping him informed, and it was not long before a rider returned with the news that the change had been accommodated and my lords had located a suitable house in that square which would serve the purpose of housing Darnley in his sickness.

As we entered the city the roughened track gradually became rough cobblestones, slippery with slush and ice. The rooftops were mostly hidden beneath a mantle of snow.

Kirk o' Field was a quadrangle of houses just inside the city walls, between two ruined kirks, with untilled fields spanning away behind the housebacks. We approached it by a narrow alley called Thieves' Row, and an icy wind blew down its channel as our horses' hooves clipped and slithered noisily over the snow-lined cobbles.

We clattered into the courtyard, our retinue of arquebusiers still bearing Darnley's litter. My husband's arm emerged from between the curtains and pointed towards the largest and most prominent house of all – Hamilton House – facing onto the square, and shouted out.

"That one is the only fit residence for a king!" he cried, but he was over-ruled and taken to the Provost's House instead.

"Why here?" he commanded.

"I have been advised it is the only one we can make ready in time, with the baths you'll be requiring. Please, don't fret any more Darnley. We are all doing our best by you."

The litter was lowered onto the steps outside and I saw my husband appear from between the damask curtains and helped up the steps into the house. He looked thin and feeble in his shift, the weight of the blankets on his shoulders making him stoop like an old man. Something about that image made me shudder and I did not know why.

It was a remote and lonely spot, made more desolate still by the prospect of the derelict church to one side, overshadowing the red-tiled roofs with its haunting shell, its nave exposed and blackened, with snow drifts piling up against the abandoned altar. Was this the beginnings of the work of Knox, I wondered? Ordering his men to rip out statues and destroy any churches which were adorned with paintings and fine sculptures? Anything suspected of being a 'graven image' was to be destroyed according to that oracle, Knox.

The house in which Darnley was to be lodged had dormer windows, crow-stepped gables, and the flagstones of the floor all sloped to one side. It smelt of damp because it had stood empty for so many years, and the doors were slightly warped so that they dragged when trying to draw them. I observed these features with some misgiving.

I later learned that the property sat on a basement which was catacombed with cellars and underground passages. I did not know this at the time, only that the place was neglected and old. Its foundations were a virtual honeycomb of cool cell-like vaults, chambers and compartments, for effective storage one must assume, although no doubt it had been used for other more nefarious purposes over the centuries.

Darnley made a great fuss about how damp and evil-smelling the place was, and in truth I did not blame him.

"This is not a suitable place for a king to lay his head," he complained, "let alone a sick king."

"I cannot help but agree with you on some points, Darnley, but we will see what can be done. I promise I shall make the place comfortable for you. You shall see."

I spoke with my page, Bastien, and the Master of the Wardrobe, and that same day additional furniture was brought from the Palace itself. Carpets, tapestries, arras, cushions, chairs and even a bed were conveyed to the house in Kirk o' Field and I supervised the preparations.

"I shall stay here too, Darnley. Perhaps not every night, but now and again, until you are better and can join us again at Holyrood."

This reassurance seemed to satisfy him for a while. I had a ground floor bedchamber set up directly beneath his own; a small bed of yellow and green damask with furred coverlets was erected in it, for my own comfort on those nights when it was too dark and cold to venture out again to the Palace.

We spent all that night decking out the Provost's bleak house in finery. Turkish carpets covered the sloping uneven floors, rich heavily-brocaded tapestries hid the damp and buckled walls, cushions of red velvet gave an impression of comfort and warmth. A cedar-wood chair with a high narrow back, upholstered in purple, was placed next to the head of his bed, together with a small green baize table for playing cards, a pastime which could occupy Darnley for hours. We even went to the trouble of having Darnley's own bed conveyed here, the one I had presented to him as a gift during happier days in our marriage. There he lay, petulant and sick, and secretly scheming, his eyes following me about the room as I attended to him.

For a week he stayed at Kirk o' Field and every evening, with a train of my own attendants, I would spend a few hours at his bedside, entertaining him, playing dice or cards, listening to the delicate trickling music of the lute or the virginals as it pervaded the smoke-filled air with its sweet resonance. I could not tell what motivated him. His eyes were shifting and fiery, especially at night. Perhaps it was the fever. When I bent to stroke his cheek or forehead, to pat his pillows higher, I smelt the rank odour of conspiracy on his breath.

Or did I?

There was a mean glint of ambition in those eyes, as there had been on the night of Rizzio's murder, and yet, a part of me believed that he was still a boy, a young man, whose appetites and passions were beyond his own control and even now in need of guidance. Still, whatever he was about, I was a match for him this time.

We were watching him. We had him in our sights.

It is true I had openly despaired of Darnley in front of my advisers and my Secretary of State, but I never outwardly condoned his death or any notion that he – or anyone else – should be harmed.

That was not my plan at all.

There was another behind all of these events. A silent other who remains shielded in mystery. The one who looks through his fingers and says nothing; the one who is always absent when trouble is afoot; the one who contrives to be neither seen, nor heard.

Of whom do I speak?

Fotheringhay Castle
October 1586

"Bothwell!"

A voice rings out as my silvery needle flies through the fabric, beautiful stitches sculpting the form of a large cat with gleaming yellow eyes.

I shake my head in silence.

"Of him, I will not speak."

"Why not?" Darnley's ghost asks me, stepping closer to the hearth.

I purse my lips tightly, reluctant to speak with this evil spectre, this intruder.

"He is not the one."

"Then who is it?" he breathes, leaning in close.

A door slams in the corridor outside and his head snaps round in alarm.

When the wood scrapes against the worn flags and Jane appears, he vanishes. I look back to where he was, startled. He is nowhere to be seen.

My tapestry waits.

Kirk o' Field
February 1567

I simply acquiesced. Not even that. I had no knowledge of what the lords were plotting between them, what they had decided.

I spent two nights with my young husband, sleeping in the hastily rigged-up chamber beneath his own. They were dark nights. I went to bed alone. A sickle moon lit the sky. The view from my window was bounded on either side by the two abandoned kirks; testimony to Knox's evil influence, even here. White snow drifted against black bare stone. One of them had no rafters remaining, as if it had been burnt to the ground, just a roofless neglected husk. I had walked there earlier in the week to investigate and seen the sad interior of the kirk, its nave filled with last autumn's leaves, newly-fallen snow, ledges and spearheads of ice against the cracked and frozen altar. They had been Catholic, these churches, declared kirks and then left to decay, the Scottish people wishing to wipe their memories clean of their Catholic past, to reach out and embrace a new religion with new laws, new prejudices, new stringent demands. The stone window-frames were without glass, empty eye-sockets letting in the rain and snow, channels through which the wind would howl on a winter's night. One steeple remained, thrusting skyward, hopelessly, uselessly, like an abandoned promise.

A new round of snowflakes fell from the night sky to land on the blackened ruins, softening their dereliction.

Darnley's health was slowly improving, day by day. He was looking forward eagerly to the day when he could move with me into the Palace once more. He claimed that he still loved me.

It was hard to believe in his claims when only weeks before he had sought to humiliate me before all the courts of Europe assembled at Stirling Castle for the baptism of our son. I reserved the right to remain sceptical.

When he grabbed my wrist and declared, "We loved each other once, did we not, Marie?" I held myself calm and aloof, outwardly pleasant. I did not know what to think. For, to my mind he had never been a devoted husband. From the minute he had secured the possibility of marriage with me, he changed, as though he had got what he wanted and needed no longer play the ardent lover. It was a hard lesson I learned.

We decided between us that he would be well enough to return to Holyrood on Monday morning, the tenth of February, and from that day forward he would share my bed and my table as we tried to salvage what we could of our marriage, even if only for the sake of our public image. It was also for the sake of our son; presenting a united front as parents would give him a more secure inheritance as monarch one day.

Sunday was to be Darnley's last day in Kirk o' Field. It was also the last day before Lent, and therefore a time of rejoicing and carnival before the long days of abstinence set in – the opportunity for a last fling, although no doubt Knox did not condone such practices. He would rather spend the entire year in travail and mourning than see his flock enjoy a single moment of pleasure in life.

My French page Bastien was to be married to Christina Hogg and I had planned a grand reception for them at the Palace, with the prospect of hours of prolonged festivity lasting into the early hours.

On the Sunday morning I dressed myself for a day of celebrations. I remember exactly what I wore, down to the last detail: a gown of rich crimson velvet with rose-red rubies glimmering at my throat and from the lobes of my ears.

At noon there was a wedding breakfast for Christina and Bastien with much laughter and merriment. I raised my glass and drank toasts to the future of the happy couple. I could see the happiness in their eyes and their demeanour as they spoke to one another and I did envy it, for I did not think their love would mar and spoil so quickly as mine had done.

At four o clock in the afternoon, as it grew dusk, I rode slowly up the Canongate to the house of the Bishop of Isles for a formal dinner to mark the Savoyard ambassador's departure from Scotland the following day. Myself, Bothwell, Huntly, Argyll and Maitland all sat at table together, with the dusk falling momentarily on the streets outside. I noticed nothing strange. I have searched my memory since and tried to reflect on whether any of those present seemed tense or anxious. I can find no clue.

After dinner we rode to Kirk o' Field, as we usually did. A long elegantly-clad train of us, still laughing and smiling, light-headed from the wine we had drunk. Thieves' Row rang with our iron-shod mounts, stamping and snorting and slipping on the uneven slabs. Bothwell was by my side, I remember that, and I felt the warmth of his presence, although

I did not interpret it in any other way than friendship and support.

We all crowded into my husband's small bedchamber, in our finery and inappropriate garb, almost too bright and festive for such a dark day, with snow on the ground outside and ice at the windows. Bothwell was wearing a suit of soft black velvet and satin trimmed with silver.

Why did I notice that?

Well, because he held my elbow firmly and steered me up the staircase to Darnley's bedside, and because I ever did have a fine attention to detail.

Darnley was delighted to see us and amused by our good-natured banter. I gave him some wine and offered to play cards with him, so we dealt out a hand of whist at the green baize table. When I beat him for the third time he grew impatient.

"You always have the advantage over me, Marie. Why is that?"

"You cannot give up yet," I urged. "Play again and you shall win this time."

"What? You think to control me thus?" His smile was strained and weak.

Bothwell stood nearby, watching.

Darnley glanced at him with plain dislike. "I'm very tired," he muttered.

"Then you shall rest," and I bent down and kissed his forehead.

It was freezing over outside and candles glimmered on the tables as I sat quietly in the high-backed chair beside Darnley's bed. The rest of the gathering began to form companionable groups, some raising their voices in a loud peal of laughter, others murmuring, chatting on volubly. Their happy circles excluded myself and Darnley – though we were the centre of this drama. It allowed us a measure of privacy, I suppose, his hand resting in mine.

At about ten in the evening someone reminded me that I had promised to attend the masque at the Palace to honour the wedding celebrations.

"We really ought to prepare to depart, Ma'am, if you wish to avoid disappointing Christina and Bastien."

It was Maitland who spoke this time.

Darnley held me back by the wrist. "Don't go," he pleaded. "Stay here!"

Maitland looked uneasy. "You made a firm promise, Ma'am."

"Perhaps just another hour?"

On retrospect, although I noticed nothing at the time, I concede now that the mood changed at that moment. Looks were exchanged.

Who was it? Maitland? Bothwell? One of them insisted that it was not possible to stay another hour, that we must leave immediately. I have searched my memory again and again to try and identify which one of them spoke at that point. They were eager that I should leave – and at once. Just as Darnley was equally eager that I should stay.

"It is only till tomorrow," I told him. "Is that so long to wait?"

I bid him goodnight and left the chamber, giving him one swift glance over my shoulder before I left.

As I stepped out into the cold courtyard of Kirk o' Field I felt the pressure of Bothwell's hand against my cloak, briefly, in the small of my back, a passing contact. It travelled through me like electricity. No words were spoken.

With bright torches burning and flaring in the night, their smoke trailing backwards in the knife-edge wind, my cavalcade made its way down the Cowgate, up Blackfriar's

Wynd, through the Netherbow Gate, then down to the Palace with the white tip of Arthur's Seat rearing behind it.

There was snow in the air.

And a sense of menace.

As we crossed the iron drawbridge into the outer courtyard, I could hear the sounds of rejoicing. A lively strain of music lilted towards me on the frozen air, reminding me for one second what it was to be young and without any cares in this world.

The doors of the Palace were thrust open; I heard the wail of the bagpipes long before I saw them and remembered how they had once wailed up to me, through the darkness of the night on my arrival here six years ago. Tonight the great yawning rooms of the Palace were filled with their sound, and it made a more cheerful melody.

Holyrood Palace
February 1567

I joined in the masque enthusiastically, pretending a light-heartedness I did not feel. The Palace was lit throughout; the hall was ashimmer and ablaze, ornate banners hung from the ceiling, fires roared.

I was dreading the next day and what it would bring, for I confess I did not want to be reunited with Darnley in my apartments at Holyrood. It was not my true heart's desire, but more a decision of management and good politics.

I danced with Bothwell at one point. I did not know what my nobility were planning this night. They did not seek to enlighten me.

It was long after midnight when I retired to my own apartments. I shed my glittering gown and my huge blood-coloured gems, and lay down in my bed beneath the canopy.

Did I sleep?

I do not remember. My brain was too overwrought with the excitement of the day.

I looked at the hearth, a faint orange glow in the darkness, and remembered how Rizzio was slain in these rooms and how Darnley had played a part in that. I wondered how I would bear to share my home with him again.

I thought about Bothwell and the pressure of his hand in the small of my back, what it had felt like to dance with him, a new sensation.

For a long time I lay in the darkness, thinking like this, until sleep claimed me.

I was woken by a terrible noise. At two o' clock or thereabouts, long before dawn, there was a vast explosion. I felt the ground tremble and the ripples of sound rent and tore apart the cold night air. I sat up in bed, wondering by what magic the extinct volcano, Arthur's Seat, was erupting once more, its lava threatening to pour down over Holyrood.

But it was not Arthur's Seat.

The whole town shook with the noise; the walls of the Palace shook, and the great black rock on which the Castle sits, silvered with moonlight, threw forth an echo of the explosion into the night. Then, it seemed, there was absolute stillness.

For many minutes nothing happened. No one moved; no one stirred.

Throughout the whole town of Edinburgh and the great halls and courtyards of the Palace, all was silent.

It was many minutes before the corridors of Holyrood burst into life. It began with footsteps pounding along the passage outside.

"Your Majesty!"

Mary Seton burst into my chamber.

Confused and still half-asleep, I shrugged on a cloak and asked my ladies-in-waiting why they were firing the cannon.

"Is the town being attacked?" I asked.

"We do not know!" came the reply.

Their faces were white with lack of sleep. There was a general air of panic at what might be happening outside, reflecting my own state of mind.

There were cries from below, and voices travelled up to me where I stood in my shift.

"Where is the Queen?"

"Sound the tocsin."

A bell began ringing as they raised the alarm. I could hear the dull tones of its clamour drifting on the night air, across the city.

Bothwell was staying at Holyrood that night, along with the rest of the royal party. He, being the sheriff of the town, was quick to take charge, and sent messengers ahead to investigate. He then followed them on foot, climbing up the hill to Kirk o' Field to see for himself. I remained at Holyrood with my ladies-in-waiting, waiting anxiously for news. A sense of deep dread and foreboding had begun to fill the pit of my stomach. It made me nauseous with fear. I did not know what news would come, but I knew it could not be good.

It was much later that Bothwell told me what he had found on his arrival at Kirk o' Field. It was still snowing as he left. The old Provost's House where Darnley had been staying was utterly destroyed, reduced to a pile of rubble. There were scorch marks and ashes peppering the snow nearby – indeed, ashes still drifted on the air along with the falling snowflakes – but of the building itself, nothing remained. Neither was there any sign of my husband. Bothwell and those accompanying him searched the charred ruins in the darkness with the aid of torches, but found nothing.

"We dug with our bare hands, Ma'am," he told me. "But Darnley is simply missing. It is to be hoped he escaped."

"But how could he?" I said. "In his weakened state?"

Bothwell shrugged.

"And where is Maitland, my Secretary of State, when I need him?" I cried in agitation, furiously pacing my rooms.

"He has had to leave town, Ma'am," someone informed me. "He was called away straight after the wedding celebrations."

The wedding celebrations? I stared at the floor. The festivities of a few hours before seemed so long ago, as if they had taken place in a different world altogether. A line had been drawn in the sand at my feet. There was Before. And now there was After.

"There is not a stone remaining?" I asked Bothwell.

He shook his head.

"I stayed at that house as recently as two nights ago. I could have stayed there last night, had someone not warned me of Bastien's wedding…"

I stopped short, arrested by this thought.

I raised my eyes and met Bothwell's gaze. He did not turn away.

"Did you search the garden?" I asked.

"Every part of it, Ma'am."

My husband had gone missing and the house he was staying in had been destroyed, not a brick or stone remaining.

Hours later I sat at my writing desk before the fire. The day had advanced and there was a weak winter sun in the sky. I was hastily dressed and over-wrought from lack of sleep when they brought me further news of what had happened.

By daylight they had searched a wider area and my

husband's body had been discovered, lying on the far side of the town wall, in a grassy area, stretched out in the snow.

Bothwell gave me the unwelcome details. "He was naked beneath his shift, but there was not a mark on him. No scorch-marks, no blood, no signs of a struggle. His poor valet, William Taylor, perished too, and was found alongside him, together with some household objects."

"What objects?" I asked.

"A chair, a cloak, a small dagger and a length of rope. It was a group of my men who found him, Ma'am. Someone shouted out and by the time I got there a small crowd had gathered, people who lived nearby. We all stared in disbelief. The townspeople knew they were looking at the King. I ordered them all to leave and arranged to have the body sent here."

I was silent.

"And my brother Moray, where is he?"

Bothwell shook his head. "He too had to leave Edinburgh on urgent business."

I gazed at Bothwell. My next words were spoken so low that I am not sure if anyone present in the chamber heard them. "They did the deed, after all… and made sure they 'looked through their fingers.'"

I was remembering Craigmillar and our discussion there, back in November when my councillors and advisers had gathered in secret to discuss the problem of my errant husband.

"Ma'am?" it was one of my ladies-in-waiting.

Bothwell glanced at me quickly as a servant entered the room to tend the fire.

"Your Majesty, you are in shock, and must rest."

"Then leave me. All of you," I cried.

My ladies-in-waiting stood at the door hesitating,

unconvinced that they should follow my command, until I insisted.

Then I sat heavily at my writing-desk, the fire at my back, and stared at the writing materials which were always laid out neatly before me, in anticipation of performing the day's business. I do not know how many minutes passed in this manner, but I neither moved nor spoke. I simply sat in silence, staring at the parchment and quills. At some point in the near future I would need to communicate with my relatives abroad, my fellow monarchs, the Pope in Rome, and I did not relish this task.

Nothing made any sense. An explosion that rocked the foundations of the town and destroyed the house in which my husband was staying? Why engineer or orchestrate such a dramatic end to Darnley's life? This is a thought which has oft troubled me. There are easier ways to dispose of a troublesome king, surely?

Why not poison? It would be easy enough to slip a harmful medicament into his goblet of wine; no one would be the wiser. After all, he was already sickening.

But instead *they* – whoever *they* were – chose gunpowder; the most profoundly dramatic, cataclysmic method possible, and one which would be sure to draw the eyes of the world to my perilous kingdom. Now…*why* would they do that?

I argued as much with my councillors. I put this to them again and again in the weeks that followed. But they had no answers – at least none which they cared to share with me.

A profound silence seemed to hang over Edinburgh like an invisible veil. No one wanted to discuss the incident. Lips were sealed.

Later that morning Darnley's body was brought to the Palace on a board. I stared at him, at his vanished youth, his wasted life. His features were white, as if cast in stone, fixed in an expression of peace – not fear – which would surely have been his real state of mind in his final moments.

I thought of his poor valet who had perished alongside him.

I had an apothecary and a surgeon attend to my husband's body. He was to be cleansed, embalmed, then laid in state in the Chapel Royal with candles burning beside his open coffin.

I spent many hours beside him. It brought to mind other bereavements I had suffered. I could not help but think of Francois, my playmate in the nursery, to whom I had been betrothed ere I arrived in France.

This loss was different. It was tinged with regret, and perhaps some remorse at the relief I felt on being free. For so long I had worried over the problems Darnley caused me; the ever-constant threat of scandal or intrigue.

Now that he was gone, I still had no peace of mind. I could not help but dwell on the fact that I too could have perished in that explosion. How easy it would have been for the conspirators to make their way down to Holyrood, snatch my little son Prince James and then rule Scotland in his name.

Who were the real perpetrators of this plot, I wondered? Who had thought to gain the most?

I edged nearer to the coffin and gazed down on him. Candles guttered next to his body. The skill of the embalmer was evident; they had even managed to conceal the scars left by the pocks. His alabaster skin was tight across his bones.

His final resting-place would be beneath the stone flags of

the abbey, down in the burial vaults through which we had crept on our escape from the Palace, the night of Rizzio's murder. There, Darnley would join my own parents and ancestors. And there, perhaps, I too would lie one day... It was a sobering thought.

I have survived my husband Darnley by twenty years, and for twenty years he has haunted me. He appears as a vigorous young man in the prime of life, while I continue to grow older and weaker; my eyesight dims, my shoulders stoop and my posture shows visible signs of age, while Darnley's ghost remains forever young, his youth preserved in death. The secret of who planted that gunpowder, who took his life at the last, died with him in his final moments. He has never shared those secrets with me since.

I bent down that day and kissed his cold lips. It was my final tribute to our dead love.

Then I locked myself in a darkened chamber to mourn, as was the custom. I was a widow again, at twenty-four years of age.

Bothwell was the only one of my councillors who remained steadfastly by my side. There was no 'pressing family business' for *him* to attend to which would require his sudden absence from the arena of power.

"Has my brother Moray returned yet?" I asked him.

Bothwell shook his head. "He has business to attend to, Ma'am. Family business, back on his estate."

My brother Moray was a happily married man. I could not imagine that he had any very pressing business that his wife, Lady Agnes, could not attend to most competently in his absence, but I swallowed the lie – as I have swallowed so many others.

"How are things in the town?"

"The atmosphere is tense, Ma'am. Master Knox grows ever more voluble."

I tried to stifle my anger. "Who do they say is guilty?" I asked.

"I do not listen to idle gossip and rumour-mongers, Ma'am. And neither should you."

Bothwell was right. There was no point in listening to the vicious slanders that flew across the rooftops of Edinburgh.

I sealed myself away for three or four days – I do not remember exactly as my memories of that period fade – but I began to refuse visitors. I grew sick and pale. I held my son in my arms, but he became distressed quickly, perhaps sensing something of my agitation, so I handed him back to his wet nurse. I did not know what to do; I wanted only to hide from the world, and I longed to avoid my responsibilities as queen.

My doctors advised me that I was in shock and should rest, so at their advice I cut short my period of mourning and went into retreat, taking with me those few ladies-in-waiting and courtiers who could make my stay comfortable. Of my Secretary Maitland and my brother Moray there was still no sign.

Make of that what you will…

Edinburgh
March 1567

March was a tense and uneasy month. I called upon the services of Bothwell to protect my little son and looked about me to see what must be done in the aftermath of my husband's assassination. Letters arrived from abroad, urging me to conduct a trial to establish the identity of the culprits and bring them to justice.

"That would be rather difficult," I told my Secretary of State, Maitland, when I did next lay eyes upon him.

"And why is that Your Grace?"

"Well…I find that many of the chief suspects attended Darnley's funeral and showed as much grief and sorrow at his death as if it were their own kinsman who had perished. One would have thought they all loved him dearly."

For it was true. Men who had never been slow to show their loathing of my husband, and had met in secret to discuss how best to be rid of him, now clamoured to express their moral outrage at his death.

Although the funeral itself was a very Catholic affair, conducted by my own priest, Father Mamaret, in accordance with the rites of the Catholic Church, my Protestant advisers put aside their religious preferences in order to attend, to kneel in piety and pray for the soul of their murdered 'sovereign'. The hypocrisy of this did not go unnoticed; it galled me deeply.

"Who do the townsfolk say is guilty, Maitland?"

He avoided my gaze.

I waited for him to speak.

"They say Bothwell must have had a hand in it, Ma'am."

I struggled to maintain my composure. "Why do they focus on him in particular?"

"They say he had a lot to gain, Your Majesty."

"Bothwell has been a loyal supporter of the crown, Maitland. I do not like to hear him vilified so. He was here at my side when the rest of you fled – on family business! I do not know how I would have managed else."

Maitland said nothing, but I noted the change of tone. Courtiers are made easily jealous; rivalries spring up over nothing, and Darnley was not nothing. This was an event of magnitude which would have repercussions rippling into the future for a long time to come. I sensed my lords and councillors would be only too willing to find a scapegoat to blame.

I ordered another solemn requiem mass to be sung in the Chapel in order to mark the end of my forty days of mourning. When I informed Father Mamaret of the decision, he had the temerity to pass judgement on my growing friendship with Bothwell.

"You must distance yourself from him, Ma'am. Can you not see that?"

"But I rely on him. He is the only one I trust."

"He has been accused of your husband's murder."

"No one has yet openly accused him. I will not listen to rumour."

"If you befriend him, you cast suspicion on yourself."

"So my cousin Elizabeth in London advises also. But do you know – she knew of the planned assassination long before I did? London has its spies, and I do not doubt she and her ministers had some communication with the conspirators – whoever they may be!"

"But it is how it *looks*, Ma'am!"

"I do not care about how it *looks*. As a man of the cloth, nor should you! I care only about truth."

Father Mamaret smiled. "Your Majesty presumes too far in advising me how best to perform my job. Careful, Marie! Remember, I did know you when you were thus high!"

I kept my temper and smiled.

"So," he added, recovering his composure. "Your Majesty will have a Mass to mark the end of the mourning period?"

I nodded. "If it pleases you!"

"You feel you have mourned enough then, Ma'am?"

I glanced at him sharply. "It is customary. Forty days in the wilderness…"

"Forty days, Marie," he said quietly. "You will be forty *years* in the wilderness if you persist in this reckless course of action."

I was astounded at his temerity.

"I have no course of action, Father. I seek only to survive."

And with that, I left him.

Relations between us were strained. I felt increasingly isolated within my own kingdom. I had but one friend and ally I could rely on at this time, and he had his enemies.

In my library at Holyrood I owned a pristine copy of *The Prince* by Machiavelli. I took it down from a shelf and scanned its pages. This was a title much loved by my erstwhile mother-in-law, Catherine de Medici, and she – no doubt – operated always with its key principles in mind.

I have made my mistakes and I have lived to regret them.

But there is one line in Machiavelli's volume which I take great comfort from.

"It cannot be called virtue to kill one's fellow citizens, to betray friends, to be without fidelity, without mercy, without religion; such proceedings enable one to gain sovereignty, but not fame."

I held the page with my finger, and gazed out of the window. The Palace was quiet at this time. There was little in the way of hubbub and activity. The mood had changed in Scotland. It has ever been a kingdom torn by faction, but there was something different about this atmosphere. I tried to pinpoint what it was. There was fear in the air, of course.

There were many who saw an opportunity opening up to snatch the crown from me, seize my baby son and use him as a pawn in the game of politics. I had to stop them from succeeding. And there was one man in my kingdom who I believed could assist me in this purpose. He had a retinue of armed followers, and he had another highly-valued quality – loyalty to the crown.

A king had been assassinated. For weeks now, many of my own councillors and men of state had debated the problem that Darnley had posed.

He was scheming with conspirators abroad, it had been said. Fuelled by resentment and grievances, what would he not do to plot my own downfall? Or at the very least to ruin my reputation abroad as far as he was able? It was essential I should keep him under close surveillance, Moray and Maitland had urged me.

No one had loved Darnley; he was hated and despised by all, yet now they cried out in indignation at his death. They began to edge away from me and align themselves with each other, like a troupe of naughty schoolboys pointing the finger.

And I was left wondering how best to manage the bungled state of affairs my kingdom had become.

I glanced at my mother's coat of arms above the window-frame, a bird pierced by three arrows, and wondered how she had managed. Marie of Guise was a woman of strength, stamina and intelligence. Her relatives in France had had no conception of how difficult her task had been, in keeping the kingdom safe for her daughter.

I mourned the passing of my mother. I mourn her still.

History repeats itself and strange demands are made of royal women. It is decreed that we must not nurture or cosset our young. We must be separated; kept apart from those we love.

I asked Bothwell to convey my little son to Stirling Castle and see him safely ensconced there, under the care of the Earl of Mar, which he did.

Holyrood seemed strangely empty in their absence, but I knew Stirling was the best place for my child.

I was beginning to grow fearful for my kingdom, uneasy in my mind about whom I could trust. Even my own confessor was proving himself to be less than loyal.

Men are changeable by nature. It was my brother Moray – with the backing of my Secretary of State, Maitland – who had urged me to pardon the exiled rebels, Morton, Ruthven and Lindsay, back in December. They assured me that if Rizzio's murderers were brought back out of exile where they languished in England, then all would be well in my kingdom. Darnley would be frightened enough to curb his behaviour and my closest advisers would stand by me throughout.

Yet where were they now? Maitland and Moray were both proving increasingly difficult to pin down.

The mood in Edinburgh was tense. The townsfolk kept to their houses, as if they were aware of the increasing factionalism and the dangers it could pose. If one happened to back the wrong side, one could lose everything. It was best to lie low and watch how the great and the good of Edinburgh played out the drama to their advantage.

Did the townsfolk of Edinburgh know something that I did not?

Vague whispers began to reach me on the air.

"Burn the witch! Burn the harlot!"

Did I imagine those voices I heard as I walked in the Palace gardens, looking up at Arthur's Seat and the Crags louring over us like a shadow?

Master Knox was preaching like fury from his fiery pulpit, showering the people with his wrath. The air was red-hot with his accusations. Not all of the townsfolk cared to listen to him. Many held him in contempt; but they knew when it was best to keep silent. Theirs was a humdrum world, filled with humdrum concerns, and they wisely held themselves aloof from the concerns of the powerful. They merely watched, and waited.

As did I.

The wolves were closing in…

Edinburgh
Early April 1567

When Bothwell returned from Stirling Castle, he came straight to me in the Palace.

I was standing before the great fire in my private apartments, trying to manage the ever-present sense of dread.

"Your Majesty…"

"How was my little son?" I asked, stepping forward anxiously on seeing him.

"He was perfectly well, Your Majesty."

"And did he cry when you left him?"

"He was reasonably contented," Bothwell said. "He was busy being entertained by the Earl of Mar's children and had no time to wonder at your absence. He is wonderfully used to the changes forced upon him."

I twisted the rings on my fingers nervously whilst struggling to hide my emotions.

Bothwell watched me closely; the look of empathy in his eyes did not go unnoticed. It moved me. Then he took me by surprise by suddenly kneeling before me, and gently taking my hand.

The action alarmed me at the same time as it did stir my blood. I gazed at him in shock.

"Your Majesty…" he hesitated then spoke my name in as soft a voice as I had ever heard him use. "Mary…would you consent to be my wife?"

He looked up at me with such frank appeal in his eyes, it quite took my breath away.

"Lord Bothwell, are you serious?"

"Never more so!"

I regarded him coolly.

"But the idea is ridiculous," I burst out. "You already have a wife! Had you forgotten?"

I could see that he was offended.

"A small impediment, Ma'am…"

"Small?" I cried out in disbelief. I gathered my thoughts. "In the Catholic Church we do not condone divorce. Your Kirk is a strange and twisted affair, to my mind."

Although I was refusing his offer, my hand still remained in his. He released it now and turned away from me. His disappointment was evident.

Recovering myself quickly, I began to protest.

"I cannot consent to your kind offer, Lord Bothwell, much as I am flattered by the attention you pay me. It would not be an expedient move to make at this stage."

"Surely, Ma'am, if you will pardon my saying so, there has never been a more expedient moment, when you have need of my support?"

"My mother had need of your support and you did not marry her!"

He looked taken aback and I wondered if I had gone too far.

Then a spark of mischief entered his eyes.

"Let us not speak of this again, Bothwell, please? I have no wish to lose your friendship."

Warm words that I hoped he would respond to.

"You value our friendship so much?"

"But of course!"

"You need my support, Ma'am. There are precious few you can trust at present."

I did not like him to draw attention to the vulnerability of my position.

Despite my refusal of Bothwell's offer, he *was* persistent. The second time he did ask for my hand in marriage, he produced a legally binding document that had been signed by many prominent men in my Council. I unrolled the parchment and gazed at the array of signatures. Then I read what the bond had to say. It urged me to marry again, now that I had been left a widow, that this would make my kingdom more secure. That if I should choose to marry soon, the Earl of Bothwell would be the favoured choice of those named in the Bond, being as he was a native of Scotland rather than a foreigner. Nowhere in the document was his wife's name mentioned. I had heard it rumoured that Lady Jean Gordon was eager to be shot of him – she had said as much herself – so perhaps Bothwell was right to say there was not much of an impediment there; but I was not of the opinion that it would be wise to marry a man who already had a wife living.

I laughed when I read the document. "I cannot agree to this, Bothwell."

"You are not persuaded a little of their arguments?"

"A little…" I conceded. "But it is not my intention to marry in haste, especially to a man who already has a wife."

A second refusal was not what Lord Bothwell had expected, and he was not pleased.

We parted, not on good terms, and this saddened me.

It was a night or two later that placards began appearing throughout the town accusing Lord Bothwell of the murder of my husband. One was affixed to the Palace gates where I could not help but see it. On it were the symbols of a hare – an image that appeared on Bothwell's family's coat of arms – and a crowned mermaid.

The import of it was not lost on me. I had it removed and burned.

Fotheringhay Castle
October 1586

More letters arrived from abroad, informing me that rumours
were sweeping across the frontiers of Europe, catching fire
as they went, claiming that Bothwell was a constant guest in
my Palace during these troubled times. Were these rumours
true, they asked? Would I risk everything for the sake of a
rough Border laird, an ambitious upstart?

Banish him, *they urged me.*

I ignored them all.

What did they know of my tangled affairs?

How could I banish Bothwell? What did foreigners know
of the terrible dangers and perils of trying to rule Scotland,
with a man like Knox at its helm?

The more dangerous my position became, the more I did
rely upon Bothwell's support.

Darnley's ghost stands sentinel at the door, watching me. He
leans nonchalantly to one side.

"He was guilty – and you know it!"

I still my needlework and meet his gaze.

"No one else sees you. Only I."

He shrugs. His silence encourages me to continue.

"I had him acquitted in a court of law. He was put to trial, along with the other suspects who were named in the placards pinned about town. There were so many of them, you see. You had so many enemies!"

Darnley glares.

"And why did you not let my father attend the trial?"

"He was quite welcome to. Lord Lennox was informed that of course he could attend, but that we could only allow six armed guards to enter the city along with him. Any more than this would pose a risk to the security of the realm. Surely he understood this?"

I resume stitching. *"He did understand it, and stayed away."*

"Exactly!" Darnley bursts out, exasperated by my coolness.

"No one mourned you, Darnley, except your own parents. If that seems cruel, then I am sorry, but I did my best by you for as long as I was able."

He cannot deny it.

"Knox had you down as an adulteress and a murderess."

"Yes, those were some of the choice epithets he used."

Along with whore and harlot and Jezebel!

"He preached against you all the time."

"So I believe. But he was no whited sepulchre himself."

"An upright man of virtue like Knox? How could you possibly think of him otherwise?"

"I had my sources. There were rumours about him too.

He was not without his faults. He was a man of passion although he sought to hide it. He hated women, and he hated the idea of pleasure or enjoyment. He thought art and beauty were not appropriate in a religious building and wanted every expression of art erased from the face of Scotland. He wanted a God after his own image. An angry God! Full of wrath!"

Darnley sniggers slightly. "Yes, it was a very angry God he worshipped. But we all tried to please him. Even you!"

"He preached such formidable sermons against me in St. Giles' High Kirk. Even when he knew the half of it to be untrue. He simply saw his chance to be rid of a Catholic monarch – and a female one at that. No, Knox was no stranger to hypocrisy."

I draw my bright thread through the weave and smile to myself. How odd it is that I should confide in my dead husband's ghost after all these years!

"So, why did you agree to marry Bothwell in the end?" he asks me, stepping out of the shadows. "If you refused him twice – why not a third time?"

The walls of my damp cell seem to retreat and fade as the memories come pouring, flooding in...

And there is no one but Darnley left to listen...

Stirling Castle
April 1567

I come now to the strangest part of my history, the part which is hardest to tell.

My health began to deteriorate and I became anxious to see my son, Prince James. With this in mind I decided to leave Edinburgh, and fetch him back from Stirling Castle where he was still in the care of the Earl of Mar. I could not bear to be apart from my flesh and blood any longer. It was unnatural to me, to be torn from his side.

As I approached the high rock across the plains, I recalled my son's baptism here, before Christmas, how it had snowed and how the kings of Europe and their ambassadors had flocked to my celebrations. The Palace kitchens had been a hive of activity then; the scent of their delicious fare had drifted across the courtyards morning, noon and night. Torches had flared along the outside corridors, and the windows of the Palace and state rooms had flickered with colour and light which could be seen for miles around.

How things had changed. Less than four months had passed and now my troubles threatened to overwhelm me.

I was lonely, isolated. My husband lay cold in a stony grave beneath the chapel at Holyrood, a man of no more than twenty-one years.

I spent a sorrowful few days at Stirling, trying to persuade the Earl of Mar to let me take care of my own son. He refused, and his refusal tore at my heart.

"Would you defy me?" I cried.

"It is not safe to remove the Prince from Stirling Castle," he informed me. "He can be protected and defended here. Can you assure the same would be the case if you took him to Edinburgh with you?"

I could not reason with him.

He remained staunchly defiant.

I spent an afternoon with my little son, walking with him in my arms, about the castle precincts, looking across the open plains. I pointed out the distant mountains, but he was still far too small to appreciate any of it, or to concentrate on anything but the pearl brooch on my cloak which he explored with his stubby fingers. The Earl of Mar did not let us out of his sight. I felt eyes watching us all the time.

The little baby prince put his head on one side and studied me intently, a mild-mannered but confused look in his eyes.

Was he wondering why I left him so often, why his life was governed by distant figures of authority who bore little resemblance to his mother?

"Mama has to leave you again," I whispered, kissing his damp cheek. "All this will be yours one day," I told him, indicating the mountains, those far pavilions that defined the edges of our world.

He did not understand me, of course. And I knew that in reality his kingdom would not consist of those beautiful mountains but instead powerful men who were difficult to control, who fought endlessly, conspired continually, and were quick to draw a dagger and blade. That was the reality, but my little son knew none of this yet.

His eyes were dull, I noticed, not particularly bright. Was this a symptom of his upbringing, the separation we bore? I did not want to see the truth, or notice the likeness to Darnley. Was this a son who would be moulded after a different image? If I was not there to protect him, how would others rear him? How would his tutors treat him?

"Your Majesty," came a voice from the shadows. "The wind is cutting up here, and the little Prince will catch cold."

"Fresh air cannot harm him!" I snapped.

"You would do well to return to Edinburgh and take care of your affairs there. You cannot afford a further absence, Ma'am," the Earl of Mar warned me.

I kissed my little son James for the last time and left him in that sturdy fortress on its formidable rock.

"I will see you again in a few days' time," I whispered in his ear.

"He will be safe there, Your Majesty," one of my women comforted me as we rode away.

I pulled my fur-lined cloak about my shoulders and hid my tears from them.

I did not know it, but that was the last time I would see my son.

It marked an ending, and I was not even aware of it.

Linlithgow to Dunbar
April 1567

We rode on, a small party of us. I did not go straight to Edinburgh, but stopped off at Linlithgow for one night. This was the Palace my father built. What had my mother made of it all when he brought her here? I do not know. There are so many questions I would have liked to ask her. Our time spent together was far too short. I mourn her to this day, and know that I always will, for we were very close despite our forced separation.

When I rode out at dawn the next day, I was accompanied by a few of my closest courtiers. It was the twenty-fourth day of April. We were heading towards Edinburgh, much to my regret. Everything in me wanted to head north instead, back to Stirling, but I controlled the impulse to do so and faced east.

However, we did not reach Edinburgh that night.

We came to the narrow stone bridge which crosses the River Almond, just outside the city. They were waiting for us – a party of about eight hundred armed retainers – on horseback. When I saw Bothwell in their midst I was deeply bewildered, confused. I did not know whether to be alarmed or relieved.

Sir James Melville was at my side and seemed uneasy in his saddle at the sight.

"What brings my Lord Bothwell here?" I asked Melville. "Did you have word of this?"

Melville shook his head.

"Perhaps he feels the need to accompany us back into Edinburgh?" I suggested, steeling myself for whatever encounter was about to follow.

Melville looked unconvinced.

As we drew near my courage failed me. There was something about Bothwell's surly countenance, the set posture of his shoulders that gave me cause for unease. His men surrounded us and I found myself vulnerable in their midst. In the chaos I became separated from my own courtiers and my ladies, until the only men I could see near me were strangers, armed and on horseback. Bothwell rode close to me and I looked at him questioningly.

"What is this, Bothwell?" I demanded.

"There is no cause for alarm, Your Majesty. I must ask you to accompany me to Dunbar Castle."

"Dunbar?" I cried. "For what reason?"

"For your own safety, Ma'am."

When I refused, he insisted, grabbing the bridle of my horse in his fist.

"I must ask that you do as I bid – Your Majesty!"

He spoke in a low voice, but there was no mistaking his purpose.

"You must ask? Then the answer is no. For the third time, Bothwell – no!"

"Edinburgh is not safe for you at the present time," and he pushed his way through the crowd, forcing my horse to follow. He pulled me away from the vicinity of my own men and Melville, until I found myself surrounded by strangers, men I had never seen before.

I spun round in my saddle, seeking a familiar face, but there was none. I had become separated from my servants and my ladies-in-waiting. There was no one near to help.

And in this wise we were forced to ride with Bothwell's army to Dunbar. I was not too unduly alarmed at first, for I was confident that Bothwell would not wish me harm, but I was bewildered and disappointed.

In the many small towns and villages we passed through, I was unable to cry out or call for help, and it would have been unseemly to do so. Bothwell had – up till now – been a loyal supporter of the crown, someone I could trust. Amongst the men nearby I did, at one point, spy James Borthwick and asked him urgently to ride back to Edinburgh and secure help from the citizens there, which I have reason to believe he did. For later on during our journey two salvoes of cannon were fired from a distance; they had little or no impact on Bothwell's intent, however. We rode on at speed to the coast.

Bothwell held my horse firmly by the bridle until we got up close to Dunbar Castle itself. When I heard the familiar roar of the waves I knew that we were near.

We clattered into the inner courtyard; walls which had once offered shelter and protection now closed around me like a prison; I began to realise that no one would raise a finger to assist me.

Bothwell looked at me. "It is not necessary that your ladies-in-waiting should stay, Your Majesty."

I glared at him. "I will not have them removed from my sight."

"They will all leave, immediately, whether you will it or not."

"Are you so cold and callous in your purpose," I asked him "that you could do this to your own queen whom you have always served so well? I cannot believe it is in you, Bothwell."

James Hepburn looked at me then and said "Begin to believe it. I did not expect you to deny me, Ma'am. Twice I did ask you and twice you did refuse. The third time…you will not refuse me. There shall be no gainsaying this."

As my servants and ladies-in-waiting were ordered to leave Dunbar, I saw the extent of how Bothwell's pride had been wounded by my two refusals.

His mind was made up and he had a force of eight hundred men to prove it.

I have borne many hard lessons in life and this was but one of them.

I had thought Bothwell was a good man; I thought I knew the extent of his faults. But I was wrong.

Once my courtiers had been sent away, I was allowed to 'rest'.

I paced the castle ramparts, looking longingly out to sea, wondering how I would bear what was to follow, how I could best defend myself.

It was but a few hours later that Bothwell came to me in my own private chamber.

We were alone, and there was no one to protect me. I looked him in the eye and said, "My Lord Bothwell, I did once hold you in higher esteem and regard than I do now – although not high enough to marry you. By forcing me to accompany you here you have not improved your standing with me."

There was a short silence.

"You have wounded my pride, Marie."

I looked at him. "You do not address me by my title?"

He smiled. "I had thought we were making good progress in our affection for one another and felt I had good reason to hope. I had thought we might follow through what had only been hinted at."

"Follow through?" I looked at him. "Hinted at? I hinted at nothing!"

"I beg to differ, Your Majesty," he said. "The Exchequer House? Do you not remember those times when you turned to me? I know the look in a woman's eye and can presume to know what it means."

"You presume too far, Bothwell."

"I think not," he said.

"You have…" my voice faltered at this point, "you have ruined what we had…"

I broke off.

"Others know what is best for you, Marie," he said gently. "You should allow us to look after your personal safety. Do I make myself clear?"

Up until this point I had remained calm. I had no choice if I wished to keep my dignity. I knew that my reputation was perhaps forever tarnished. Women are chattels to be bought and sold; even a monarch, a queen ordained by God, is no exception and can be bargained for like coveted goods.

Men rule this world we live in and it is their laws and priorities which hold sway. We merely bear their children and their pain, and try to make the best of it.

What happened next is hard to describe.

I made a move towards the door, but he barred my way.

"I wish to leave," I cried and began to push myself past him in a blind panic, but he did fling me so hard that I hit my head against the bedpost. It was then I began to realise what would follow.

Bothwell seemed taken aback at his own violence. He made a move to apologize but I slapped him away.

"For your own good, Ma'am, it would be best for everyone if you were to oblige me by becoming my wife."

And my consent, apparently, was not what was needed.

He forced himself upon me.

Fotheringhay Castle
October 1586

Darnley claps his hands in slow motion, as if congratulating my performance.

"I don't believe you."

I lift my tapestry and continue to sew in the firelight, calm in the telling of my story.

"Believe what you like."

Dunbar Castle
April 1567

Sir James Melville and others were present in the heavily-fortified castle of Dunbar while I was held against my will, and not one of them burst into my private chamber to defend their queen and demand she be freed and taken back to Edinburgh.

Besides, it was now too late.

I did not tell anyone what had happened. Abduction is an ugly word, and an ambiguous one. Men like Knox have made it so. Women of my position in life know that the shame of it is too great – so we keep it to ourselves. The secret dies with us. We go to our graves with it sealed away in our hearts.

Instead I did raise my head high and bore my fate.

In a letter I wrote to Elizabeth, I spoke true when I said, "Although we found his doings rude and strange, yet were his answer and words gentle. As it has succeeded, so we must make the best of it."

If I search my own feelings I cannot deny that I had never found his company objectionable before now. I had sought him out; found his person attractive, his presence a comfort.

I had never suspected in my worst nightmares that Bothwell would force himself upon me.

I had trusted him.

But something in me changed towards him.

He would need to ask my forgiveness.

And ask it, he did.

Give it, I did not…

Not at first…

I then went on to point out the obvious.

"I am a widow, Bothwell, but you still have a wife. It does not matter how much you coerce your Queen or claim the backing of your supporters – it is a nonsense you speak of. The prospect of any marriage between us is impossible."

Bothwell shook his head.

"A minor obstacle that can be dealt with. Lady Jean Gordon has no strong wish to remain married to me."

"In the Catholic Church marriages are not so easily annulled."

Bothwell shrugged, as if it were a small matter.

"Then we will ensure this is not a Catholic marriage!"

We spent almost two weeks at Dunbar, isolated from the rest of my court circle. Bothwell ensured that we shared the same bedchamber and I allowed myself to sink into the trap that had been made for me.

We slept together, ate together, lived together, and waited…

Sometimes Bothwell walked with me along the battlements where I liked to retreat for some 'air'. The wind was so strong up here that it swept back my cloak and hood and almost blew me from my feet. I watched the surf endlessly crashing and pulling back, far below in a relentless rhythm.

At one point I went up there alone, despite – or almost because of – an ominous horizon. While I stood there I felt the sky darken, moment by moment. A storm was imminent.

What is going to happen? I wondered, as the clouds met overhead and day turned to night.

I did not move. I wanted to stay and witness the cataclysm.

Bothwell suddenly appeared at my side and insisted I take shelter below, while above us the sky cracked and a deluge drowned the ramparts.

Once inside an inner passageway, where the wind still howled, I shivered, drenched in every part.

"What are you about, Marie – in this?" He had taken to calling me by my French name, as a sign of affection.

I blinked away the rainwater from my eyes and saw his face swimming in a blurred fashion before me. Was he real, or imagined?

I thought I saw concern written there.

Then he did something that took me by surprise. He pulled me quickly towards him and stroked the damp hair from my face. It was as if he suddenly saw for a moment the toll his actions had taken upon me.

"Marie," he murmured.

He kissed my forehead then put me aside again. His actions merely confused me further. I did not know what to believe.

"Come, we'll escape the storm inside."

But there was a worse storm coming. One we would never escape. I knew this as I watched the torches guttering against the darkened walls, slick with wet.

Life was beginning to race ahead of me, like a stallion out of control, and I struggled to rein it in.

Those twelve days became a strange dream-like retreat in the end, from all the cares of governing. I almost gave up, sacrificed control. Part of me had no choice. Although spring was not far away, that ferocious ocean surged and moaned like a wild beast, so that fountains of spray continually shot almost as high as the castle ramparts.

One morning I woke with a familiar feeling in my body. I felt leaden, exhausted. Nausea pervaded every fibre of my being, and although I was not physically sick, every sense seemed to be invaded by it. Everything I looked at, touched, smelled, came to me through a miasma of sickness.

I told no one. This was a child conceived out of wedlock. It would be a bastard, like my brother Moray who had ever resented the fact. I thought of Knox back in Edinburgh, his insufferable glee and triumphalism if he ever got wind of my predicament, and I struggled to hide my condition even from Bothwell.

Pregnancy does not agree with me; it makes me grow despondent.

Bothwell was restless, nervous. I could sense this during our nights secluded together in a high chamber.

I do not know what Bothwell noticed. He was too bound up with his own ambition. He had once been a favourite of my mother's, Marie of Guise, and he had foolishly fixed his sights upon her daughter. What had seemed like endearing loyalty had become something else entirely.

"Marie," he said at one point. "You need me now. When we return to Edinburgh, the world will be waiting for us, and you will need me by your side."

I looked at him, and wondered precisely what would be waiting for me out there.

When I rode back into Edinburgh almost two weeks later, it was with a heavy heart.

What I had already suspected turned out in fact to be true: I was with child. There was no alternative, and I must salvage what I could of the situation.

Edinburgh
May 1567

The sea fortress receded into the background as we made our way towards Edinburgh. Dunbar is a memory, a stain on my conscience, and only I know what secrets took place there. I confide in no one, not even the ghosts who inhabit my lonely chamber here at Fotheringhay; not even my Catholic confessor will ever know what unfolded behind the scenes.

Bothwell kept me there for twelve days, and in that time no one made a move to defend me – not even Melville, or Maitland, or my brother Moray.

During our enforced seclusion Bothwell had become gentle, even apologetic, almost, but he insisted it was for the best and almost persuaded me of the fact.

He had a purpose in mind. "With me by your side, Marie, you will be stronger, safer."

I did my best to believe him. There was at least some truth in his assertion that with his army at my disposal I could defend the throne for my son. Certainly no others had rushed to my defence.

While we remained at Dunbar, Bothwell sent instructions through to Edinburgh that a divorce should be obtained from the law courts. Word came through that Lady Jean was in agreement; she was happy to see the proceedings rushed through in all haste.

I recalled that she had been reluctant to marry Bothwell, having been promised to Alexander Ogilvie, and still held that man in great affection. She was no doubt relieved to be shot of a partnership which had ever been irksome to her.

By the time we left Dunbar I was suffering from morning sickness. I was left with little alternative. My plight could not be mended other than by agreeing to marry Bothwell, father of my unborn child.

We entered the town through the West Port, in as discreet a fashion as possible, and travelled up the steep cobbled Bow to the castle on its platform of polished black rock. A strange hush descended on the people who saw me pass by. Did they know I was, in part, a captive queen?

Bothwell still held my horse by the bridle all the way. As I looked to left and right, I saw the townsfolk line the streets and stop what they were doing to stare. I saw looks of pity, confusion and bewilderment on their faces.

I had no choice but to endure. How could I tell the world that I – a ruler by divine right – had been coldly taken by a man I trusted? The world does not listen to women, even those ordained by God to rule. As the world knows, it is always the fault of the woman. She must take the blame, bear the shame.

The drawbridge was thrust down with a reverberating creak of straining timbers; we passed over it into the mouth of the castle and the heavy doors clanged shut behind us.

Bothwell proposed that we should remain in the castle while the banns were being called. He did not relish the thought of staying in Holyrood until he could be sure of his position.

I felt like a prisoner on that windswept summit, the hostile town stretched below me. Bothwell had a retinue of professional armed arquebusiers ringed round to 'protect' us.

"I have never felt quite so heavily *protected* in my life before, James," I ventured to remark.

The sarcasm of this comment was not lost on him.

We kept to the rooms in the south-east tower, where I had given birth to my little son one year before. There was a strained atmosphere in the castle which the few servants permitted to remain near me remarked upon. I still longed to have my ladies-in-waiting with me, but Bothwell refused. He promised that they would be part of the household once we were safely established in Holyrood as a married couple.

I protested, but in vain.

Was there any comfort to be had in this relationship?

I reflect on it now that the years have passed. Bothwell has become a fading memory, but he once loomed large on my horizon. He changed the course of my destiny.

I cannot deny that as the days went by there did begin to be some warmth in our physical relationship. I was isolated, cut off from my friends, with only Bothwell to keep me company. He showed concern for my welfare; at length I began to return the warmth.

But it was a bad beginning, and as such, it would be hard to fix.

Up in the tower, I took time to sit at my desk and wrote to the foreign heads of state, including Elizabeth, informing them of my decision to marry Bothwell. I needed to argue the case as I could appreciate their protestations, but the one salient point which I forebore to mention was my abduction and subsequent pregnancy.

I hinted at it between the lines, but whether they recognized the import of it, I do not know. Elizabeth was genuinely horrified at the dangerous position I had been placed in, but she did not know that I was with child.

No one knew.

At this point I had not even confided in my ladies-in-waiting because they had not yet been allowed to attend me. There were now no friends nearby I could tell.

The facts of the matter are these. When a woman is coldly taken against her will, she is expected to marry her attacker in order to rescue her own honour. There is no other way forward. Otherwise she is damned. Look across Europe, and even among ladies of the nobility and crowned heads of state, the same holds true. It is, however, rare for a man like Bothwell to have the audacity to abduct a queen and force her against her will.

I couched my letters in words which did hint at my predicament, and explained that it did seem that my advisers and councillors were keen for me to marry a Scotsman rather than a foreigner, and one with adequate forces at his disposal. This being the case, Bothwell seemed a likely candidate.

I got no encouragement or support from my old friends and relatives in France. I was almost too tired and worn down to care about what foreigners abroad might think.

I had a rugged country to control, one which my mother before me had also struggled with. I saw that I would need to concentrate my efforts to rescue the situation and use what troops I had at my disposal to strengthen my position. It was imperative that I should stop factions from rising up and brewing more trouble.

If Bothwell could help me with that, then so be it!

Knox refused to publish the banns of marriage, of course. Instead, he preached fire and brimstone from his ugly pulpit and the people had no choice but to sit and listen. If they were Protestant they filed into the High Kirk and endured his wrath. A storm of torrential abuse against me was unleashed, as far as I could tell.

I wept tears of frustration, but Bothwell told me to remain calm. "Knox can be dealt with once we are married. You will not need to endure his abuse for much longer."

"And yet you tell me that you prefer to be married by Protestant instead of Catholic rites? How can I agree to that?"

His face hardened. "Do you recall when you arranged my first marriage, to Lady Jean? You could not persuade me to marry under the Catholic Church then, and you will not do so now."

"If we wait for Knox to declare the banns of marriage, then we will be waiting for ever and by that time…" I stopped myself short and realised that my hand had drifted instinctively towards my belly.

Bothwell was watching me carefully. If he guessed, he said nothing.

Our quarrel raged on, so that the servants could hear, and I was left alone in my chamber, weeping. If I could have found a way out of my predicament, I would gladly have taken it, but there was a child in my womb. And that child did not belong to my dead husband. It was Bothwell's and he had but lately been married to another.

♛

The atmosphere in Edinburgh was explosive. John Knox was preaching like fury from his pulpit. Bothwell – although he was never a godly man – attended a service at St. Giles' High Kirk. Afterwards he informed me that Knox took the story of Ahab from the Scriptures and screeched it above the heads of his gathered congregation until no one had known where to look.

"Ahab did not walk in the way of the Lord, and look what happened to him," he shrieked. "He took a wife. Jezebel – who tempted her husband to commit wicked atrocities. Elisha said 'and the dogs shall eat Jezebel, and there shall be none to bury her!'"

Bothwell laughed as he related the story, but I was not amused.

The tension up at the castle increased as Bothwell rushed to secure his plans.

When we quarrelled he threatened to return to Lady Jean.

"Are you aware that some say I am not even divorced from Lady Jean Gordon, that she is my true wife? I could return to her, in fact, and abandon you to your fate."

He became cruel in order to secure what he wanted.

I have a notion that he must have known I was pregnant. He knew I was afraid that my reputation would be ruined.

"So, my Jezebel," Bothwell laughed. "We are to be married soon."

I turned away from him and murmured, "I need no approval from Master Knox."

As I gazed from the windows of the castle that night, I felt the hostile town ranged below me. So many had proved fickle in the end, even my confessor Father Mamaret. Bothwell was my last ally. When the moon broke from under the cloud cover I could see that the waters of the Firth were etched with ripples. A path of silver led to the horizon. If only I could vanish into that horizon, I thought, but I do not have that luxury.

Father Mamaret was still residing at Holyrood and I sent word to him that I had need of his presence. Word was sent back that the pious father regretted that he found himself indisposed, but would try to attend when he was able.

Stung by the rebuffal, I waited till the next day and repeated the request. He came that afternoon, but in no great hurry it must be added. A fierce wind blew from the Forth and he met me in the tiny, whitewashed chapel of St. Margaret on its bluff above the city.

I knelt in the darkness before the candle-glow.

He had the temerity to ask what I expected of him.

"God's blessing," I replied.

"I will give you His absolution, Your Majesty, but not His blessing."

I kept my composure, and listened carefully to what he had to say.

"You cannot go through with this marriage, Your Majesty. A Protestant marriage? You must save yourself before it is too late."

I frowned at him and considered my words before replying. "I have always freely forgiven those who have sinned against myself. When Rizzio was murdered and my own life was threatened, I forgave the perpetrators of this deed at the instruction of my own councillors. Why am I then never to be forgiven?"

"Your husband lies dead in the Abbey!"

"And who put him there? Not I! I know who is guilty

of Darnley's murder. Others have blood on their hands, including those who sit in Parliament and dare to pronounce upon others."

"I am not concerned with their sins, Mary, but with yours. You cannot marry Bothwell under the rites of a heretical kirk when he has a wife of his own unlawfully – *unlawfully*, I say – divorced."

"If I must compromise on the religious rites of the ceremony, then it is a necessary evil."

"I understand what you feel you must do, Mary. But you must do what is right, and you will find that what is right is also politic."

Around us the shadows moved in the candlelight.

"It would be politic to marry Bothwell. It is my duty to protect the monarchy."

"And you think this action will protect it?"

"I am with child," I burst out.

Father Mamaret paled and said nothing for some moments.

Eventually he rose, made the sign of the cross, and murmured, "May God have mercy on your soul!"

Then he left me.

I knelt alone in that tiny, whitewashed building before the glittering painted icons, while a merciless wind howled outside. I prayed to my ancestor, Saint Margaret, who had spent many long hours worshipping in this chapel. My whispers filled the darkness.

Saint Margaret did not reply.

Holyrood
May 1567

Bothwell, on observing my distress after Father Mamaret's visit, took me aside and made to offer some comfort.

"Do not fret, Marie," he told me. "You need no priest's blessing. What makes him such an intermediary for God?"

I regarded him in silence, this rogue soldier of mine who had worked his way into my affections, won my trust, and then taken me by surprise when I least expected it.

"Am I a good son of the Kirk, for instance, of any Church? Tell me."

"You should ask yourself."

"I do ask it of myself. No priest can refuse you the right to be forgiven. It is not in his power."

"I was talking of the true Church," I whispered, gazing out at the distant waters of the Firth.

"So was I," I heard him breathe at my side.

The day before our wedding I made Bothwell the Duke of Orkney and the Lord of Shetland and all the Isles, placing the ducal coronet on his head with my own fair hands, trembling as they were. It glittered on his brow, a small token of our pledge to one another – such as it was.

Bothwell had become kind and reasonably attentive. He had good reason to be, I suppose.

Tomorrow we would venture down to the Palace where we would be wed.

It was the middle of the night when we made ourselves ready for departure. It was Bothwell's idea to leave before dawn.

What I did not know was that I was leaving that castle for the last time, never to enter its impregnable walls again.

The iron drawbridge was thrust down and we rode slowly down the stony Castle Hill. Bothwell rode beside me, and in our wake was a long winding train of armed men, hooves slithering and skittering dangerously on the steep cobbles from time to time.

A pall of silence, so thick it was almost tangible, hung over the city. No lights showed behind any of the shutters; no one was astir at this hour. Our journey went unremarked.

Holyrood waited for us, its twin towers wrapped in secrecy and silence.

We clopped quietly into the courtyard at a walking pace, dismounted, and left the grooms to attend to the horses. Then we entered the Palace in a mood of subdued gloom. It was too early to be of good cheer. The sun was not even beginning to lighten the sky.

I was dressed in mourning, my alabaster face made all the

more pale by the fall of my black veil and sombre draperies.

We walked down the panelled corridors to the Great Hall, the same where I had wed Lord Darnley.

How my fortunes had changed! Now beside me was James Hepburn, the Earl of Bothwell, handsome, engaging, roguish, someone I had thought to trust.

Now…I did not know what to think. All I knew was that he was the father of my unborn child.

There were no guests present. The Protestant Bishop of Orkney presided. None of my own family were there. Moray was nowhere in sight, as usual. He had fled Edinburgh long ago.

A makeshift altar had been erected, and a small brass lectern stood to one side. I thought wistfully of the Chapel Royal, with its paintings and icons and sculpted splendour.

The wedding ceremony was short and abrupt, according to the austerity of the Calvinist Reformed Kirk. There was no organ and no Mass, and I hid behind my veil.

There was no music, either. Just the words themselves, falling flat and hollow onto empty silence, a ceremony which Knox himself would have been proud of. There were a few short spoken promises, an exchange of rings, and the pact was completed, the bargain sealed. Performed surreptitiously and with all due haste in the darkness of the early hours.

I remember the Bishop of Orkney preached a long sermon, this being his chance to shine and carve out a place for himself in the new order, so he thought. I paid little attention. This ceremony was not as momentous as the Bishop supposed.

As the Bishop droned on in his dull monotone, he suddenly made reference to Bothwell's 'past life', his former sinful ways.

I glanced sideways at Bothwell and saw his dark gaze fixed pointedly on the Bishop, giving nothing away.

After the service there were no masques or banquets. We were too nervous for that kind of celebration. It was a tense atmosphere. We left the Great Hall and went straight back to our chamber. I was exhausted, having risen at such an early hour.

It was still only five o' clock in the morning and we did not open any of the shutters. When the sun rose, I did not see it. My head ached with lack of sleep. By the time the shutters were thrown open, a cold grey drizzle had set in.

That morning a letter arrived from Rome. A page delivered it to me directly where I remained cloistered with Bothwell. I read it in silence and let it fall at my feet.

"What is it?" Bothwell asked.

"It is from the Pope. He informs me that he is breaking off all relations with me."

Bothwell did not react at first, which quietly enraged me.

Eventually he shrugged. "It is not the end of the world, surely?"

"Not for you, perhaps. You are not a Catholic."

I waited. Still he did not react.

"Don't you understand? Can you not see what this means? I might as well be dead."

He got up and came towards me. "We are married now."

"Do you not see how much I have lost? Family, friends, everything. They will not accept our marriage – despite this ritual we have conducted today. Life will not go on as you want it to."

"This is just the initial uncertainty. One day all this will be in the past."

"This will never be in the past," I insisted, retrieving the letter from where it lay. "Perhaps this is only the beginning."

I knew that if the Pope chose to excommunicate me, the rest of Europe could do as they pleased. Anyone could plot for my downfall. I would never be safe again.

"This is my punishment," I murmured. "I am justly punished."

Bothwell watched me, perplexed. "Justly?"

"I have forsaken my own Catholic faith…to please you!"

It was not long before our voices rang out, echoing down the corridors so that, no doubt, the servants could hear our quarrel.

I dashed away my tears and tried to harden my heart as I had done so in the past.

As I sit here incarcerated in Elizabeth's castle, I think on my three husbands. Which of them earned my love or respect? First there was sexless Francois, who loved me as a sister. We were raised together in the nursery. He never awakened any physical love or passion.

Then there was Darnley, who did at first awaken my delight, but just as quickly quenched it with his irrational depraved behaviour.

Then there was Bothwell, who charmed me with his dark eyes and his rough embrace. When my person was threatened, he rushed to defend me, and in doing so won my heart. What I did not know was that he had another purpose in mind. He wanted the crown, and now I was beginning to realise it.

He had deceived me, played a double game, just like the rest of them. I have been ill-used.

There were no fireworks after this wedding. I did not replenish my wardrobe either, except to have a dress relined and an old black cloak embroidered with gold braid. My wedding gift to Bothwell was some genet fur with which to trim his dressing gown, a symbolic gesture to acknowledge his rise in station. I did not feel inclined to be lavish with extravagances we could ill-afford.

At noon there was a wedding breakfast. I had sent out a proclamation that the townsfolk were permitted to watch us from the courtyard for their entertainment if they should so desire. It was an attempt to include them in the pageant, but I regretted it the instant the command went out. I did not feel like being observed, my spirits were so low.

Bothwell and I sat out our ordeal in the dining-room on the first floor, our chairs scraping awkwardly against the floorboards as we sat down. We had been quarrelling all morning and there was a mood of tension between us as we avoided one another's gaze. We had left our quarrel unresolved and it nettled us both.

Bothwell tried to relieve the mood with a false heartiness at times. He rose from his seat at one point and shouted down to the assembled crowd below who had wandered into the courtyard to observe us.

"Make merry," he bellowed. "Share with us this cause for national celebration!"

A cheer went up, but there are always those who will cheer at anything. I noted that an enterprising vendor was weaving his way between the people selling burnt toffee and other sweetmeats.

For a moment I envied them their ordinary poverty – strange to say – although these people were not the true poor. They had shelter at night, a hearth to cook food upon. I had seen others in the vennels much worse off than these folk;

poor souls who lay in the mire and the dirt, whisky-addled in an attempt to dull the pain of their condition. I had seen it on those nights when I walked abroad after dusk with Darnley, in disguise.

But I did not wish to think on that. I focused on my plate, but found it hard to eat. I was still suffering from nausea.

Bothwell tried to engage me once or twice with a witty rejoinder, but grew frustrated when his attempts fell on parched soil. We fell instead into laconic silence, lifting the food to our mouths like wooden puppets.

At last, Bothwell stood up, pushing his chair back almost violently in his frustration.

"I consider we are done with this wedding breakfast. I can eat no more. You?" Then he turned to me, his queen. "You are done also…Ma'am?"

I inclined my head slightly.

He held out his hand to me, which I took, and raised me up from the chair where I sat. I was glad this pantomime was drawing to a close, as I was growing increasingly uncomfortable under the gaze of the townsfolk. I felt that many had gathered out of curiosity rather than genuine support for our cause. The doings and proceedings of 'great folk' are ever a cause of wonder to the poor, and I do not doubt that we offer them entertainment of a sort.

We went to the window and bowed to the crowd, who released another desultory cheer then we retired from the public gaze.

My mask of cheer instantly dropped. I could disguise it no more. My misery was complete.

That afternoon I heard it whispered that Father Mamaret was leaving for France. Bothwell was discussing it with one of his men when I came across them in the outer chamber.

"What news is this?" I asked.

There was nothing in this room but a long polished table, paintings on the walls, and no fire set in the great hearth, it being May.

"It is Father Mamaret. He is leaving. I came across his valet, packing. They intend to leave for France as soon as possible."

"Why was I not informed of this decision?"

No one replied.

"I must go and say farewell to him!"

"Wait!" Bothwell stopped me. "Don't you think it would be wise to leave well alone?"

"He came with me to Scotland, eight years ago, and has been with me ever since. Why would I not bid him farewell?"

Bothwell stood aside with a shrug and said no more.

My Catholic confessor's office was at the furthest end of the Palace from my own rooms, next to the Chapel Royal. As I stood outside I heard movement from within, chests being shifted and dragged across the boards.

I pushed open the door onto a scene of ordered chaos, towers of books spilling across the floor, one or two servants busy at their work of packing eight years worth of accumulated possessions. The icons and religious paintings that had once graced the walls had been taken down, leaving grey, discoloured rectangles as evidence of where they had hung. It was a depressing sight.

"I heard you were leaving, Father Mamaret." I looked him pointedly in the eye.

He avoided my gaze.

"You thought to leave without a parting word, after all these years?"

He struggled with his composure and I could see that my directness and honesty made him uneasy. He rallied, however, in front of his servants and said, "Forgive me, Your

Majesty, but I thought we had concluded our business the other day."

"Did you?" I said. "So you are leaving for France? You must feel very glad."

"I cannot deny that I shall be glad to see the shores of my own country again, after all these years. It has been a long time for an old man like myself."

"Pah! You are not so old, Father Mamaret. It has been a long time for me too. You must send my warmest regards to my relatives in France."

He bowed his head. "Your Majesty. But you must not pine for France still."

"I do not pine!" I retorted acidly.

He carried on as if I had not spoken. "This is your adopted country now, Ma'am. Here is where your duties lie."

I stared at him. "I am well aware of where my duties lie, thank you, Father Mamaret."

He looked alarmed for a moment.

"I wish you God speed on your journey!" I said, before turning my back on him.

I heard him beginning to utter some words, "Ma'am…" but it was too late. I had swept away from him.

Bothwell had been right. It had been a mistake to visit him. He did not hanker for my farewells.

As I moved away down the corridor, I heard the door being closed behind me by one of his servants and I stood a moment to listen. That door closed on a childhood of memories and trust. If I had any unfinished business with God, I would deal with it myself. My salvation was in my own hands – where it has always been.

Bothwell was correct in as much as no one truly needs an intercessor to mediate between themselves and God – even in the Catholic Church. My psalter, prayer book and rosary beads would suffice, and my own earnest prayers to a benevolent God.

Father Mamaret left Holyrood for the port of Leith that day, and from there sailed away to France. I never saw him again, nor received any letters from him, despite our shared experiences over the preceding eight years of my reign. I never wrote to him either, having no desire to do so. I have learned the hard way which servants are deserving of my loyalty.

Before supper Bothwell and I took a turn in the grounds for some air. The days were getting longer and I liked to enjoy the twilight time. I have a dislike of being confined indoors for long periods of time, and this was especially so when I was a young woman. The great mound of Arthur's Seat reared up behind us and there was a brisk wind. It was cloudy and cold but the sun broke through in intermittent shafts, bathing the black crags in a golden glow. I already felt uneasy in my heart as we neared the Palace gates. Something drew me, attracted by a dark shape pinned there.

Bothwell pulled me back, but I resisted his efforts.

A placard had been fixed to the Palace gates – a new one – tied with rope.

I drew close to inspect it.

A mermaid, her silvery blue tail curling out behind her, bare to the waist, long auburn hair flowing unchecked down her back. She bore a crown on her head. Beside her was a portrait of a hare, symbol of Bothwell's Hepburn lineage. There was a message this time, in clear Latin script which I could translate with ease.

Wantons marry in the month of May.

I looked about the empty grounds as if to locate the suspect then turned back to Bothwell, my husband.

"What does this mean?"

He was silent as he cut the placard down.

"There is another's hand behind this," I murmured quietly.

I thought of all those courtiers and advisers of mine who had chosen to absent

themselves – Maitland and my brother Moray among them.

"Pay it no need," Bothwell said, but I knew he was angry.

Rebellion
May 1567

The start of our married life was marked by three lonely weeks spent in Holyrood. The Palace had emptied itself as if a plague had swept through the corridors. Its rooms and corridors echoed to our solitary footsteps. Everyone fled, even those who had been close to me.

At night sleep forsook me and taking a candle, I would walk aimlessly through the great echoing chambers. I stood at the top of the staircase, looking down through the gloom. It was here they had dragged Rizzio's body, thrusting their daggers into him as they went. I could still hear his cries. They had dragged him along as if he was a lump of meat – until he fell silent – then they thrust him from a high window and flung his corpse onto the cobbles below.

Then I thought of Darnley's body being brought back here after the explosion at Kirk o' Field, how he lay still and white on a board after the embalmers had made him ready, and how young he had looked.

As a woman I fail to understand why violence should be resorted to so readily. It grieves me.

I glanced at the portraits of my own ancestors. Long chiselled noses, arched brows, superciliously cold eyes. What advice had they to give me? I had never known my father and his forebears; I had been parted from my mother at the age of five. I felt utterly oppressed by loneliness. I was surrounded by ghosts. Dead voices were the only ones I heard. It was perhaps at this point in my life that I first began to feel haunted.

The fireplaces in this Palace were vast, great yawning caverns one could stand up in, but none of them were lit. There were no servants left to tend them, and the season was not cold enough.

Holyrood had become a giant mausoleum, filled with monuments to the dead rather than the living. Those parties we had once held, the convivial evenings when we gathered in my small turret chamber to play cards and listen to music, left a faint indelible echo on the air. Those days were gone, together with their warmth and optimism.

My courage was failing me. The rooms and staircases and corridors seemed to be teeming with the past.

Most of the nobility had fled Edinburgh and were seething in almost open revolt, in far reaches of the kingdom, plotting against me. I was left only with the protection of Bothwell's men.

I took my candle and drifted back to the bedchamber where Bothwell lay.

I held my candle aloft and studied him. The glow must have wakened him because he reached out a hand and murmured. "Come to bed, Marie."

"I am restless," I whispered.

He opened his eyes, and fixed them on me. "You are safe here now."

I lay down beside him, and felt the warmth as he wrapped his arms about me.

"If only you had not forced me…" I whispered, "I believe I would have come naturally to love you if you had allowed me."

"Pah! We are here now, are we not?"

I asked him then if he was ever troubled by ghosts.

He did not know what I meant.

"What will we do?" I asked him.

He did not answer for a long time.

"We will wait."

We did not have much longer to wait. The following day our eerie peace was disturbed by an unexplained sound; the slamming of heavy oak doors below and the pounding of footsteps echoing up the staircase and along the corridor.

Bothwell's hand was immediately at his belt, locating his dagger.

I waited, remembering other nights when an intruder had forced their way into my private apartments.

A breathless dark-clad figure stood in the doorway, gazing at us.

We stared back.

On his livery was embossed the device of Lord Borthwick, which I recognized instantly.

"I have been sent to warn you…" he began.

"What news?" Bothwell said.

"The confederate lords are advancing on Edinburgh with a vast army," he cried.

One word breathed through the room.

Rebellion.

"They claim that they are intending to free Her Majesty from the clutches of the Earl of Bothwell."

Lord Borthwick's messenger paused for breath before continuing. "My lord urges that if you remain here at the Palace, Your Majesty will be a prisoner within hours, and Lord Bothwell will be killed."

It had come to this. I was a fugitive in my own kingdom.

We extinguished the candles and I threw a riding cloak over my shoulders, then we fled from the Palace without taking any possessions. We left everything behind. Except for one thing.

My prayer book and psalter, with its soft leathery covers and its crisply illuminated pages, was attached to my waist by a chain, as it still is, and from it I would not be parted.

As we hurried down the staircase the sounds of our own armed guards drifted up to us from below and this was some comfort and encouragement.

The confederate lords were greedy for rebellion but I had an army at my disposal which was renowned for their skill in battle. I was not without protection and I would not allow those men to overtake me.

I was, however, anxious for my son at Stirling. What if they got to him first and kidnapped him?

Outside, the courtyard began to fill with the reassuring clamour of men at arms, the jangle of harnesses, the stamping of boots, soldiers mustering for action.

Bothwell and I mounted our horses and rode away from Holyrood without further ado. When I glanced back at its windows, the Palace presented a bleak facade.

I remembered how I had first set eyes on it seven years ago. Now it seemed deserted, haunted almost.

We rode up the Canongate in the darkness, the houses silent on either side of us. Dawn was a long way off and as we clattered up the Royal Mile towards the Castle the rest of the town lay shrouded in an unearthly stillness. Not a chink of light appeared behind any of the shutters. When I glanced up at those grey tenements, I felt the weight of my own loneliness.

We approached the iron drawbridge over the steeply slanting cobbles and waited for the doors to be thrust open to admit us.

Instead, all was as silent as the grave.

Its grim dark walls excluded us.

We waited; the horses restless and impatiently pawing the ground.

Bothwell shouted up at the man in the postern to allow us entry, but a disembodied voice cried out of the darkness.

"I have been given orders not to allow anyone through tonight, sir!"

"What?"

There was a pause.

"But this is Her Majesty the Queen. Now open the gates at once."

"Sorry, sir," came the reply.

The rebel lords had already sent word through to Edinburgh to warn the warden not to allow us protection inside its walls. They wanted us defenceless.

I gazed up in silence at its dark mass, its gates apparently closed to me.

"Let me speak to the Keeper, God damn you," Bothwell bellowed. "The man is under my command. Now open the gates at once to Her Majesty the Queen."

"Sorry sir, but I have been given my orders already."

The voice quavered a little as he spoke, but Bothwell's men could not get at him, safely inside the castle walls as he was.

I had given birth to my son in that castle; now I was forbidden to enter.

"We must ride to Stirling," I said. "I must be with my son."

Bothwell turned his horse about. "They will not touch the Prince," he said.

"But I must be reunited with him."

"If we ride to Stirling, we may run the risk of encountering their guards. Stirling is too near Edinburgh."

"But…"

We stood outside the castle, our horses restless and nervously pawing the cobbles. I could see the weaponry of Bothwell's men glinting in the darkness around me, but it was useless without the protection of castle walls. We had no shelter, no refuge, and my enemies were moment by moment advancing on Edinburgh.

"Borthwick Castle," Bothwell said. "We will ride there first, and after, try to raise enough troops to make it to Stirling."

My thoughts raced. What if the rebel lords held my son hostage and forbade me to see him again? They could capture him and choose a Regent amongst themselves. The fact that I was their anointed Queen did not carry any weight with them.

We turned our horses about and raced from Edinburgh. Once in the saddle and galloping at speed through the darkness, my spirits lifted. I would not let these rebels defeat me. I would see them to the doors of Hell and back.

I had no time left for tears or self-pity. Revenge was my purpose.

Borthwick Castle
June 1567

We rode on through the night for mile after weary mile, across the bare-backed hills, until we came to a deep fertile glen. Here I saw the twin towers of Borthwick rearing up grey above the dark foliage.

Lord Borthwick's castle stood entrenched in its own wilderness, a vast tumbling undergrowth, quite unlike much of the rest of Scotland. That night it was varnished with a bright film of moonlight. It was perched on a rocky eminence and moated around by the waters of the Gore. This, we felt, would offer adequate protection.

My heart was sore with thinking of my son in Stirling and I was equally troubled by the babe in my womb and the fatigue I did feel. How would either of these two creatures fare in this kingdom of mine, torn as it was by strife and factionalism?

Lord Borthwick met us in the inner courtyard with such warmth and hospitality that I was deeply moved.

"No one knows we are here," Bothwell informed him.

"And nor shall they," Borthwick breathed. "You will be

safe here, Your Majesty, until we can muster enough support to challenge the confederates. They are men of evil intent. Turn-coats. They have no real beliefs, other than the thought of saving their own skin and lining their own purses."

Then he noticed how pale I was and the way I held myself, in pain almost.

"Come, Your Majesty needs rest. I will instruct the servants to make a chamber ready for you."

As we walked across the hall to a winding stone staircase I heard him murmuring to Bothwell, "Her Majesty seems exhausted."

"She has been unwell of late, and the strain is beginning to tell…"

Their voices faded as they moved away from me.

He led us to a high chamber at the top of a turret, connected to the main rooms by a very narrow staircase.

"Your Majesty will be safer up here," he indicated "in case you should have need to hide from our enemies in the night."

I glanced at him.

"They will not think of coming here, Your Majesty," he assured me quickly. "Of that, I am certain. You are safe in our hands."

"And if they do trace us here?" I asked.

Borthwick turned and looked me in the eye.

"Then we will defend you, Your Majesty."

I bowed my head in gratitude. Once alone, I lay down in the small chamber to sleep as I was truly exhausted.

Bothwell must have joined me during the night, for come morning I found myself in his arms.

A servant knocked at the door with a pitcher of water.

I had no clothes other than those I was wearing when I fled Edinburgh.

I rose and looked out of the narrow slit of the window at the greenery of the glen beyond. There was no glass in any of the windows here. I had lain all night calmed and soothed by the sounds of nature from outside, the background rumble of the River Gore, the constant trickle of water from a burn nearby, the shriek of an owl, then the beginnings of birdsong as the dawn chorus got underway, the odd flutterings and stirrings among the trees. I felt at peace for an instant, and yet my eyes began to search the undergrowth for any rogue movement which might indicate danger or an intruder.

It had become unnaturally hot during the night, temperatures steadily rising. It was strange weather which we were not accustomed to experiencing in Scotland, and my gown felt soiled with sweat.

I made to clean myself with the pitcher of water as best I could, having no ladies nearby to help me. Bothwell watched in silence. Somehow, the normal protocols of our life had been stripped away and we were left with this intimacy.

Summer had thickened the ivy clinging to the high stone walls and tendrils of it poked through the bare window. There was also convolvulus, white trumpet flowers, folding in on themselves during the night and opening again by day. Their snowy bloom whitened the green beneath our window and their musky scent drifted up to us.

At midday Bothwell and I descended the spiralling stone staircase and found that Borthwick and some of his retainers were waiting for us in the great hall below. A table was laid with victuals and a jug of watered-down ale.

My nausea had left me and I suddenly realised how ravenous I was. The flight from Edinburgh had given me an appetite and I fell upon the food offered.

Borthwick, the perfect host, poured more ale into our glasses.

"What do you suppose has happened in Edinburgh, in our absence?" I asked Borthwick.

He hesitated before replying. "They will have surged into the capital by now, taken possession of the Castle, the Palace, the Exchequer House."

"Then they hold the keys to my kingdom," I said.

Bothwell and Borthwick were silent. They could not offer me false hope.

"We will defy them to the last, Your Majesty. We are not done yet."

"What do you imagine their intentions are, Borthwick?" I asked.

It was a few moments before he ventured to speak. "I think, Ma'am, that their motives are mixed. There are men among them who were close to Your Majesty at one time."

"And where is Moray in all of this?" Bothwell asked.

Borthwick nodded. "I do not wish to alarm Your Majesty, but it is possible they plan to use Prince James – as a pawn."

I felt the air leave my chest and I half-rose in my chair, unable to still the panic I felt. "I must somehow make it to Stirling Castle. My Lord Bothwell, we have to…"

"First, we must defeat our enemies, Ma'am. Then we will ensure that Prince James is safe. If we ride to Stirling now, we ride straight into their trap. They will be waiting for us, expecting Your Majesty to do just that."

"We will play a waiting game," Bothwell said. "They'll not outwit us, Mary."

I marvelled at his confidence.

"How dare they use my son and rise up against their Queen – in his name."

All day we waited.

"They will not find us here," Bothwell insisted. "We will send out scouts and see what they are about!"

A tangible pall of heat lay heavy on the air. I looked out the crack of the window onto the great lonely glen beneath.

That evening, with a furtive moon rising over the treetops, we sat down to another meal in the banqueting hall. Its high stone rafters arched above us in the gloom like the buttresses of a giant cathedral.

The servants were kind and when the heat became intense I bade them take their rest.

The long windows overlooked the deep glen beneath, which fell away in natural tiers and terraces. It was lit by moonlight. Inside, candles threw colossal shadows up the bare walls.

Sitting here, soothed by the taste of the ale, I could believe that everything would be alright, that my son and I would be reunited; my followers would ensure that those who rose against us would be dealt with.

Those few hours at Borthwick Castle were a small respite. I remember them well: the atmosphere, the seclusion, the sense of peace despite my great troubles. It was a haven, I suppose, and I have not forgotten the man – Lord Borthwick – who provided that haven.

However, there was one disadvantage to Borthwick Castle. Surrounded as it was by the waters of the Gore, the roar of water could obscure other sounds. This made me uneasy.

It was as we sat at table together, by candlelight, that our peace was disturbed. I chanced to glance out of a window at the darkening glen and thought I saw a flash of movement in the bushes beyond, something glinting.

Borthwick was sitting back at his ease, glad to be entertaining his Queen and her consort. I sat rigid, peering into the dark where shapes and outlines were becoming more vague.

I stood up and moved towards the window, just as one of Borthwick's men burst into the hall with the news that the rebel lords had been seen in the glen.

"They've surrounded the castle walls!" he declared.

Borthwick's countenance changed and he rose in silence to follow his steward out onto the staircase. "I will speak with them." he said, as he left.

Bothwell and I were left to wait alone in the banqueting hall. His face was pale in the smoky candlelight.

"I am well punished for having loved you," I murmured.

He looked at me then glanced away. We heard voices below, but could not make out the import of their dialogue.

"They will not hurt you, Marie," he said after a while.

"You cannot be certain of that!"

Borthwick returned in a few moments. His countenance was grim. "They are requesting that Lord Bothwell be brought out to them," he said. "They are suggesting that their quarrel is not with the Queen, but with her husband."

"And do you believe them?"

Borthwick shrugged. "It is true I would not trust any one of them with my own life, let alone Your Majesty's."

I glanced at Bothwell.

He looked wary; I saw in his face a shadow of doubt or suspicion. He expected me to feed him to the lions, to abandon and forsake him. I saw it all in an instant, and in that same instant my heart contracted and expanded. He was the father of the child in my womb and as such, I would not forsake him. I had married him against my own wishes; it had been a matter of coercion, but I was not without affection for him and I would not deny the man as my husband. I did not like to see him look so fearful.

I took Bothwell's hand and spoke to him hastily. "You must escape alone. Now! Otherwise they will never let you leave here."

Then I turned to Lord Borthwick. "Do they know that Bothwell is here?"

Borthwick shook his head. "I told them I had no guests, but they refused to believe me. They just repeated their demand that Lord Bothwell be given up to them."

"Then there is still time."

Bothwell turned to our host. "Is there another way out of the castle?"

"There is a postern in the southern wall. It leads out onto a steep escarpment of loose stones. They will not expect anyone to exit from there. If you can negotiate the scree and make your way to the bottom, then keep to the undergrowth and trees on that side, you may escape notice."

"It is true that they will not expect me to escape alone," he said.

The banqueting hall burst into movement. As we hastily equipped Bothwell with a pouch of water and some oats, a cloak and weapons, he turned to me and began to issue instructions.

"Mary, if I manage to evade the lords outside, I will make my way to Black Castle. Meet me there in three days' time if you can. Then we will ride on to Dunbar and from there send out a summons across Scotland to muster an army against them. The Catholics in the north will rise up."

I nodded, and whispered "Black Castle. In three days' time."

"Borthwick here will give you an armed escort. You will not be alone, but go in disguise. It can be done, Mary."

Then he kissed me swiftly on the forehead, and was gone.

We watched, breathless, from the southern wall as he sped

down the side of the steep escarpment. I listened for the sound of a cry and the clatter of men-at-arms, but there was nothing, just a scattering of loose stones as they clattered downwards. I held my breath again. Would that alert any guards posted nearby?

I watched the darkness swallow Bothwell. He was on foot and alone. When he was finally out of sight I turned back to my host, Lord Borthwick. "Let me speak with them!"

I went out alone onto the battlements of the tower and gazed down on the cluster of rebel knights gathered beneath.

They fell silent at my sudden appearance. Perhaps they were surprised that I went unaccompanied.

I looked down on them, their weapons glinting in the moonlight. I scanned the crowd carefully. I could see Morton, Ruthven and Lindsay among their number, the very same who had murdered my friend Rizzio, and whom I had pardoned on Christmas Eve at my son's baptism in Stirling, on the advice of Maitland and Moray. The cruel irony of them appearing here now, below this castle, to threaten me, was a bitter pill to swallow. I had shown them mercy, as requested by my closest advisers: they themselves had undoubtedly had a hand in the explosion at Kirk o' Field which killed Darnley – and yet here they were now! They had the bare-faced audacity to challenge me here in my own kingdom, and claim to 'free' me from the clutches of my husband.

I called down to them through the gloom. "What is it that you want with me, gentlemen?"

There was a ripple of unease among them before Lindsay spoke. "Our quarrel is with the Earl of Bothwell, not the crown!" he bellowed up the steep side of the castle walls. "Send him out to us…Ma'am!"

"I will do no such thing!"

There was more movement below and some discussion. Then another, Kirkcaldy of Grange spoke. "We are here to request Your Majesty to abandon your husband and accompany us back to Edinburgh!" came the cry from the darkness beneath.

"For what reason?" I called.

"We have occasion to believe that Your Majesty is in thraldom…"

"I am no one's captive, Ruthven – other than this crowd massed here below. That is the only threat I feel – although I thank you for your *consideration*."

I oiled the final word with plenty of venom.

"We must insist, Your Grace, that you meet our request. Abandon Bothwell here and return with us to Edinburgh!"

"And why on earth do you imagine I would comply with such a *request*? Am I a subject that I should take orders from you? I do not think so, my lords."

Lord Borthwick, apparently unable to bear this abuse of my person any longer, suddenly appeared on the ramparts beside me and shouted down, "The Earl of Bothwell will be long gone by now. He escaped early this morning."

There was a pause as they allowed this piece of information to sink in.

"And why should we believe you?" Ruthven called back.

"The man is a scoundrel!" Borthwick shouted. "What would you expect?"

We heard the jangle of harnesses and the pawing of the horses against the ground as Lindsay turned in his saddle. "You have no choice, Your Majesty. You will need to comply in the end! You must leave Bothwell to his fate and come with us!"

"I shall not abandon my husband at your bidding!" My voice rang out across the darkness of the glen.

"It will be to your own destruction!" he roared back, his voice bouncing off the tower and echoing in the depths of the lonely forest behind him.

I stayed up on the battlements, listening until the last of them had begun to move away.

"I do not trust them!" Lord Borthwick said at my side. "They will not go far."

"Let us hope Bothwell has escaped!"

I wondered if I would ever see Bothwell alive again.

Journey to Black Castle
June 1567

Not all of the country was against me. The Protestant lords – and Knox, of course – resented the idea of a Catholic queen and took great delight in trying to bring me down. But there were others in Scotland who did not approve of their rash actions and were not fond of Knox's heretical diatribes.

The odds seemed stacked against me, here in this remote corner of my kingdom. However, I was not yet ready to be controlled by my enemies. I would resist them with the last breath emanating from my body.

We waited until we could be sure that the rebel lords had disappeared, then the following night I prepared to make my escape. I borrowed the clothes of one of Borthwick's retainers and in my room in the tower I shed the gown I had been wearing since I left Edinburgh. With my height and slender figure, it was easy to pass myself off as a young man. I am quite broad across the shoulders and have a narrow waist. In my youth I was very agile; I would think nothing of riding all day in the saddle with hardly a break.

My nausea had left me and I felt focused.

One of Borthwick's female servants attended to me and passed me a small, distorted looking-glass.

"Thank you, Meg," I said, and smiled. She had been kind to me since our arrival at Borthwick's castle, and I appreciated this.

"Do I pass as a young man, do you think, Meg?"

"Easily, Your Majesty." she murmured.

I stared in amazement at my reflection. It was Darnley's ghost who stared back at me. We were cousins of the same blood, he and I, and the resemblance shone through, as I stood there dressed in the garb of a young nobleman. My long auburn hair was bound tightly beneath the brim of a broad velvet cap and I had a great warm plaid to arrange and wrap around my person. This would be my only bedding for the night, as I ventured across country on foot along the most remote paths we could find.

"I wish that My Lord Borthwick would let me accompany you, Ma'am. There will be no female company to offer you comfort."

"That's a kind thought, Meg, but it will be best if I go alone. It is a dangerous journey."

"Will you be safe, Your Majesty?"

"I have every intention of remaining so, Meg." I smiled, "I have no desire to fall into their hands…"

Meg looked angry and muttered, "Traitors and cut-throats! They would sell their own mother if the price was right."

Borthwick had chosen a young guard to accompany me.

"He will defend Your Majesty with his life. Your Grace has nothing to fear," Borthwick assured me.

I bid goodbye to his servants and retainers who were

gathered in the great hall. The expressions on their faces were sombre; I knew that they feared for my safety and I was grateful for this show of deference and support.

Then I bid farewell to my kind host in the darkness of the inner-courtyard, the shadow of the tower looming over us. "I will not forget your kindness," I told him.

I could hardly see him in the shadows now, but I heard him murmur, "Your Majesty deserves better than this!"

"God bless you. It will be an adventure," I assured him. "I am in no doubt that I will arrive in one piece at Black Castle and we shall meet again to rise against our enemies. And then you and your kind will be rewarded," I finished.

We turned away into the darkness, my young guide and myself. Like Bothwell, I was on foot and almost alone. We slid our way down the steep side of the escarpment, listening out for returning horses the while.

We floundered across the moat, and struggled up the other side through the wild greenery of the glen. My clothes were damp and dripping with fetid river-water.

"Do not worry, Your Majesty," my young guide, Euan, assured me. "Your plaid will dry quickly enough in this heat."

I looked at him. I could not believe that he alone was the only soldier to protect me against the hostile forces ranged against us. The thought seemed incredible; if the rebel lords could have known how vulnerable I was at this point, they would never have left their post outside Borthwick's castle but swooped upon us like a hawk.

We stumbled on through the undergrowth, while the bats did glide in the air around us, and the owls screeched.

We had not gone many yards when I saw something that made me freeze. A figure standing out stark against the trees.

A guard had been posted here.

I crept backwards and motioned to my guard who had seen him also. We crouched low and watched the solitary figure. He was watching and waiting, but he had not yet seen us.

We carefully retreated, back the way we had come, and took a different route, cutting south-east away from his line of vision, treading warily, softly, desperate not to make a sound. But it was inevitable. A twig snapped underfoot like a pistol shot in the darkness and we froze.

The figure turned his head, but he clearly was not as vigilant as he ought to be. He yawned in boredom, having assured himself that this was merely a sound of the night, and continued his vigil.

We crept on in relieved silence.

When we were confident that we had put a good enough distance between ourselves and the sentinel in the trees, we stopped and listened. Complete silence met our ears. An owl screeched and I could feel the skin on the back of my neck prickle. I was aware of the swoop of leathery bats' wings, gliding almost silently on the night air. The whisper of them caught my ears now and again.

We remained cautious in fear of other guards posted in the woods. They might well be watching for the flurry of an escaping figure on horseback. They would not expect Her Majesty to venture out into the night alone and on foot, disguised as a man.

We walked on in silence all that night. My guide was able to follow the direction of the stars and moon, and used these to navigate our way in the dark. When day broke we lay down to rest in a hollow where we could be confident no one would pass. I lay my head in the heather, wrapped the plaid around me and slept. When I woke, we drank river-water and I ate the oatcakes that Euan offered me. Then we continued our journey.

We saw no one.

I was alone, other than this one companion who guarded me. Part of me was exhilarated by the journey, despite the hardships of hunger and thirst, and sleeping rough on the heather. The anonymity of it held a certain charm. I had shed the trappings of royalty.

At last. If only for a brief moment.

When night fell again, I wrapped the plaid about me and lay on the coarse heather which prickled and scratched my back. As I gazed up at the star-filled sky I felt free, despite the fact I was evading my enemies, men who would seek to capture and imprison me if they could.

I felt humbled by the grandeur and ferocity of this wild landscape through which we forged a path. I was dispossessed, more naked than the day I was born. For at my birth I could already boast a great number of titles, honours, castles, future responsibilities, my life mapped out before me…whereas now I had nothing but my wits to guide me, as well as the expertise of my faithful guard Euan.

The summer-scorched land around me was wild and remote. I loved it. I felt unencumbered, even in my distress, capable of flight. Maybe a small part of me wanted to stay in that wilderness, eating plain oats, sleeping on heather in the open air, the friendly sky as a canopy above my head.

It could not last, of course.

I was never free to be myself, but was destined from birth to carry the burden of royal responsibility.

It was an arduous and difficult journey. Often I wondered if we were lost, and partly I did not care. Perhaps I would never be found again, but would remain here forever, wandering the countryside.

We headed due east and kept our heads. We hardly spoke.

On our fourth night in the open, exhausted in every muscle and limb, we spied a stark fortified donjon on the skyline.

Euan stopped and pointed ahead.

"Black Castle," he said.

Bothwell had promised he would be waiting here with horses and an escort to ride us to Dunbar. I laboured on through the gloom and the castle keep loomed larger above me. The drawbridge was down and we walked cautiously forward, two lone figures in the dark with all this oppressive silence around us, uncertain of what to expect.

Suddenly from the portcullis a figure leapt forward, taking us by surprise.

I gasped and Euan murmured evasively, "Her Majesty has come for her escort."

The shadows seemed to come alive with more figures breaking away from the walls and assuming the shapes of humans and horses.

I heard a familiar voice amongst them. "It is alright. She has come!"

Bothwell's voice.

He came towards me.

"I half did not expect to see you here!" I said.

"You did not?"

"I was not sure if you would have met with disaster along the way."

"I promised, Marie, did I not?"

"Promises are easily broken. I have learned that before."

He led me towards the horses. "Come. There is no time to rest."

"But Her Majesty is tired," Euan protested.

"We cannot take that risk. We need to leave immediately.

We have horses ready. Can you manage the journey, Marie?"
he asked me.

"I am exhausted."

"We need to reach Dunbar before they close in."

"Then let us leave now."

"My wife has a fighting spirit," Bothwell announced.

And so we continued our journey from Black Castle and
thence to Dunbar, with hardly a pause. I was merely glad of a
horse to ride and the compulsion to flee did keep the fatigue
from overwhelming me completely, despite the burden of
what I carried in my womb.

As we rode on in the dark, a tiny doubt occupied my mind.
When we paused at a burn to allow the horses to drink, I had
occasion to speak quietly with Bothwell, away from all the
others.

"When you left me, Bothwell, were you sure that I would
escape the confederate lords? They were ringed all around
Borthwick Castle."

"I know your ingenuity, Marie. I knew you would outwit
them."

"You could not have been certain."

"You have done it before. And you will do so again."

"And what if I hadn't escaped? What if I had fallen into
their hands?"

I could feel his eyes on me in the darkness, his hands
loosely holding the reins. "Then I would have raised an army
to rescue you."

Would that I could believe his lies!

And yet, they were not lies, merely misplaced confidence.
He did try, I heard, even from the Netherlands where he fled
in the end.

But here in Fotheringhay I gave up believing in Bothwell
long ago.

It is many years now since his death, and I wait to catch a glimpse of his ghost. So far he has never haunted me here in my cell. His restless soul, it seems – unlike those of Knox and Darnley, and my brother Moray – is strangely at peace.

Dunbar
June 1567

It was a relief to be riding swiftly over the cumbersome ground instead of stumbling on foot. To ride was like flying, and it is painful to me that I am largely deprived of this occupation since I became Elizabeth's 'guest'. In my youth I rode like any man, and better. It was one of my greatest pleasures in life.

My horse flew through the night, skilfully clearing rocky obstacles, never stumbling, never faulting.

Bothwell had sent out scouts to check the way ahead was safe. One of them came back with the news that a rebel contingent were still on the prowl in the area, so we took the long route to Dunbar, skirting the Lammermuir hills to the north. We hoped this would throw them off the scent.

It was three in the morning when I saw the sturdy fortress of Dunbar etched in black against the horizon. The sky behind was just beginning to catch fire, spilling its radiance across the sea.

Bothwell was riding ahead of me, but he turned in his

saddle on seeing the castle and shouted a command to the men at the back. As he did so he caught my eye.

The castle stood proud and substantial on its ridge of irregular black rocks. Dunbar would ever more occupy an ominous and ambiguous place in my memory. Here Bothwell had forced himself upon me, making marriage between us inevitable.

Had he been patient and asked for my hand in marriage a third time – would I have accepted, persuaded by the growing warmth of my feelings? I have reflected on this often. I shall never know, of course, for Bothwell chose a different course of action. He was not a patient man. He was impetuous, impulsive, passionate.

A man with flaws.

Our horses were damp with sweat and my whole body was racked with fatigue, aching with exhaustion.

Once inside we sat down to a makeshift meal like a group of hungry fugitives, hastily devouring our food, too exhausted to talk. I could hear the surf pounding the rocks below, while dawn streamed through the narrow windows in golden threads.

There was a mood of optimism and cautious excitement. We had plans to raise a great army from here and recapture my capital. The rest of the country, the Catholics in the north, would rally under our banner and join forces with us to ensure that the crown remained safe from rebellion. Our ranks had already swelled since the night we fled Edinburgh pursued by the rebel lords. Many had joined us and more would follow. We had sent word out, urging all royalists to muster under Her Majesty's banner at Dunbar.

I looked at the men gathered in the great banqueting hall. There were noblemen and low-born alike, sitting at table together without respect of origin or lineage, a liberating freedom engendered by necessity. We were merely reacting to the moment, and all differences were expunged.

I felt reassured, moved by the readiness with which the country had responded. As I watched these men eat together, I felt queen of this country more than ever before. I could lead my men into battle and lead them to victory. My breast was full of unwomanly valour.

I have yet to see my sister Elizabeth display such physical bravery in the face of danger. Although I was with child, I did not allow this to hold me back.

As the day progressed, and more men streamed into the castle, I took myself off to a quieter room to gather my strength. Bothwell joined me. We could hear the distant rabble from the banqueting hall, the murmur of numerous voices and the clatter of utensils.

"The men are hungry," I observed.

"Aye, and ready for a fight! What is troubling you, Marie?"

"When you left me at Borthwick, part of me did not expect to see you again," I murmured.

"I know. You told me. What did you expect?"

"I know not."

I added, "If I am honest, I thought you might take your chances alone. I thought you would be in France by now, safe from all of this."

"And leave you to face the consequences?"

"Why not? It has happened before."

"But not by me. I have never abandoned you yet, have I, Marie?"

I was silent.

"You do not trust me!" he said sadly.

"I am not sure what I think. It is hard to trust a man who…" I hesitated, seeking the right words, painful as they were to speak, "forced himself upon me."

"I thought we had resolved that issue?" he said impatiently. "What else was I supposed to do if you would not see sense?"

"Let us not discuss this now," I said.

"Gladly!" he muttered as I swept past him.

The next day the whole of Dunbar rang to the sound of metal against stone. Heavily-armed troops surged through the courtyards and corridors of the castle. The entire fortress resounded with it.

There was a mood of tense excitement, nerves and fear under a hot summer sky. Temperatures continued to rise. It was hotter than I had ever known Scotland to be, since my arrival seven years earlier.

We went to sleep long before dusk, knowing that at dawn we would ride out early to meet our fate. Preparations had been made. We planned to advance on the rebel army before they had the opportunity to advance upon us. We would choose the battle site and thus gain the advantage.

I slept in Bothwell's arms that night though I did not know it would be for the last time.

He tried to erase my fears with easy assurances. "Just look at all the men who have gathered under your banner, Marie. You have so many supporters. They will not let you down."

"But the others," I said. "They are so determined." I shook my head. "Do you think that even if we win the day tomorrow, they will ever leave us alone?"

"Think of victory," he said. "Not defeat! God has promised us a victory tomorrow."

"I have never taken you for a religious man before now, James."

"I am not!"

"What will we be certain of this time tomorrow?"

At first light I was woken by the swell of the waves against the rocks and the sounds of noisy preparation below. Although it was not yet dawn, it was already too warm, a sultry closeness, which did not bode well for battle.

What would this day bring?

Carberry
June 1567

I rode out before dawn at the head of a substantial force, leaving Dunbar behind. I was clad in armour and the attire of any fighting soldier.

Carberry Hill is a name I shall never forget. The Battle of Pinkie had been fought on the site of this hill, twenty years earlier when King Henry of England was launching his bloody raids over the border, and a trench still lay at the foot of the incline as evidence, like a raw wound in the landscape. It was these raids which had forced my mother to pack me off to France at the tender age of five, for my own safety. We had been separated ever since, other than those two visits she made to the French court. Was this an ill omen, that we had chosen such a site for our encounter?

We had heard that the rebel lords had left Edinburgh and were advancing upon us, so we lined up on Carberry Hill in readiness, the trench before us like a slit throat. My army covered the crest of the hill, the silver of their armour glinting in the early dawn light. I sat astride my horse, beside Bothwell, the rampant red lion of Scotland floating on the air above me to mark my position among the troops. I turned my head and looked at the men either side of me. No one spoke. We stood still and waited for the enemy.

There were no birds calling, despite the heat and the early hour.

It was hot and close, and I felt my nerves build.

We could hear them long before we saw them, their kettledrums pounding as they slowly advanced. The hairs on the back of my neck prickled, but we stood our ground. The noise was distant but loud, thrumming through the earth and making the trees shake where they stood.

From our elevation above the plain we could see the countryside for miles around and between the trees I began to see movement. The rebel army was coiling like a snake through Musselburgh. The beating of their drums was terrifying and I could feel the fear rising in the men around me.

I could also see the Pinkie Burn winding its way in peaceful loops between banks of willow, sedge and reeds, and then the densely wooded banks of the Esk further away, but closer still came the ranks of the rebel army. On and on they came, as the sun began to rise behind them.

"How many of them are there?" a voice muttered.

There were murmurs of apprehension from our own army, and a cautious silence as we viewed the opposition. It seemed to take them an age to advance. They came on and on and then finally stopped on the other side of the trench. A white silk banner was borne above their heads.

I screwed up my eyes. "What is that?" I asked.

Bothwell conferred with his men and someone handed him a field glass.

"There is a picture and an inscription, Your Majesty!"

"And what does it say?"

Bothwell hesitated before replying. "I think it is meant to represent your husband, Ma'am."

I looked at him, askance. "My *husband*?"

"Your *last* husband, Ma'am!"

With some reluctance he went on to explain, "It shows him lying on the ground next to the house at Kirk o' Field, with your little son, Prince James, kneeling beside him, praying."

"Praying?"

There was a silence.

I snatched the field glass from him and peered through it. "How dare they use my son in this fashion?"

I could see a banner unfurling from the little Prince's mouth with the words '*Judge and Avenge my cause, O Lord!*' painted upon it.

My countenance grew pale. "They take my son's name and claim to be acting on his behalf, as if he seeks to avenge the murder of his own father? When it is they…*they* who sought Darnley's murder in the first place? What *hypocrites* are they?"

I remembered Craigmillar and our secret meeting, all organized and convened by my brother Moray and my then Secretary of State, Maitland – he who could now be seen mingling with those gathered below.

The hypocrisy felled me in one blow. I could barely catch my breath. They were claiming to fight their battle in my son's name.

Fotheringhay Castle
October 1586

Here in this damp, chilly chamber, the fire smouldering low in the grate, I have had time to reflect on the vicissitudes of life and the conclusion I have come to is this. If they were seeking to avenge anyone's cause, then the God they serve is unjust.

I am not afraid.

I have suffered so many injustices at the hands of men that my rage has turned cold inside my icy breast. I am done with men like Maitland and Morton and the rest of them. I have nothing more to say to them.

When the last trumpet sounds, I will confront my God and demand to know why he has withheld his compassion all these years while my tormentors and captors were allowed to go free?

Is that a sin?

To demand the truth of God?

To demand answers?

I do not understand why those men felt able to accuse me when they themselves were guilty of the crime. Their souls were blackened with the deed, their hands bloodied. Darnley's blood was smeared all over their consciences, and yet they felt able to stand on their moral rectitude – with Knox's backing – and accuse me!

I have had years in which to dwell on these injustices, nights in which to pray for guidance and absolution.

My gilded prayer book hangs still at my waist. I open its delicate pages to extract what comfort I can.

I kneel and I pray, but the answers are few.

Carberry
June 1567

The sun rose higher in the sky and neither side made a move.

I could make out Morton below, moving amongst the ranks of the mercenaries, clad in silver armour. I could see his dark brow, the long beard flowing over his breastplate. I took my sword out of its sheath and felt the heavy weight of it, hot metal hissing through the air. How I longed sometimes to have been born a man – like my brother Moray.

My hatred for that man, Morton, was so intense I thrilled at the idea of spilling his blood. For a brief, dizzy moment I imagined myself running my sword through him, pinioning him to the ground.

But there would be no blood shed that day.

As the sun steadily climbed higher in a cloudless sky, it shone directly into our eyes. It began to glint against the armour, blinding us with its glare.

The men grew thirsty and hot, but there was not a bit of shade to be had on Carberry Hill. When we chose our site, we had not anticipated the heat or the need for shade.

When I rode out of Dunbar that morning my spirits were high, but it was not a noble battle we fought. Neither side was eager to engage in combat. We confronted each other across the Pinkie Burn, wary and hostile.

A stalemate.

We waited.

They waited.

Hours passed and nothing happened, although the men grew thirstier and hotter beneath their armour.

Towards midday as I rode through the ranks, I realised they had lost their enthusiasm for a fight. I noticed a group of them break away and wander off in search of shade. I hoped the rest of the men would not notice this defection.

In contrast, the forces below looked rigid, stern, ready for a fight; their white standard borne above the standard-bearers' heads with an air of self-righteous determination.

They were liars and they were hypocrites, but they were deadly serious.

They knew how to manipulate the facts to suit their purpose. They had stolen the advantage, manufactured a masquerade of lies to support their 'cause'. Their only cause, in fact, was rebellion, greed, the grasping of power.

At noon a party of horsemen detached itself from the main body of the troops below and rode towards me bearing a flag of truce.

"What do they want?" Bothwell muttered.

"We shall find out shortly," I replied.

Maitland was at their head and when they were still some distance off he dismounted and walked on alone, on foot. The harsh glare of the sun bore down on us all and he laboured his way slowly, looking hot and dishevelled.

I sat down on a block of stone to receive him, weary with the heat, and waited for him to come to us.

It seemed to take him an age, but at last he reached the summit and came towards me.

Then he dropped on one knee.

I looked at him. "I am surprised at this show of obeisance, Maitland. It is not what I would have been led to expect of you, lately, considering recent events."

"Your Majesty," he mumbled, mopping his hot brow with a handkerchief.

"We are unused to such heat, I fear," I offered politely.

"Indeed!" he said.

"So…you have come to ask…what? My forgiveness for your actions?"

"Ma'am," he eyed me coldly. "I have come as a mediator."

I opened my mouth to exclaim, "Oh, have you now?"

But he continued – "To ask that you abandon Bothwell, and having done so, the confederate lords do promise that they will then gladly acknowledge you as their Sovereign."

I paused, and waited, gathering my composure. It took an effort of will to contain my rage.

"Do they?" I said. "How very kind of them! I was under the impression that I was their Sovereign no matter whom I should choose as my husband – it being an unchangeable fact! I was also under the impression that the Sovereign need not be dictated to by the very same men who murdered…"

He interrupted me at this point. "I have not come here to quarrel with you, Ma'am. I have come with a view to peace."

I stared at him.

How to outwit such an oily manipulator of the facts? After all, I knew his worth. I had appointed him my own Secretary of State because I knew him to be a man of diplomacy and tact, deception and subterfuge. Do those qualities contradict each other? In Maitland they did not. He managed to balance the half-truths, lies and distortions and transform them into a reality of his own making.

"I am merely trying to acquaint you with the facts, Your Majesty."

"I know the facts, Maitland," I answered drily.

"This is what the confederate lords have stated as their truce."

"Truce?" I laughed. "Have you forgotten our meeting at Craigmillar?"

I looked him in the eye, but he glanced away, down at the rebel hordes below with their banner suspended in the windless air.

"Do you remember how I was allowed to remain in ignorance of the deed? What else did you decide that night after I left you all? How much did you keep from me, Maitland?"

He looked a little awkward, although I was wrong if I imagined him to be contrite.

"To rid me – and Scotland – of the problem of Darnley and when that was done, to rid yourselves of your monarch?"

"All of this is irrelevant, Your Majesty. What matters now is that…"

I cut him off. "What matters now is that you – and they – are gathered below, in defiance of your Queen."

"I am merely their spokesman," Maitland answered flatly. "If you wish to be restored then you must leave Bothwell. Declare him unfit to be your husband."

"And give myself over to an army of rebels?"

"Those are our terms."

"You care so much about Darnley's death, Maitland, when you were one of those who organized the same?"

"I care for the security of the realm. It is my job."

"And who appointed you?" I asked him.

"I am, of course, indebted to Her Majesty, it goes without saying, for allowing me to retain office, but I am obliged to remind you that I held office before you arrived on these shores."

"Ah, is that it?" My eyes glinted. "I am a foreigner still? And if I were more like my sister Elizabeth, down in England, I'd have sliced your head off for a traitor long ago."

He paled in shock. "Traitor is a strong word!"

"I trusted you, Maitland."

He faltered for only a moment. "Our cause is merely this. To avenge the King's death and bring the King's murderers to justice."

He and I both knew the emptiness of those fine words.

"You know as well as I do that half the men down there are guilty of Darnley's murder." I watched him. "Such hypocrisy doesn't worry you? Even before the eyes of God?"

"It is for your own safety, Ma'am!" he added weakly.

"For my own safety?" I laughed. "How you do turn things about, Maitland! It is for my own safety that you have taken up arms against me?"

Then I stood up and spoke loudly. "If you seek justice against the late King's murderers, you know where to find them." I glanced down at the enemy lords ranged below us. "Look to yourselves!"

Then I turned my back on him.

Bothwell had watched this exchange from a distance, but he came forward now with a proposal.

"If their quarrel is with me and not with Her Majesty then why not settle the affair by single combat? Select an opponent from within your own ranks, and I will fight him."

Maitland glanced at Bothwell with obvious disdain and looked to me for confirmation.

"I won't allow it," I said. "I will not be dictated to by rebels and traitors. Let them look to their own consciences."

Maitland rode away, disappointed.

"Why will you not let me fight in single combat, Marie?" Bothwell asked. "It could settle the affair without prejudice to yourself."

"Because I do not believe them. They seek to humiliate me."

The sun was directly overhead now and I could feel a blinding headache pulsing behind my eyes. It was oppressively hot. As I glanced around I realised that more of our number had melted away. Our forces were slowly diminishing, some drifting towards the Pinkie Burn to quench their thirst but not troubling to return. As the afternoon wore on, my courage began to fail me, and my hopes were dashed.

Far beneath us I could see they were taking Bothwell's offer of single combat seriously and lists were being drawn up.

I glanced upwards and saw that a line of enemy horsemen had cut off our retreat to Dunbar. They had crept round to the back of us to ensure we could not escape.

We were surrounded.

"It's hopeless, Bothwell," I said, calling him to my side. "Look!"

"I have no choice," I murmured. "We must accept defeat, or compromise."

"You cannot trust the rebel lords, Marie. You said so yourself. I tell you, let me fight one of them in single combat."

I shook my head. "No, Bothwell, they would not allow it to rest there. We must seek a different compromise. I am still their queen, their Sovereign."

I looked at him sadly with a dawning realisation in my eyes. Whether or not Bothwell knew it, those men below –

massed against us in their hundreds – would not allow us to remain together. The confederate lords would never accept him as my husband. With him at my side, I could not remain Queen. I needed to compromise.

I swallowed.

I felt suddenly bereft. I could not bear the thought of being alone, without his support.

He looked about. "We have lost a battle, Marie, but we have not lost the war."

I blinked away tears. "I am going to parley with Kirkcaldy of Grange. Of all the men gathered below, he is the most honourable. I know him. He is a gentleman and a man of his word. With him, I will reach a compromise."

"You cannot do this, Marie."

"I must. You know there is no other way."

He glanced around at the depleted forces. Those that remained were tired, hot and thirsty, weary of the consequences.

I called a messenger towards me and sent him down to the opposition, asking Kirkcaldy to come alone. We watched as the single rider approached the troops below and waited for their response.

"I will come for you, Marie," Bothwell said. "And I will raise another army. Be sure of that."

I nodded. "I know you will," I said.

The response did not come as quickly as I would have liked.

It was six o'clock in the evening when Kirkcaldy rode up the hill on his black charger. As I watched him approach, I felt Bothwell touch my arm. It was the last contact I remember having with him, before we would be severed forever.

Kirkcaldy ignored Bothwell when he approached, and spoke only to me. He knelt before me, his head bowed.

I watched him in silence.

When he had straightened again I spoke as calmly as I could.

"Avenging King Henry's death is a poor excuse for taking up arms against your sovereign, Kirkcaldy!"

He coughed and spoke quietly, "Your Majesty, it is said that you have allied yourself with a murderer."

I shook my head. "Bothwell is no murderer and I do not *ally* myself with him. He is my husband. We are lawfully wed. He is the…" I almost went on to add that he was the father of my unborn child, but something stayed my tongue.

Kirkcaldy softened. "If you will only come over to the Confederates, Ma'am, I can promise you – with my life – that all will be well, and the quarrel ended."

"Yes, Maitland said as much, but you know, I find it hard to trust his word of honour. That is why I have sent for you. I have reason to believe you are more a man of your word."

"Your Majesty," he said, lifting a hand to his chest. This was a gesture I have never trusted in a courtier and I should have recognized it now – but I did not. Perhaps Kirkcaldy truly believed that he could help matters.

"I am ready to consider their proposal," I said. "But what of Bothwell?"

"What about him, Your Majesty?"

"Will he be allowed to go free?"

Bothwell was watching and listening to this exchange, eager to interrupt, but Kirkcaldy would not look at him or acknowledge his presence.

There was a short silence.

"I cannot promise," Kirkcaldy began awkwardly.

I interrupted him. "Then I cannot agree to your terms. That is my condition. That Bothwell be allowed to go free."

I had an ulterior motive for such a request. There was my

concern for Bothwell's well-being as the father of my child, of course, but in addition to this was the half-conceived idea that I would have need of his support in raising an army once we had left the field of battle. All was not lost and I was far from giving up. I merely wanted the day to end without bloodshed or deadlock.

Kirkcaldy's eyes opened wider. He had evidently not hoped for as much as this. "Your Majesty can count on my word of honour."

"He will be given a safe conduct and allowed to leave the country if he wishes, unharmed?" I asked, following up my advantage.

"You have my word!"

Once free, Bothwell might be able to gather support from the Catholics abroad.

I turned my back on Kirkcaldy and approached Bothwell. "They will spare your life if I give myself up to them."

"It is madness. I don't trust him." He glanced at Kirkcaldy over my shoulder. "How can you be certain they will not try to depose you and act as Regent over your son?"

"I cannot be. But I have to take that risk. There is no other way, otherwise neither of us may be able to leave the field alive."

I glanced at Kirkcaldy wearily over my shoulder. "Tell the confederate lords I agree to their terms."

Kirkcaldy visibly swelled beneath his breastplate, so elated was he with his success. Where Maitland – the prince of diplomacy – had failed, Kirkcaldy, a down-to-earth knight, had succeeded.

I could not help but notice the gleam of satisfaction in his eyes as he turned to Bothwell, shook his hand and said, "I'd advise you to depart as quickly as you can. I give you my word you will not be followed or opposed."

How the men do reach their agreements, how they do ratify their bonds. It is often a language which excludes women, even those of us – like Elizabeth – who rule them.

Then Kirkcaldy mounted his charger and sped off, back to the enemy troops waiting below.

Once we were alone Bothwell turned to me, a look of remorse in his eyes. "All is not lost, Marie. We will see each other again soon."

"I think not," I murmured.

He took me in his arms then, a last embrace, while the tired soldiers of the two armies looked on. Bothwell did not care what they thought. He mounted his horse, and leant down to me. "I will raise an army," he whispered.

I said nothing, but watched him as he rode away.

For the first few yards I could almost believe this was not happening, but as he grew more distant I was hit by the powerful realisation that I really was alone. There was no one else on that lonely summit I could turn to.

The sun had not yet set, nor the heat of the day faded. I watched him – a solitary figure becoming smaller on the horizon. Then he was gone.

I had half-hoped that he might look back.

He did not.

I never saw Bothwell again.

I had reliable information afterwards that he spent some months trying to raise an army for me, but he was unsuccessful in his efforts. He fled to France and died ten years later in a prison cell in Denmark. They say he died a madman, fettered to a stake. Rumoured reports found their way to my secluded tower, for the story of our romance had become the stuff of legend and myth by then, but I listened with only half an ear. I knew to trust not such rumours. The warmest heart grows cold with waiting.

I entertained hopes for the first couple of years. I listened for the pounding of hooves, the jingle of a harness, but it never came. In the end I turned to other, fresh followers to champion my cause. I was never short of admirers who fell under the spell of Mary Queen of Scots. There have always been those ready to risk all for the sake of our cause.

I mourned Bothwell.

I mourn him still, to some extent.

But of him, I never speak.

No one will know the truth. I breathe not a word of that private and most intimate of stories. Except perhaps to the forlorn ghosts who haunt me here, and they will not repeat it to a living soul. I can be certain of that.

Since his death I have oft wondered if he would appear in ghostly form, along with the others – Knox, Darnley, Morton, my brother Moray. But there is no sign of him.

It is my hope that Bothwell loved me enough to leave me in peace.

Fotheringhay Castle
October 1586

Darnley's ghost detaches himself from the shadows and leans towards me.

"I didn't come here to seek vengeance, or to hurt you."

"You've nothing to seek vengeance for, Darnley. I never did you a wrong turn, and I certainly had no hand in your murder. If there were a court of law here now, they could acquit me of any part in it. If they had a mind to."

He sniffs and reaches out a long white finger towards the missive on my table.

"What's this?"

I turn the parchment away from him.

"More plotting?"

"If others should plot on my behalf, what is that to me? Can I control it?"

Darnley's ghost smiles.

"You are a canny one, Mary. Always were."

You think?

"Bothwell stays away because he doesn't love you. Never did."

Darnley's words sting. I remember when Bothwell was my friend, and the one loyal supporter I could rely on.

I try to hide my disappointment.

When Bothwell took me to Dunbar Castle, and I found out what his real motives were, it was a rude shock to the system. But it is not something I care to share with Darnley or anyone else. That is a secret I will bear with me to the grave.

When they tell stories of us, and sing songs and invent ballads about us, they will be merely guessing. I will not apprise them of the facts. I will not tell them of how my heart was broken – not because he left me, but because he did not wait to win my hand by fair means. He stole it instead. By fair means or foul, he decided he would have me. It could have been by fair means if he had exercised just a little more patience. That was a shock I struggled to recover from. But none shall know of it.

Abduction and ravishment are not topics for polite conversation.

I lift up the parchment that lies curled at my side.

"You are a very persuasive phantom, Darnley. But I do not believe you are really here."

He sighs.

"Besides, it makes little difference in the end. If I escape from here…"

"What do you mean, escape?"

I ignore him.

"Do you still dream of escaping?"

"I was very good at it, in the past. There were a few times

I slipped the net when they least expected it. I am skilled at it."

"You are being foolish, Mary."

"I have letters sent to me. And I reply."

"Letters?" he scoffs. "Do you think they have not been intercepted and copied before they go on to reach their destination? Lord Burleigh knows what he is about. He even plants the ideas in your head, and you do not know it. They have a whole wad of evidence against you."

"I care not."

"If you put your hand to that letter, Mary, you will die."

"It is nothing, merely a proposal. And I am agreeing with it – that is all."

"A proposal to rock the throne of England?"

"To escape from where they confine me! Is that wrong? Would not any sovereign do the same?"

He shakes his head.

"Besides, my actions are endorsed by God."

"My murder had the blessing of Parliament, but that did not make it right."

"Parliament is not the same as God, Darnley. You ought to know that. Divine law is another matter entirely."

"So you make up your own laws which are above those of man?"

"Don't be facetious, Darnley."

"You are misguided, Mary. And your dreams of escape will see you ruined."

"I am ruined already."

"Then they will see you to the scaffold."

I shrug. "It would be a welcome end to all my sufferings on this earth. My sorrows have been legion. Even our son denies me. If I could hasten my end, I would gladly do it. For in my end is my beginning."

Darnley gazes at me.

"What do you mean by that, Mary? Do you mean to become a legend?"

"I mean nothing. I mean only that I will hold my head high to the very last. And neither you nor anyone else will gainsay me. I have nothing to fear, and nothing to be ashamed of before God."

"Truly, Mary?" he asks.

I look at him, this unwelcome phantom who can never rest in peace.

"Truly."

Behind us we hear a door opening on heavy hinges. As I turn my head I hear Darnley's voice whisper, "I believe you!"

And that is the last I hear from him.

He is gone, vanished in the darkness.

Would that the rest of them would leave me in peace!

As the door opens wider to admit Paget and Jane Kennedy, my fingers reach out nimbly to hide the evidence. The scroll of parchment with Babington's proposal upon it is secreted safely within the folds of my clothing. It would be wrong to trust those closest to me, for it would put their own lives at risk.

My little dog Geddon paws the flags at my feet and nestles closer.

"Jane, I think he needs a walk."

"I will take him, Ma'am."

Carberry Hill
June 1567

When Bothwell was no longer visible on the horizon, I slumped onto the block of stone that had served as my throne all day.

The sun was beginning to set, gilding the treetops and the distant turrets and spires of nearby Musselburgh. I was hungry and thirsty, having eaten nothing since before we left Dunbar at dawn. It was still unbearably hot, even for this time of year.

I watched with indifference as Kirkcaldy left the rebel army beneath, having discussed with them our terms, and then came riding back up the summit to fetch me. He was quite the hero of the day. The other confederates were delighted with the success of his efforts although Maitland was perhaps a little put out.

"Ready, Your Majesty?" he gently prompted.

"I am ready."

I mounted my own horse and suffered him to lead it by the bridle as we made our way slowly down the hill.

By the time I reached the enemy troops, I glanced back up

at Carberry Hill to see who remained. It was deserted. They had all fled.

As we drew closer to the line of soldiers, I began to feel the first stirrings of doubt and misgiving. Had I made a mistake, a fatal error? Their faces looked stern, not kind. I waited for one kind word, for one of them at least to show some small sign of homage to their queen, but there was none forthcoming.

They showed me no respect.

They were loyal instead to Knox's tyrannical diatribe against the *Monstrous Regiment of Women*. He had won. He had coloured their hearts and minds.

I had been betrayed.

I began to hear faint whispers and murmurs.

"Burn her!"

The blood left my face and neck, but rage took hold of me.

"Burn the whore!"

I could not believe it.

I turned to Kirkcaldy then and said to him, "Is this your word, Kirkcaldy? Is this your honour?"

He glanced at me almost apologetically then melted away into the background to be replaced by the rabble of soldiers who surged forward. They pressed in on me. They had their white banner, with my own son on it, praying for vengeance. I leaned forward and grasped it in my fist.

"Is this what you believe?"

I pushed my way through the press of soldiers, a worthy opponent to any of them. They were cowards and I forced a passage through to where I could see Morton in the crowd.

I managed to get close enough in the confusion to cry out, "What is this then, Morton? I am told this is an attempt to seek justice against the King's murderers. And yet I am also told you are one of them!"

Lindsay appeared at my side then and I grabbed his hand. "I swear by this hand which is now in yours, I shall have your head for this. I shall see my revenge!"

Lindsay choked on his wrath, but felt unable to say aught in reply. I did not give him the chance.

I am ashamed to narrate what happened next, for it does not put my own subjects in a good light. It reveals them as cowards and turn-coats, lily-livered and vulnerable.

Perhaps we are all vulnerable, that is the kindest thought I can muster.

Before long I found myself surrounded by the ordinary soldiers who – at the command of their superiors – were permitted to vent their spleen on me. There were whispers and sighs, which grew to a tumult.

"Burn her! Burn the witch! Burn the whore!"

When I heard that word *witch* I trembled.

I could not see any of my former councillors and courtiers. Of Maitland, Kirkcaldy, there was no sign.

Lindsay came before me and held up the white banner. "This shall be borne before you on your journey," he said, his eyes like slits in his reddened face, "as evidence of your crime."

"My crime, Lindsay? What about yours?"

But he was gone, coward that he was, leaving the banner in the hands of those lesser soldiers who were happy to do the bidding of anyone who paid them enough. Mercenaries – every single one.

It was thus I found myself being forced from Carberry, site of that former battle, twenty years ago, all the way back to Edinburgh. I suppose it was a spectacle of amusement to some of those citizens who came out to stare: to see a queen so humbled, brought so low, is a pantomime not to be missed. Whatever their own thoughts or views on the subject, who would not want to stare?

This journey lasted from seven in the evening until ten o' clock at night. I was paraded before them, jostled and jeered at by the soldiers, the white banner with its self-righteous claim searing itself upon the minds of those who looked on. A piece of successful propaganda, it was a lie that has never been fully investigated. A murder mystery, which remains unsolved in the public imagination although I knew the answer long ago, as did those in the Scottish court who had signed bonds and secret agreements, who had conspired together to have Darnley removed. Having removed him they needed a scapegoat to blame. And while Knox was pointing the finger, what better scapegoat than a weakened sovereign? The Protestants were in ascendency and they knew how to pave the way.

We crossed the old narrow bridge of Musselburgh as the sunset bled its crimson crisis across the sky. On through the village of Niddry we rode, past the towers of Craigmillar where they had plotted at first to be rid of Darnley, where they had held secret meetings to discuss the threat he posed to the security of the realm. And all the way the soldiers – an ungodly rabble – taunted me with their insults. It took all my dignity and courage to hold my head high and ignore them.

We entered the city by one of the southern ports and they compelled me to ride past the ruins of Kirk o' Field. Did they truly believe that it was I who had plotted to blow up the house where he stayed, until not a stone was left remaining on another?

Lindsay, demon that he was, ordered the soldiers to pause here so that the Queen "could take stock."

I glared at him in disbelief, the man who had – along with others – burst in upon me in my private chambers only fifteen months before and slaughtered Rizzio in my presence.

But there was yet worse to come.

In the distance I could see that Knox, ever the opportunist, had chosen this moment to mark his victory and triumph over me. He ventured out from his web with a pack of mischief-makers at his back.

"Scotland has been bewitched!" he roared. "But now, by God's edict, I break that spell. I set the people free from their bondage that she…" he almost screeched now in his excitement "has put us under. But no more oan it, lassie. No more. Ye've had your day!"

I looked at him in astonishment, this consummate actor with his ghastly performances.

"What an angry God you serve, Master Knox," was all I said, but it was spoken so softly beneath my breath that I doubt he heard. He was too busy shouting withal.

"And now, let us pause to reflect on the sins and crimes of our sovereign!"

Lindsay stepped forward again, to stir up the rabble. "This is where our King met his end! Let us serve his memory by punishing the perpetrator of this dark deed!"

"Burn her! Burn the witch! Burn the whore!"

If I write this narrative in my own blood, will you believe me?

The procession moved on again, towards the town. I saw people pouring out of their houses, leaning from the windows and crowding the outside stairheads, but they did not join in flinging curses at me. They merely watched in astonishment.

"Leave her be!" a voice cried from above, and I glanced upwards hopefully.

I could not locate the owner of the voice.

They were too afraid to counter this rabble. Those who conveyed me through the streets of Edinburgh were the ones with the weapons in their hands, the weight of armour at their disposal. No one would dare defy them.

Any who still loved their Sovereign would need to wait a while before daring to express loyalty.

Night had fallen by now and I was fatigued beyond bearing. No one at this stage knew that I was with child. I carried my burden in silence.

Now that we were within the town I looked forward to regaining the sanctuary of Holyrood where I could at least rest from the inspection of the crowd. But instead of taking me to the Palace as Kirkcaldy had promised, they led me on, through the dark and narrow vennels to the Provost's House at the head of Peebles' Wynd, near the Cross. This was a bleak bare building, opening off a stair called the Black Turnpike.

I was then led down the steep stair and thrust into a small chamber, cell-like in dimension, thirteen feet wide and eight feet high, no bigger than an outhouse. There was one narrow, barred window, high in the wall, through which I could see the cobbles of the street and feet passing by.

I would have no privacy here.

I watched in shock as they banged the door shut behind me, and left me there. When I turned about I saw that I was not alone. Two armed guards stood in the darkness behind me. Evidently they were to share the room with me for the night.

I sat down on the narrow bunk provided and wept.

I had borne as much as I could bear.

As I dried my tears, I heard movement and noticed a handkerchief being thrust towards me.

I looked up.

One of the guards proffered it while the other stood by, looking at his feet awkwardly.

I thanked him.

Nothing more was said.

"I am thirsty," I said after a while.

The same guard rattled the bars and called out to those posted nearby. "Her Majesty is thirsty."

"If you show her too much compassion, they'll not like it," the other muttered.

"I care not! Look at her. She's undone."

"What are your names?" I asked them, through lips that were cracked and dry.

They hesitated. Perhaps they had heard tell of my ability to escape any trap.

"I only ask because you have been kind."

"*He* has been kind," the guard said, gesturing at his partner. "Not me!"

I made no remark to this, but when the other guard managed to procure a jug of water for me, I drank from it thirstily. It was dusty and impure, but to me it tasted like nectar.

The Black Turnpike
Edinburgh
June 1567

W hat little light there was fell into my cell through the bars, and through that barred window I could hear heavy footfalls on the stair. I glanced up in hope, espying the glint of armour in the gloom.

I took heart at first, but then I saw the owner of that shining breastplate. Lindsay's dark face appeared at the window, fixing the white banner in place.

"In case you should forget why you are here – Your Majesty!"

His dark outline blotted out the light for an instant then he left me. I was too exhausted to utter a rebuke. I lay down and closed my eyes against the wash of moonlight that filtered through the bars.

I could hear the confederate lords sitting down to supper in another part of the house, eating, feasting and drinking. Perhaps they were toasting their success. My stomach rumbled in protest. I had been offered nothing to eat or drink, except what the guard had procured for me.

Inside my womb I felt the child stirring and my thoughts flew to Prince James. Was he still safely in his nursery at Stirling Castle? Would the Earl of Mar protect him? Anxiety swept through me in waves and there was no comfort to be had in that bare cell, with the two guards watching from the shadows.

I heard movement.

When I opened my eyes I saw that they had lowered themselves to the floor and were sitting upright with their legs stretched before them.

They would need to sleep, as would I.

I glanced at those bars at the window, at the locked door.

Could I convince one of them to set me free?

Was Bothwell even now arranging a few loyal soldiers to enter Edinburgh by stealth under cover of darkness? How would he know where to find me?

Towards midnight I slept.

The early grey light of dawn filtered through the bars. I woke with a start, opened my eyes and blinked. I had not dreamt it then. This was the stark reality.

The guards still slept, their legs stretched out, though they had been commanded not to.

I picked myself up and reached up to the bars of the window. I could not quite see the stern black buttresses of St. Giles' High Kirk, even when craning my neck, but I knew it would be there, bathed in the early rays. I watched as the High Street slowly came to life.

I held my breath.

The world looked so beautiful outside, even in its poverty and misery and viewed from this angle, my eyes close to the cobbles. And yet I was confined behind bars.

The cruelty of that burnt into my soul, where it has left a mark ever since.

For nineteen years I have suffered the terrible torture of being imprisoned. I have longed for freedom, but longed in vain. I grow old by degrees and am quite diminished by age, which has come early due to my straitened circumstances. For nineteen years I have prayed to a merciful God, I have lifted my needle and thread and stitched elaborate tapestries for which I am renowned. And I have tried so hard to forgive those who have sinned against me, for it is what the law of God demands.

But it is not easy. Vengeance is never far from my heart.

My little dog, Geddon, is the most reliable companion I have. My servants are kind, and if my end comes soon I will remember them in my will. Let it never be said that Mary Queen of Scots does not repay her servants with kindness, nor pay her debts. I will speak to my brother-in-law in France and request that he pay them any wages they are owed, and although the Catholic princes abroad have not been able to free me from captivity, I know that my brother-in-marriage will fulfil my final request and see that my servants are paid in full. This will be some comfort to me.

Paget, Jane Kennedy, Elizabeth Curle…they have served me kindly at the last. However, I am aware that they sometimes think me 'touched' or mad.

I am not mad, merely haunted.

If I had fresh air, regular walks when I wanted, if I was free to choose my place of residence, this incarceration would be easier to bear. As I lift my needle and begin to sew, the bright threads slip through my fingers, and my thoughts slip through the air like gossamer, winged angels in flight.

A secret code finds its way into the letters I write. I labour still for a bright new future. I think of my son and how he has not cherished his mother's memory, but chose instead to believe the lies against me.

He broke my heart.

They took him from me: they moulded him in their own image.

My brother Moray got what he wanted in the end. He became Regent over my son for a time. I heard from ambassadors and the like that his tutors beat him at the command of Morton and others. They once gave me a portrait of my son when he was a child, and I saw in his eyes and his pale face that he was dealt with harshly. I could read it all there as clearly as if the artist had whispered the truth in my ear.

I focus on my future.

Elizabeth little suspects how one day soon the earth will be rocked beneath her feet.

Twenty years ago, in the Provost's House at the top of Peebles' Wynd, just off the High Street, I gazed out at the black cobbles steaming in the early morning sunrise, and I longed for freedom with a hunger that only the young can feel. I wanted to be outside. I cared for nothing but my freedom – and my desire to see my son again. I could see no further than that.

I remembered how Bothwell had come to my aid fifteen months before as we escaped from Holyrood during the night. He had waited with horses beneath the churchyard wall and we had galloped away under cover of darkness. Darnley had ridden ahead, terrified that Morton, Ruthven and Lindsay would catch up with him. He had good reason to fear those men.

I heard whistling.

Someone was whistling in the dawn sunrise as they rolled a cart along the street. How I longed to be free of the burden of royalty in that moment, and how I longed to be just like them. I could not see their faces, but I could hear the rumble of cart wheels. Then I saw a little boy clad in rags, his face full of mischief and hunger. He grabbed a small bannock from a passing cart and disappeared.

I watched the High Street going about its business; I listened to the voices, the sounds of wheels and horses' hooves, and I waited.

The guards were changed, and those who took their place were less kind. They did not speak to me and I did not speak to them.

Towards the middle of the afternoon I saw a figure descending the stairs, his hat pulled low, and I recognized the face of my brother.

"Moray," I cried.

When he made as if to walk on I called out. "Would you ignore me?"

He stopped and turned. The door was unbolted and he came into my cell.

I am ashamed to say that I wept on seeing him. "If you had been here, my brother, none of this would have happened! They would not have treated me so."

In my desperation it did not occur to me to wonder why he was always absent whenever there was conspiracy afoot.

"I have not been able to wash or change my clothes," I said. "And they have threatened me. They have said that they will burn me. I am not afraid to die!" I added. "If that is their wish."

"You will not die, Mary," he assured me. "They'll not burn you."

"Will you help me, my brother?"

He avoided my eye. "Did you renounce Bothwell?"

"I asked if they would let him leave the field unharmed. That they did. I will not renounce him, for he is still my husband in the eyes of God, and in the eyes of the law."

"Then I cannot help you," Moray said flatly.

I stared at him. "He is also the father of my unborn child," I said, admitting what I had so far never breathed a word of.

Moray stopped, and frowned. "Bastard!" he corrected.

I looked at him, taken aback.

"He is the father of your bastard."

"And you would know about that, of course?"

Moray was angry. I had touched a raw nerve. "He was never lawfully separated from his wife. Your church does not recognize this so-called marriage of yours."

Suddenly the scales fell from my eyes and I realised who was my real enemy in all of this. It is always the one you least suspect. Always.

A sudden memory of Maitland at Craigmillar Castle saying, *"After all, Moray here will look through his fingers at the deed, and say nothing!"*

My brother was always absent from Edinburgh on business whenever conspirators came knocking at the door. If there was trouble brewing, if a fight broke out, if the rebels ever got the upper hand and scored an advantage against me, Moray was nowhere to be seen.

I had often said to Bothwell, "Someone else is behind of all this. I will find out who."

As the years have passed I have even suspected Lord Burleigh and Elizabeth of engineering my downfall. Cecil did not want me in power. A Catholic Queen? Just over the border? I think not.

Keep your friends close, but keep your enemies closer.

"It was you," I breathed, looking at my brother. "It was you, all the time."

He said nothing.

"But you visited me in France. You encouraged me to return to Scotland. You said they were waiting for me."

"And waiting they were!"

"Then why?"

"When I asked you to join me in Scotland, I expected you to be biddable, open to advice…"

"To do as I was told."

"I did not expect a queen who would–"

"Make her own decisions?" I began to laugh and he thought then that I had descended into madness. Perhaps I had.

I was mad enough still to entertain hope.

"But what of my son?" I cried, as Moray walked away from me. "I need to know that he is safe. I want to see my son!"

My brother did not reply, but left me in my cell with the two guards looking on.

Holyrood
June 1567

Night fell.

Eventually I heard footsteps on the Black Turnpike stair and figures darkened the window. The door to my cell was thrust open.

I lifted my head in hope, but my visitors were not a welcome sight.

Lindsay entered, with Morton close on his heels. What he said next gave me cause for relief.

"We are taking you to the Palace," Lindsay offered abruptly.

I stood up. I had nothing to take with me, other than the clothes I had worn when I left Dunbar for Carberry – the garb of a soldier. Gingerly, I walked up the Black Turnpike stairs in their company and out onto the street. I was weakened by my ordeal and relieved it was over.

I mounted the horse that was tethered there, waiting for me, and we rode slowly towards the Palace. The streets were deserted, but behind closed shutters I could see chinks of candlelight glowing. I felt excluded, shut out.

A low night mist swirled about the Palace grounds when we passed through the gates. I rode into the inner courtyard and dismounted.

I was escorted through the corridors. Our footsteps echoed, hollow on the air. Very few candles were lit. Each room oppressed me with its silence and emptiness, no one to welcome me home, other than my few ladies – and what could they do against the brutish behaviour of men like Morton and Lindsay?

The Palace was filled with ghosts. Voices which had once clamoured here left their echoes: the soothing sound of musicians, laughter, warmth, celebration – all had faded away, leaving only the residue of happy memories behind. It haunted me to realise those days were over. During my glittering reign at the Scottish court there were troubles aplenty, but I had dealt with them. I had conquered, but in the end the sea of troubles overwhelmed me. The waves rose higher until they engulfed me.

I glanced at the portraits on the walls of my ancestors.

We walked on in silence until we reached the north-west tower, and in the familiar rooms with their bright tapestries draping the walls, my ladies-in-waiting stood gathered together nervously.

They ran towards me when they saw me and I held each one. It was a tearful reunion. Mary Seton and Mary Livingstone wept as they told me how much they had feared for my life.

I comforted them and assured them the danger was over, that no one would separate us again. There was not much opportunity to talk, as we were not left alone. Lindsay stood in the corner watching us, a great brute of a man. A handful of women were my only friends, and the only barrier against these violent men.

"Her Majesty is hungry and thirsty," Mary Beaton spoke up forcefully. "She needs to change her clothes and wash, and will require privacy to do so."

Lindsay sneered and shook his head. "She can do what needs to be done here."

"But…" Beaton protested.

He turned his back and stood at the door.

I was permitted to change my clothes in the dressing-room and washed as best I could with the help of my ladies who expressed shock at the state of my body, the bruises and cuts from the several days' journey I had endured through the wilderness. Supper was being prepared while I made myself ready. Soon I was dressed in a black velvet gown, its softness caressing my shoulders. A white veil floated about my face, and around my waist hung my familiar prayer book. Beaton and Livingstone found my jewels in their chest and dressed my ears and throat in pearls. It seemed a long time since I had worn the trappings of a queen.

I appeared in the doorway with my head held high. Lindsay turned to look at me and said nothing.

When supper was ready I sat at the foot of the carved oak table which I had eaten from so many times before, and the silver candelabra was lit so that a soft golden light flickered over the tapestries on the walls.

I felt uneasy.

As I lowered myself in the chair to eat Morton came and stood behind me like a pillar of stone. I could feel his presence, his hands placed firmly on the chair-back.

So – I was still a prisoner.

Being famished, I ate quickly, as fast as I could, trying to ignore his menacing presence and what it might mean. Lindsay stood to one side, watching me, his hands behind his back, his legs apart.

When I was still only halfway through my meal they told me that I must be ready to make a journey.

I lay down the fork I was holding. "To see my son at Stirling?"

Lindsay did not reply.

"Where am I to be taken?" I asked, growing fearful now.

"It is not your business to know."

"I must have time to pack a few things, some personal belongings. Clothes and linen and…"

Lindsay stopped me. "You will be provided with everything you need at your destination."

Then he came towards me. My ladies watched as he lifted the pearl necklace which Beaton had lately fastened, and ripped it from my throat.

"You'll not have need of these," he barked. "Or these." And he wrenched the pearls from my earlobes, the rings from my fingers and the other few jewels I had donned only moments before.

My ladies leapt forward to protest, but it was no use. No one would listen to them.

An armed guard entered and without acknowledging my presence announced to Morton and Lindsay that the horses were ready for the journey.

I was gruffly told to get to my feet, and when I refused, Morton hoisted me up by the elbow.

"Her Majesty has not finished eating," Livie cried.

"Too bad," came the reply.

My supper lay half-finished on the plate.

"You must let us go with you," Beaton and Livie pleaded, but they were torn from my side. When they wept in protest, Lindsay shouted at them to desist. In the scuffle that followed I felt my mind become blank with fear and shock.

"Her Majesty will take no servants of her own on this

journey!" he bellowed, and I was led away, listening to the cries of Beaton and Livingstone fading along the corridor behind me.

Wherever my journey's end might be, I wondered for a moment if I was intended to arrive there alive.

As fresh horses were being saddled in the courtyard I looked about nervously. It was becoming clear to me that no one else would appear, there would be no other familiar faces on this journey. Morton and Lindsay would be my only companions, with a small guard of armed soldiers.

My brother Moray was notably absent. In his favour I can only conclude that perhaps he had no stomach for this, and did not wish to see his sister in this state.

As we rode in silence through the quiet streets of Edinburgh I longed to cry out and rouse the citizens, to tell them of my plight, but what could I do?

Two men I feared more than anyone were to be my only escorts.

The darkness of the night pressed down on my shoulders and I felt the weight of it, particularly as we left the town behind and ventured out into open countryside. An eerie silence descended, punctuated only by the sound of our horses.

I looked at the backs of these men – Morton and Lindsay. They had murdered Rizzio and then they had murdered Darnley. My brother Moray did not like to get his own hands dirty. He organized others to do his killing for him. They were ruthless killers.

We rode on through the night and no one spoke. We seemed to be heading north and this gave me cause for hope. Perhaps we were making for Stirling after all, where I would be reunited with my son.

But as the hours passed I began to doubt. I slowed my

horse down, complaining of fatigue, glancing the while from left to right.

My eyes swept the darkness, hoping against hope there would be a rescue attempt. Perhaps my ladies had been able to warn others. And then there was Bothwell; he was out there somewhere, a free agent.

I listened hopefully for the pounding of hooves.

Lochleven
June 1567

As our dark journey continued I soon realised that I was not being taken to Stirling.

I would never see my little son again.

We rode fifty miles north that night, past Stirling and up into the heart of Kinross-shire. We came so close to my son's nursery that it broke my heart. I could make out the dark crags on which the castle sat, looming in the near distance as we crossed the flat carse.

The sight pierced me. So close, and yet so far.

When I realised we were not going to stop here, I pleaded fatigue and hoped for a rescue.

None came.

I have often said that Scotland is a country that inspires me with its bold landscape and majestic mountains, but that night it was a cold and unforgiving place, filled with terrors. I reminded my captors that I was with child, but they allowed us no pause. We kept going until the sky began to show signs of lightening at the edges.

At the first peep of dawn we arrived beside the still waters of Lochleven. It was vast and lay like a sheet of grey steel before me. I remember the utter stillness. Far out on the loch was a small island covered in trees, and among those trees was the dour castle of William Douglas louring over its miniscule kingdom.

I knew the Douglases. They had threatened my life on the night of Rizzio's murder. Morton was a Douglas. My husband Darnley had been their kinsman.

This then was my destination. A bleak inescapable fortress in the centre of these black waters – a loch that stretched twelve miles across – with the dark Lomond hills surrounding us on every side. It was isolated, remote, far from any help.

I was helped down from my horse. With the grey morning mist swirling and eddying about us, we stood on the edge of the water and I felt the unbearable stillness pressing down on me.

It was just before sunrise. The black, faceless castle on its island was partially obscured by trees, but I could feel the innate desolation of the place.

My heart failed me.

They meant to keep me a prisoner. They did not mean me to leave. How would I ever engineer an escape from the banks of that tiny island where my every movement would be observed?

We crossed the loch by boat, the waters glimmering as the dawn came on. The mist hung in scarves and ribbons – six miles of granite-grey water, as still as glass, before the solitary inaccessible fortress of the Douglases loomed up large above me, its towers ready to receive me and purge me. This was where I was to begin my long years of imprisonment.

The tall iron gates shut behind me with a resounding

clang that has reverberated down the years. It was a sound that shattered the silence.

I have spent the rest of my life as a prisoner, locked up in the rooms of one drab castle or another. To begin with it was Lochleven, then I spent the remainder of my days in exile in England. One castle is much the same as any other.

They forced me to abdicate; they threatened to drown me in the loch if I did not sign. Then they made my brother Moray Regent over my son.

William Douglas and his wife were harsh gaolers, but there was worse to come. Bothwell's child did not live to see the light of day. I miscarried twins while incarcerated on that island.

My talent for escape continued.

I managed to evade my captors and left Lochleven disguised as a washerwoman – but the boatman recognized my hands and took me back. A few months later I escaped again. But when no one – not even Bothwell – came to my aid, my courage failed me. So I crossed the Solway Firth and threw myself on Elizabeth's mercy, hoping she would take pity on my plight.

A fellow sister sovereign, like herself, opposed and in danger.

But this is where my story ends.

I have nothing more to tell.

As I languish in my lonely cell, I entertain the ghosts of my past and stitch for them my tapestries. It is a narrative in gold and silken thread, telling the many stories of my life.

I doubt that I shall ever return to Scotland and this makes me sad.

It was a deadly inheritance, after all, the Scottish crown... nothing but a circle of deadly barbs, threaded, looped and woven together, one sharp thorn above another.

Ghosts never haunt the innocent.

I have not ceased hoping, I have not ceased wanting what my Guise uncles taught me to want. As my needle flies swiftly and patiently through the bare canvas, ornamenting plain linen with glittering designs, I sit with my gaze fixed on Elizabeth's throne. I have my hopes and ambitions yet. I have supporters to champion my cause. I am a Catholic monarch in a world that cries out for order and redemption. I have my little jewelled prayer book at my waist, my rosary beads and yellowing crucifix. I have my knights in shining armour waiting in the wings to rescue me still.

I long for freedom.

Every day I long for it.

She has kept me incarcerated here for nigh on twenty years, and I am sick with longing.

I shall sweep her off that eminence on which she now sits. It is mine by divine right. I shall avenge myself on my dear sister and cousin Elizabeth.

Fotheringhay Castle
October 1586

*My little Skye Terrier Geddon begins to bark. I lean down
and pat his wiry head.*

Who is this now? What intrusion do we have here?

*He steps forward in sky-blue satin, vain and impudent as
usual, although softened slightly with experience.*

The experience of being dead?

*"So that is it?" he asks. "The truth and nothing but the
truth?"*

*I stab the needle through my tapestry and meet Darnley's
gaze.*

"I swear!"

*"And the famous Casket letters they produced at the
trial?"*

*"You mean that charade that Lord Burleigh rigged up to
try and establish my guilt?"*

"The same!"

"Forgeries, for I did not write them."

"But they were in Bothwell's hand!"

"They took letters we had each written, cut pieces out and replaced them with others to make a convincing argument. Many of those endearments were addressed to another woman – not I! I liked Bothwell , indeed – before he forced me against my will – but I did not commit adultery."

Darnley says quietly, "It makes for such an interesting story – the queen who had her own husband murdered in order to marry her lover. They will be telling it for years."

"Lies, distortions and half-truths" I murmur. "They have slandered me so effectively even my own son believes them."

"Our son!" Darnley corrects me. "They will not forget you, Mary. You will become legend. Myth!"

Darnley leans forward. "How many times did you escape from captivity, against all the odds?"

"Not this time…"

"Why do you think they are so nervous and set such a ferocious guard upon you? They are terrified you will escape. Loose in the kingdom you pose an enormous threat to Elizabeth."

I try to hide a small smile, but Darnley has seen it.

"You are plotting still. Be careful, Mary."

"I have had so long to think on vengeance. Someone has been scheming against me from the very beginning, engineering things."

"Have you never understood?" Darnley tells me.

"Understood what?"

"Moray was behind it all."

"I know that…"

"And behind him, was England. The whole thing stinks of England. Lord Burleigh was funding Moray in an attempt

to undermine you. Think about Kirk o' Field. A massive explosion to draw the attention of the world and to put suspicion onto the Queen of Scots. Why else would they blow up a building? A touch dramatic, was it not?"

I stare at Darnley's white spectral face.

"Cecil," I whisper. They funded Moray and encouraged the Protestant lords to cause trouble for me, promising them rewards.

"It was coming from England all along," Darnley says. "Elizabeth knew about the Rizzio plot before you did. She knew also about Kirk o' Field before it happened."

"But why?" I whisper, thinking of the terms of endearment, the little gifts I had exchanged with my sister queen in the early years.

Darnley shrugs. "To neutralize the threat from the Stuart monarchy."

"And why Moray?"

"He turned against you as soon as you married me. That was enough to make him an enemy, even when he pretended to be your closest adviser."

My brother deliberately engineered a state of affairs which would leave me friendless in my own realm, despite the affection he did once bear me and which I bore towards him. But Elizabeth...?

My plans for vengeance seem more than ever justified.

"You need to watch Lord Burleigh. And Walsingham. They have spies everywhere."

Suddenly the door to my chamber opens and Darnley whips round, alarmed.

Jane Kennedy enters.

"Good Morning, Ma'am."

"Good Morning, Jane."

"I thought I heard voices earlier?" she says.

I gaze at her, feigning innocence.

She does not see Darnley's ghost who regards us both coolly from the shadows.

To her, he is invisible.

"It will be different soon, Jane," I murmur. "Great changes are coming. I can feel it."

Jane Kennedy folds clothes at the fire, smiles with her back to me.

She is distracted by her task, a quiet woman who follows instructions and does as she is bid.

"I'm sure, Madame," she murmurs.

Fotheringhay Castle
February 8 1587

They came for me at nightfall, just after we had finished dining.

Jane Kennedy had not had time to gather the plates before we heard a commotion downstairs and heavy footfalls echoing obtrusively outside.

They burst in without ceremony. Lord Burleigh was among them, his eyes full of delight.

Jane shrank back and my little dog began to bark.

Lord Burleigh lashed out at him with his foot, but this did nothing to quieten Geddon who snarled.

"Come, Geddon," I said, and motioned my valiant little soldier to my side, where I offered him comfort.

Then I rose to meet their gaze.

"What have you to say to me, gentlemen?"

I knew what was coming, and wanted only to show them an air of courage and defiance.

Lord Burleigh cleared his throat before he spoke, and I stared at the point of his beard as it worked up and down.

"We are here to advise you of your sentence, Madam,

that you are finally condemned to death by our sovereign, Elizabeth, and her Estates. You will be taken from this place at eight o'clock in the morning, and executed in the Great Hall."

Jane Kennedy and Elizabeth Curle drew in their breaths sharply, and Didier my porter cried out before he could stop himself.

"I have suffered much at the hands of my cousin, the Queen. Tell me, on what charges am I condemned? What is it you have found against me?"

Lord Burleigh met my gaze.

"The Catholic faith and your assertion of your God-given right to the English throne are the two issues on which you are condemned."

I smiled.

"You must leave me, gentlemen. I have much to do before dawn."

Lord Burleigh and his companions stared at me, as if expecting something more.

"I said…leave," I commanded them.

And they did.

This last gave me much satisfaction.

I have spent the remainder of my last night writing letters to my relatives abroad, chiefly my brother-in-law, the King of France, and ratifying my will.

But when that was done, I turned to my confessional diary, the journal that Jane Kennedy did encourage me to write.

Long before dawn I hand it to her.

"This is yours, Jane. To do with as you wish."

She does not quite meet my gaze. But she takes the journal from me.

Alex Dye

Inside it are my secrets.

"The true version, Jane," I tell her, and smile.

If truth be told, I have never quite trusted any living human, in the end.

There is only one I trust, and him I scratch behind the ears. He nestles close, my little Geddon. Betrayal is not a word he understands.

He will go with me tomorrow to the Great Hall. I can hear them building the scaffold. Their hammering is but a faint echo, but still it keeps me awake.

I have no wish to sleep.

I will hide Geddon in my skirts and none shall stop me.

It is my only hope, that I conduct myself with dignity.

Fotheringhay Castle
February 10 1587

Didier, Elizabeth and I have been left to clear the chamber.
We are no longer wanted or needed here.

Didier says that he will take Geddon, and give him a good
home.

I look around this barren room and feel its emptiness. It is
dark and cold without any life in it. My Mistress's voice has
left no echoes behind. She is gone.

If I believed in ghosts I could fancy that she breathes still,
that the poems and songs she wrote fill the dusty air.

But I do not believe in ghosts, and her voice is forever
silenced.

Her tapestries are packed into a chest made of oak. Like
a casket, it will hold her dying thoughts. Impossible now to
unravel.

But I have in my possession one last gift.

I pick up the journal and place it among the folds of
tapestry which she spent so many years and months carefully

working. Then I change my mind, lift up the lid and remove it again.

At nightfall, when the others have left, I light a fire, then I draw a stool close to the hearth.

On my knee is the journal – my Mistress's last thoughts, her most intimate secrets. With this, I could tell all.

But I think of her little dog Geddon, and how she said that 'Betrayal is a word he understands not.'

To be poor is hard.

Who would not sell their soul for the security of lasting riches, or the assurance that they will not be tortured or slain?

I do what I must.

I lean forward, and feed the pages of her journal to the flames until the last page crumbles to dust.

No one knows my name.

Historical Note

In October 1586 Mary Stuart, Queen of Scots was found guilty of plotting to overthrow Elizabeth. She denied all the charges and stated quite categorically that if others were to manoeuvre on her behalf, then there was little she could do about it.

Sir Anthony Babington was a young gentleman and a Catholic, who championed Mary's cause and wrote letters to the Scots Queen, promising to help her escape into freedom. What both he and Mary did not know was that their letters were being intercepted by Sir Francis Walsingham, who had possibly also interfered with the correspondence. When Mary signed her name to her final letter, Walsingham knew that he had her. The Queen of Scots had walked unwittingly into a trap from which she would not escape. She had unknowingly incriminated herself and the proof could be set before Elizabeth so that she could no longer avoid the inevitable, and must have her cousin charged and executed.

Whether Mary actually knew what she was putting her name to is unclear. She certainly wanted to secure her own freedom, but it is doubtful she would have agreed to the assassination of Elizabeth I. What is clear is that Walsingham and Lord Burleigh were not above tampering with the evidence.

Elizabeth was reluctant to sign the order to have Mary executed, but would later claim that she signed it amongst a pile of other papers and had not been aware of its import.

Mary was executed on 8th February 1587 in the hall at Fotheringhay. She spent the night before her execution writing letters and making a will, to ensure that her servants were paid any wages they were owed. She claimed that she was glad to meet her fate, as it would be an end to all the sufferings and sorrows of the Scots Queen. It took the executioner three blows with the axe, and afterwards her little dog Geddon was found to be hiding in her skirts. He had been a comfort to her at the very last.

"In my end is my beginning."

Acknowledgements

I would like to gratefully acknowledge Clare Cain and everyone at Fledgling for their input.

The idea for this book was first planted in my head unconsciously when I was a child and read *A Traveller in Time* by Alison Uttley. This is when the mysterious figure of Mary, Queen of Scots first sowed a seed.

I have read many books with regard to Mary Queen of Scots since I was in my early twenties, when I first began this novel. In particular Antonia Fraser's *Mary Queen of Scots*; John Guy's *My Heart is My Own: The Life of Mary Queen of Scots*; and more recently, *Mary, Queen of Scots: Truth or Lies* by Rosalind K Marshall, *Crown of Thistles: The Fatal Inheritance of Mary, Queen of Scots* by Linda Porter. *Mary, Queen of Scots and the Murder of Darnley* by Alison Weir, *The Captive Queen of Scots* by Jean Plaidy and *The Little Book of Mary Queen of Scots* by Mickey Mayhew.

This is a work of fiction and it goes without saying that any mistakes or errors are my own. I would also like to thank the many friends who have always encouraged and supported me - no one should feel left out from that acknowledgement. Also Judith Nye, who was there at the beginning when I first conceived this novel, and tramped the streets of Edinburgh in search of inspiration.

My own parents, who are no longer with us but who definitely deserve a mention for the huge encouragement they always gave me, and their belief in me. I wish they had been here to see this labour of love finally emerge. My brother Nick Gollaglee and my sister Liz Kumar, also my aunt, Beryl Foreman, for all their love and support. Lastly, but not at all least, my two children, Micah Nye and Martha Nye, and my husband Joe Austin for all their love, patience, support and just about everything.